Catching My Breath

Three Stories

Joanne McLain

C.J. Prince

William C. Thomas

ISBN: 978-1475165470

Front cover artwork by Janine and Michael Thornton, *thorntonartworks.com*

www.catchingmybreath.com

Dedication

For all wounded women

who have lost the rainbow in their hearts

and can't hear the angels speak

but learn

that from the abyss, there is only up

Contents

Foreword

The change starts when you make the decision that, this time, I'm packing my own bags on this journey of life. All the other choices come into play after that big one. These three stories all involve young women in the process of learning about that packing: what to take with, what to leave behind, who to talk to about it all.

It isn't easy, this process of packing and carrying our memories, hopes and dreams, worries and fears. There's no way to pack it all so the pieces fit snug together—something is always jittering about inside, unsettling everything and eager to get out. Sometimes we just need to let it go.

The three women in these stories, Gwyneth, Dannah and Lisa, all start out by doing their best to shove deep down inside themselves emotions and memories that just won't stay packed up. Each one learns how to take some control of what they carry along and how they want to pack it. Along the way, they also learn a few things about sharing the burden.

The people we love aren't always the ones who know how to love us back. That always hurts. We need to learn how to protect ourselves and nurture ourselves, and sometimes we need to put distance between ourselves and the ones who hurt us (a few feet or a lifetime), but the worst choice we can make is to stop loving at all. These stories are about the choices we make every day on this journey that either lighten the load or add more stones to it.

That first step is a hard one, recognizing that we have choices to make, but the next step can be harder: giving those choices a voice so that we can unpack a little more from our bags of useless stuff. These three stories are also about speaking our truth, even when we're not really sure what that means. Step by step we make choices, not just when to speak our minds, but how and why. Each burden we unpack makes the next step a little easier, so we go on.

The characters in these stories are all fortunate to be living in Fondis, in the heart of Colorado. It is a strange place: if you see it with everyday eyes, you will find a ghost town. But if you open the eyes of your soul and listen to the stories carried on the wind, you will find yourself in a mythical town *somewhere in a state of mind. It is a place where odd things happen to good people, and the best packed bags somehow come undone. A great place to find yourself and a great place to lose yourself for a while, too. We invite you to set down your bags, settle yourself into the community, and listen.*

Transformations

Joanne McLain

Samhain / Snake Drifts Within

I found myself in the garden without really thinking about it. A storm was coming in and I knew this would be my last chance to harvest anything above ground. Usually we would have a killing frost before now, but this year had been different. It was already Halloween and flowers were still blooming. By evening, however, it would snow.

The old movements came hard: bending was a chore itself, and straightening up again required new learning. As I carefully busied myself picking leaves of chard, I noticed movement at my feet. A tiny gardener snake was sluggishly coiling down into a hole. I stooped down and picked it up for a moment to watch its quivering tongue sense for danger in my hands. It looped its tail around my finger like a ring. Snakes mean transformation, I thought, but not the graceful transformation of chrysalis into butterfly. Just the itchy shedding of tight, worn out skin in order to grow.

I let the little snake slide from my hand down into the ground, faster now from the warmth. It disappeared down the hole, ready to hibernate until spring. I would not be hibernating, but I didn't feel prepared for the winter, either.

Before everything changed, I had been fascinated by the old beliefs and customs. I loved reading about how my ancestors honored the turning of the year and I was happy when we moved to the hills just outside Fondis, a place where the old ways were still alive and honored along with newer beliefs. I knew that the ancient Celts started the new year at sunset on Samhain, now called Halloween. I remembered a seminar from the university where I had taught writing. Epona Maris, a local poet, had said that the Celtic

1

day starts with the night and the year begins with the "dark half," a time of introspection and looking within. This means that each year is birthed from the dark night of the old. A time of spirit voices and traveling the deep paths. A time of living with death. I had been living with death since the accident, but I knew I needed to travel deeper through the dark to reach whatever life held for me beyond it.

At least I had a head start on this process: I was traveling into the dark with my changes already begun. From one moment to the next, I had found myself alone with no family, no job, no secure income and no idea of what I would do about all of that. I was changing in ways I couldn't control or even understand, leaving me with an empty sense that I should be doing something active about that, or at least deciding how I felt about it, not just crawling through the fog of each day. I should be deciding how to live my life, but I couldn't find the energy to do that. So, for the moment, I decided to pick chard.

November / Fox in the Snow

There was a time when I had a place in the world. I was married and was establishing myself in a steady career that seemed to make some sort of difference in the world. I was learning what it means to be a mother. I had friends and purposeful activities, a welcoming home. Time can unravel the surest of cords.

I had a husband and a baby daughter, both lost in one day to a drunk driver. I survived, but the weeks of physical therapy on my twisted body left me without a job or the ability to return to the work I knew. And the weeks of grief shut the door on well-meaning friends. The phone would ring, I would think of picking it up, but didn't. The messages on voice mail were cheery, but hollow and distant. I knew I should return the calls, but rarely did.

The house was empty even when I was there and the garden gradually filled with blown snow. I watched through the window for hours as the drifts built before deciding that I really should do something more useful. I moved the laundry from the washer to the dryer, then went back to the window. I could see the vague outlines

2

of my reflection: pale hair, gray eyes, white skin. My father had named me Gwyneth: "white-browed." When I was a child, other children called me "the ghost," and claimed I would disappear into the air if no one looked closely at me. It felt like the truth, now.

I turned and picked up a framed photograph. "Steven," I said, tracing my husband's form with my finger. "Kelly," I added, touching the baby's face lightly. "Gwyneth," that was me, but no more me than the flat picture in my hands was Steven or Kelly. Empty of life.

I don't remember, but I think most of November went that way, with no energy, no motivation, no desire to change. I was hibernating within the confines of my house, drifting slowly from room to room, picking up and putting down objects that somehow did not connect to memories. When I moved, my muscles and bones spoke to me painfully of limits and caution, yet I was restless within my bounds, unable to settle to any activity, even aimless ones. The few times I left the house, to buy groceries or visit the doctor, I avoided human contact as much as possible and returned home quickly, as if the house were a refuge, not a memorial to what I lost.

Somewhere, deep in my unconscious mind, the little snake from the garden had found a place to start shedding its skin. I had a vague sense that, if I could only wriggle out of the shreds of my old life, I might be able to grow a new one. I had no idea where to start, except to follow the course of days down into the dark pattern of the year. Sometime during those early gray days is when I first saw the fox in the snow.

I was staring out the window, as usual. It was late afternoon and the scattered rays of sun touched here and there across the light drifting of snow in the garden, with the brittle stalks poking up through it. There was a flash of rust behind the faint yellow horseradish leaves, then a pair of sharp black eyes looking back at me. Before I could move, he was gone.

I put on my coat to go outside for the first time that day and carefully walked down to the garden as the sun set. The paw prints were barely visible but they were real. I touched them with my fingers as the ground faded into deeper gray. For a moment, I felt connected to something.

Each day after that, as I went about my routine, I was drawn to the window, to actually look for something, not just look out. There was nothing the next day, but on the third evening he returned to the garden, sitting quietly under the rose briars as if waiting for me to look. The last light of sun shone through his fur.

That night, I dreamed of foxes, startlingly bright after weeks of vague nighttime images that quickly faded with the dawn. They flashed quickly across the back of my sight, leaping gracefully, swishing their broad tails behind them. Sniffing the air, bounding into the sky to pounce down on mice, snapping their narrow jaws. They were full of life, full of fire. I reached my hand out to touch soft fur, but they were gone.

I was standing in an open field, cold in my nightshirt and bare feet. I turned around and saw the fox in the snow, sitting quietly behind me. His black, knowing eyes watched me, his teeth gleamed as he laughed. "Learn to live alone," he told me, "or you will never live at all."

"How do I learn?" I asked.

"Turn around and look," he said as he glided away, stepping gently across the frozen ice of a stream. "That's the only way you will live." I turned around and looked. I saw my garden, iced over for the winter. I stepped down the bark-chip paths and looked at the dead growth. When I got to the leafless stems of the rose briar bush, I knelt and scraped the sheltering mulch away from the base. There was a faint hint of green. I carefully covered it up again with mulch: I had winter still to live through, and I was not ready for the green.

I woke in my bed with the pearl gray of dawn about me, cold air flowing through the gaps in the bedroom window frame. Getting up slowly, stretching cautiously to warm my frozen bones, I decided to try walking beyond the garden that day.

December / The Language of Crows

Strings of lights were going up on the houses in the valley about me as I ventured out for a walk in the cool sunshine. By the beginning of December, I was walking down my long driveway to the mailbox each day, pausing for breath before limping back up to the house. I had a staff, carved with swirls of Celtic interlace, that I had

4

bought years ago at the Renaissance Faire and it served me well as a walking stick.

I had decided to venture further down the road today, to guess what my neighbors' Christmas lights would look like after the sun fell below the horizon. The air was pleasantly crisp on my face as I walked, staff firmly in hand. My muscles warmed to the slow pace, my twisted legs found a hesitant rhythm. I felt at peace.

As I rounded a corner, on the side of the road I saw a few black crows shifting about, flapping their wings as they gathered about some object of interest.

I remembered that, when I first moved to Fondis, I was fascinated by the language of crows. At first, I puzzled over what they were saying to each other in their sonorous voices, but Epona Maris taught me the clue to translate crow talk when she announced in a writing workshop that crows are spiritualists, enlightened by the Buddha and various Hindu yoga masters. Crows love to draw attention to the moment: "Be Here Now, Here, Now" they caw to each other from the treetops. Then they practice their walking meditations as they carefully attend to the roadside suffering of the world.

I smiled a bit, remembering the laughter and community of that workshop, but, as I walked closer to the crows, my mood shifted. I could see them piercing their beaks into something dead. I hesitated, then continued walking. I refused to let them stop me as if they owned the road.

Up close, the sight of death scattered about the roadside, picked apart by insensitive beaks, was enough to make me slow my already fragile pace. I shuffled close enough to see what they were eating, unable to simply turn back and ignore it. I caught the flash of russet fur against the frozen weeds in the ditch. I could see clearly enough that it was the remains of a fox they were picking over. The nearest crow slid his beak into the mess and pulled up shreds of muscle. He looked at me with sharp, dark, knowing eyes.

I turned and walked as quickly as my stubborn legs would carry me back home, back to the shelter of walls around me. When I closed the door tightly behind me, however, it was not enough to shut out the memory of tattered fur, dried blood, cracked white bones. I tried not to think of the graceful flash of red fur beneath the rose briar in the corner of my garden, but even straight brandy with Vicodin would not shift the memory and sleep came late with no relief.

That night, crows walked through the garden in my dreams, shuffling their wing feathers, dipping their heads to caw at me: "Be here now!" they repeated their pattern relentlessly through the night.

"Why?" I finally yelled back at them, causing them to rise in a flurry of black wings, glide about to land in the garden again. They wouldn't answer me, but one circled back to land heavily on the fence post near me. "You are not your body," he reminded me.

Somehow the shifting black wings turned into dark rain against a windshield. I caught my breath as I helplessly watched the headlights slashing into the car again, just as it had before. I heard the crash, the screams, the shriek of tearing metal, but my mind refused to follow that track further into the dark.

The dream shifted abruptly to another memory: I found myself in the central hall of the Fondis University Cultural Center, cell phone held to my ear, arguing with Steven as I walked restlessly. "When are you coming home?" he had asked in that moment torn from the calendar of my pre-accident days. "I need you here with me."

"I need to be at the poetry reading tonight," I told him, trying to capture a tone of certainty. "My students are counting on me."

"Don't I count with you anymore? Since you took that job, I hardly see you." His words became a pounding drumbeat in my ear, intense, demanding, unyielding. My nervous steps took me round a corner into a sunlit gallery. I stood still, eyes drawn to a painting on the far wall: a kneeling woman, hands pressed against the earth, body straining to stand up. From her arching back, the faint hint of feathered wings rose to the sky.

The painting wavered through my tears as I said "I have to go now" and turned off the phone. I walked closer, lost in the image. Even the swirled "Dannah" signature held meaning, if I could only look long enough.

"Lots of emotion in that painting," Epona said, standing softly behind me. "Her body is heavy with sorrow, yet her spirit rises." She placed a gentle hand on my shoulder. "Dannah painted that for the Women's Crisis Center fundraiser. They're a good group of people to know."

I didn't know what to say, so we stood quietly together for a while, looking at the painting. A small plaque below it gave its title: "Love's Burden."

I woke to gray snow blowing against the house. I struggled up from the bed and stumbled to the kitchen to make coffee.

The next three days, I went past the window every few moments, looking to the garden, hoping but telling myself not to hope, reminding myself why it was a bad idea to hope. I knew that I worried about the fox because it was a safer target for my concerns than my deeper wounds, but I worried anyway. The first two days were empty. But on the third, just before the last faint glow of sunset ended, he was there, briefly, under the bare rose branches. Before I could draw breath, he was gone.

After that, I was determined to walk down the road, crows or not. Sometimes the road was empty; sometimes they laughed at my distractedness, with their mantra of "Be here now." I did my best to learn how.

January / Owl Flies Deep

The Great Horned Owl came to the garden so subtly that I scarcely noticed her. The sun had just set, so she was soft gray alighting on a gray pine branch against a gray sky. Only her brilliant yellow eyes showed the spark of life. I turned to go back into the house, unable to take the next steps she would show me on the path through the woods. Inside, I made a pot of tea but drank none of it. I went to bed early and did not dream.

The next morning, I shuffled about, pretending to tidy things up, but moved about in aimless patterns. I avoided the window most of the day. That night I went to bed but didn't sleep. Morning came with gray clouds, more snow and more attempts to avoid the pain I knew awaited me in the woods by the garden. In the dim afternoon, I heated water for tea and poured it into my familiar old teapot, reaching for the comfort worn into its handle. Trembling, I dropped it on the kitchen floor and watched the shards spin across the room. By nightfall, I gave in, put on my coat and walked slowly down.

She was there on the branch, as before, silent as the faint snowflakes that shifted through the frozen air. "Hello," I said, determined to break the stillness. She swiveled her head about to look at me and clicked her beak. She never blinked. I looked down at the base of the tree where the outlines of a baby swing dimpled the

7

snow. It had fallen sometime in the summer and I had no reason to hang it back up. It felt safer to look at the owl.

We stood quiet and looked at each other for a long moment, then, without warning, she slipped from the branch and fell upon a mouse in the leaf mold below. The mouse squeaked abruptly; silence returned. Holding the mouse in her beak, she looked up at me, then thrust herself into the air and was gone. I returned to my house, but it was long before I went to bed.

That night, she glided silently into my dreams, spiraling about me, talons reaching out to pierce through me. I felt a claw strike my heart and I squeaked helplessly as the mouse. "You are dead," she hissed through her beak, just before it gripped the back of my neck. My hand closed about the feathers of her wing as I spiraled down into the darkness. It was soft as a baby's skin.

I found myself surrounded by fire in the shape of a car. The rational part of my mind informed me that the car had not burned, so this would not be a true reliving of that moment. The deeper part of my mind disagreed. I raged against the moment in a way that I had not been able to when it happened. As before, I felt the pressure of the metal against me, the fragments of glass sliding across my face, trailing streaks of blood. I felt no pain, but could not move anything but my left hand. My breath was loud, even with the crackle of flames about me. I strained to hear other breaths, any sign of life next to me, but heard nothing. "That isn't right," I told myself. I remembered that Steven had been breathing raggedly at that point, moaning softly against the steering wheel crushed to his chest. It was only after the fire department cut him out of the car that he died.

I reminded myself that this was a dream, but it was a dream with power to make me face what I had avoided for so long. The Paramedic reached through the broken glass to touch my face, as before, and spoke meaningless words of encouragement as the Jaws of Life ripped through steel. I felt the hissing pressure of oxygen in my nose again, then the hands that laid me flat on the board, felt for my pulse, stuck the needles into my arms for the IV's. I tried to close my dream eyes against the next sight, but was helpless. As they pulled me out of the wreck of the car, I saw again the twisted metal that crushed into the car seat and the tiny fingers that spread motionless against it. I screamed, as I had that night, until the remembered wash of morphine sent me back down into the dark.

I woke, or half woke, in the dark, with fever rivers running along my skin, sweat sinking into the sheets. I trembled suddenly with cold, but the wet sheets were no comfort and there was no one to wrap me in warmth. My body ached but I couldn't get up to take medicine. Outside the window, I saw a snowstorm raging but I heard nothing.

"There now, little white-feathered one," I heard my father say, in the soft voice he had used when I needed comfort. The voice I had not heard since he died when I was seven.

"Daddy?" I whispered, my voice too dry to carry sound. There was no answer.

I don't remember how long I shook with chills or burned with fever, alternating discomforts in the dark. I vaguely recall faint brightening of the clouds outside the window before the darkness returned, the long night of midwinter spreading through the window into the bedroom. Sometime near the next dawn, the fever broke and I looked up with clear eyes.

The owl was perched on the headboard looking down at me, swiveling her head to look along the tangled length of the bed. Lifting her wings slightly, she drifted down to the pillow beside my head and looked closely into my eyes. "Would you prefer to be alive?" she asked.

I thought a moment, but felt the first stirring of health returning to my muscles. "Yes," I whispered past cracked lips.

That's good," she said, and slid her beak gently through my hair before she disappeared. "Very good." For the first time since the accident, I cried.

Trembling, I got up, drank water, managed to shower. I went to the door I had avoided opening for months and opened it. I sat down in the rocking chair next to the crib and looked at the stuffed animals scattered on the floor. The keening grief sliced through me and I wept.

I sat for hours with my memories, touching the lacy blankets, the mobile of sparkling fish above the crib. I picked up the rattle that had fallen on the floor. As I set it on a shelf, I noticed the little stuffed owl toy I had bought when I first learned I was pregnant. When Kelly was teething, the owl had been her favorite toy to chew on.

It was late afternoon before I felt strong enough to put on boots to break a trail to the garden, but my body felt washed clean and made new, my skin tingled with every touch. My heart was quiet. I stood by the pine trees near the garden and looked for her, but she did not come. As the twilight spread down the hills and the full moon rose, I heard her voice calling softly. I looked behind me and found a gray feather, soft as baby's skin.

February / A Pair of Deer

There were two of them in the garden one morning, eating the dry stem tips of the rose bush. I thought to shoo them away, angry that they would damage my roses, but paused. Two Whitetail deer, male and female together, which was odd at this time of year. They were thin beneath their fuzzy winter coats, despite the slight thickening in the middle of the doe. They looked at me with eyes that knew the winter was not near to ending and drew a little closer to each other as I paused by the garden gate. I watched their breath fog in the chill air for a bit, then left them to their meal and walked down the driveway instead.

I knew by now to expect dreams that night. The deer were there, looking at me with questioning eyes, legs trembling with the need to run. When I approached, they bounded over the garden fence to the trees beyond. My dream body leaped after them, without a trace of the twisted awkwardness I had come to accept in daily life. I felt the cold wind tingle on my bare skin. Among the pine trees, the pale doe turned to look back at me. "Follow as you can," she said, and ran after the buck. I followed, drifting effortlessly in her wake.

I caught up with them in the clearing by the pond. The doe froze, eyes wide, as the buck turned and brushed passed her. Snorting, he lowered his head and charged at me. I couldn't move beyond trembling as I felt his antler tines pierce through my chest. His breath was warm on my skin as I fell to the snow. "It's only your heart that is wounded," he said, as my blood warmed the snow beneath me. "You must give all of yourself." He lowered his antlers again and I felt the tines rip into my groin, my navel and my solar plexus. A third thrust pierced my throat, my forehead and the crown of my head.

Whirling energy flowed through my blood at each point he had wounded. My body shivered in waves as I lay on my back in the

10

snow. The doe lay down beside me to offer her warmth as I bled into the frozen ground. "Love's burden," she whispered.

I looked up and saw my husband standing above me, looking down at me. "Steven," I whispered. "Why am I here?" He looked irritated.

"You shouldn't have taken that job, teaching at the university," he said. "I told you not to. I made enough to support all three of us."

"That isn't why," I said, hearing the whining noise fill my voice. "I needed me..."

"You needed me enough when I married you. You said I saved you." I could hear a plaintive tone underlying the anger in his voice, a note that I never heard when he was alive. Had it been there all along, I wondered, with me not listening for it? Steven looked down at his clenched hands, a movement I had always interpreted as his stubborn refusal to listen to my needs. Now, with my distracted awareness, I could see that there might be more behind it.

"You couldn't live without me. I pulled you out of the mess you'd made of your life and you were so grateful."

"I was grateful. I am grateful. That just wasn't enough."

"I was never enough for you."

The pain started deep in the wounds the buck deer had torn into my flesh, spreading in waves until my body could no longer contain it and it spilled out with my ragged voice: "You made it clear that I was never enough for you. You cut off my life, made me live through yours, and then you left me alone!"

He didn't answer, just turned and walked away, pulling the heat from my body after him until I was drained of all feeling. The doe touched my cold cheek with her nose.

I felt myself drifting down, filling the earth with my essence, until all of me was drawn into the welcoming ground. With no strength left to question the experience, I left myself open to everything with no boundaries between me and the world. My senses flowed outward, raw from the scrape of life against them until the earth cradled me.

The next morning, I woke with the sense of something new within me, silent roots unfurling from a deep-hidden seed. The sun reflected off the drifts of snow in waves that felt like heat. I left a pile of cracked corn between the garden and the trees before continuing my daily walk on the road.

March / A Choice of Rabbits

The first edges of spring entered the garden, punctuated by wet snowfalls that disappeared the next day. I started to rake the garden beds, planning what would go where: peas by the south fence, carrots under them, poppies by the gate. Last year, the garden had suffered from my absence; I wanted to make up for that, now. As I raked, I felt the rays of sunshine warming my back, promising more to come.

I was only able to work in the garden for an hour or so at a time, so I paced myself, going back to the house to rest before returning to the work. It felt good to have something constructive to do.

By the time I had cleared the vegetable beds, the sun was sinking to the horizon on a late March afternoon. In the grass by the pine trees, I watched a pair of rabbits dancing. They would chase each other in circles, then one would turn and leap into the air, twisting above the other, facing in new directions. I couldn't tell which was chasing and which leading at times. I laughed and surprised myself at the sound. The rabbits paused in their courtship to look at me, quivering still as they waited for a signal of my intentions.

"Go on," I said to them, and sat down on the garden bench, hoping to look less threatening. They hesitantly set about resuming their dance, then forgot me in the act of finding each other. Eventually they fell apart and hopped separately into the woods. I picked up my tools and walked back to the house to make tea.

I dreamed that night of the doe rabbit giving birth in a nest softly lined with fur she had pulled from her belly. Seven fragile pink kits struggled against each other to find the source of milk and warmth. As I watched, the one on the end (a runt, I presumed) got shuffled out to the cold edge of the nest. Waving little pink legs, it toppled over and rolled out, lying alone in the cold darkness of the world.

I reached a hand out to pick the kit up, but stopped. What if the mother rabbit would reject it because of my scent? While I paused, I saw the fox watching me from the edge of the pines. "Choices have consequences," he said.

"Do I choose if it lives or dies?" I asked him.

"It could be your choice, or it could be mine," he answered, walking a few steps closer. "But there are always choices."

I looked again at the rabbit kit. "If I place it back with its mother, she might reject it."

"She has a choice, as well."

"But the little kit has no choice: it's too young to move that far."

"Did you choose to place your child in harm's way that night?" His yellow eyes were large and bright in the darkness that surrounded us.

I saw the night, the rain, the car with us inside it. Steven was driving, as always. We were on our way home from one of the boring parties he had to attend in order to rise in the electronics business, and I had to attend as his supportive wife. Only I wasn't good at playing that role. I was much better in a classroom or as a solitary writer, with words between myself and the criticism of others.

I never knew what not to say. I don't remember what it was, but I had said the wrong thing, again. Steven said nothing as I buckled Kelly into her carseat. That was his pattern, to hold me captive by his unspoken anger. I could feel the tension rising, knew there was nothing I could do to ease it, knew that anything I said would trigger the explosion, but said it anyway: "Are you sure we should drive home right now? What about the storm? The dirt roads..."

"You don't think I'm capable of much, do you?" His voice held the threat of grievances that would build into a tower of thunder clouds until the lightning struck.

I gripped the door handle as I felt the tires skid under me. "Steven, please slow down, the road's too slick..." but he just stepped harder on the gas pedal as he drove us into the night.

I hunched over, hugging my knees, and pressed my forehead hard against them, realizing as I moved that I was on the ground by the rabbit nest. "I did not choose, yet it happened," I told the fox. "Now I can't choose to undo what happened."

"So your choice does not control the world," he answered. I looked up as he sat down and gracefully swirled his tail about his paws.

I closed my eyes a moment, hoping for inspiration, then shrugged, picked up the rabbit kit and placed it back with its mother. "And if we sit here talking any longer, the cold will make any choice of mine academic."

I left before I could see whether the mother rabbit rejected her kit, or whether the fox enjoyed a quick meal. It might have been cowardice, but it was my choice that night.

April / A Wandering Goose

The garden began to grow. Green tips of pea plants began their twisting path up the fence and spears of onions were long and thin as lace-knitting needles. The sun began to linger a bit longer in the sky each afternoon, as if sorry to end its conversation with the grass. The air was softer, but the ground still hard and cold.

I was gradually digging a new bed for potatoes one early afternoon when I heard a hissing noise behind me. Startled, I twisted awkwardly about, holding the garden fork like a spear.

A large brown goose confronted me, neck quivering and bill jabbing toward my legs. "Hey," I yelled at him and whacked him in the chest with the fork. He stumbled back, confused.

As if he had been caught in a social gaffe, his manner became apologetic. Head bobbing low to the ground, he shuffled toward me, sinking to the ground at my feet. I laughed. "Well, hello then," I told him, "pleased to meet you. Are you here to help me dig?"

He got up and marched along the garden paths, investigating each bed, mumbling to himself and nibbling on stray bits of grass as he patrolled. I left him to his survey and went back to my digging. Every now and then I stopped to talk to him, if only to hear the sound of my voice in the open air.

When I paused to rest my back, he lifted his head and honked loudly. I turned to look and saw a man standing by the garden gate.

"I see you found my gander," he said, "or he found you."

I stared at him for a moment, forgetting what I should do with a human guest. "Oh, please come in," I finally said. He entered the gate and walked up the path in a far less threatening manner than had the goose, but I found myself trembling. I sat down on the bench, still holding the garden fork, and stared at him.

Perhaps he recognized my apprehension since he stopped halfway down the path. "My name is David," he said. "I just moved into the house down the road."

I gathered my wits somehow and said "My name is Gwyneth." I paused, realizing I should say something more. "I'm sorry I'm rude—I don't talk much to people these days." I thought about how that must sound. "I mean, I haven't been out much." That didn't sound much better, but I couldn't think of what else to say.

He just smiled. "May I sit down?" he asked. I moved to give him room on the bench. "Thank you," he said. "Not like it was much of a walk to get here, but it's nice to just sit and enjoy the sun." He looked around. "You have a beautiful garden."

"Thank you," I said, and could think of nothing more to say. I watched the goose, who was now walking up the path toward us. David held out his hand. "He hasn't settled into his new home yet, unlike his girls."

"His girls?" I asked.

David laughed. "His two female companions—they are already trying out nesting sites, but he has to wander the neighborhood before settling down, I guess." The goose came up and laid his head gently in David's lap, seeming to enjoy the fingers ruffling his neck feathers. "Some geese don't take well to moving. I'm not sure I do, myself."

I looked at him questioningly and he smiled. "Divorce," he said. "Not final yet, but we agreed that she gets our house so I had to move. I wanted a place that would be good for the kids when they're here."

"Kids?" I asked.

"Two—John and Amanda, eleven and nine."

I thought about them, for a moment, about the idea of babies growing to be children, soon to be teenagers. I could feel the weight of a half-grown girl on my lap. My fingers curled to hold her to me.

"How about you? You said you live alone."

His words caught me and pulled my thoughts out of the spiral they had begun to follow. "Uh—I do—now."

"Now?" he asked, with a tone that was gentler than the word.

"I had a husband. And a baby, a daughter. Kelly. They died last year." Last year, as if it were a long time past.

"Oh," he said. His fingers paused their stroking of goose feathers. "I'm sorry." I watched his fingers, quiet against the soft brown feathers, but I felt the warmth of his eyes watching my face. "I can take my goose and leave," he offered.

"No," I said without thinking. Then, when I thought, I laughed. Looking up, I saw him laughing, too. His eyes were green.

"I didn't mean it like that," he said, still smiling. "I just don't want to cause you more pain."

"It's alright," I said slowly, considering. "I think I can talk about them now."

Haltingly, I told him about the accident, the vaguely remembered funerals I attended in a wheelchair, the pins in my hip, the weeks afterward at the rehab center, and about coming home alone. And, since he listened, I found myself talking of times before: my wedding to Steven, the first few months of living in our new house, Kelly's birth, teaching at the university, planting the garden. I didn't tell him much about Steven.

I paused, thinking I had said too much, but he just watched me, then gently touched my hand with his, much as he had stroked the goose's feathers. For a moment we sat quietly together, apparently both lost in thought.

"Let me break some of that hard ground for you," he said, and took the garden fork to attack the prospective potato bed. I watched him work for a while in silence. His movements were both graceful and effective. Eventually, the sun was setting behind us and the goose grew restless with the coming dark. "I'd better take him home," David said.

"Yes—there are foxes here," I said, thinking of my winter visitor. "I hope you have a sturdy fence around your goose yard."

"The first thing I did when I moved here," he said as he picked up the gander. Between flapping wings, he turned back to me. "I don't have much in the kitchen, but I would be happy to cook you dinner," he offered, tucking the goose's head under his arm. "Not goose, although I'm tempted right now." The goose stopped struggling.

"Tomorrow," I said, then watched him walk down my driveway and disappear at the bend of the road. The air grew cold and I retreated to my house for the night.

I felt unsettled as I ate dinner and got ready for bed. I wanted to get to sleep so I could dream. I wanted some clarity in dealing with this stranger to my life. More than that, I wanted to know what to do with the feelings that were edging out from under the frozen ground inside me. I settled into bed with expectations of visiting geese, but found myself alone, waiting by the empty garden in my dreams. "Where are you?" I asked, but heard no answer.

16

I looked around. The pine trees formed a dark ridge against the sky, the driveway a pale trace along the ground, leading outward. I decided to follow it, barefoot in my nightshirt, as the dream would have me. The goose would be in his yard with his "girls" I reasoned, so of course I wouldn't find him wandering in the dark, even with dream logic.

I walked down the driveway, over a hill and saw David's house below me. "I'm here to talk to the goose," I told myself, and ignored the house. The gander was, as I expected, in the yard. Like all geese, he slept lightly and woke at my breath of presence.

"You are here," he said, unnecessarily, so I answered: "Yes, I'm here."

He got up and paced the yard. The two female geese snuggled closer in the straw he left behind. "What do you want?' he asked.

"I thought you were supposed to tell me that," I answered. He hissed, perhaps a laugh.

"How would I know what you want?"

"I thought you were my animal guide tonight," I said.

He paced about in irritation. "What you want lies in the house," he said.

"I thought you didn't know what I want."

He hissed again and stalked back to the shelter. Once he had settled himself between the female geese, he looked at me with clear, sharp eyes. "Do you want to live alone?" he asked. "What eggs are you warming now?"

I felt a sudden heat between my cupped hands and held it close to my belly. "Perhaps one," I said, "but no telling when it will hatch."

He curved his neck down to rub against the crest of one of his mates. "Your choice," he said, "but guard it well." He closed his eyes as if sleeping, but I knew better.

"Thank you," I said, and drifted on. My eyes went to the house beyond. I meant to walk back toward my own bed, thinking my nighttime lesson over, but found myself drawn onward. "Just a brief look," I told myself. "It's not real, anyway."

There was a faint light in one of the windows, so I drifted through it into a bedroom, the bed occupied. I wondered briefly about the nightlight, then decided I would not want my own nighttime habits examined at this time.

He was sleeping, alone. He looked childlike, as most of us do in sleep, curled about a pillow. I wanted to touch his hair to comfort him, but the thought sent me drifting backward. I watched from the

17

window for a moment, then went home, to my own bed, to sleep. I woke in the gray light of dawn but lingered in bed, remembering. Once the sun rose, I was up, filling the coffeepot for the day.

The rest of that day I spent in the garden but had little practical result to show for it. By late afternoon I went back to the house, showered and put on a dress for the first time in months. I almost took it off, but didn't. I looked at my wedding ring, almost took it off, but didn't. I brushed my hair and looked out the window, hoping for a sign.

As the sun was setting, I gathered staff and shawl and walked down the driveway, careful of my hip, then on down the road. By the time I reached his driveway, the pain had slowed me to a crawl. Suddenly he was there, his arm through mine, helping me to the house. I leaned against his shoulder in relief.

"I'm sorry, I should have thought to pick you up in my car."

"No, I need to walk more—that's the only way it will get better."

Inside, he settled me in a chair and went about the preparations for dinner. He was graceful and efficient in the kitchen, too, I thought. Dinner was a pleasure. The food was good, the wine stimulating. The conversation drifted about the various topics two people share when they are learning about each other.

Eventually, my body tired and I knew it was time to go home. David offered to drive me there, but I wanted to walk in the moonlight. Despite my protests that I would be all right, he walked with me, his arm through mine, strong and sure.

At my doorstep, I turned and thanked him for the evening. He slid his arm from under mine, then lifted his hand to touch my face, his thumb resting lightly on my lips. His eyes held mine for a moment. "Goodnight," he said, then walked down my driveway. I slept deeply that night and remembered no dreams.

The next few weeks were a pattern of days spent in the garden, most evenings enjoyed at his house or mine for dinner. I was generally content with what the moment held, but at night I sometimes felt a twinge of apprehension. I knew what the past held and knew I had not dealt with the bulk of it. I did not know what the future held and I wondered about a man who so easily moved into my life. He was graceful in that, as well.

I found myself thinking about that one morning in the garden, when, startled, I looked up to see a single crow on the fence post.

"Be here now," he cawed, bowed lightly, then flapped off to the pine trees.

"I will do my best," I answered.

May / Meadowlark Sings

The fields were singing with joy as the sun rose. It was an early May morning and the world was new. The meadowlarks were singing all around me in the grass. The garden was growing strong with peas, cabbage and broccoli. Near the bench, the first rose buds lifted their tender lips to the sun. I breathed deep as I settled poppy seeds into the ground.

David came to the garden as the afternoon sun slanted through the pine trees. He helped me finish planting the poppy seeds, smoothing the soil over them, then we sat together on the bench and admired our work.

"I'm leaving tonight—I'll be gone for a few weeks," he said. "Some business to take care of." I presumed, but would not ask, that the business involved his wife.

"When will you be back?"

"The first Friday of June. I'll be bringing my kids with—you can meet them, come for dinner that night."

"I would like to meet them," I said, but was thinking of other things. The meadowlarks continued to tell the world of their blessings. We sat silently and listened to them.

"I need to go," David said finally, then stood up to leave. I stood with him, looking into his green eyes. He smiled, pulled me to him and kissed me as I leaned into his warmth. I felt sure of myself in the strength of his touch.

Later, as the sun set and I made tea in my kitchen, I thought of that moment and breathed deep.

That night, I lay awake in bed for longer than usual, looking at the patterns of stars in the window, wondering about the future. Eventually, I fell asleep. I found myself lying on my back in the garden. Under my open hands I could feel the newly planted poppy bed. My skin warmed in the sunlight that streamed down on me and I

19

stretched my arms and legs to welcome it into my muscles and bones. I closed my eyes and breathed deeply of the rose-scented air.

I settled down into the soft ground below me, relaxing my shoulders, letting my legs fall away from each other, my lips part. I felt his touch, soft as the lightest breeze at first, then growing more insistent as my breath quickened, my pulse beat harder into the ground. We came together with a flood of sensation that fluttered with the wind like rose petals, then sank like water into the reaching earth.

I opened my eyes and I was alone in the garden. Sitting up, I looked about me to find a meadowlark on the fence post. He opened his bill to the sky and sang. Into the silence after the song, I spoke: "Do you bring me a message beyond simple joy?"

He fluttered down to the grass next to the garden and I saw, sheltered from casual sight, his mate on a nest. She lifted her breast for a moment to show me two eggs. "Shelter your joy on the ground of your own heart," she said as she settled back down. "Or else it will break."

I lay back down into the bed of poppies that had grown about me as I listened. Their red buds began to unfurl in the sunlight. I felt my breath slow and deepen as I fell into dreamless sleep for the rest of the night.

In the morning, I welcomed the sunrise in the garden, listening to the meadowlarks in the grass around me. Behind me, in the Ponderosa pines, a crow cawed: "Be here now."

"I am," I answered, then set to work pulling weeds.

June / Toad Dives Into the Water

June brought the first blades of corn bursting through the garden soil. The weeds also grew like they were desperate to prove themselves. I diligently pulled them each morning, then, more often than not, found myself walking through the pines, listening to the breeze playing tunes through their long needles.

I told myself I should start looking for work: there were some things I would be able to do now, at least on a part-time basis, and money was growing short. But each time I thought of driving into Fondis to pick up a paper or visit the employment center, I found myself walking in the fields instead.

I had not come to resolution by the time David returned. "Come to dinner tonight and meet the kids," he said, so I came to dinner. The food was good as always but, despite a sparkling white wine, the conversation dragged.

David seemed at a loss for words as he went about preparing and serving. John, a lanky boy just turned twelve, looked much like his father, with black hair, green eyes and a soft smile. He answered my questions about school and sports freely enough, between bites, but offered nothing.

Amanda did not smile as readily. I could see the promise of the woman she would become, with long lashes and high cheekbones beneath bright auburn hair. She was polite, but no more, throughout the dinner, questioning me silently with her dark eyes.

David tried to draw her out with a story about their visit to Lake Fondis that morning, but she remained closed within herself, not quite accusing. After dinner, as I turned to leave, I caught a glimpse into her face as she looked at her father. Her sorrow spoke painfully to my own. I wondered why David had invited me to dinner on the first day his children were in his new home. I wondered why I had agreed to come.

David's children spent three weeks with him, then returned to their mother. I met with them occasionally, but the wall remained in place. I spent most of my time working diligently in the garden: watering, weeding, picking the early harvest, then eating it alone.

The toad emerged from under a squash leaf as I was watering one evening. He sat there, unmoving, watching me. I dribbled a little water on his warty hide and he puffed out his throat in thanks. I laughed. "Would you like a kiss?" I asked him, but then the thought of it chilled me.

Steven had hated toads. "Nasty, crawly things," he called them. There was an evening in early summer when we had decided to eat dinner outside on the porch. I held the bowl of stir-fried vegetables against my pregnant belly while Steven carried the wine glasses out to the table. A little toad was hiding under his chair. Scowling in disgust, he had stepped on the creature, smearing it across the cement. When I started crying, Steven had held my shaking body close, smoothing my hair until the tears passed. "The silly moods of pregnant women," he said, then kissed me hard.

In my dream that night, I was lying on my back under the spreading squash leaves, their vibrant blossoms arching into the black sky above me. The toad scrambled out from a hole in the ground, then hopped onto my bare shoulder to croak into my ear. "Look beneath the surface," he advised.

"Beneath the surface of what?" I asked.

"The surface of what you feel."

"There's just pain under what I feel."

"Your skin is dry," he said as he crawled onto my neck. "You can't feel the world through dry skin." My whole body shivered as I felt his webbed toes scratch against my earlobe. Fear was rising in me faster than I could build walls to close it in. I tried to tell myself that it was just a dream, but I had learned enough to know better.

"Dry is safe," I told him, then I shuddered as I felt the dirt under me turn into water.

"Dive into it," the toad ordered.

"If I do, I'll drown."

"You are hard and dry as mud in drought-time," he countered as he tangled himself in my hair. "Dried mud can't flow, so nothing lives there." I screamed as he pulled me under.

I sank backward into the dark. I couldn't breathe. Desperation filled my mouth with a rush of water until an unseen force slammed into my solar plexus forcing me to gasp it in. My lungs filled with the heavy weight as I sank down. I couldn't see, couldn't hear beyond the scream of my blood, couldn't feel my body as I fell.

With a shock of transition, I was sitting at my work table, grading students' papers. It was late but the air was still hot from the day. I could hear Steven walking up to stand behind me. I tensed, remembering that night. He came closer and started rubbing my shoulders.

"It's late and you're tired" he whispered. "Come to bed."

"I have to get a few more papers done for tomorrow," I found myself answering, just like that night.

"Not tonight—tonight you're mine." His hands were in my hair pulling my head back, his mouth covering mine, biting my lips.

"Now," he demanded, voice harsh, breath rough against my cheek. I froze, my hands gripping the table edge, but he pulled me up, forced me around, pressed my back to the table. I could feel his hand pulling my skirt up to my waist as he held me down with his weight. "Be a wife to me," he said. I felt him force my legs apart, felt him thrust himself deep into me. My breaths came hissing through my teeth, my hands slapped helplessly against his back, until they clenched without my conscious will against his shoulderblades, pulling him closer to me.

Afterward, he left me alone, thighs trembling as I pulled my skirt down, sat back down in my chair and stared blindly at the papers scattered across the table. I would not feel it, I would feel nothing. It was a mistake to feel. Numbness was easier.

I gave up. There was nothing in me left to struggle with. I was swallowed by the dark mouth of the water that rose around me and took me within. The toad found me there, floating in darkness. "I was wrong," I told the toad. "But I don't know how I was wrong. I should have fought him. Or maybe I shouldn't have fought him at all, shouldn't have worked at the university. But that made me feel real. Maybe I should have told him how I felt—but he wouldn't have listened. He never listened to me. I wanted to feel real, feel myself, feel whole, not just Steven's wife—but that's all he wanted of me, wanted me for." I felt the panic rising in me, but this time I refused to shut it out. "Damn it—I knew better then that! Maybe I couldn't have stopped him. I couldn't stop him. But why did I have to let my body feel good when he did that to me?"

The toad just floated serenely by my side, watching me. "You can choose again," he said. "If you want to. Your spirit is soft enough now."

Choice. I was different now. I could choose to be different. I looked back at who I was, what I had done, what had been done to me, and something in me melted. I chose to forgive myself. At the moment I chose, I found release. All the world rushed into me and filled me to overflowing, then circled out and around again in a pulsing spiral of life, death, rebirth. I laughed hard, choking at first, then looser.

I woke and took a clean breath of air.

July / Snake in the Thunderstorm

July brought thunderstorms and heat.

I watched the play of lightning among the clouds that teased the earth with scattered drops. Standing in my doorway, I felt the tingle of electricity along my skin, smelled the expectation of ozone on the swirling wind. There was a rising urgency in the air that woke an answering tide within me.

Finally, a crescendo of thunder spilled itself into rain, sinking deeply into the dry ground. I walked into the rain, raising my face and hands to it, feeling it sink into me like it sank into the earth. I followed the track of a snake as it flowed effortlessly through the wet grass, parting it smoothly.

After the storm, the clouds softened and faded to the east. The sun shone as if it had held the sky alone all afternoon. Feeling the rising heat, I returned to the house to strip off my rain-soaked clothes. I dressed in a thin blouse and cotton shorts, then walked barefoot to the garden to pull weeds before the soil baked hard again.

That evening, David joined me in the garden. Weeding and watering done for the moment, we sat together on the bench to watch the sun set. He put his arm around my shoulders and gently pulled me to him, as he had not done since before his children's visit. I felt his breath flow across my cheek; my brief thoughts of resistance melted into the heat. "Your hair glows like fire," he said, as he ran his fingers through it, holding a handful up so each pale strand fell through the slanting sun rays.

I could feel the fire race across my scalp and down my spine. His lips soft on my throat sent another sheet of flame through me, his fingers on my blouse traced swirling sparks around my nipple that hardened to his touch. I gasped, unable to speak, just clutched his waist and arched toward his hand as he pulled my blouse slowly off my shoulder, then traced the exposed curve of my breast. Helplessly, I watched the sun sink deep within the wide pupils of his eyes, mesmerizing me into stillness in the first light breeze of dusk.

I arched with fire again as his hand trailed lower, resting for a moment between my thighs. As he lingered there for a while, I moaned deep in my throat, aching to feel him move deeper, but he paused, quiet. I found his lips with mine and parted them for my tongue to thrust as I pressed the length of my body against him.

"No!" he said as he pulled back, sliding his hand from between my thighs. "No—I'm sorry." His breath was ragged in his throat. "I shouldn't have done that to you." I could see his shoulders shake with effort.

"Why?" I managed to ask, feeling my own muscles shake with need as my leg slid away from his.

"I promised Amanda that I would try to work things out with Tracy—her mother." His long, gentle fingers clenched. "I promised—but I want to make love to you!"

He looked at me, long and lost, as the last glow of sunset faded in his hair. I felt the cool night against my bare breast. I knew that all I needed was to touch him and he would be mine. My choice.

"Go to her," I said, as gently as I could. He stood to go, but paused; I could see his body still struggling with need for mine. "She is the mother of your children."

As he walked the garden path, a snake wound away from his step. David reached for a stone; I said, "Don't—just let it go." The snake slid among the poppy stems, their wet, red buds trembling as it passed. David was gone. I pulled my clothes where they belonged and walked to my house.

I had no true sleep that night. I lay naked and sweating in the heat, windows open to the night air and sheets scattered on the floor. I knew the snake would visit me and felt relief when he finally came, sliding gracefully up from between my thighs, across my belly, to curve around one breast. He looked at me with dark, unreadable eyes, tongue quivering. "You are changing," he said.

"Life is changing around me," I countered. "And I don't know what to do about it." I felt petulant, but also felt I had the right to be. It occurred to me, like a flash of revelation, that maybe I was just going crazy.

"Life is change. Certainty is death. Which do you want?" He flickered his tongue lightly across my cheek and down my neck, sending cool shivers behind it.

"I want enough certainty to stand on, enough to keep my head above water while life does whatever it wants to do to me."

"Whatever it wants?" he asked. "Do you have no choice?" his tongue brought my nipples flaring to life, set my blood rushing achingly through my veins.

"What choice have I had so far? The choice to accept what's done to me? The choice to feel pain or try to wall it up until it breaks through to me anyway?" I could feel the walls I was rebuilding in me and the pain rising within them. "I tried to open up and feel, but it just keeps hurting."

"What is pain?" he asked, his scales moving smoothly across the skin over my heart as he rose to look at me, eye to eye.

"Pain is when everything I care about is taken away from me."

"Why do you care?"

"Because I can't stop caring."

"Because you are alive."

"Then maybe I should die."

He turned to nestle in a loop between my breasts. "That will come, in time. Until then, you will care, and feel pain for it."

"Why? Why do I have to hurt so much?" At that moment, I could feel nothing beyond the aching hole I had fallen back into.

"Pain and joy share the same knife blade. Learn to use it or it will cut you to the bone."

My hand curled as if to hold that knife. "I am lying here, talking of pain with you, when I could have been feeling some joy with him."

"Pleasure is not the same as joy. You can tell the difference by the aftermath."

It bothered me that he was right. "I know that. That's why I sent him away."

"You are learning to speak your truth," he said, then bit me at the hollow of my throat. The pain radiated in waves throughout my body.

I woke to find menstrual blood staining my sheets. I got up and stumbled to the shower, coughing. The warm water slithered like snakes down my skin as I let myself cry into the soothing flow of water. As the day passed, I found myself absently rubbing at the base of my throat, until the dead skin peeled away in patches.

The next day, I found reasons not to visit the garden, but went instead to stand under the pine trees as the heat of the afternoon began to ease. I knew he would come to talk to me then, and I preferred to meet him beneath their shade.

I followed a path to a little pond, sheltered among the trees. I could see the tracks of animals that came to taste the water. Standing on a stone by the water's edge, I traced with my toe the curves left by a snake in the drying mud. I could feel David's presence behind me without turning to see him.

"I'm sorry," was the first thing he said.

"I know," I answered, sitting down on the stone, looking at the water.

"I don't really know what I want." I heard him move a few steps closer to me.

"Perhaps you just don't want to choose. If you let someone else make a choice for you, you don't have to be responsible for what comes of it."

When I looked up at him, his eyes were distant, clearly thinking about what I said. "I know I don't want to hurt you. Or my kids."

"So you don't choose, and hurt us all. Hurt yourself, too."

"I know I owe them something more than I've given them so far. I owe them a family." He cupped his hands in front of his chest, looking down at them. "Tracy and I will just have to learn how to make it work."

I stood up to look right at him, finally, wanting to see the green of his soft eyes one more time before he left me. "Don't look back," I told him. He didn't as he walked away.

I sat back down by the pond for a while longer, watching a dragonfly skim its surface, watching the shadows of the trees deepen the hidden places below. My fingers rubbed absently against the rough skin at the base of my throat. Behind me, a crow laughed.

It was near dark when I looked up to see the fox watching me from across the water. For a moment, we watched each other. I didn't know if he would speak to me outside of my dreams, but I heard his words in my mind: "So are you coming back to your senses?"

I felt the hard stone under my hands, heard the faint breeze whispering through the pine needles, smelled the vanilla scent of sun-warmed pine bark, tasted salt on my lips. "Yes," I answered, "But I'm not sure yet if I want to."

"Follow as you can," he said, then slipped between the trees and was gone.

August / Cougar Hunting

The August sun was unrelenting. There was no hint of rain for three weeks, but at night the heat lightning would play about the sullen sky. I took to walking in the pine woods in the early mornings, in the first gray light of dawn. When I realized I was avoiding the garden, I spent time watering the drying plants, but was soon drawn to walk the woods again, restless. My skin itched; the flaking spread from my throat to my chest as I rubbed it without thinking. I could not settle comfortably with any task.

The little pond shrank gradually in the heat, concentrating the animal tracks that ringed it. One hot morning I found the tracks of a cat, wide as my palm. I felt a shock of fear and looked about me, but saw nothing.

I could see her in my dreams that night, gliding smoothly along the ground, muscles bunching to launch her powerful body up the bole of a tree, flashing eyes looking down at me. I heard the harsh rush of her breath as she ran past me, but she did not speak to me. I stood alone, shaking with apprehension, but nothing came of it all night.

I spent the day in mundane chores, unable to concentrate on anything for long. The itchiness in my skin spread across my back and down my stomach, never letting me rest until I doused it with pain pills in the night. As I slept, my skin tightened, pulling hard on the muscles and bones beneath it, merging in my restless dreams with memories of hospital nights spent counting the minutes until dawn.

Again, in dreams, I felt her heat, watched her confident passage, but she would not talk to me. I could not read a message in the tracks she left behind on the floor of my nightmare hospital. She brought no relief for the aching tightness I felt within me.

The third night, I called out to her: "Talk to me, damn you. Don't just leave me here to burn!"

She turned gracefully, looked into my eyes. "Burn you will, whether I talk or not."

"At least give me some company, then," I said, feeling the flames grow within me. "Don't leave me alone with this pain."

"Then run with it," she answered, and leaped on my shoulders, driving me down until I felt four legs hold me up. I ran, following her. I felt the power of muscles sliding rhythmically under skin, felt the heat build within me until the flames roared through my throat.

She slowed until I paced even with her steps. "Feed your hunger," she commanded. I could feel it rising within me, pounding in my blood. I saw the buck deer in front of me, antlers proud against the stars as I slid quietly toward him through the dark of the trees. The musky scent of him filled my mouth, fueling the raging flames in my throat.

Abruptly, the night was sliced by rushing headlights behind him: a car approached uncontrollably on the rain-slick road that suddenly appeared under us. I sank to the ground, unable to move to save myself.

"No," I screamed, the sound piercing through the glaring light, shattering it, unlocking my muscles at the same time the buck deer gathered himself to run.

My whole body burning, I ran, leaped, felt my claws dig deep into the muscles of his back as he shuddered, bucking desperately. I held on, feeling the flames spill from my throat. I sank my teeth into his neck, felt the soothing flow of blood in my mouth as he stumbled and fell crashing to the ground. My body trembled with release as his trembling ended beneath me.

I woke in the dark, body cold and slick with sweat, breathing hard. I sat for a moment, pulling my conscious thoughts into some sort of order, gradually recognizing that I was in my home, in bed. I tasted blood in my mouth and felt the shock run through me, driving me up and outward. I stumbled outside, barefoot on the trail that ran into the pine woods, forcing my stiff body to move past the pond, up the hill.

Heat lightning raced across the rainless clouds above me, followed by rolling thunder. I felt the electricity scatter across my skin as I climbed the hill. Near the top, the adrenaline washed out of me, leaving my hip aching. I limped on, determined to see what lay on the other side.

The deer was lying where I had left him in my dream, throat torn, dead eyes looking up to the flashing sky. The crackle of lightning swirled around me, raising the hairs on my arms. I turned quickly, sensing her behind me. She was beautiful and powerful, flowing and graceful, eyes flaming green in the shivering light. She watched me, quiet, the dark tip of her tail flicking behind her.

I stood and faced her, feeling the anger rising in me again with the beat of thunder in my ears. Lightning flared around me. I bared my teeth, not caring that hers were more deadly, and stepped toward her. She dropped her gaze, turned to leave. "The kill is yours," she said. "Feast well."

I stood alone on the hilltop, drained empty, bare feet growing cold. Even the lightning faded into darkness. I looked again at the dead deer, then at the cougar vanishing into the pine woods. "The feast is yours," I told her. "My thanks for the lesson." She paused to look over her shoulder at me, then she was gone.

I knelt carefully next to the deer's head and traced the curve of his antler with my fingers. The last of the heat lightning shimmered along the tines. "I'm sorry," I told him, wondering if his spirit could hear me. "I will do my best to honor what you have taught me."

As light as the breeze that whispered through the pine needles, I heard his voice circling around me: "I live in you." The night sky faded into predawn softness as I stood, turned, and walked slowly home.

I made coffee, stood drinking it by the window that looked toward the garden. All of the burning anger I had felt seemed to have settled into my skin: it was all-over-hot, tight and itchy. I took a cool shower, standing under the pounding water, eyes closed. I could feel my old, dead skin pulling away in shreds, flowing down.

September / Butterfly Music

The rains finally started in the first week of September. I stood in the garden, letting the misty drops soak into my tender, new skin. A few shafts of late afternoon sunlight found their way through the clouds. The sunflowers glowed and crystal beads slid around the curves of pumpkins and winter squash.

I found words crowding into my head, asking to be written down, a sensation I had not felt since before the accident. I went into the house to find paper and pen.

The phone rang for the first time in weeks, startling me. "Hello," I somehow remembered to speak into it.

"Gwyneth—it's Mary. I'm sorry I haven't called in so long."

I thought for a moment. Mary Lucero taught Biology at Fondis University. "It's o.k. I haven't called you, either."

"Well, I could use your expertise," she said. "I'm writing a book on the way our local wildlife is adjusting to urbanization, and the way people are adjusting to the presence of wildlife. I could use your help with the wording of it. You know me: a science type, not writer material. I bet you have some personal experiences that would add color to the book, too, living where you do."

My first impulse was to say "No, I'm not ready," but I wasn't sure what that really meant. "Sure," I said instead.

"Great! Let's meet to hash things out—how about Thursday?"

I paused before answering—what day was it now? Not that it mattered: I had nothing on my schedule, no matter what day. "O.K.," I answered, figuring I would turn on my computer and find the date.

"Should we meet at your place?" Mary asked. "I've never seen it and I'd love to."

"O.K.," I said again, wondering if the house looked good enough for company.

"Ten o'clock sound good? Oh—and I'd like to introduce you to Brendan, who's going to illustrate the book. He's a great artist, works part time at the university."

What else could I say, but "O.K.," again? I hung up the phone, found pen and paper and went back to the garden, aware that the flow of life had suddenly pulled me back into the stream.

The wind was picking up, drawing clouds from the west, bringing a quick chill into the garden. I sat for a while on the bench, writing whatever came into my head, until the sun was firmly packed away behind lowering clouds.

As I stood to leave, I noticed a fluttering of butterfly wings among the last of the summer poppies. Walking closer, I saw that it was a Monarch, not just one of the faded Painted Ladies that passed through each fall. It had been blown off course by the wind, most likely, and unable to raise itself out of the tangle of stems because it was cold. I freed it from the poppies and carried it to a sheltered corner near the house, where the sun warmth still lingered.

"Sit here a moment," I told the butterfly, "and I'll get you something to drink." By the time I returned with a shallow plate of watered honey, its wings were already beating harder. It uncurled a shiny black proboscis to taste the honey.

"Good?" I asked it, but got no answer.

31

I watched as its wings pulsed and straightened, ready for flight. Each tentative wingbeat resonated deep in my chest. As the butterfly launched itself into the wind, the sun dipped below the cloud curtain, throwing shafts of gold across the ground. The butterfly disappeared into the light, but I could still feel its wingbeats drawing me out of my body like a cord along the slanting light. It felt like music within me, singing me home.

I dispersed among the sunrays, sliding in straight paths pouring ever upward, drawn into nothing but streaming light. I felt peace and little else, except the gentle pull upward and onward, light but insistent. The universe sang with many blended voices around me, drawing me in.

Then the sun dipped below the mountains and the night began. I felt myself crouching again before I could see though my eyes. When they adjusted to the dimness, I saw that I was on the hill past the pond, between the trees, with no body sense of how I had arrived there. I stood slowly, stretched muscles to the sky, and walked home.

On Thursday, Mary's car pulled into the driveway, marking fresh tracks into the gravel. "It's so good to see you!" she cried as she got out of the car. "I can't imagine how bad this year has been for you!"

I had gone through some anxiety thinking I wouldn't recognize her, but as soon as I saw her—a petite Latina with long hair—it all came home.

"It's getting better," I told her, shaking her hand. "How is your new department head doing?" I asked, dredging up a faint memory.

She chattered for a bit about university politics while I watched Brendan step out of the passenger side. Tall, broad shoulders, sandy hair. But as he turned to greet me, it was his intense hazel eyes—framed by eyelashes many women work hard each morning to acquire—that drew my attention.

"I'm Brendan O'Donnell," he said, stepping toward me with his hand outstretched. As my hand slipped into his, I felt a flow of warmth up my arm. My whole body hummed with energy as I stood there, staring at him until the moment broke and we stepped apart.

I don't remember what he said then or what meaningless social grace I responded with, but I know I invited them to the house for ice tea since the day was becoming hot for the season. We sat together on the porch for a while, talking about little things until Mary brought us to the point.

"I really appreciate that you're taking the time to go over this," she said, as she handed me her draft manuscript. "I know it's rough, but I hope it's not too hard to slog through."

I just laughed a little and took the papers. I flipped through a few of them, recognizing the awkward phrasings and convoluted patterns from prior examples of Mary's work, bringing my past along with them in a rush of memories. "Give me a week and I'll get the revisions to you," I said.

"A week? Is that enough time?"

"I don't have much else to do right now."

An awkward silence followed. I knew that Mary would end it, uncomfortable with the tension. "It's going to be wonderful working together again, and I'm sure you'll love Brendan's artwork. He and I have been travelling all around the outskirts of Fondis: up on the ridge, around the springs, on the cliffs, in the canyons, everywhere there's animals and people. I have some great interviews, too. You wouldn't believe what that weird Deirdre Moon told us about the unicorn she thinks is living in the canyons!" She laughed, but Brendan just smiled like he remembered something private.

Mary chattered on, not noticing. "And Epona Maris! She tried to get us to believe that the animals all talk to us like psychics, or something like that. I know she's fun when she does writing workshops at the university, but that went a little too far! I guess that's what living alone in the woods and writing poetry all the time will do to you!" This time Brendan saw that I noticed his private smile and broadened it to share with me. I wondered what Mary would think of my wildlife experiences, if I told her.

"We got a lot more useful information from Roger Rural—you know, that farmer who writes for the paper," she went on. "He's been watching the wild turkeys in the forest and says that they make all sorts of elaborate calls to tell each other when to worry about people coming near and when it's safe."

"We got to see a beautiful flock coming down to the river that morning," Brendan added.

"Absolutely beautiful," Mary emphasized. "Well, I'm sure Brendan would love to look around your land a bit, maybe sketch a few pictures," she said, patting him on the arm.

"Only if I'm not intruding," he said. "It's a remarkably good area for wildlife around here. I imagine you must have had some memorable encounters." Something must have shown in my face—I have never been good at hiding what I feel—but Brendan just tilted his head a little with one eyebrow raised. He knew I had stories I could tell, but didn't push for them.

"I can show you around the fields, if you want," I said, and led them both on a little tour.

Brendan looked like a little boy hunting for frogs when he saw the pond. "This is great," he said, bouncing a little on the balls of his feet. "This would be the perfect place to observe at twilight—if you don't mind," he added quickly. I laughed and decided that I didn't mind.

Mary seemed more interested in the old barn behind the house, within a fence that we had meant to repair, before the accident. "Look at this," she said, smiling at Brendan. "Maybe you could talk Gwyneth into renting her pasture for your horse!"

Brendan looked quickly at her, frowning. "I don't think now's the time to bring something like that up."

"But you were saying that you really need a new place for the horse, and wouldn't this be perfect? The grass really needs cutting, and there's nothing like a horse for that! As long as the fence is fixed, of course."

"The pasture is nice," he said, "but I think it's kind of an imposition on someone who's barely met me." He turned to look at me, straight in my eyes. "I'm sorry," he said. "You don't need to consider it."

I wondered why he felt the need to apologize, but then wondered if this was really why Mary had brought Brendan to see me. I realized that I had been standing there, watching them talk as if I were just an observer. I brought my thoughts back to the question at hand. "Why don't we get to know each other a bit better as book collaborators before we talk about who moves in? I haven't even seen your drawings yet—maybe I won't like them." Realizing how that might sound, I tried to lighten it with a smile.

"Maybe you won't," he echoed, smiling too.

Behind him, a crow landed on a fence post, dipped her head and cawed: "Be aware!" Brendan pulled out his sketchbook and pencil to capture the pose. His fingers moved with surety.

The crow flapped her way back to the trees and Brendan closed his sketchbook. "Well, alright," Mary said. "You two are big kids and can work things out without me interfering anymore." She turned to walk back to her car. "I'll see you in a week!" she called back to me.

"Did I offend her?" I asked Brendan.

"I doubt it," he answered, laughing, "but I'm going to hear all about it on the ride back into town. If you let me come back tomorrow evening, I'll fill you in."

"Fine," I said, feeling a faint sense of anticipation that I couldn't quite define. "Just before sunset?"

"Just before sunset."

I listened to the car's tires chuckle through the gravel on its way down the driveway, then went to the garden to check for tomatoes.

That night, I went to bed thinking of horses, but dreamed of butterflies. The air was filled with them, swirling about in chaotic patterns that I could almost understand. I lifted my arms and they surrounded me in a vibrant haze. "Come inside," I told them, and breathed them in. I was filled with a flurry of music that danced about inside me.

I spent the next day alternating between editing Mary's text and working in the garden. I felt a pleasant hum within my body, my energy building and setting to work in a way that had not happened for far too long.

The last sunlight was filtering through the pine needles when Brendan's truck came up the driveway. I carried a basket of squash to the porch then walked over to greet him.

"Mary is so excited that I'm coming back here," he said. "I know it's obvious that she has match-making plans, so I want to state right up front that I'm not asking for anything beyond professional courtesy from you."

"Nothing else?" I asked. "How about some ice tea while we watch the pond?"

"I'm willing to bend the rules for ice tea," he answered, laughing. "But that's it."

"Watch out—you're on a slippery slope. What starts with a little ice tea could lead anywhere. But I promise I won't push you down that slope."

"Contract accepted," he said, and balanced his glass with his sketchpad and pencils as I led him down the path to the pond.

We settled between two rocks with a good view of the pond. As the sun faded from the trees, everything around us became shadowy. The pond glimmered faintly in the afterglow. The scent of

Evening Primrose drifted from the pale masses that surrounded us. I felt content with the moment, open to whatever might come.

The fox was there at the pond's edge across from us, as if he had always been there, watching us. "How do foxes do that?" Brendan whispered, sketching his casual pose. The fox smiled.

"It's just magic," I answered. Brendan glanced at me, then went back to sketching. I watched the pencil lines become an insolent fox on the page. "Magic," I whispered again.

Brendan returned before dawn the next morning to watch meadowlarks and warblers begin their morning rituals. He left me to my peace during the day, returning to watch by the pond in the evening. I enjoyed sitting quietly with him watching the world transition into night. The owl called to me from a pine branch over Brendan's head one evening. I watched her glide silently into the darkness, knowing I was not alone, knowing there were paths opening before me, but knowing I could choose.

Brendan found cougar tracks by the pond early one morning as the night-chill began to lift from the water. "Look at this," he called to me, but I could tell by the tension in his body what it was he saw. "They follow the path up the hill," he said when I got near enough to see the prints. "Where does it go?"

"I'll show you," I said, and led him up the hill. I had not visited the hilltop since the buck's death and I was hesitant to take Brendan there now, but I was learning that it's better to face challenges when they are presented to me.

There wasn't much left of the deer beyond scattered bones and the elegant tracery of his antlers. I could feel a little of the anger that had burned in me that night, but it was a banked fire now, illuminating the walls that surrounded it, walls that now had doors that I could open when I needed them. Brendan was watching me with curious eyes, but he did not ask. I knelt down beside the empty skull, touched the antlers that rose from it. "I'm sorry," I said, echoing that storm-charged night. "I'm sorry, Steven," I added, "and I forgive you." Behind me, I could hear Brendan take out his sketchpad, but I didn't mind. It felt appropriate, somehow, like a memorial. Afterward, we walked quietly together back down the path.

There was a simple pattern to the next few days. Brendan sketched frogs in the pond, crows in the trees, hawks in the sky and he carefully followed a skunk up the path. I looked up from my work in the garden one day to see him standing by the gate, sketching me as I picked shell beans. "Not much wildlife here in the garden," I told him.

"You'd be surprised," he answered, continuing to sketch me. I went over to look at what he had drawn and saw my face, sharp-boned and angular, framed by pale hair that ended in owl feathers. The elegant brush of a fox's tail was draped across my shoulders. "Is that how you see me?" I asked.

He shrugged and looked down at what he had drawn. "Close enough," he said. "I don't think your nose is really quite that long, though."

"You seem to have too much time on your hands," I said. Why don't you find something useful to do, like mend the fence?"

"With what—a pencil?" he asked, holding one up and waggling it.

"There are tools in the work shed. Figure them out."

Smiling, he put his sketchbook into his pack and walked behind the house to the work shed.

A few hours later, I carried the pitcher of ice tea and a couple of glasses back to the pasture. He had done good work in that time: all four corner posts braced and a section of t-posts straightened. I set the tea on a table in the shade and he seemed happy to take a break.

"You're sweating," I told him. "I guess sketching pictures doesn't build your muscles much."

"I used to be in great shape when I did massage therapy full time," he answered, sipping his tea. "The university schedule really cuts into that."

"You did massage?"

"Still do—when I can. Energy work, too." He saw my puzzled look and added: "Clearing the energy patterns in and around the body. I've always been able to see energy patterns in people—animals too. That's why I have a horse, by the way." I just looked puzzled again, trying to track his thoughts. He laughed. "She was abused by a previous owner. She's a mustang, from the open range. I really felt for her, coming from that freedom to a cage complete with whips and chains. The horse society rescued her and asked if I would work with her: trauma recovery. I'm more used to working with humans, but I couldn't say no when I saw her."

I thought about that, sipping my tea: trauma recovery. Recovering from trauma. "Why do you need a new place for her?"

37

"She's been living at the society's ranch, but they just took in a herd of starved horses so there's not much room." He looked at me for a moment before continuing. "Besides, she still needs time to herself. Time to recover."

I realized that I had already chosen. "I know something about time needed to recover," I told him. "And I know something about being abused." It was the first time I had used that word in reference to myself. I wasn't sure how I felt about what that meant, but sharing it with Brendan had felt all right. "I suppose she and I could help each other."

"She's already been good for me," he said quietly. "I have a few wounds to recover from, too." I wanted to ask, but was afraid to say anything, so said nothing.

Brendan broke the silence: "Remember, we have a contract."

I looked blankly at him, so he added: "professional courtesy. You don't have to give me anything beyond that."

"And I won't push you down that slippery slope." We shook hands, as if sealing a deal. I felt the thrill of energy flowing into my body again. "So what is her name? I can't just take in a guest without proper introduction, you know."

"Do you know Brighde NicEoghainn and Shining Owl Maris, the two old women who run the rescue society? The ones most people call 'Epona's crazy grandmothers?' They like to name each of the horses they take in. It doesn't matter what name they might have been called before—they say a horse needs to know its 'true name' if it's going to make a new start in life."

"That makes sense to me," I said, wondering if I had a true name waiting somewhere for me to claim it.

"They named her Foxheart," Brendan said. "She certainly looks like a fox, as you'll see. And she has a subtle heart."

Brendan finished his tea and went back to work on the fence. I sat for a while longer, just listening for music in the pines and watching him.

October / Traveling by Horse

The fence was fixed, the barn cleared of junk, the trough filled with clear water. Foxheart explored her new home. She was a ruddy bay paint, with elegant black ears, slim black legs and streaks of white in her mane and tail: very foxlike. She also startled at the least movement, nostrils flared and muscles primed to run. The wire fence seemed a fragile thread to hold such wildness within.

I stood away from the pasture so as not to frighten her as Brendan walked with her, voice softly encouraging her, hand gently stroking her neck. Slowly she settled into his calm, letting him lead her. I found that my own muscles had tensed, my hands were clenched under my arms, watching them. I breathed deep, unfolding myself as I watched Brendan's hands slide across her smooth side, then cup her chin as he held her eyes steady with his. She lowered her head to the manger, tasted the hay that waited for her, and sighed. I sighed, watching her.

Brendan came to stand with me, outside the pasture, watching. "She is beautiful," I told him.

"You wouldn't have thought that when I first saw her. She was so thin that I could almost hook a finger under her ribs and she had rubbed her hair off in big patches. I couldn't get within ten feet of her without dodging a kick, even though she couldn't walk without limping. Whenever she heard someone coming, she would wedge herself into a corner of her stall, sweating and shivering."

"You've done amazing work with her," I said, watching him as he watched her.

"She wanted to change; I could feel that as soon as she let me into her energy field."

"How do you do that—connect with her energy and make it flow the right way?"

"It's not that I make it flow; I just hold open the possibilities for her to choose."

"Show me," I said, not really asking. I needed to know. He stood still for a moment, watching me with wide eyes, then slowly held out his hand. I laid mine on top of his and felt the flow instantly. It started with a faint hum but grew stronger, filling every secret place inside my body, folding around me like a warm shawl. I sighed again, giving myself up to the feeling, leaning toward him so close that I could feel the warmth surrounding his skin as well.

"I can't..." he said, breaking the contact by pulling his hand from mine. I stumbled, feeling like I was dropped from a cliff.

He shook his head, holding his arms tight around his body. "I'm sorry—I barely know you and I'm afraid." I just stood there, suddenly numb. He took a step back, looking down at his hands. "It's not about you," he continued. "I don't want to be set up again by whatever it is—God, spirits, the universe—that throws me in with people who are hurt. I felt your pain from the moment I met you—not just the physical pain, which is a lot. The emotional pain. The spiritual pain."

He turned to look into the pasture, gripping the fence post as he watched Foxheart explore her new home. "I went to massage school in large part so I could learn to set boundaries on what I feel from others, and it helped. For a few years I thought it was enough. Then I met Sharon. She was hurting from her last love and seemed vulnerable. I couldn't help opening up to her, giving to her until she took everything and left me.

"After that, it was a relief working with Foxheart, feeling her honesty." Brendan looked suddenly into my eyes. "I don't understand what I feel for you," he said. "It's not about whether I'm attracted to you or you to me. It's about being me. I don't know anything about what I want, now. I loved Sharon, felt we had a strong relationship. I trusted her with everything. But she was a user. There's a term for it: 'psychic vampire.' She drained me and moved on."

I felt like I was frozen in place, numbly watching him as he poured out a stream of emotion. I felt I might drown. "Why didn't you tell me?" was all I could think to say.

He shook his head. "I wanted to say something to you from the beginning—I can feel some sort of bond between us, not just the pain, and it scares me. I keep feeling like I have to make a choice that will determine the rest of my life. I'm not ready to choose." He turned suddenly and walked a few steps away. "I need to go now—I need some space to think this through. But I'll be back tomorrow morning to take care of Foxheart. I'm sorry—it's the best I can do right now."

I said nothing. I watched him walk away, not sure what I felt or what I should do. I had thought I knew the path I had chosen, but it had fallen out from under me. After a while, I went down to the garden and sat on the bench.

I heard hoofbeats in the driveway. I turned to see Foxheart walking into the setting sun. She paused to look at me, whickered softly, then continued walking. I followed her as quickly as my body would allow, not thinking beyond the need to keep her from losing herself. She turned down the road, hesitantly following it past David's old house. I noticed the For Sale sign as I passed. We continued down the road, Foxheart pausing at times to sniff the air or crop a bit of grass in the ditch, as if she knew I was struggling to keep up with her.

She turned into the mouth of an arroyo and followed it up into its source. I followed as best I could, watching the last sunrays shift away from me. It would soon be dark and I was not familiar with this path, but I knew the moon was full and would soon be rising above the hills. I kept going, hoping that would be enough light to see me through.

The arroyo was filled with the orange glow from the sunset, so intense that it was hard to see. I felt my body fill with the light, softening and flowing outward. "Not now," I said and slapped my hand hard against the side of the arroyo to ground myself. I walked carefully, my hand touching the sandy wall as it rose above me until it closed off the sun. I traveled into the blackness, hands reaching for the surety of the walls, feet shuffling across the uneven surface, seeking enough balance to continue. It felt like more than an hour, but time acts strangely in those circumstances. Every now and then I heard the sound of hoofs in the sand.

All of a sudden, the hoofbeats multiplied, the echoes rising around me, ringing off the arroyo walls. I could see nothing, but I smelled the sharp scent of horse sweat, felt heavy shoulders sliding past where I stood, frozen. I wanted to run, but there was no place around me that was not filled with the presence of unseen horses.

Then the moon rose and I could see. I was surrounded by moon-grayed horses, snorting and slick with sweat as if they had just been galloping hard. I held still, afraid I would be trampled if I moved. Suddenly, from the middle of the herd, Epona Maris appeared, bareback on a prancing mare. She saw me at the same moment.

"I'm sorry," she said, shifting her mount closer to me, which broke the flow of horseflesh around me like a stone in the stream. "There's never anyone here," she added. "Not that you're nobody—just nobody before you."

"I've never been here," I told her. "But I'm looking for a horse." She looked around her, as if just noticing her companions. "I followed her up here," I added, "But I think I lost her."

"Call to her with your heart," Epona said.

I thought about my heart but shied away from the pain that had returned to it. "I'm not sure I can."

"You can. You made it here."

I put my hand above my heart, as if I were saluting the flag, and felt the warmth of it. "Foxheart," I said softly; the horses around me shifted and I saw her.

"I am here," she said, as she walked to me and rested her head against my shoulder.

"She was at my grandmothers' place, I remember" Epona said. "She's an excellent guide to the otherworlds."

"She led me here, but I don't know where I am."

"You are in the moment you have created," Epona said, as if that solved my confusion.

"I don't understand—I just found this place."

"You don't just find your belief—you create it."

I felt more lost than found at that point, and not sure of creating anything. "I don't know how to get back home," I told Epona.

"Follow me," she said and turned her mare toward the rising moon. The rush of horses around me pulled me along; I found myself on Foxheart's back, clinging to her mane and hoping I wouldn't fall.

The horses galloped through the forest then swirled about a campfire in the middle of a clearing. I slipped off Foxheart's back and collapsed next to the fire. "Would you care for some tea?" an old woman asked with a Scottish burr, handing me a cup before I could respond.

I took the cup and looked into her deep gray eyes. "Where am I?"

"Wherever you want to be, dearie" she answered. At that moment I realized I had no idea. I just sat there, holding the teacup and crying. "There, now" the old woman said and handed me a lace-edged handkerchief. I watched Epona gracefully sit down across the fire from me, next to another old woman who watched me silently. Her long braided hair was black shot with silver; the firelight slicked the broad planes of her cheekbones.

"These are my crazy grandmothers," Epona said, making the old women cackle. "Grandmother Shining Owl is a Fondis Medicine

Woman and Granny Brighde is a Druid. I come to them whenever I no longer want to be lost."

"What am I looking for?" I asked them, not knowing what would be right to ask.

"Yourself, of course," Granny Brighde answered. "Not that any of us ever find ourselves, but we have a fine time with the journey."

I let the breath out that I hadn't realized I was holding. "I'm tired of riddles," I said. "I've had nothing but riddles for a year now, riddles with no real answers. I try to figure it all out, then realize I have nothing figured. I'm just tired."

Grandmother Shining Owl smiled. "You draw lines in water then wonder why they disappear."

I shrugged my shoulders. "Then how do I learn to draw lines in stone? Or at least sand."

"Even the stones flow with time," she answered.

"Then I am lost," I whispered.

"All you need is to go back to the beginning," Granny Brighde said. "Find the loose end of the tangled yarn and start winding."

I looked down at my hands and found a thread of moonlight crossing my palms. I curled my fingers around it, rose up and followed its path. "Back to the beginning," I said, then repeated it louder.

"Surely the beginning is a fine place to start," my father said. I could see his face where the moonlight flickered among pine needles, his familiar smile traced with the simple lines of childhood memory.

"Daddy?" I asked, still not believing.

"I'm sorry I left you so," he said. "I know I failed you, like I failed everything I cared about."

"What do you mean?" I asked. "You didn't fail me, you just died."

"All the more a failure," he sighed. "I should have been there for you as you grew to be a woman. Your mother did the best she could, of course, but she is not one to share her heart, you know."

"She never shared it with me."

"You and I, we have Celtic souls. We know how souls call to each other. Your mother was deaf to that music, no disgrace meant to her. She may rest in peace now, but you and I are restless with the knowing."

"What can I do about it?" I asked, feeling the restlessness he spoke of rise like the tide within me.

"Don't choose my path," he answered. "Don't run from what calls your spirit. You have a light within you that I lost, like I lost everything because of my fear."

"What fear?" I shivered and hugged my arms tight.

"The same one you hold inside you, my girl. The fear that the tide will sweep you out to sea and you will be forever lost. The fear of letting yourself open to the world."

"I don't know how. You left me and I'm lost."

"Not lost, my little white-feathered one. Not lost, just afraid to fly into the wind." He spread his hands wide and I could feel the breath of wind in my hair. "Not lost. I could have taken that chance. I know now that my life was worth living, despite what I feared. I could have chosen to keep struggling through it, but I chose to accept my failures instead. I thought I would end it all, but I just made things worse. I am sorry I hurt you so."

I could barely see him as the moonlight wavered through the tears in my eyes. "I miss you, Daddy. I love you."

"I love you, too," he said, his voice fading into some unknown distance. "Please forgive me."

"I thought I forgave you long ago," I said, but he was gone.

I turned and walked back to the campfire. "What do I do now?"

"Untangle the thread, dearie. Set the poor man free."

"I don't know how."

"Just start with the loose end, remember, and wind it up, little by little."

I didn't know what to say in return, except: "I want to go home but I don't know how."

"You have what you need inside you," Epona said as she slipped back onto her mare. "Just follow the moon." She leaned forward, sending all of the horses galloping back to the forest except Foxheart. The old women faded into the night, along with the campfire.

I have what I need inside me, I thought. What do I need? I looked inside myself and found that I was doubtful but whole. "This is who I am," I told Foxheart. "I am an instrument and I can feel the universe flowing through me like a song." She just snorted and stomped one foot. "Let's go home," I told her, turning toward the moon. It was setting at a different angle than Epona's path, but the slope was manageable, even with my bad hip. I started to walk,

Foxheart pacing beside me. The moon glow covered both of us, filling my eyes to overflowing. I felt the energy rise in me again and flow through me until I was running on four hoofs, drumming a pattern into the earth. Foxheart followed me home.

By the pasture gate, I stumbled, fell to the ground as a human again. My body ached with a throbbing pulse as powerful as my hoofbeats had been. I was too tender to move beyond curling into a fetal position and closing my eyes.

The night grew cold. I opened my eyes to see my breath drifting into the air. Foxheart stood near me, her breath flowing about me like a shroud.

I woke up again in the faint lightening of predawn with frost lacing my hair. Brendan was there.

"Gwyneth—what happened? Why are you out here?" he asked, kneeling beside me.

I looked up at him but had a hard time focusing on his face. "I followed Foxheart," I told him, "then she followed me. But I couldn't go any farther."

"Oh God," he said. "I'm sorry—I must not have latched the gate well. She has a talent for getting out. I am so sorry."

"I've heard that word too many times in my life," I told him.

"Then I'll stop saying it and do something useful instead. Just let me get Foxheart into the pasture—and latch the gate properly." I felt him leave, then return to pick me up and carry me into my house. I rested my head against his shoulder and fell back asleep.

I woke up alone in my bed. I watched the sun shine through the window and felt its warmth fill my skin, not wanting to think past the moment. I felt calm, despite the ache that clenched my muscles into tight knots. My fingers traced their own way into the pattern of the afghan covering me, searching for loose threads to follow. As I tentatively stretched my arms, I realized I was wearing my nightshirt. Brendan must have changed me into it as I slept.

As I was pondering my state, Brendan walked into the room with a steaming teapot and two cups. "I hope you don't mind," he said. "I was going to just put you on the couch, but you were so damp and cold from the frost. I decided comfort would be better than decorum."

"Thank you," I said, not sure what better words to use that would convey my meaning.

"How do you feel?" he asked as he set the tea tray down next to me.

"I feel good for some reason, even though my body feels like a tightly woven Celtic knot."

"Let me do something about that," he said. "Can you turn over on your stomach?" I could, barely. I felt his hands on my shoulders: firm but gentle, flowing with energy. "Just lie still." I did, sinking deeply into the sensation. I felt my muscles stretching and lengthening, felt the blood running freely through them. I felt his energy flowing like light into me, setting me aglow like he was the sun shining through me. I was filled to overflowing, sending ripples of energy back into his hands, completing a circle of light. I heard a deep humming that seemed to come from everywhere around me. I felt my whole being flowing into it, my spirit stretching toward a myriad of other shapes, but settling back into my own body. There was no better form to be in right then. I was at home in my skin and enjoying it. It took a while for me to notice that he was no longer touching me.

I sat up and took the full teacup he offered me. "I don't know how to be in the world anymore," I said without thinking. Brendan just sat quietly on the bed beside me, watching me.

"I thought I knew how to be—before the accident. But I've been learning that I didn't know, I was just pretending. Now I understand that, but I don't know how to live true." I felt an intense need to tell him everything I had done, everything I had felt and thought during the past year, and before. I told him how I had learned to understand Steven's intense desire for me to be part of him, my tentative moves toward independence through work, the painful results of our conflicting needs.

I told Brendan about the fox in the snow, the owl, the crows, the cougar, all the other animals that had taught me how to live again. I even told him what it felt like to flow into other shapes and the strange place filled with horses where I had followed Foxheart and spoken to Epona's crazy grandmothers. I told him about what my father had said.

When I finished, he was quiet for a moment. "You should write all of that down," he said. "I think it's the sort of life experience that will deepen from retelling it."

It struck me that, as a writer, it was odd that I hadn't thought of writing about this. "I will," I told him.

Brendan swirled the last of his tea about in his cup, watching it as if reading the future. "On my way here this morning," he said,

"I'd decided that I would tell you that I need to keep some distance from you. I had it all neatly figured out, but then I saw you lying on the ground out there, looking like you were dead."

I sighed. "I had wanted to tell you that I'm strong now, that I don't want to be another person in pain that needs your help. Now I should say that I'm sorry."

He shook his head. "I don't know what you want of me, but I'm not ready to even start thinking about a sexual relationship. Or anything else that implies."

There was a flicker of warmth growing inside me. "That's ok," I said. "I'm trying to learn how to be with myself, first. I think what I need most right now is a friend."

He smiled for the first time that morning, easy like a child smiles. "Friends. It's hard for me to trust, but I keep finding that you're like Foxheart: I don't feel used, giving to her."

I smiled, too. "Remember: professional courtesy. Now that we've pushed each other down that slippery slope."

At that, he laughed. "Professional courtesy. Maybe a little more." We laughed together, then Brendan went out to tend to Foxheart. I got dressed and went outside to stand in the sunlight, enjoying the world.

Samhain Again

A year and a day. I thought about that this morning as I sat down to write of my journey through it. I wrote for a few hours straight, caught up by the rhythms of storytelling. I will have strong material to work with in my next counseling session at Whispering Pines Mental Health Center. I have learned that the benefits of telling my story to non-judgmental ears were too important to pass up and I am determined to write the next few chapters of my life with a clearer voice than I had in the past. As I tell my story, I am growing the skills for choosing what I need and what I want in my life. I am finding that it is a process much like growing a garden: effort and knowledge must work together with time and nature to produce fruit.

In the evening Brendan picked me up and we went to a Halloween party at the studio of Nirvana, an artist friend of his. We were told to dress up as the most important lesson we had learned during the past year. I came as myself. I had fun.

After the party, Brendan took me back home: as usual, he knew that I needed time to myself. I am working on finding the balancing point between time alone and time with others, enjoying both. Mary's book about wildlife is finished and off to the publisher. I'm starting to teach writing at the university again, thanks to her enthusiastic recommendation. I wonder at times about my relationship with Brendan and how it will grow, but, reliably, the crows come and tell me to be in the moment.

Tonight I wrote for a while then walked out to the garden. I felt comfortable standing among the dark rustling of dried leaves, imagining what would grow next spring. When I felt ready, I walked slowly through the pine trees and watched the stars move across the surface of the pond. I walked up the path to the hilltop and felt the wind against my face.

"A beautiful night it is," my father said, coming to stand beside me.

"A beautiful night, indeed." We stood for a moment watching the world.

I turned to look at his shadowy face. "I learned something new," I told him.

"Have you now?"

"I learned that the essence of life is choice. If I don't choose, I die to the world, little by little. But if I choose, sometimes it hurts. Feeling the pain is better than not feeling at all."

"I'm proud of you, child."

"I know what I have to forgive you for, and I forgive you as much as I love you."

The owl flew silently past, a thread of moonlight trailing behind her wings. I walked alone down to the pasture to stand by Foxheart in the darkness. Everywhere, the music filled me.

I turned to walk back to my house and saw the fox, leaping into the air. I could feel his joy.

I am filled with the world now, alone but not alone.

Canvas Angels

C.J. Prince

Don't let the hand you hold
hold you down.
Julia de Burgos, *El Mar Y Tu*

1 /

My rainbow fingers are long.

Index finger, lapis blue. Thumb, poppy red. Middle finger, orange sherbet.

Ring finger, ponderosa green. Sweet pea pink pinky. My finger nails are brushes flying over angel wings above an airplane. I do not know when the dream ends and the canvas begins. I paint.

Sunset hazy crimson, sapphire lake-blue, smudges of apple-green paint under nails, dream images emerge. Angel falls from the sky into the oils, onto the canvas. Color brings me momentary peace. I paint. Or does the image paints itself?

A deep inner calm chases away my feathers and merry-go-round mind, filling me with a lake of clouds. I live in a chicken coop, old one now made home with sweet Half Moon cat lifting a paw to my tattooed ankle. Pet me, pet me now. Lift me up. I scratch behind Moonie's ear with a bare toe. Kitty cry dissolves into a purr. Lift me in your strong arms. Even as I think of cat demands, I am reminded of Zip. Bad times, past and present, usually dissolve when I paint, and Zip was a palette of bad.

"Dannah, who would live in a chicken coop?" Mama said two years ago when I rented this place from the Colonel. Now I glance at the paint-chipped windowsill and admire the texture. I would, I told Mama. I would. She'd called from some faraway place, again said she was glad I was no longer with Zip. She didn't say anything more about the Coop. Finding a place to live had been one of her problems too.

I step back, pick up my water bottle and stare at the painting. Take a drink. Unframed paintings hang canvas to canvas on the slatted Coop walls, stacked behind the couch near the narrow door that leads to the tiny bathroom. I have to scoot my knees under the sink to sit on the john or ease into the narrow shower. All my artist supplies are shoved under the couch that also serves as my bed with a sleeping bag and down comforter. The mini kitchen is just a corner of the room with a round bar table and two chairs that I picked up at a garage sale.

Now, the angel image pulls me back to my dream memory. The brush swirls, streaming across the canvas. Ordinary days start at night. "Night owl," my friend Nirvana says. "You have the hoot and the eyes of one." Yes, night owl. The dance of the Muse comes when it will, usually in the midst of the stars. My best friend Nirvana is an artist herself. She knows that artistic madness knows no clock. Dusk to dawn, turpentine vapors swill about me, an ether of creativity and passion. Linseed aromas calm my feverish brush. It's past midnight. I'll work until three. No later than four, I tell myself, guessing I will actually see the sun rise if this storm blows through.

Alone but not lonely, I fall in with Half Moon cat-cat's rumbling purr, the white noise of creativity. I work amongst the stacks of canvases, some raw, some finished—like parts of me—revealing stages, places, thoughts, dreams.

"I've got your number," Zip had said. Zip is my ex. Well, not mine. Just the former husband who was once so handsome and persistent, I couldn't resist. "You're number one in my book, baby," he'd said. I fell into the well of illusion, the flames of passion, the high of praise. No one else had ever wanted me that way.

Grannie told me to beware of certain things, bad men and moose in rut. Moose used to wander the Bijou Basin in Grannie's youth. Guess she knew how dangerous they could be. Moose or meece, mice and rice. Short grain brown rice is nice. Brown as a bunny, Zip was, but not always nice. I noticed his dark eyes following me. He called, offered to meet me at the library—that seemed a safe space to meet a man. Male angels sometimes flitted into my dreams—mostly not.

Dreams on canvas, a safe place to capture them. "Stupid dreams," Zip had said. That once handsome man deteriorated into a haunting of himself, a fearful, cocaine snorting ghost. When he found meth he totally lost me.

"Full of fancy, my wild child," Grannie used to say and chuckle. "Draw, my wild Dannah girl. Here." And she'd turn over an opened envelope, usually a bill, and hand me a pencil. I would release the images raging in my head; I'd draw the dragons and faeries that helped me as a young girl

Not that I ever believed in any of it, not god, nor faeries, certainly not angels, nor santa. The beings were there to distract me and distraction calmed me. Even after I married Zip. When I'd retreat into my art, he'd get crazy. Sometimes he'd tear up watercolors, smash his fist through a canvas. Once he sliced a butcher knife through a Madonna and child painting. Another time he slung ketchup on an angel head, broke the wooden frame with an ax and threw the shambles in the trash.

In the beginning I wanted to please him in any way. What was love if not that? Now I need a magnifying glass to find love. You can save money but you can't save love. Grannie loved me. She taught me to draw. She bought me colored pencils and watercolors. Grannie was good to me. I could weep now missing her. How full she made my life.

Find the angle, the design, the shadow, the shades, the hues. Find them all in your soul, she'd said. How do you know you have a soul? How do you know true love? How does electricity work? Lots of things I don't know. Electricity went out in a snowstorm and I painted by candle light. A strange shadowy portrait loosed itself onto the canvas that night. When the lights came back on, I turned them off to finish the painting.

Girlfriend Harrie says I'm obsessed with painting. "So what?" I say. Nirvana understands my obsession. Only another crazy artist would. Besides Harrie is the most anal-retentive friend I have, hardly a paragon of normalcy.

"We all have character gifts," Grannie would say. "That's where we are different. Our gift." I didn't understand then. Maybe not now, either. Just me and the cat living in the Colonel's renovated chicken coop. Together we'll find our gifts. Moonie's gift is catching mice. Leaves the entrails at the front door. My gift may be my obsession. Time will tell if I can really survive as an artist. Got fired from the last waitress job because I was late. I couldn't leave the canvas unfinished and worked until I signed it. Sold it the next day, too. Nirvana said it was a sign. I was being guided. Guided away from serving high class wine to low class customers.

Moonie twines between my ankles, yowls that special meow. I let her out, breathe in the chilled dawn air, lean against the aged

51

wooden doorframe and watch the snow swirl. My life is stable now. My toes are cold. Pull the door shut. It sticks, swollen with the dampness. Return to the dream painting, that angel hovering over an airplane, protecting it. It is almost complete. Moonie will want back in soon. She'll jump to the window ledge and paw the glass to get my attention.

"You always think you're right," Zip'd said. He'd shut the door to the bedroom in that little house we rented over on the west side of Fondis. "Revealing diary," he'd said, snapping it shut. He moved toward me. "Shut your eyes, Dannah." I was afraid. Afraid to shut them, afraid to keep them open. Afraid of what he'd do, afraid of what he'd done. Images on canvas, far safer than words in a journal.

I shake my head, dropping the memory. Back to the canvas. Angel flying over an airplane in the mists. If an angel could leap off the canvas and help me, maybe I'd be safe. All night, since the dream, the three by five foot canvas comes to life: angel guarding airplane. The wind is a knock on the door. Uneasiness flitters in with a draft. I look up.

I'm my usual mess. Oil paint on my hands, elbows, apron pocket filled with brushes. The knock hammers faster. Not wind. I look at the door and decide to ignore it. I'm afraid. I pick up a finer brush, dip it in linseed and then starlight blue. I steady my hand, swirl my signature into the left hand corner.

Pounding on the door now. I grab an old cloth, dab it with turpentine and rub at my fingers. Fumes fill my nostrils. A lump forms in my throat. It could be anyone, really. The door knob jiggles. I don't want it to be him—ever. He shoulders the door open. The chill that crawls my spine is more than wind.

Zip. He's no longer handsome—his chiseled face marred by a scraggly beard. Still, those blue eyes. Haunted now. Then, that familiar grin.

"Don't come in." My shout is a whisper. I grab the long handled brush from the turpentine tin and swing it. A gray stream drips on my feet, flails toward him but misses.
He pushes past me. Drops his shabby backpack. "Got any wine, baby?"

"It's almost morning," I protest, my voice too weak to mean anything.

"When did you care about the time of day? How about a joint?" He gives me that raw, I-need-you look. I shake my head, step back.

"Amethyst threw me out," he says. "I'm staying here."

"So did I." I dare the words, ease away. I trip over a kitchen chair, steady myself against the counter.

"That was a long time ago, Baby." He grabs my wrist, pulls me around the tiny kitchen table, close enough now to smell the reek of stale booze, cigarettes and something deep and sour. "We always had good times, Dannah. Remember? Remember all the good times? Remember when we danced on the pool table at Charlie's Bar? Remember when I stole a tractor and drove you up the bluff and we had a six pack or two? Remember..." His arm tightens around my waist.

Pushing away, I open cupboards and begin searching for something to do, anything to stop my skin from crawling. Remember when I lost the baby?

"Peanut butter?" I pull out the almost empty jar, find an old box of Wheat Thins. My hands are shaking.

He jerks at his crotch. "You know you want me, little girl. You're the only one for me. Always have been, always will be." He leans down to kiss my lips. I turn my head and his lips catch cheek. Dry, cracked lips. I remember when they were soft.

I sit down. The tiny kitchen, my kitchen is my space. He's too much, too big for it and I know his hunger wants more than crackers. He is there next to me, his hand grabbing at my breast.

"No, Zip." I pull away but he grabs me and drags me toward the couch. I fight him but he throws me on the sleeping bag, tosses books, sketches and tools aside.

"You always did sleep with a god damn library." His blue eyes harden, then shift to a cold, make-believe nice. "Tell me a love story." His lips quirk.

I feel the corner of a book pinch my back.

"Do not touch me," I scream a whimper. I lift my hand to scratch at his face, but he grabs and twists my arms. Nails scrape his shoulder.

"Bitch." He snarls. "Snow makes me hot. Now, tell me a story." He shoves a book at me. I open it. Shakespeare's Sonnets. He pulls off his red plaid shirt revealing a thin, bruised torso. He's on drugs, still, again. Coke or crack or meth or some crazy illegal thing ruining what good might still linger in his heart. Once I gave him my heart. He destroyed that too.

53

I open the book, aim, then slam it toward his face. Knuckles clip my jaw. My eyes rest on the far wall unseeing, a fuzz through wet eyelashes.

"Now. Read."

With quivering hands, I hold the book. My voice trembles.

"From fairest creatures we desire increase, that thereby beauty's rose might never die..."

I might die. His body odor makes me gasp. I flip a page. Eyes track words, tongue speaks but I do not hear.

"Grant, if thou wilt, thou art beloved of many, but that thou none lovest is most evident..."

His sweat drips on my cheek. I turn my head, try to wipe it off.

"Read." He growls the command.

I turn away from the rage in his eyes. He has himself out of his jeans. I hold the book in front of my face, try to jerk my knee toward his groin. He pins me.

"Read."

I flip pages, mouth words.

"So I, for fear of trust, forget to say the perfect ceremony of love's rite..."

I know he'll never get out until he gets in. Inside me. I know it, fear it, crash out of my skull, mumbling Shakespeare's words while he peels off my panties.

"Dannah, the guys at the pool hall said you sold a painting. Where's the money?" I moan, shake my head, no. It pounds, he pounds. "God damn bitch," Zip mutters. "Where the fuck did you hide the money? Son of a bitch."

My eyes feel sewn shut. I vaguely follow his voice. The book falls from my hand.

Finished, he pulls out. "Get up, Dannah. Get the money." He slams my head against the wall.

I hear myself sob. Roll to my side, cover myself. Can't move. I hear him rummaging around my tiny kitchen, emptying drawers, tossing tubes of paint. Something bounces off my forehead. Focus through eyelashes. Zip is looking under the couch, inches away. I squeeze my eyes shut, hear him step into the bathroom, look inside the toilet tank. Consciousness slips in and out. He scuffles, lurches and drags something through the door. He's gone.

"Nirvana?" I croaked into my cell phone. "I need help. Zip..."

"Dannah? You're breaking up. Where are you?"

"Home. At the Coop. Where are you?" My voice quaked into the cell. I hadn't moved from where Zip left me.

"Highway 24. Coming back from Simla. You sound awful. What happened?"

"Nirvana?" Gone, her cell lost in a black hole of Zebulon County. Dialed Harrie. I ached all over. I needed help. Not 911 help. Just friend help. The phone rang and rang. Damned voice mail. I mumbled something and hung up. Harrie is always too busy.

I'd be better dead. A shroud already draped my body, hid my not-soul. Shroud of protection, shroud of invisibility, shroud of denial, shroud to hurry me off this planet.

I eased off the couch. Where did he go? At least he is gone. What if he comes back? Why did I ever open the door? Crazy addict. How could I forget? I need to get out of here. If he comes back, he might kill me. I doubled over in pain, collapsed to the rubble on the floor.

My body was filthy. I pulled myself up, walked like a stick figure to the bathroom. Undressed. I moved as if I'm in a real, cloying black shroud. I leaned over the toilet, gagged but could not vomit. I am empty, disconnected, numb. Shower. I must shower. I want clean water flowing over my body. My skin crawled, flesh repugnant. Not enough soap in the world to dislodge the slimy feeling. I turned on the water, leaned against the tiny bathroom sink, drifted as steam filled the room.

"Dannah? Oh, shit. Look at this place. Fuck." I heard Nirvana before she opened the bathroom door. "Here you are. Look at you. Dannah, look at me." Nirvana's hand touched my cheek. I flinched, opened my eyes.

"Uh...shower," I mumbled.

"Later." Her voice took command as her eyes circled the Coop. "We're going to see Dr. Talia now."

"No. Yes. I don't want to see anybody.." Nirvana always thinks she knows what to do. Fingers to my bruised lips, I resisted the urge to upchuck.

"Never again. Never fucking again will I trust a man." Never. Like I'd never said that before. Shit. An old mantra I needed to live now.

"Dannah Hannah Banana," Nirvana crooned, touching my nose. She helped me to the couch. "Zip?"
I nodded.

"Start at the beginning." Nirvana's voice was quiet. She squeezed my hand. It hurt. The lump in my throat grew.

I started to tell her about the dream painting and Zip's arrival. I hated to let anybody see my wounds, to give away my vulnerability, but I couldn't help it. I sobbed. Nirvana pulled me into her arms, dabbed at my cheeks with the edge of her shirt.

"Listen, Dannah. Full penetration?" She handed me a box of tissues.

I nodded, so ashamed I couldn't fight him off. I blew my nose.

"Possibility of pregnancy?" She pushed a strand of hair from my eyes.

"You know I can't get pregnant." I sobbed. At least one thing I don't have to worry about. A hysterectomy. Just lift out my parts, take away my children. Put me on hormones that might cause cancer.

"Shit. I'm sorry, Dannah. I forgot. What about AIDS?"
"What? I don't know……He wanted money," I sobbed. "I won't get that commission check until next week. I don't have any money. He didn't find any money." I blew my nose again.

Nirvana nudged a wastebasket toward me. I dropped in a mound of damp tissues. She scrolled through her cell numbers, pushed the call button and sat down next to me, all the while holding me while she talked to the doctor's office. I rested my head against her shoulder, trying to get comfortable, faded in and out.

The shroud clung to my face. I couldn't catch my breath. No breath, death. Dying. I'm so close to dying. Nirvana squeezed my hand. I could still feel. She rubbed a thumb over the back of my hand. I took a deep breath and choked.

It was just before the divorce that the black drape obscured my vision. The first time I felt it, I was just a kid. A little girl hiding from Daddy. Then Daddy left us, Mama and me. Black cloth wrapped me tight whenever I was threatened.

"I'm so stupid. Shit." I started to cry again and she let me sob. I'd married Mr. Scum Ball—that's what everyone in Fondis called him. On an impulse, I'd said "I do," thinking he was Mr.

Right. But I was wrong. Totally wrong. I had married Mr. Wrong on a whim. What was the matter with me? He couldn't hold down a job. Drank. He promised me everything and delivered nothing. He even took advantage of my friends. Made a business deal with Nirvana and then absconded with all the money Nirvana made on the sale of a big sculpture.

Then he'd just disappear, be gone for a long time and when he'd come back, he'd look worse than an un-neutered alley cat. I lost my car, my Grannie's house and eventually my job because of his drug use. I stuck it out for as long as I could. I thought everything would be okay after the divorce.

Nirvana eased me into my bathrobe. Somehow she got me to Dr. Talia Master's office. I hate going to the doctor and I hated it even more today. Talia Master occasionally comes to the Womyn's Group, so I know her on a first name basis.

"Thanks for getting her in right away," Nirvana said.
The doctor office smell triggered my gag reflex. I caught my breath, covered my mouth with my hand. Breathe slowly, Grannie used to say. It didn't help that I knew everyone. The nurse had pity in her eyes, or worse, resignation, like I couldn't change. It isn't true. I can change. I will never let this happen again. I know that. Breathe, I said to myself. I just needed to breathe.

Talia's nurse Caroline showed me to the exam room, pressed a button on the CD player and soft new age music filled the room. Nirvana eased off my robe and clothes. Caroline helped me slip on a paper gown and sit on the table. It hurt to sit. I eased back and she put soft, wooly socks on my feet and tried to make me comfortable. I'd never be comfortable again. I felt so stupid. I didn't want to see anyone and here I was with Nirvana and Caroline. Talia Master opened the door wearing a pristine ecru pants suit, aqua silk shirt and a strand of pearls. A stethoscope dangled from her neck.

"I'm glad you came right in, Dannah," Talia said and glanced at Nirvana. "I'll do an exam and then I want to do some basic tests for sexually transmitted diseases." She pulled on rubber gloves.

Talia glanced at my fisted hands and turned to Caroline. "Chamomile tea, please." Caroline nodded and slipped out the door. "Do you want Nirvana to stay?"

"Yes. You know I hate those icy cold metal things," I shuddered in advance of the intrusion. "They were probably designed in some medieval torture chamber by a man and I've been tortured enough down there."

57

"Problem solved, Dannah. We use disposable plastic speculums now, and I have a special unit to heat it to body temperature. I'll be careful." She moved the crinkly gown past my knees. I tightened up and winced.

"Take a deep breath. Relax." Her voice was soft. I drew a shallow breath. My head hurt, my body screamed pain. It's weird to have a friend nudging around in your private parts—but at least someone I can trust.

She made a tsking sound between her lips. "Abrasions and tissue damage. I'll need to use a swab, take a culture to send off to the lab."

Caroline returned with the mug of tea. Talia didn't look up. "I'll let you know if I need your help, Caroline." Caroline left the room again.

"There's some damage here. I'm going to look for *Trichomonas*," Talia said, and moved toward a microscope on the counter. "I'll give you a prescription to cover it just in case. Then we have to wait for the lab results before we can determine anything further."

I stared at the mobile twirling pansy purple and dandelion yellow above me. Dolphins and birds edged together in a slow twirl like an Escheresque sculpture. If only I were a dolphin swimming free in the sea, a bird in flight. If only Zip hadn't hurt me. A phone rang.

Talia slipped the cell phone from her pocket. "Yes, Harrie. We're in the back exam room. Bring your bag." She turned to me. "Is it alright if Harrie joins us?"

I nodded. The more the merrier. I couldn't even smile. It hurt my face. My jaw and eye were swollen. I could feel the skin taut like a water balloon.

Talia wrote something in my chart. "I thought Harrie's homeopathic skills might be helpful." She continued to write in the chart.

Caroline came in and then Nirvana handed me a mug of tea. I eased up on an elbow, took it. The liquid was warm and soothing. How can chamomile calm you down when it tastes so vile?

"Dannah, rape is a serious crime to be reported." Talia pursed her lips. "Press charges. Stop him."

"I let him in." I gulped and cast my eyes away. "The door wasn't locked. It's my fault."

"You haven't looked at yourself have you?"

I forced my fingers through my unruly hair and found the tender spot on the side of my head. It was sticky Matted blood. I knew I looked a wreck. No sleep. No makeup. Old clothes. "I didn't fix myself up today."

"That's not what I'm talking about. You're ripped and torn. I can prescribe a pain med plus some cream but I'm afraid you'll be sore for some time." She moved to a drawer and returned to my left side. "I need to do a blood draw." She twisted a rubber strip around my arm. "Take a deep breath and let it out slowly."

I turned my head to the right. There was a poster of a red hibiscus ablaze with faeries dancing about the yellow stamen. I hardly felt the needle go in my left arm.

A soft knock on the door and Harrie entered. She was carrying her old black leather doctor's bag. I knew it was filled with homeopathic remedies. I tried to smile at her—happy to have her there. I couldn't.

"Good Goddess. That bastard." She ground the words out, shaking her head. "How are you, Dannah?"

"Not great."

Talia handed me a mirror and I sat up slowly. I figured I was sore from not having had sex in so long. Plus he was pretty rough with me. Angling the mirror, I saw what they saw. Black and blue marks and swollen flesh and... I looked away, but not at them. Bile rose in my throat.

"Not just there. Bruises on your arms, shoulders. And look at your breasts," Talia instructed, her voice terse. She touched my head.

"Ow."

"Abrasions need to be cleaned," Talia said. "Harrie, give her something for shock."

Harrie rummaged in her bag. "Damnit, Dannah. Why didn't you say something on my voice mail. It could have been anything." She pulled out a small brown vial and tapped out a single white pellet. "*Arnica*. For shock. To stop bleeding. I want you on it all day, every hour. Open your mouth like a little bird. Tongue up." She tapped a pellet into my mouth. "Now, hold the vial, too. Even holding it, you'll get the vibrational healing energy by keeping it next to your skin."

I'd heard all this homeopathic mumbo jumbo before. How I could let this happen? Again. I closed my eyes and dropped my chin to my chest, ashamed. It hurt.

"Now this," she said, tilting up my chin. "*Ledum* for the battering. You probably need *Ruta* and..." She let out a great sigh. "That asshole. You'll need something else. I have to think about it. Maybe *Pulsatilla*. Dannah, I'm so sorry this happened to you. Tomorrow I'll give you some *Aconite*. For seeing the unacceptable."

"But it's my fault. I shouldn't have..."

"Shhh. It's okay." Nirvana handed me the mug of tea again. I sipped, scrunching up my face.

"I know, but you can't backtrack and undo the past. We've all made mistakes in judgment." Talia was futzing with vials. "I want you to take some western meds too." She glanced at Harrie. "My call. Our patient needs both. Remember what we agreed?" Talia interlaced her fingers. "Western meds interwoven with alternatives. Find the balance to best suit the patient."

Harrie nodded and pulled out a tube of homeopathic cream. "Traumeel cream. It will help the bruising. Avoid putting it on the open wounds," she instructed. Carefully she began to apply it, starting at my jaw and working down.

"My jaw?" I yanked up the mirror to see the swelling taking an odd hue, my face and jaw misshapen Oh, yeah. He'd hit me.

"There, there, Sweet Pea, it's okay. You're still in shock." Harrie was crooning, murmuring gently as she worked her way down past my sore shoulder and eventually to my ankles.

Talia buzzed for Caroline.

"Bring the camera," Talia said.

Caroline was an acquaintance. I trusted her, but still felt uncomfortable with her seeing me in such a state. She entered quietly, holding a small digital camera.

"Full body shot, limb shots and tight shots," Talia instructed.

I tried to ignore her—paparazzi when I least wanted it.

I didn't realize how sore I was all over. I leaned back on the exam table. Caroline took more pictures.

"He doesn't like my hair short," I said. "Said I looked like a dyke." An image from the rape flashed in my mind's eye. "He grabbed my hair and shook my head..." Tears puddled in my eyes and I couldn't go on.

"Where was Half Moon during all this?" Harrie asked about my beloved cat.

"Half Moon." Jerking up from the table, I tossed the sheet aside and stumbled to my feet, pulling at my gown. "I have to find her. She went out. I don't remember her coming back in. Shit.

What if an owl got her? What if Zip... ?" I couldn't finish the sentence.

"Dannah. Calm down." Harrie reached for my arm.

I flung her hand aside and grabbed the sweat pants Nirvana handed me. "I've got to find my cat." I tried to tug them up. My head throbbed. I couldn't stand anything touching me down there. I sobbed and my head hurt more.

"Dannah, here's your robe. And wrap this blanket around you. Nirvana will take you home. You'll probably want to wear loose clothing or a skirt for a few days," Talia said.

"My cat..."

Nirvana handed me my old plaid robe and helped me button it. "I'll take you home," she said. "We'll find Half Moon. Don't worry."

"Dannah, here are your prescriptions. Stop at Fondis Pharmacy on Main Street. I'll let them know to put it on my account." Talia was all business. That was good. I didn't want sympathy right now.

"Here," Harrie said, "put these in your pocket. I'll remind you when to take them."

I stuffed the homeopathic vials in the robe. "We'll have lunch first. You need something to eat."

"Harrie, I have to go home. I have to look for Moonie." Why didn't anybody understand?

"Dannah, we'll go look for your cat. Harrie, why don't you pick up the meds and grab some lunch and meet us back at Dannah's?" Nirvana said.

3/

"We'll find your puss in boots, Dannah, and then we're going to my place where that thug won't find you," Nirvana said.

Nirvana knew all the back routes to avoid midday traffic jams in Fondis and soon we pulled up next to the Coop. Hollyhocks tilted in awkward directions outside the front door, the flowers persisted even after last night's snow. The zinnias lay flat along the side of the coop.

The Colonel stepped out of the big house and waved. His white undershirt was tucked precisely into his old army pants. His posture, military straight, defied his age, in his seventies, I guessed. He pulled on an old Army jacket and crossed the yard toward us. I didn't want the Colonel to see me like this. He marched to the garbage can. I couldn't face him.

The faded petunia-red Coop door stood ajar. Fear bubbled in my throat. Nirvana shouldered ahead of me and I followed. I leaned against the doorframe and gasped at the mess. When I'd fled, the shroud was still blinding me. Now, I limped from object to object, seeing everything—the table turned over, tubes of paint strewn everywhere, shattered glasses, a broken lamp. Things were in such disarray that I didn't know what was there and what wasn't. I didn't care.

"Moonie," I said in my cat voice, soft as a purr. "Moonie?"

I heard a car pull up and turned toward the open door, alert. Harrie came in with a paper bag of prescriptions. "Pizza will be delivered," she said and then looked around. "Oh, my Goddess. What a disaster. I'll help you clean it up. He must have been looking for money," she said, righting the tipped over canisters and a salt shaker.

"Money for drugs." I groaned. The tiny corner kitchen had a small sink and short counter. The stove was apartment size with two burners. A narrow window looked out to my garden. My eyes tore around the living area. "Oh, no." The painting was gone from my easel. "Shit." My eyes searched everywhere amongst my scattered possessions. The big canvas had dominated the room and now I could hear the scream of its absence.

"Here's a long velvet skirt, Dannah. It will keep you warm," Nirvana said.

"The painting's gone, Nirvana. Son of a bitch." I sobbed.

"Damn that bastard. Here. Put on the skirt. You'll be more comfortable. We'll get your painting back." Nirvana pulled the elastic waist wide and dropped it over my head. Then she slipped my arms into an old sweatshirt hoodie and pulled up the zipper. Shit. Zipper. Zip. I'll have to get Velcro.

Harrie was already folding towels, picking things up and putting them in order.

"I wouldn't do that," the Colonel's voice barked from the door. "Evidence. I called the police. Some young hoodlum must have gone berserk in here." His eyes narrowed as he looked at me. "Or was it someone you know, Dannah?"

I looked away from his watery eyes. The Colonel was a father to me and I hated to disappoint him.

"Zip, huh?" The Colonel had been there for me after the divorce, and helped me out by letting me rent this place. If I were late on rent, or missed a month, he let me run errands to make up for it. I dropped my chin. "Today is my day for raking leaves. Can I do it later?" I said.

"Forget the leaves. You're wounded." He led me to a chair he righted and helped me down. Outside, the sounds of cars screeching to a halt. The Colonel jerked away.

"That must be the MP," he said.

The next half hour was filled with questions by uniformed officers, a Victim Advocate and Talia's lawyer, who advised me to say nothing. The Colonel stood by my side, occasionally putting his arm around me to comfort me. Harrie wanted to know when she could clean up.

"Where's Nirvana?" I said. "Did she find cat-cat?"

Then the photographer from the Fondis Daily showed up.

"Enough," the Colonel barked, shielded me from the camera as he guided me across the yard to his big, old Victorian house.

"I can't. I have to find Half Moon," I said, pulling back to look for Nirvana.

"Forgot to tell you not to worry, little lady. That cat of yours is sippin' milk right now in my kitchen. When I saw what had happened in your house, I scooped her up and settled her in my kitchen. Sari is cooin' and pettin' her plenty. Oh, yes, I left your door open just like I found it. I watch enough cop shows to know not to destroy any evidence. Now come inside." Sari had been his housekeeper since long before the Missus passed. She still looked after the Colonel. Sometimes me.

Harrie had followed us. She shook her head. "We have to get her out of here, Colonel. Take her someplace where that son of a bitch won't find her."

"Moonie's not back there," Nirvana said, rounding the corner from the back garden.

"The Colonel has her," I said, and limped through the rose garden and up the back steps of the old Victorian house, pausing to lean against the Colonel when my feet slipped on ice.

63

Inside the kitchen, Moonie was curled in the full, round lap of Sari Thompson, kneading and purring. She didn't even look up at me.

"You rascal cat, look at you," I said and eased down, resting my head in her warm, soft fur. I sobbed. Sari stroked my hair and made a sound. Moonie shifted. It hurt when I stood up. "I can see you're happy enough, silly cat-cat. You scared me. I was worried to death about you." She closed her eyes and purred.

"There's the pizza guy," Harrie said, looking out the window. "I'll be right back."

"We'll take good care of that cat of yours, young lady. You girls go along now and eat. Be safe," the Colonel said.

4 /

The three of us sat at the breakfast nook in Nirvana's studio, a renovated fire station. Harrie handed me a paper plate with a slice of pizza. I wasn't hungry.

"Dannah, stay here tonight," Nirvana urged.

"Or my place," Harried chimed in. "Then I can help you with your homeopathy treatment."

I'd never stayed overnight at Harrie's. Far too tidy for me. "I don't know what to do." My voice sounded weak even to my own ears.

"You have a choice, dear Dannah. My place or here with Nirvana," Harrie said. "It is not safe for you to go home tonight. The Colonel will take care of your cat." Harrie patted my hand.

"I want to talk to you about my new sculpture anyway. And Panther will give you cat company. Stay with me," Nirvana said.

"Okay." I turned apologetically to Harrie. "Do you mind?"

She shook her head. Her cell phone rang. She answered it, listened and spoke briefly before switching it off.

"That was Talia. Her uncle Tucker Master, you know, the Fondis chief of police, is keeping an eye on the Coop—watching for Zip."

∞

I was jumpy. I'd taken all the meds and remedies recommended. Still I kept looking for Zip out of the corner of my eye whenever there was any movement. The shroud fluttered around my body, protecting, masking and helping me delay, deny the truth. Nirvana helped me take a sponge bath. Then she gave me a soft rose pink silk nightie to wear. It didn't seem her style. It looked brand new. I curled up in a cloud of soft blanket on her bed. Breathe in breath out. Breathe, I said to myself while Nirvana put classical music on—anything to block my mind chatter. I drifted.

"Violin," Mama said, "you should play the violin." But I played with color not strings. Strands of color tied to my heart break—a broken heart floating in my bruised chest. You will not cut me again. And I jumped. A thread tied to my center snapped.

"Stop it, Zip." The dark man of winter hiding in snow. Now I hide from him. "Do not come in here," Mama said. Her pretty dress tumbled over the couch. I crouched down, peeped through the crack in the bedroom door. Inside adult pleasures not fit for a child's eyes. A child runs, chases a dog. Together they run away far into the painless place of dusk. Soul child, she called me. "Grannie, can I have a cookie?" I said.

"Cookies for the soul child," she said. "My grandchild wants more, more of everything." But things don't equal love. People love me. Me looking at Grannie. "Grannie, did you have a Grandpa?"

I startled awake—a soft hand on my forehead.

"There, there, Dannah. I just stopped by to see how you're doing. You're mumbling in your sleep," Harrie said.

I sighed, turning a little, moving slowly because of the pain.

Harrie unscrewed a homeopathic vial and slipped a little white pellet under my tongue.

I let the sweet pellet dissolve. Her eyes were peaceful, caring. The knot in my throat felt smaller. "I'm fine," I said. "I feel safer now." I looked away. The dream images flickered in and out.

5 /

I heard Nirvana close the blinds of the fire station's front windows. Her clogs clip-clopped across the cement floor. She came into the bedroom and sat on the side of the bed rubbing lotion into her hands. She always complained of tiny cracks from clay. Her hands hurt more in winter. "They haven't found Zip. If Zip knows you're here...well, we just won't give him a chance to look in my tall windows."

"Zip wouldn't come here, would he?" I had a sudden desire to vomit and turned my head to the side. Turning hurt and now my head did too. I had to think of cat-cat. Nirvana rubbed my shoulder.

"He's out of control," Harrie said, as she came from the kitchen with a mug of broth. "Talia thinks he's bipolar. I don't think we should take any chances. Try to sip on this, little one."

I couldn't swallow anything. Nirvana's cell rang. I studied the high ceiling while she talked. Her space was huge, ideal for a sculptor. Nirvana created this cozy bedroom by setting up screened panels. Along with the spacious bathroom, twenty artists could sleep here.

I felt my two friends stir. "She's exhausted," one of them whispered.

"Um hmm. Good. She'll relax and get some sleep. We can both do some Reiki." I sank deeper into soft flannel sheets under a pile of down comforters. A soft energy tingled my feet, surrounded my head, radiated down my spine. More of their mumbo jumbo but it worked.

6 /

"Oh, God." Swords fly through the air. I dive to the ground and huddle in a ball, quaking as rapiers slash and strike nearby. Lightning bolts shatter the night. Zip's sword rips through the airplane. I hear the fierce howling of beasts. I swing my arms to ward off flashing metal.

"Dannah, Dannah. It's okay, honey. I'm right here. Wake up, Dannah." Nirvana's voice finally broke through the nightmare.

"I must have fallen into a pit of swords in my dream," I said, my heart racing. I forced my eyes open to see her beautiful face. She stroked my hair and chanted softly.

"C'mon. Let's take a walk to the kitchen," Nirvana said.

I eased out of bed. Walking with her arm around me, Nirvana guided me to the kitchen area. Her cat Panther yowled and rubbed my ankles. I wondered how Moonie was doing.

"Cocoa or chamomile tea?"

I wrinkled my nose.

"Oh, I remember, picky one. No chamomile—unless it's an emergency."

"I had enough chamomile in that mug at Talia's office to last a lifetime," I mumbled.

By the time I'd finished the cup of hot cocoa, I'd stopped shuddering. "I haven't had a nightmare in two years. Guess I am pretty freaked out. I'm sorry to get you up in the middle of the night." Tears leaked from the corners of my eyes. I sniffled and wiped my nose with a tissue.

"Most people in shock think they're okay," Nirvana said.

"Silly me. I didn't notice."

"That's better. A little cryptic humor returns. Chocolate to the rescue," Nirvana said.

Harrie padded into the room. "What's all the racket?"

"I thought you went home," I said.

"We decided on a slumber party. I'm sleeping on a cot in the studio," she said. "Good thing, huh?"

I stood, unsteady, and leaned into their arms. "I just don't understand how Zip could be so crazy," I said.

"Nobody understands crazy, little one. I'll get my cards," Nirvana said, "come on back to bed."

Harrie held my hand and I followed her, happy to settle back under the covers.

"I don't put much faith in that airy fairy stuff," I said, as Nirvana lifted a worn tarot deck from an old dresser.

"Faith is not required, dear friend," Harrie said and grinned at me. "Let's see what the cards have to say."

Nirvana unwrapped the cards and shook out a large square of purple silk on the bed next to me. The two of them settled beside the bed, Harrie on a straight backed chair and Nirvana on a nasturtium red exercise ball.

"After all, Dannah, this is Fondis." Nirvana giggled. "Did you see the story about the Fondis faeries in the National Inspirer?"

I shook my head. Most of the women in our group talked about all this New Agey stuff, but I really didn't have time to indulge in it. I was too busy keeping my head above water, selling my paintings and paying the bills. Lots of people said my paintings were very spiritual. I always thought, whoever buys it can believe whatever they want. Just pay me the money.

Damn Zip. If only he hadn't taken the airplane painting. I'd hoped to show it to a pilot who saw my work at the last Fondis Bank Art Festival. The angel/airplane painting came in a dream, and when I'd mentioned it to the pilot, he'd said he wanted to see the finished product. The proceeds would have covered next month's rent. I would strangle Zip with the shroud, if I could.

"Where did you wander off to?" Harrie poked me.
I jumped.

"Oh. Sorry about that. I forgot you were all bruised." She leaned over and air- kissed my shoulder.

"I'm black and blue all over. What fun could I be?" I said.

Nirvana smiled and left the room, returning with an ice pack. "This will help. We do have to remember to tend to her, Miss Harrie." She handed me the ice pack and sat on the exercise ball. Nirvana shuffled the cards, blew on them, cut the deck and laid out cards, face down.

"Okay. All settled? I'm going by impulse here. I'm going to lay out two lines of cards. One for you and one for Zip."

"I don't even want to think about him," I said.

"But he did get you into this mess, courageous one. We need to get some perspective here. So, this card is you. This one, Zip. Under you is how you feel now. The same for how he feels."

I rolled onto my right side and noted that it seemed to be the only place without any bruises. Harrie grabbed an extra pillow and eased it between my knees. I relaxed more.

"This is you," Nirvana said, turning over the card to reveal a blindfolded woman holding two swords. "Wow. You can't see where you're going. You're feeling unbalanced by the weight of the swords. Uncertainty abounds. You have difficult decisions to make and you have the tools to make them. Good girl."

I closed my eyes. The blindfold felt like the shroud.

"You're spaced out, Dannah," Harried said, tapping my pinky finger.

"She's overwhelmed." Nirvana looked back at the cards. "She needs time."

Overwhelmed, I thought. I didn't need a deck of cards to tell me that.

"And she's suppressing her feelings," Harrie said, looking directly at me. "You feel unable to make a move, right?"

"Well, why don't I just take off the damned blindfold and use the swords?" I asked, my tone, snotty.

"Exactly," they both said. That eased the tension and we all laughed. I hated it when they examined me and yet I knew they were trying to help.

"Now, let's take a look at Zip." She flipped the card to reveal beggars in front of a church window. Weird, I thought, knowing how he hated church. I wondered what they'd say now.

"Zip is full of troubles. He's out of money, doesn't have a home, feels like he has to beg for the things he needs. And he's depressed." Harrie said. She picked at the edge of the card. "This card supports my sense of his imbalance. He's out in the cold and wanted to use you to save himself. The only person that can save him is himself," she said, peering at the card

"He will just keep using you," Nirvana continued. She turned over the next card—a man leaning against a tree. He looked grumpy. There were cups nearby. Maybe it was Zip's drinking habit, I thought.

"He feels dissatisfied and bored. He has no money and he has no ambition. He can't focus or get his life together. He resents it and everyone else."

"He's very withdrawn, Dannah. You can't help him. Do you know that?" Nirvana's voice sounded far away.

I didn't know what I knew.

"This is how you feel," she captured my attention again. "The Nine of Wands. You're protected, surrounded by wands. You must stand your ground and know that you can create anything you want. But you must protect yourself. Be able to resist attack."

They still thought Zip was out to get me. They were making more out of this than I wanted. At least they hadn't talked about making a police report regarding the rape. I wouldn't go for it, I knew that much. Nobody believed a woman who reported rape. Oh, she's making it up, they'd say or, she had it coming. I've heard it before. No way was I going to put myself in that position. I was so out of it when the cops came to the Coop. Maybe it was all out of my hands already anyway. I put my head down, closed my eyes and began to drift off.

Swords and blindfolds. Fold the clothes. Keep your knees together, Mama said. Don't flirt with the boys.

"Dannah, you're slipping away again. You really need sleep, girlfriend." Nirvana touched my hand and gave me a reassuring look. "You will have to rely on your own strength, even though Harrie and I are here for you."

They flipped some more cards over and I heard their voices but couldn't track the words. The pictures on the cards blurred. I closed my eyes.

7 /

Later in Nirvana's bedroom, Harrie squatted to pull open the door to the wood burning stove. She crumpled newspapers into tight balls and layered them, adding kindling, not randomly but what seemed to be a specific crisscross pattern. I settled into a big overstuffed chair with floral upholstery, taking care to sit so the sore place wasn't pressing against the cushions.

The fire crackled and burned beautifully as Harrie closed and secured the door. "Water. We all need water," she said. "Especially when we're healing."

"Right-o," Nirvana said and pulled a soft fleece coverlet off the chair and tucked it around me. "I'll be back."

"Here, take this," Harrie said, opening a homeopath vial and tapping a single pellet into the lid. "This is *Aconite*. For seeing the unacceptable. And shock."

I was confused.

"The rape fills your mind. You have a keen imagination, Dannah. Even the pictures in your mind cause a physical reaction."

I nodded. "Plus that nightmare."

Nirvana returned with a tray of cheese, crackers, chocolate truffles and water.

"Cheese before chocolate. Right?" I said.

Nirvana lifted a questioning eyebrow.

"Something about the protein ratio? I don't remember."

"I think we'd had this conversation before," Harrie said. We all laughed.

I kept laughing and laughing until I was crying. And then I cried until I was laughing again. Harrie pulled up a stool. "I'll do your feet."

"Chocolate and a foot rub. Thank you." How quickly I grabbed a splinter of good and stretched it like a canvas waiting for angels to cover the pain of life. I wiped my face with the palm of my hand and slouched down, pulling the blanket under my chin as Harrie settled to work the reflex points on my feet. I focused on Harrie's strong hands, pushing away thoughts of Zip, of the pain in my bruised body. Still the shroud settled around me. I ignored it. I ignored everything. Didn't my yoga teacher say "be here now"? My feet felt good in the here and now. Tingly. Alive and relaxed. If only Harrie could massage the pressure points inside my head.

Nirvana's cell rang. She mostly listened, then closed the phone quietly and looked at me, her face pinched. "That was Talia. She's still at the hospital."

"What? Is it Zip?"

"Dannah, he's in critical condition. Zip ran naked through the woods. He ran across the road just as a truck was rounding a bend. He wasn't killed, Dannah. They don't know if he'll make it. He's in ICU."

"He doesn't deserve to make it," I growled, immediately sorry I had said such a vile thing. "I didn't mean that." What was the matter with me, I thought. I know he hurt me, but he's sick. Crazy sick. Out of control sick. Dangerously sick.

"It's okay, Sweetie," Nirvana said. "We're all angry with him."

"It's not okay," I said. "What about the driver of the truck? Was he hurt? I can't believe Zip hurt so many people. Asshole jerk." I can't forgive him and I can't help him and I feel sorry for him and I hate him—all at the same time.

Harrie glanced at Nirvana. Nirvana bit her lip.

"What?" I hissed.

"Talia said the driver is fine but the Colonel is in the hospital," Harrie said.

"The Colonel is...?" I said quietly. "What happened? Did Zip hurt him too?"

"He's doing fine. They stitched up a gash on his arm and are keeping him overnight for observation. He's just stressed out, Dannah. He'll be okay."

"What? Tell me what happened." My jaw clenched.

"Zip went back to the Coop. The Colonel saw him and probably gave him military orders and...well, the Colonel's arm was ripped open in the struggle." Harrie shook her head. "An ambulance took the Colonel and Sari to the hospital. Talia checked Sari out too, told her to go home and rest. They both will be fine."

"What happened to Sari?"

"She's fine, Dannah. She insisted on going with the Colonel. They'll be fine."

She crossed her fingers. "We have to go to the hospital," I said, tossing the throw off my lap. I climbed gingerly from the chair. "What? Either you drive me or I'll drive myself."

8 /

The shroud clenched my neck. Harrie drove like a crazed banshee. I clung to the armrest, keeping myself upright as she rounded icy corners, the high beams lighting the skeletal tree outlines on the Fondis bypass between Nirvana's Firehouse Studio and the hospital.

"How are you doing?" Nirvana said from the backseat.

"Fine." I blotted tears with the back of my gloves and pulled up the plaid blanket Nirvana had tucked around me. Snow swirled into the slash of windshield wipers. I sniffled.

"Tissues in that compartment between our seats. Fondis University Hospital is the best in the state. The Colonel's got a very strong constitution. I think he'll be fine," Harrie said. A deer leapt onto the road, almost crashing into our vehicle. Harrie braked. The car swerved, dovetailed. The deer bounded across the street. In the headlights' beam, I saw his antlers collecting fresh snow flakes.

I let out a breath I didn't know I was holding. "Good driving, Harrie." My heart was racing.

"Helps to have a good car, too." Harrie said. "You know, I should have figured this out long ago. Zip could use *Hyoscyamus*."

I was used to her random inserts of homeopathic jargon. I just wasn't at all sure I cared right now or wanted to talk about him.

"What do you mean?" Nirvana asked.

"Remember I told you Talia thought he was bipolar."

"Yeah. He'd never been diagnosed, but he sure was moody, up and down and a little crazed in-between. When I first knew him, it seemed exciting but for years he was just whacked," I said. "Maybe he always was and I didn't see it. Jumpy, you know. When he'd get that tick in his face, I could hardly look at him."

"Involuntary motor motions. One of the symptoms for *Hyoscyamus*. Plus I've seen him pick at his clothes. Another symptom."

"Oh, God, yes. It made me crazy. There wasn't a bit of lint or cat fur or anything there. He couldn't stop. I complained about it once. That was one of the first times he hit me." I pressed my lips together. The shroud fluttered over my nostrils, snuffling my breath.

Harrie rambled on about homeopathy but I couldn't stay focused. My stomach knotted and my mouth was dry. Tears kept leaking from my eyes.

∞

The three of us rounded the nurse's station by the critical care unit. Betty, the head night nurse, looked up and smiled

"I've been expecting you. Hi, Harrie, Nirvana. You doin' okay, Dannah?"

I nodded. I couldn't smile. Strong medicinal odors ripped through my nostrils. I covered my nose with a tissue.

"Dr. Master was just here. Colonel Klaus was given a sedative. You will be able to see him but he may already be sleeping for the night. I'll have his nurse tell you when you can go in." Betty glanced at a monitor. "Mr. Caruso Smith was in ICU. They must have moved him."

I turned away. I didn't care where Zip was. Just the Colonel. Nirvana and I followed Harrie to the waiting area and sat in uncomfortable orange plastic chairs. I got up, limp-paced down the darkened hall.   First light brightened the hospital windows. Morning. I'd lost all track of time. Snow blanketed the streets but no longer fell. I stopped, staring without seeing at the eastern end of Fondis slowly coming to life after the night's snow.   A siren screamed the day awake.

A street car glided out of the hospital station toward the Metroplex which housed the elderly and people of all ages who were financially unable to put a roof over their heads. I'd lived there for a few months the first time I left Zip.   And again later, before the Coop. It's a nice place—with security.

Since then, I'd done a lot of things to make a living.   Even volunteering. I figured if I could give back to everyone who helped me out, I could turn things around.   In some ways it did.   I was delivering Meals-on-Wheels when I met the Colonel.   I delivered to the elderly woman next door.   The Colonel was there once.   After that I stopped to chat with him too. We took to each other right away. After a while, I'd deliver his neighbor's meal last and go to visit the Colonel. Sometimes I'd read to him. He taught me to play cribbage.

That's when he offered me the Coop.   He said I reminded him of his daughter who died when she was twenty.   He was more than any faded father image I carried in my head and so, he became my surrogate father and I, his surrogate daughter.

The front door was the only door into and out of the Coop. My home and my studio and my entire life contained in a revamped chicken coop. Sounds kooky but the rent was reasonable.   Okay. Cheap.   The Colonel and his wife converted it years ago as a guest cottage. Then she died. That's when everything went awry with Zip and the Colonel decided to rent it to me.

"Dannah," Talia spoke softly, touching my elbow.
Abruptly I turned around. "Talia, is he okay?"

"Yes. You can go in and see him now. He's sleeping but you can talk to him—even if he doesn't respond."

I followed Talia down several corridors, twisting and turning until I no longer knew where I was. One step after another along a red line, footsteps echoing in the still hallways.   Harrie's heels clicked; Nirvana's tennies squished. I still had on slippers. They scuffed.

Talia stopped at a closed door. "We'll wait out here.   Let me know if you need anything." Talia stepped aside and I pushed open #491.

Colonel Marcus Klaus was hooked up to tubes and monitors and looked like a paper cutout of himself. Pale and lifeless. His cheeks were sunken in, a few white strands of hair twisted astray. Even his bushy ears seemed to sag.

"Colonel. It's me. Dannah." I watched the rise and fall of his chest. I think he took a deeper breath when he heard my voice.

"I'm so sorry this happened. Did they tell you Zip is in critical condition? " I paused, thinking I'd seen his lips move. He was probably cursing. Why did I mention Zip?

"You're going to be fine. You picked a good place to have a night's sleep. Plus they'll check you out to make sure you're A-OK." It was one of his terms. Shit. I didn't know what to say to him, didn't know if that were true. But he might as well think he really was going to be all right.

"I know you can't talk to me right now. But I can talk for both of us. You know you changed my life. I really didn't have much regard for men until I met you. You know my father left Mama before I was four. I don't remember him." What I did wasn't worth remembering. I leaned a hip against the edge of the bed and watched him sleep.

"Does that bother you?" I touched his long, bony fingers. "I don't know why I even married Zip. Obviously, he wasn't the best thing for me. My counselor at Metro said he was toxic. Guess he was toxic for a bunch of people. Both Talia and Harrie say he's bipolar. What did your generation call it? Manic-depressive? Well, he's both."

His lips lifted ever so slightly.

"I saw that. You can hear me, can't you? I knew you could. I want to thank you for everything you've done for me. You gave me a second chance when there wasn't one." I slipped my hand under his, holding it carefully. Two wounded souls together. That was probably a little dramatic. Souls go along with angels in the "To Be Determined" file.

"When I was a little girl, I dreamed of having a daddy who would read to me. I loved it when I delivered meals to your neighbor while Sari was back east taking care of her sister. When you read Shakespeare to me, it made sense." I smiled and patted his hand. Then I caught my breath, hating Shakespeare now.

"Then remember that big snow storm we had a couple of years back? You started reading Dickens's *Oliver Twist* and we all took parts, Sari, you and me. That was the best snowstorm ever."

The old man opened his watery blue eyes. I leaned forward.

"I remember," he whispered.

9 /

Harrie went home to feed her cats. Nirvana drove me by the Colonel's place to check on Sari who seemed to have weathered the storm better than we all expected. Moonie was well fed and quite content. I wanted to stay with her but Nirvana insisted that I go back to the Firehouse for a few days longer. I was so tired and achy I didn't argue.

The drive back was slow going. Snow blew into drifts and the roads froze down into layers of ice. Aches and pains in my body raged. With my mind on the Colonel, I'd forgotten and denied my abused parts.

When we got back to Nirvana's, I crawled into her bed, still wearing the silk nightie, a robe—and a pair of sweat pants I don't remember pulling on. She tucked me into a dreamless sleep.

∞

Sometime later, a hand nudged my shoulder. I rolled over and opened my eyes. "Loren," I exclaimed.

"Dinner's ready. You've slept the day away, honey."

I stretched. Every muscle in my body ached. I stared at him. Darling Loren, with perfect blue eye shadow and mascaraed lashes, gazed at me with concern.

"What?" I said.

"Come have dinner with Nirvana and me and I'll tell you good stories." He stepped back, giving me a hand. I took it and eased out of bed.

"They better be good," I said.

I headed for the john. It burned to relieve myself. I looked up at the oval mirror across from the toilet. Black and blue and green marked my skin like a bad painting. My red curls were matted worse than Moonie's fur after a field romp. The toilet paper felt like sandpaper. I washed my hands, leaned into the sink and cupped water onto my face. Everything felt tender. Then I padded down the hall to join Loren and Nirvana in the breakfast nook.

Nirvana ladled out bowls of potato leek soup. It smelled delicious. I sighed.

"The police sergeant finished his shift at Talia's and another man took over," Loren said. "They're still going to keep a watch on Talia's house–and here—and the Coop for the next week in case Zip hasn't crawled off and died in the woods somewhere. You know he just up and walked out of the hospital?"

I didn't. "Shit. That means he's on the loose. Weren't you going to tell me a story? I don't want to hear about the villain." I lifted an eyebrow. It hurt.

"Yeah, sorry. I have to tell you about Marshall. He's the sergeant I met up at Talia's last night," Loren said.

"Um hmm. You got the hots for him?" I bit into a buttered biscuit. It was warm and flaky—soothing.

"You're no fun at all, Dannah. Am I that obvious?" Loren grinned.

"Uh huh," I said between delicious bites. "Still, tell me all about him."

"He started it really. Can I resist a man in a uniform?" Loren said. "You should feel his biceps. Hard as cement but his skin is soft as..."

"You felt them?" Nirvana touched Loren's bicep and grinned.

"Loren? What was it? A one night stand?" I really didn't want to hear about sexy bodies right now.

"Definitely not a quickie. He just talked about body building and staying fit as a cop. He stayed for a while after he got off duty." Loren dabbed soup from his red lips. He smiled, or was it a smirk?

"So?" I really was curious now.

"We have a date." He sat back, grinning and looked at his hands. "I need a new manicure. You know, I think he might be the one. Can you believe it? Me and a cop?"

They laughed. I had to stifle a broad smile. My lips stretched my skin too much and I couldn't endure the pain—even for Loren.

"Oh, but I don't have anything to wear," Loren said. Want to go shopping, Dannah?"

"Get a grip, Loren. You know I hate to shop. Call the fashion queen—Talia."

"Oh, I couldn't. She's so busy with all her doctoring and charity work."

Nirvana was already out of her seat to fetch her cell phone. She dialed and handed it to Loren. He got up and paced back and forth in front of the towering firehouse windows, talking, listening and then squealing with delight.

"Dannah, you're brilliant. Talia has more clothing than the Goddess. She thinks we're the same size and wants me to look through a whole section of evening wear. I'm in heaven. A new boyfriend and the hottest clothes closet in town." He blinked away tears. "Gotta go, girls." He grabbed his coat, waved air kisses and left.

Nirvana put away the food and filled the dishwasher before we went to bed.

10 /

The next morning sunlight shimmered off snow, glaring through the window. I squirmed and rolled over to ask Nirvana a question. I found a note on her pillow.

"Off to pick up welding supplies. Call if you need anything. Love, Nirvana"

Rolling gently out of bed, I headed for the bathroom to relieve myself and find a toothbrush. As I sat on the pot, I studied the old fashioned bathtub with claw feet and decided what I'd do after breakfast.

A new toothbrush and special homeopathic toothpaste sat next to the sink with a note in Harrie's precise scroll. "XOXOXO from Harrie."

I circled the old fashioned bathroom, scrubbing my teeth. The inside of my mouth was tender. Fresh towels were stacked on the narrow counter next to a small zippered case. Harrie had been to the Coop to retrieve lotions, perfume, eye shadow and mascara, lipstick and foundation. She knew me so well. I needed my beauty supplies. Even if I couldn't touch my face. My stomach growled.

I was stiff, sore in expected places, achy in others. My neck was tight. Even in slippers, my feet could feel the cold of cement floors. I walked into the breakfast nook and filled the teakettle and put it on the burner. While it heated, I snooped around for something to eat. The kettle whistled. I turned it off and reached for a mug hanging from a hook under the cabinet. I dropped a Red Zinger tea bag in the cup and filled it with scalding water. Finally I sliced a grapefruit in half and cut along each section. Sitting at the old Formica table, I stared at Nirvana's latest sculpture while I ate the sour fruit. Once I finished the grapefruit half and squeezed the last drop of juice, I opened a Chocolate Fudge Clif Bar and broke off a piece. Tea, dunk, bite. Delicious.

I wandered back to the bathroom and ran hot water into the tub, pouring in a dollop of lavender and citrus bath oil. Life was pretty good at the moment—unless you started to think about the details and I wouldn't. I eased into the tub and let the foamy water rise around my aching body.

I didn't have a job, didn't want a job. The painting I was hoping to sell was missing. If my dream were accurate, maybe even destroyed. Mostly my dreams aren't, so I'm trusting that the painting will show up, that I can find the number of the guy who was interested in it and make a sale. That would carry me through the end of the month financially.

My body was bruised and hurting. If Zip were dead, he couldn't hurt me anymore. Or anyone else. I immediately felt guilty that I'd let that thought glide through my brain. But it was what he deserved. Poor guy. He really had a nice side to him. I don't know what makes him so crazy. When I got out of the marriage I thought I was free from his madness.

I slid my head back, dunking my hair under water. While lathering in shampoo, I wondered if his ex-girlfriend knew he'd been in an accident, was in the hospital escaped and now was out on the run. I can't even remember where she lived. Was it New Mexico? Or Montana? I know he'd said. I just couldn't remember. He'd probably hurt her too. There was an old letter that he'd written somewhere at the Coop. Rinsing my hair under the faucet, I reached with eyes closed for the conditioner. Maybe she still loved him. Maybe she'd want to know.

I soaped and shaved my legs carefully, avoiding the bruises. I wondered what she was like. I had to find her address. What was her name? Pearl? No, but a gem. Diamond? Amber? No. Amethyst? That was it. The last name still eluded me.

I had to get back to the Coop and check on it. Go to the hospital, check on the Colonel. If Zip died, would there be a funeral for him? Did I care? Who would go? Wouldn't that be terrible to die and have no one show up at your funeral? Maybe that happened to really old, old people, the last one of their generation to die. I wasn't going to be like that. I'd keep making younger friends. I didn't know what my ramblings meant. Who cared about funerals anyway? If you were dead, you were dead. You'd probably be chatting with angels with any luck and not even notice who was at your funeral. All those folks still hampered by a body. Like I believe in angels. I eased out of the bathtub.

"Get a grip, girl," I said to my steamy reflection in the mirror. I dried off—dabbing, patting carefully with a big soft towel. I needed more than a grip. I don't believe in angels. Just the ones on my canvas.

I took a slow assessment of myself. My face looked less tired than yesterday. The swelling and bruises might be hidden by makeup. Finger bruises on my arms where he'd shaken me; a bruise along the side of my neck. From hitting something? Or him strangling me? Black and blue marks on my hip bones and belly. Inner thigh bruises going yellow-green. Bastard. He didn't deserve a funeral. I hoped he was bleeding to death in a ditch.

I hid the circles under my eyes with foundation and did my best to put on a mask that wouldn't show what I was going through. Fear, dread, pain, recovery from rape. My eyes showed the truth. My sunglasses were at the Coop. I could pick them up when I looked for the letter.

A stack of clothes leaned against the straight backed chair in the oversized bathroom. Nirvana must have grabbed some of my clothes when she went to the Coop. Long sleeves, long pants. Just what I wanted to cover my body. I eased into a drab gray turtleneck and a pair of black sweats. No underpants. Loose, saggy clothes not tight on body parts. White socks. Birkenstocks. Red down jacket and knit cap. I was good to go—but no vehicle. Usually I love to walk and the Coop isn't that far from the Fire House Studio. Today it was a chore just to walk around Nirvana's huge space.

I could call someone but hadn't I been enough of a bother? I looked out the window—snow and wind. I yawned feeling exhausted by the idea. I pulled off the stocking cap, stretched out on the bed and dozed off.

Wings stroked my lips encouraging me to speak. The shroud tightened around my throat. I gagged, awaking with dry heaves. Stumbling to the bathroom, I hung over the toilet to no avail. I sipped a glass of water and headed back to bed, first pulling the mini blinds to shut out the offending light—then pulling the covers over my head.

Time passed. I heard Talia and Harrie come and go. Nirvana asked if I wanted food. I groaned and sank deeper into my cocoon. The shroud opened, unfurled and stretched into a dark tunnel. I slid into an abyss. Nothing mattered. I was nothing.

∞

"Never mind. I'll talk to her." I heard a familiar voice coming from the kitchen. I rolled over. The shroud jerked against my face. Harrie handed me the cordless. "It's Sari Thompson." I rubbed a hand over my forehead and took it.

"Hello?" I tried to sound strong.

"Dannah. It's Sari. I figured you'd want to know the Colonel is home and doing fine."

I opened my eyes. The shroud was gone. "Hi, Sari. I'm so sorry about the Colonel. I've been kinda out of it but I'm feeling better now. Thank you for letting me know."

Sari talked on about Moonie. I sat up in bed. I ran my fingers through my short hair. The scalp wound throbbed when I touched it. I tried to focus on her words. If I could just stay in the present, I wouldn't sense the shroud.

"So, don't worry about that puss in boots. Or the Colonel. Dannah, I've got to run now. You take care."

11 /

Nirvana and I stood on the back steps to the Colonel's laundry room shivering in the cold wind. Sunlight sparkled on the fresh snow-covered shrubs and bushes. The Coop looked small and unfriendly. I couldn't look at it. I turned to the back door.

"Knock again," Nirvana said.

I did and then I just stood there wondering why I hadn't gotten back to the Colonel before now. I should have been giving Moonie long, scratchy strokes along her spine. Disjointed and disconnected, I shrugged my bruised shoulders just as Sari Thompson opened the door.

"Oh, come in, come in, girls. Let me get you cookies and milk. The Colonel's out for a walk around the park. You'd never know he had a run in with that scoundrel of yours." She frowned, perhaps aware of her error.

"He's not mine," I said.

"Of course not, dearie. Sorry. I didn't mean anything by it," she paused to open a cupboard and set two blue and white plates on the counter. "I was afraid the Colonel had a heart attack caused by that gash on his arm. Zip went crashing right at the Coop door. Of course, it's locked, so he fell in the snow. Next thing I know he's headed through the rose garden. I'm keeping this door locked now. And so should you." She paused and took a breath.

"Sari, I'm so sorry." My eyes puddled as I reached for her hand.

"There's more. When he pulled open the screen door, I was right there, took my wet mop and pushed it right under his chin. He stumbled backward down the steps. Landed in the snow. Then the Colonel yelled out 'What's all the ruckus?' and came into the kitchen. When he saw it was Zip raising a fist to me, the Colonel started to run, slipped on the wet floor and went down." Sari shook her head.

"Are you okay, Sari?" Nirvana and I said it in unison.

"Oh, girls, I'm fine. And the Colonel scrambled up from that floor, shaking his fist. And that hoodlum starts back up the steps. You should have seen 'em. Zip was yelling something and the Colonel was swearing to beat the band. I handed the Colonel the mop and I grabbed the broom. Kitchen commandos, girls. We both pushed that good fer nothin' right into a snow bank and slammed and locked the door. That's when I called 911 right there on the wall phone." As Sari talked, she poured milk and put an aqua blue plate of cookies on the kitchen table. She spoiled the Colonel—and me— with her baking. I stuck a finger into the still warm chocolate chip cookie and licked.

"Anyway, I saw the Colonel was bleeding right through the rip in his sleeve. Think he caught it as he fell and grabbed that infernal towel rack and down he went again. I knew his blood pressure was up for sure. Mine too. So, off to the hospital, the two of us when 911 got here. We both were fine. They gave him a bunch of tests—since last spring when he had that heart attack, they keep an eye on him. Said it was good he was there. His ticker needed monitoring. They gave me some pills and I came home. Haven't had time to take any pills myself. Glad the Colonel is back home."

"I'm sorry this all happened and I'm so glad it wasn't serious," I said. "What do you mean monitoring?"

"They did a heart scan and want to keep an eye on him. See. It all works out for the best." Sari brushed her hands across her faded apron.

"Where's Moonie?" I looked at her favorite spot on the kitchen window sill.

"Gone for a walk with the Colonel," Sari said.

Nirvana chuckled.

"What? She could get lost. Cats don't go for walks like dogs." What if Zip got Moonie...or the Colonel.

"Well, you know the Colonel misses that little ol' dog of his. Stopped walking completely after that ol' pup died. Colonel needs more exercise. I've been tellin' him that. Then the doc insists on it. So, I says, why don't you walk the cat? He scoffed at first and I forgot about it. Next thing I know, he's got your cat on a leash and they're off for a jaunt around the block. Cat happy as anything. Colonel comes in with rosebuds in his cheeks. More cookies, girls?"

I shook my head. I couldn't imagine Moonie Cat on a leash. I'd have to wait to see it. I dreaded going to the Coop but I wanted to get it over with too.

∞

"Your place looks great," Nirvana looked around.

"No kidding. I hardly recognize it." Harrie had cleaned the Coop, putting an order to the place that I'd never achieved. I wondered if I'd be able to find anything.

"Do you want anything? Tea?" I said, opening a narrow cupboard. My tea was no longer there, nor were the cups in their usual place. I couldn't find anything. "Okay. So, let me think. How would Harrie put it together?" I opened and closed cupboards. My spices were alphabetized in the cabinet next to the two burner stove. My plates, saucers and cups were stacked by size and color. She'd restocked my tea supply and many boxes of tea were in a cupboard under the counter, next to the oatmeal. "I haven't had milk and cookies since I was a Girl Scout. Sari's a sweetheart. But a cuppa tea will be good." I smiled at Nirvana.

She'd taken a seat on the couch. Soon we were settled with mugs of tea.

"Show me your recent paintings." she said.

I nodded, and got up slowly. I turned in a circle, looking for a stack of paintings. Behind the sofa, Harrie had organized my paintings by size and color. Smaller ones were stacked on the hat shelf in the closet.

"I've been so preoccupied with my sculpture I haven't even been to the Art Co-op meetings, let alone seen anyone else's work." Nirvana looked apologetic.

"We're all like that. Not to worry. I'll show you some of my new stuff."

It was the incentive I needed. Focus on my creativity, not my destruction. I slid a stack of eight by tens from under a little table. "These are impressions, moments I captured quickly." There were many angel paintings in various colors, shapes and positions that I'd created as prototypes for various paintings.

"Here," I said easing out two twenty-four by thirty-six paintings, "are a couple yet to be framed. I have that show coming up soon at the Faerie Arts Gallery."

"You better get painting. What if you sell out at the Co-op this month?" Nirvana asked.

"An artist's dream, right? To sell out," I said. "That will be the day."

"I saw Deirdre while I was out this morning running errands," Nirvana said.

"Our airy-fairy writer who lives on the bluff?" I laughed.

Nirvana nodded. "She said to give you a message and that it had to be exact." She closed her eyes. "Let's see—oh, yes—The faeries like you. They've been working with your guardian angels to cleanse the Coop." She paused, as if she were listening to Deirdre. "They've been with you a long time and would like you to acknowledge them. Your disbelief discourages them. Some of them have left already. There is a small group who have been with you for lifetimes. Spend some time with them, Dannah."

I nodded. "Thanks for the delivery but you know I just can't go there."

"Here, let me help you," she said and lifted one end of a large painting from behind the bed. I jiggled the edge but it was tightly wedged in. "We have to scoot the couch out first." Nirvana is all muscle, I think, and had it moved before I was even ready. "This is the latest. Except for the one that was on the easel." I clenched my jaw, shying away from the emotion that leaked toward my tear ducts.

"Wow," Nirvana said. "You'd never know you weren't the woo-woo type. Besides, Deirdre means well."

"It's not woo-woo, really. This is another one I dreamed." A mermaid sat on a ledge, deep on the ocean floor, a cave rising up behind her. The colors were the hues and shadows of the deep ocean—a place I'd never been and could hardly imagine.

"Deirdre would think it so realistic," Nirvana said and laughed. I smiled without it hurting too much.

"Realistic? It's a mermaid." I shrugged.

"Think about it, Dannah. Deirdre has a point. You paint angels you see in your dreams. She sees faeries in the daylight. Not much difference really."

She helped me slide the paintings back behind the couch. The thought settled in another hidden pocket of my mind.

∞

"I'm looking for Zip's girlfriend's number or address," I said to Nirvana and slowly turned looking at my tiny home. "It's on an envelope. He sent me a letter when he first started living with her. I think he tried to make me jealous. As you know, it didn't work." Harrie had done a good job of cleaning up. "You look in the table," I said, showing her how the coffee table was really a chest. Opening it, I groaned. I used to know exactly where everything was. Now it was too orderly to find anything. "It's got to be here somewhere."

I went to the small desk that served as a bedside table and pulled out the drawer. A stack of paperwork. Good. Maybe it was here. I was certain I'd put it in the desk. When? Last month? Six months ago? Or before that?

"Her name is Amethyst," I said. The last name still wouldn't come.

"Amethyst Green?" Nirvana asked, holding up a letter. "Here we go."

"Yes. Nirvana, you found it," I said, grabbing it out of her hand. "The postmark is hard to read. I wonder if she still lives there. I could go check it out on the internet at the library," I said.

"You need to get a computer. I need to get my computer fixed," she said.

"One of these days. Wanna come to the library with me?"

"I really need to get back to work on my sculpture. I can drop you off. Then you can give me a call when you want a ride home."

"That's okay. I'll take the truck." I hoped I was up to driving. My old pick-up truck was parked off the alley on the far side of the Coop. I wanted to be alone to think.

"Dannah, I support you in taking back your life. Please be careful. Full of care. Each day you are stronger. Please also know when to ask for help. Call me when you need to." Her eyes fired into mine with love and concern and permission to be myself.

I smiled, a tiny smile that didn't hurt too much.

12 /

I found the truck key in the silverware drawer. At least Harrie hadn't moved that. I planned to drive to the library and then head up to Talia's to thank her for all her help. If I remembered right, it was her day off.

Obviously Half Moon cat-cat was getting along fine without me for now. I was relieved that the Colonel was feeling so good. Silly old guy, walking my cat.

I threw some clean clothes in my fraying green backpack, found my miniature Winsor Newton watercolor box and a small pad of 180 pound paper, locked up the Coop and headed for the truck out back. This may not have been the brightest idea. Shifting gears was painful in my private parts, along my thighs. I drove down tree-lined streets, missing the leaves of autumn that had already fallen in piles of gold, now mushy baby poop brown.

I stopped at the small branch office of the Fondis Public Library, showed my card and signed in for a half hour on the computer. Fortunately it wasn't crowded and I didn't make eye contact with the few people in the stacks. Search: Amethyst Green, Chimayo, New Mexico. Bingo. There she was. Nirvana had been right. Amethyst had a new address. I copied it and her phone number and signed out.

∞

I drove along narrow streets on the west side of town past tidy, quaint houses and neat yards. I hung a left on Panorama Drive. The paved road curved up toward the bluffs rather steeply. Half way to the top, the engine began to lose power. I shifted, floor boarded the accelerator but no increased action. "Damn." I gripped the steering wheel. I'd been doing my best to keep up my dear ol' clunker. Double damn.

I didn't have my cell phone. How spacey can I get? What's wrong with me? I should remember these things. Did I charge it at Nirvana's? I just can't remember.

I eased off on the narrow shoulder, sliced the tires so it wouldn't roll, and turned off the engine. I climbed out and stood on the roadside, wondering which way to go. A sharp breeze edged under my collar. It was a long way to the top, where Talia lived, steep and winding. I'd best head back toward the stables at the base of the road and hope to find a phone there. I walked to the passenger side of the truck and rummaged around in the glove compartment, finding a stocking cap and mittens. I put them on and started walking back the way I'd come, toward Fondis.

I heard the car before I saw it and jumped off the pavement. As my feet hit gravel, the jolt wrenched up through my body, slapping my core and leaving me breathless. The Mercedes, exceeding the speed limit, braked, squealing as it came to a stop.

"Dannah Davidson, whatever are you doing here?" Talia asked as the window slid down.

I was so glad to see her, I just giggled.

She shook her head. "Still stressed, I see. Get in."

I did, pointing out my stranded vehicle around the next curve. "Can I borrow your cell phone? I forgot mine."

"That's why you didn't answer. Did you ever consider that someone might be worried about you?"

I looked at her in blank astonishment. "Of course not. Why?"

"Well, I'm just glad you're okay. My cell's in my bag there on the floor by your feet."

"Talia. I'm sorry. I didn't mean to worry you. I need to call Sam's Garage and have the truck towed again."

"His number is on my phone list," she said.

I dialed and the woman who answered promised to have it picked it up in ninety minutes. "Oh, yes, the keys are in the ignition. Nobody can steal it. It won't move." I giggled.

Talia pulled out, spinning gravel as she took off up the hill.

I was silent as Talia drove to the Palace, my nickname for her home. As I looked at the Ponderosa pines lining the road, I thought about Zip running wild, mad and naked through these woods. Now where is he? The road twisted with tighter curves upward.

Talia drove into her garage and closed the door with an automatic clicker. "I need to shower and change. Why don't you take a rest in the guest room at the end of the hall?" Tiny bells jingled from her cell phone. I went to the kitchen and got a glass of water. I was feeling woozy.

"That was Sam at the garage. He says your transmission is out," Talia said. "He couldn't get ahold of you and wanted me to give you the message."

"Shit. That sounds expensive." We walked into the great room and I flopped on the sofa, wincing, and stared at the ceiling trying to figure out what to do.

"It is. You'll have to decide if you want to keep that old truck or not."

"I've been keeping it up—spending money on it all year so it would be dependable. If I start over, I'll just have someone else's problem vehicle and then what?" I shook my head.

"I remember Loren suggested the auction. He bought a car there once and it lasted three years," Talia said.

"Yeah, and Harrie bought a car there once and it didn't last a week," I said.

"You don't have to decide anything right now," Talia reminded me. "I'll think about some options for you."

I loved coming here to her huge kitchen, formal dining room and palatial décor. As Talia went off to her bedroom, I peeked into the formal living room with huge windows looking down over Fondis. I'm not sure I'd choose to live in a place like this if I had the chance but it's great to visit, the view inspiring no matter the time of year. If I painted landscapes, I'd sit outside and paint from one season to the next. I prefer being inside with the angels. Outside or inside my mind can be dangerous. Too quickly I unravel into dark thoughts. I want to choose another way.

Choice is a weird word. Choice of where I'd wanted to live always seemed happenstance. First Mama told me where we'd live; then I was just with Grannie and finally Zip who moved like a grasshopper. I'd lived in every part of Fondis. No choice. It wasn't my choice to lose my baby. It wasn't my choice to be raped. It wasn't my choice to have my truck break down. Maybe when I was a kid I thought I had choices. Jeez, there it was. I thought it. I'd said it in my head. I was raped. The word is a dark dagger toward my empty womb. Nirvana was right. I'd been repressing the word and the anger it slapped in front of me, behind me, battering the air I breathed. I tried to skip away from all its implications, tried to slip away from the damage it had done.

I imagined myself skipping in the wind. I used to love to skip and let my hair fly as I'd skimmed over the grass, my feet light as butterflies. The skipping impulse left me sometime after I married Zip. He ground his passion out like cigarettes, his greedy lust used against me, pressed against my body, me feeling so lonely, so hungry, tingling in imagined love. I said I loved him and I did want to love him. But he always dripped contempt like a leaky faucet.

The pregnancy transformed me, our child growing toward my heart, that unknown seed. Seed that I would hold in my arms, nourish at my breasts. My tears became a deluge when I lost that baby. Maybe she was my only hope for love in this life.

Her death hovered over me every time he hit me. The memory of me, quivering, slinking away into invisibility is always with me. Yes, my pain was invisible. Oh, I'm fine, I'd say to whomever asked. Yes, I'm just fine.

But I wasn't. Say the truth, the voice in my head would shout. Then I said it softly, whispered it into an empty hospital room. His voice had been loud, full of anger when he found out I was pregnant. His only true gift to me was my baby and then he took her away. I'd collapsed with the force of his punch landing me hard on the floor. Pain in my head. Cramping pain in my belly. Then nothing until a nurse said, "She's awake, Doctor."
And the doctor stood there all white and official. "You lost the baby."

"You mean I lost my life," I said and began to weep quietly, pushing down, down into the darkness all the hatred I had for him. Hell is living life with Zip. Zip, short for Zipper, because he always wanted to pull it out. He thought it was funny to tell me about his name. Like his name made him a sex god or something. Aloysius Caruso Smith was his real name. I think. After a while everything seemed like a lie so I started to disregard anything that came out of his mouth.

When I left the hospital, I just wanted him out of my life. Friends urged me to get a restraining order to keep him away. He'd still come after me, find me, get me, hurt me, they said. Afraid to sign anything, I was helpless to act on my own behalf.

Terrified, I went home without a baby. Empty arms. Rivers falling from my eyes, I went to bed and stayed beneath the covers. Months in bed, the soft place where people die. I wondered if Mama ever lost a baby and where she was now. Probably someplace in Europe with her new boyfriend.

I'd had to figure it out by myself and now this. At least Zip isn't around now. I opened my eyes and looked around Talia's guest bedroom. He escaped from the hospital so maybe he's even dead. I'm still alive. And every day I'm getting stronger. I don't like wishing it, but I do; I wish him gone from the planet, buried in some cold grave where he can't hurt anyone ever again.

14 /

Talia stepped into the doorway of the forest green guestroom.

"Dannah, let's do some cranial sacral work. It will help balance your physical body in a gentle way," she said.

"What's wrong with my cranium?"

"I'm not sure anything is wrong with it. But you did have a severe blow to the side of your head and neck. I'm always concerned about contusions to the head. I'll put my hands on you and feel the rhythms and adjust them. Sometimes it's a subtle thing like the cranial sacral rhythm that throws other things off—like all the fatigue and forgetfulness you're experiencing. Let's go back to the spa."

"Okay." I was feeling confused but I trusted Talia. I gimped along the plush carpet and followed her to a room with a massage table, sauna and little altar with white sand raked in a labyrinth pattern. A statue of Kwan Yin stood above the sand by a tiny twisted tree.

"Spend the night here, Dannah. I'll call Nirvana and let her know. Now, take a deep breath and relax."

I eased on the warmed massage table. Candles burned on tables in the four corners of the iris blue room. She adjusted a foam roll under my knees and covered me with a dandelion yellow silk cloth. My eyelids felt heavy and closed, fluttering as she circled the table, mumbling phrases I couldn't catch, and making hand gestures.

She was murmuring or humming and I drifted off, trusting my old friend to touch my body. Images came and went. Soft music filled the room, harps and birds chirping, frogs singing, the wind over water. She placed gentle hands on my head.

"Your aura is ripped in several places," her gentle voice washed over me. "And you're leaking energy at the solar plexus chakra, the place of self-confidence and will. I'll be working on that first. Then we'll check your cranial rhythm."

I thought of the times I'd hidden in Grannie's closet. Of course, she knew where I hid from daddy. She'd find me nestled amongst her finery, sitting on the floor next to the rows of leather shoes and all her lacy special things. She'd ease down onto the floor with me and tell me stories.

"Open the treasure chest," I'd say and she'd get up, stand on a little stool and lift down the big leather case, slip the key from her apron pocket and open the lid. Treasures we oohed and ahhed over.

"Costume jewelry," Mama would sneer when I told her.

"No. Diamonds and sapphires." Hidden beneath the gaudy flower pin, the plastic clip-on earrings, were her real jewels, the pearls her mama gave her. I have them now and keep them hidden in a false bottom of my painting box. Zip never saw them. My treasure had been the baby. And he'd taken her away. Gradually the angry images shifted into a pond with reeds growing along the side. A boy and girl sat on a log and dangled their feet in the pool. I woke myself up with a snore. Talia was no longer there.

Talia pampered me with dinner before I settled in the guest rooms, decorated in hues of cottonwood green. She showed me the television behind a sliding panel. I glanced at it. That would surely activate my fears. News, news and more news. All bad news and bad news reminded me of Zip. I'd seen his bristled mug on TV more than once. He'd been caught on a security camera robbing a liquor store once and was jailed for robbery and resisting arrest. I didn't know where he was but he wouldn't be around here now. I didn't want to think about him. Just the mellow magic my body felt and I'd like to hold onto that feeling.

"Actually I would like to fall into a good historical romance and forget about the present."

"Oh, I just finished one by Hannah Oakley that I think you'll like. You know she used to live in Fondis? She lives in Seattle now. Just a sec. I'll get it for you. Then I'm ready to turn in." Talia went to her bedroom and returned with a paperback.

"Thanks, Talia" I said and took the book, *Carriage Secrets*.

"Sleep tight," she said and kissed my forehead before leaving.

I turned on the nightstand light, dowsed the other lights in the room and settled in to read about Cornelia Carmichael in 1780 England.

15 /

The next morning Talia dropped me off at the Firehouse Studio. It looked like Nirvana had worked through the night. She was sleeping on top of the bed in rumpled coveralls. I was still tired. I placed a blanket over her and climbed under the covers. We both slept. Memories, not angels chased my dreamtime. I was half awake, remembering...

Nirvana and Harrie had been out jogging. It was their New Year's resolution that year. I would have laughed if I hadn't been crying. Both of them hated jogging. I could see the pained expressions, the hobble in their gait and then they turned and jogged right up to me sitting on the front steps, a pink baby blanket snuggled around my shoulders.

Plopping down on either side of me, they panted like winded horses. Nirvana wiped sweat from her brow. "We miss you in the Womyn's Group," Harrie said. "Why don't you come back? You make us laugh. You know, you've got that wry sense of humor and we love your creativity."

"What's wrong, Dannah? You look like shit," Nirvana interrupted. I hardly paid attention to either of them. She grabbed my freezing hands and examined the creases. "You haven't been painting. Come on, girl, get up. We're helping you out of this funk."

Somehow they managed to get me to Harrie's place, bathed me, and dressed me like I was a baby. They didn't know I'd lost the baby. I hadn't told anyone. Finally I blubbered out the words. Nirvana insisted that I stay with her so I could paint in her studio. I didn't want to paint. Nirvana challenged me, coaxed me, encouraged me. I don't remember how many days I stayed with her then.

It was my blue period. I listened to the blues and painted with blue. When I ran out of cobalt, I painted in teal. The colors of blue slid through my eyes like a kaleidoscope: cyan, azure, turquoise, powder blue and slate blue. Old penny copper blue, cornflower blue, whale blue, delft, sky, royal. Lake Fondis blue and oh, the St. Louis blues.

A few angel paintings during that time but mostly I painted babies. Women and babies, mother and child, a nursing baby, the Madonna and baby, pregnant Mary Magdalene. All in shades of blue.

Then one day my body was no longer black and blue. I had the two of them to thank for that—and the Womyn's Group. I gave Harrie the first angel painting. It's still hanging in her neatnik living room.

The Womyn's Group helped me apply for a divorce, helped me see the value in a restraining order. I didn't see Zip for a long time, but I was fidgety nervous in public, looking around for him. I expected him to round a corner on Main Street—or show up next to me in line at the grocery store.

When I rented the Coop, Nirvana insisted that Athena, her German shepherd, stay with me. Then Half Moon kitty found me and Athena went home to her own cat and artist. I missed that sweet dog after she died almost as much as Nirvana did.

That Half Moon cat had curled into me with a deep and resonate purr that healed my wounds. I no longer wanted to die. I just wasn't sure if I wanted to live, or even knew how to live.

The angel dreams came more often, a visitation, Talia called them. They came in a rainbow of colors. And slowly life changed. I still didn't like to be in public, in large groups or in a crowd. I volunteered at the Women's Crisis Center. Sometimes I just cleaned toilets. Other times I answered phones. I taught painting classes. The Womyn's Centre sponsored an art show featuring the creations of abused women, heart wrenching, powerful images erupting from canvases.

A year went by and I was still afraid of running into Zip. Once I thought I saw him coming out of a bar at dusk. It was someone else but it freaked me out. When I heard on the great Fondis grapevine that Zip was in L.A., I breathed a sigh of relief. He had a cousin there and drugs were easier to access.

Knowing he was no longer in Fondis, I felt more relaxed. I was more comfortable with folks, even went out to eat occasionally. Life was good. My paintings were in several galleries. People liked them enough to buy them.

Most people think of this town as a tourist attraction or they come for the spectacular parades and gallery walks. But we're just real folks here. Yes, even in Fondis, there are abused women. I painted a woman crouching, picking up shards of glass, a child's wide fearful eyes peering out from behind her. The threatening man's shadow is all you see of the implied action, a hovering danger to mother and child. A philanthropist bought it for a women's shelter in Texas.

I'd always looked at body shapes and textures, light and contrast. Made sketches. I wonder if I'll ever draw men again. Maybe I could live celibate. It would be safer that way. I trusted my women friends. I could never trust a man again. And why should I?

I remembered the time Zip broke my left arm. Maybe if I'd had as much to drink as he had, I wouldn't have felt the excruciating pain— fortunately, I was sober and dialed for help.

Old memories and recent ones merged and needed to come up now and be purged for good. I could not imagine even shaking hands with a man. I was just freaked out. I was glad to be with Nirvana.

16 /

The next morning, Nirvana dropped me off at Sam's garage to pick up a loaner Subaru. I drove back to the Firehouse, trying to figure out how to shift gears. I asked her to drive back to the Coop with me. I needed to start being in my own home, feeling safe. We both finally had enough sleep and she offered to help in the garden. I was glad for her company. I wanted to be home but I didn't want to be alone. She followed me through the weathered garden gate. I should paint it, maybe honey amber or ketchup red.

I nodded as she bent to deadhead a chrysanthemum. We'd planned a short gardening session and then have lunch with Harrie.

"Nirvana, I'm so glad you're here with me." I smiled at her as we wandered the soggy flower beds. The small garden was fenced with chipped white pickets and faced the Colonel's rose bed with the best southern exposure. "You're my garden angel. I don't even know where to start."

"We need to mulch the roses for winter. You can collect the marigold seeds now or let them drop of their own accord. Same with the hollyhocks." She scrunched up her shoulders and dropped them. Welder's shoulders, she called them. "Alyssum. All your annuals will provide you with seed for next spring. Except hybrids."

"Even petunias?"

"Yes. I've even had them re-seed, but it's easier to buy sets in the spring." She bent down and picked off a marigold seed head and rolled the spiky seeds between her gloved fingers. They tumbled to the ground.

"I'd like to do it the natural way," I said. "It would be more natural to just let the seeds fall to the ground, wouldn't it?"

"The problem with the natural way, that is, scattering them or letting them fall with the whim of the winds, is that the birds eat them. So, if we're going to scatter them, let's cover them up with some top soil. Since the snow has melted, it's good to get it done before the next storm comes in."

I walked back toward the Coop where I stored bins of compost and top soil, filled the wobbly wheelbarrow with rich, dark earth and pushed it down the garden path. I was still aware of aches and pains in my body but working in the garden healed my mind. My body felt better doing something physical. Pushing the heavy load, I knew my muscles would get stronger. I could feel Nirvana keeping an eye on me.

Dropping a kneeling pad on the path next to the dried sweet pea vines, I eased to my knees. I pulled one weed and then another, making a clean area before I plucked a marigold head, broke it apart and scattered the seeds. I pushed up with my hands. I wasn't too good in a squat position. Nirvana was stuffing mulch around the roses. We worked in silence but my mind was jabbering with thoughts. I moved to the next bed, grabbed a shovel and hoisted manure. Sacks of manure were still just shit. And, shit, I could dig all the way to the center of the earth and still not escape. Yes, the fear in the creak of the wooden floor, the wind rattling the window panes, the unexpected sound of a car in the alley behind the Coop, the fear that another day would rise and I would not have changed. I knew I had to change or die.

"I'll leave this between us so we both can nab some compost," Nirvana said, groaning as she heaved a fifty pound bag onto the pathway.

We worked quietly for some time. Birds chirped and settled at the bird feeder. Poor little winged ones must have missed my daily feedings. I'd remember to fill the bird bath. The garden was peaceful and I knew in a place deep in my heart that it would be okay to spend the night. I wondered if Her Highness Half Moon would be willing to join me. Spoiled kitty.

"I'm getting ideas being in your garden, Dannah," Nirvana said. "What if I sculpted a glass scarecrow sculpture? Would you be willing to let me experiment and put it here? It probably won't be ready until late spring."

"That would be great. What happens if the glass freezes? Won't it break?" I said wondering if it would keep Zip away as well as the crows.

"Not if I do it right. After all, your windows don't break from the cold, do they? This will be a good opportunity to test out the environmental possibilities of the new techniques I'm working on. Because I don't have a garden or even a bit of dirt at home, I can't do it at the Firehouse."

I nodded. It was surrounded by cement. She had a few potted containers in spring but mostly came to the Coop for down-in-the-dirt time.

"What time are we going to meet Harrie?" I asked. I never wear a watch, just feel the angle of the sun and get a sense of the time of day.

"I forgot to tell you. She's going to swing by here and pick us up. The girls' lunch out." We laughed. We never called ourselves girls. Women, that's what we were. Strong women. I want to be a strong woman.

We continued cleaning up the garden beds, each lost in our own worlds. Clouds drifted across the November sun. The morning weather report promised a light snow this afternoon. I'd need to grab a heavier jacket before we left for lunch.

∞

"Sorry, I'm late, girls," Harrie said as we climbed into her SUV.

"No problem," Nirvana said. "We finished our chores and had time to scrub up."

Harrie looked fabulous in a tailored suit and boots. I wore old jeans and a sweatshirt with an old down vest. I still wasn't at all sure about being out in public, seeing anyone who might know what happened. Nirvana, always dependable for the unusual, wore her garden clothes, faded denim bib top with a flowing mirror cloth blouse beneath. A Moroccan camel hair cape wrapped around her shoulders finished her ensemble, Nirvana style.

"I'm famished. Lunch is my treat, girls." Harrie said as she pulled the car unto the Ute bypass.

"What's up with you?" Nirvana said. "You're grinning like the Cheshire cat, Harrie."

"I can never keep a secret from you. I have a date tonight." She pulled into Ye Ol' Fondis Tea Shoppe. "Is this okay with you? They have great sandwiches."

I turned my head to see what Nirvana thought. She smiled from the backseat and nodded to Harrie's image in the rearview mirror. I didn't really want to go inside but they climbed out of the car, chattering. I pulled my wool scarf up over my chin, tucked my stocking cap over my ears and dropped my head as we walked to the door. We settled in a booth with cracked burgundy naugahyde.

I gazed unseeing at the plastic menu. This was a busy restaurant and I was afraid to look around, afraid I might see someone I knew. I didn't recognize the waitress who bounced up to the booth with a cheery smile. Harrie ordered a club sandwich. Nirvana asked for a veggie burger. My eyes rushed over the menu and I ordered a tuna melt. Harrie looked up and waved at someone coming in the door. A blast of chilled air blew in.

"Hey, Mac," she called.

I glanced over the booth. A tall, broad shouldered man walked toward us. He wore an overcoat and scarf and was pulling off leather gloves. "Harriet," he said, shaking her hand, rather formally. I took a drink of water and looked at my reflection in the mini-juke box.

"Great to see you back in town," Harrie said. They talked about something business sounding and I pushed the salt and pepper shakers in circles on the green Formica table top, wishing for a pencil so I could sketch. "Sorry, Mac. I'd like you to meet my friends." She introduced us and he shook hands with Nirvana and repeated her name. I clenched my hands into fists under the table and nodded. He had some kind of accent "Dannah," he said. I glanced up and he looked directly into my eyes. He was the kind of man I might have noticed in the past. His smile lifted me out of myself for a nano-second. His eyes were sparkling sapphires, the blue of Lake Fondis in August. Don't trust smiles, I thought and pulled the scarf closer.

"Nice to meet you," he said as the waitress brought our food. He looked at each one of us again. I couldn't remember his name. I asked the waitress for a pencil. "Give me a ring, Harriet, and we'll go over the details," he said.

He left and I turned my attention to the plate in front of me. "I'm sure I've told you about Mac. Interesting guy, Scottish. Consultant for a chain of assisted living facilities," Harrie said and picked up a wedge of her club sandwich.

I wasn't very hungry. I stuck my finger in a glob of melted cheese on the side of the faux English patterned plate made in China and stuck it in my mouth. The waitress returned with a pencil. I pulled a napkin from the silver holder and began to doodle.

"Okay, Harrie, back to your date tonight. Tell us," Nirvana said. I didn't look up. I wanted to hear but part of me really didn't care.

"I had a meeting and ran into the bank to make a deposit. Tad Duncan was coming in as I went out. You know him? The new VP. Well, we sort of floundered at the door, him coming, me going, in that round about. Somehow we both managed to be in a cubicle at the same time and we went a full circle before we both got out on the sidewalk, laughing." Harrie gesticulated with her hands, her long fingers graceful.

Nirvana and I laughed at the image of it.

"And you have a date with him?" I said.

"No. Weird thing. Another man came up just as I reminded Tad who I was and he introduced me to this mortgage broker who just flew in from L.A. named Jonathan Jacobs. Tad almost directly asked me to show him around town tonight. He wanted me to give Jonathan the Colorado experience, Fondis style. He said he was busy and couldn't do it. How could I refuse?"

"I'm not sure which one you're more excited about. Sounds like you and Tad had a great moment together," Nirvana said, and wiggled her eye brows. I sketched her profile.

"I probably would prefer to have a date with that handsome Tad guy, but it seemed like I was doing him a favor. So, he owes me one." She chuckled. "Jonathan will only be here overnight. He flies out of Fondis International at 6:00 a.m. He seemed pleasant enough but not my type. It will be a change. I'm planning on having a good time." She flashed her broad smile. "C'mon, let's go to the rock shop. Then I have to dash home and get beautiful."

"Dannah, you can do this. You are filled with courage and don't hesitate to call me if you need anything," Nirvana said, emphasizing the last word as Harrie dropped me off. Snowflakes fell from a darkened sky. I unlocked the Coop and went in. Home. It did feel like it, just a bit too clean and crisp from Harrie's tidiness and cold like nobody lived here, but home, nonetheless. I turned on the floor lamp and the kitchen light and plugged in the electric radiator heater. I wanted to visit the Colonel, to gather Moonie into my arms but I didn't want to come back to the chill of seeing my breath in my own house.

Even though I was just going next door, I locked the door behind me. I stopped at the garden gate, looking at the lacy feather snow gathering on the garden rows. Snow equaled spring green. Heading up the path to the Colonel's back door, I noticed the thorny rose bushes, stark stems glistening white. Sari Thompson answered the back door and her face crinkled into a smile. The Colonel sat by the wood stove, his feet propped up on a log for a footstool.

"Dannah," he said, standing. Sari ushered me to the kitchen table, covered with a red and white checked cloth and then busied herself at the counter. When she turned, she carried a mounded plate that made me smile.

I took a bite of warm apple pie with ice cream dripping down the sides. Sari was filling a glass of milk for me while Half Moon sat smugly on top of the refrigerator cleaning her face and slyly watching the activities.

"I wanted you to know I moved back home," I said. "I know Zip hasn't been found—but the police think he left town. Probably headed for his ex-girlfriend's house, if he's not dead in a ditch, that is."

The Colonel nodded. "That's where he should be. Good for nothin' bum."

"Now, don't go and get upset, Colonel," Sari patted his shoulder.

"Hummph."

"Colonel, I have something special in the garden I want to show you," I said.

"Yup. I noticed you out in the garden with that gardener friend of yours. Weren't you cold out there?"

"You don't miss a thing, Colonel," I said. "You remember Nirvana. She's knows more about gardening than she does about sculpting. And Harrie gave me a piece of rose quartz. It took three of us to haul it with the wheelbarrow." I laughed, thinking of Harrie, Nirvana and I as we'd maneuvered the huge chunk of stone into place. Afterwards, Nirvana went off to dinner with a friend and Harrie to her date with the guy from out of town. And I had a date with a cat. I hoped she'd get over feeling abandoned or maybe she preferred all this special attention from Sari and the Colonel.

"I can't thank you enough for taking care of Moonie, Colonel. It's been a rough time for me. I couldn't have done it without you."

"Pashaw," he mumbled or something like that. "You're a strong gal. All I did was pet the cat." He sat down in the chair across from me, picking up his coffee mug to study it.

"I don't know if Half Moon will even want to come home." I couldn't imagine my life without a cat, without Moonie.

"Demanding cat, that Half Moon. Why I had to take her for a walk every single day. She'd caterwauled at the door if we didn't go right on schedule. Pain in the caboose, that cat is," the Colonel grumbled.

Half Moon circled in place, flicking her tail at us as she repositioned herself.

"Well, I guess you won't miss her when I take her home, huh?" I lifted an eyebrow.

"Of course not. Too high falutin', that cat is. Don't know how you keep up with her."

At first I thought he was joking but then I worried that he was serious. Maybe Half Moon had been too much for the aging military man.

"I'm sorry. I thought maybe you enjoyed her."

"Harrumph."

"Colonel, sir, now don't be so ornery. You're upsetting the girl. Go on, tell her," Sari said, picking up my empty plate and glass.

The Colonel glared at her and then up at Moonie who jumped down and pushed against the Colonel's ankle. Then, with one agile movement, she landed lightly in the middle of the table. She twirled, flashing her tail across my nose. I laughed. Then she tail-whacked the Colonel.

"What's going on, Colonel? She seems upset with both of us."

"Well, Dannah, your friend here was missin' you. I could tell. She knew I wanted her to stay on. I didn't know how long you'd be gone and I got used to cat company. Doesn't talk back like Sari, here."

She made a sound in her throat, giving the Colonel an exasperated look.

"We went walkin' every day, your cat and me," the Colonel continued. "Suited both of us. She took to a lead better than any canine I ever trained." I could hear pride in his voice and relaxed a little, wondering what was coming.

"I knew you'd be along soon' enough to take Moon Face home."

Moonie batted my hand, claws retracted. I reached out and rubbed behind an ear, waiting for a purr.

"Well, now. I see you two are properly getting reacquainted," the Colonel said.

"Colonel, tell her," Sari urged.

"Tell me what?"

"I got my own cat. There." He crossed his arms, his lips a thin line.

"Your Moonie didn't like any part of that," Sari said. "We've had to keep them separated for the past few days. They only get along when the Colonel takes them both for a walk." Sari shook her head.

"You walk both cats on leads?" I couldn't believe it.

He nodded, got up and pushed the swinging door into the dining room.

"C'mon, Private." He shifted his voice up an octave. A black cat streaked past his feet and skidded across the polished linoleum. Moonie hissed, hair bristling like a porcupine.

"That's the Private," Sari said. "Better take him back in the dining room, Colonel, until Dannah leaves." She suppressed a giggle with her hand and winked at me as the Colonel bent to pick up the twitterpated cat.

"Time for us to go home, Moonie," I said.

"And it's about time," grumped the Colonel.

Sari and I exchanged a glance. I stopped at the back door, turning. "Colonel, if you need an extra companion for walking, I'm sure Half Moon will be up for it." Cuddling kitty in my arms, I walked down the back steps and headed home to the Coop rubbing my chin in Moonie's fur.

I woke up feeling great. There's nothing like sleeping with a purring cat to soothe a restless soul. No nightmares, either, which was a relief. I hoped the day-mares would stop too. I laughed out loud as I imagined a herd of wild horses, mares, and reached for my sketch pad.

Like I'd promised Talia, I'd kept my appointment with a counselor. I wondered what the difference was between a counselor, a therapist and a psychologist. Maybe it's just what you say to people if you don't want them to think you're whacked. Mentioning a counselor sounds so proper and nice. A psychologist is way too close to a psychiatrist for comfort and then everyone knows you're in big trouble. A therapist sounds like you've got deep problems.

When I finished breakfast, I drove the borrowed Subaru over to the Zebulon County Medical Center. The receptionist had me go through a door, the kind with a wire criss-crossed window pane that looked like trapped chicken wire and then down a long hallway with green gray carpeting to Room 231. There he was. Tall, skinny, hawk nosed and unsmiling. My assigned counselor. During the hour he questioned me, he kept his eyes on the computer. He never looked at me and I wondered how he could read my body language. And since I was having issues with men, or at least one whacko, then why go to a male counselor? He entered a bunch of stuff on the computer while I answered his questions. Or avoided them. It wasn't long before the shroud dropped over my head, blocking my speech. I imagined I'd be better off in a deep conversation with Nirvana or Harrie. I kept running my fingers through my short curls and fidgeting with the zipper on my hoodie.

When we were finished, he said I needed to see a psychiatrist and he wanted me on some kind of meds for depression. I found him very depressing. Once I got out of there, I drove around in a funk. I needed to walk to clear my head. I pulled into a parking lot and got out of the Subaru, locked it and began to walk. I just followed my feet, scuffing leaves, kicking pebbles and frowning at the pavement. It was far more productive than the hour I'd spent with Mr. Geek.

Eventually I found myself in front of Nirvana's loft and walked down the side of the building to the alley entrance. She had Tina Turner cranked and didn't hear me enter. Nirvana was standing on a high scaffold, her head covered with a Darth Vader-like welding hood, working on the form of a woman.

I settled in a chair and watched her, feeling amazed at the tools she needed to create her art and the heights she had to go to weld. Soon Panther, her sleek black cat, was curled in my lap, purring and nudging my hand for attention. This was real therapy, unlike that pop psycho-babble with Mr. Hawk Nose.

Nirvana paused, placing her torch in a holder and pushing the hood back off her face to stare at her creation. I remained silent, not wanting to distract or startle her when she was up so high. She turned, like she'd heard my thoughts.

"Hey, Dannah. Be right down." She turned off the welder, set her hood and gloves in a bin attached to the triple-tiered scaffold and climbed down with the speed of a monkey.

I laughed. "You're too funny, Nirvana. Sorry if I'm interrupting your work."

"No problem. I needed to take a break. This is the piece I'm going to attach the stones to—after talking to our friend Silver at the rock shop, I realize I can have slabs of a stone cut in a particular size and then I'll line them up along her chakras. I'm really jazzed about this sculpture." She grinned as she stared at the sculpture. "The Chakra Goddess. That's her name."

Panther hopped down from my lap and circled Nirvana's ankles. "He thinks I work too much." She laughed. "How's it going?" She turned, focusing all her attention on me now.

"Oh, you know. I just saw the counselor, therapist guy. He said I'm depressed."

"Who isn't? What did you start working on when you went home? Most artists I know are depressed if they're not in the midst of some mad creation."

"I never thought of that. You're probably right. I'm carrying my watercolors around like some kind of talisman, but I haven't painted a thing. I haven't even sketched anything besides doodling on a napkin at lunch. Oh, and a cluster of mustangs this morning. It's like my fingers and brain are disconnected. You're much better therapy than that clueless counselor I just saw. You really do understand me." I told her about my dismal session with the Nose.

"Better to go see the psychiatrist. I've lived with Prozac and without it. It's better with. It may not be the right thing for you, but you'll never know if you don't show up. Once you accept how bad life feels and one pill makes you feel so much better, then you're willing to experiment."

"I didn't know you took meds," I said, studying her, trying to see if I could tell she was on an anti-depression medicine. "I was so

103

upset I just started walking and my feet brought me here to the Firehouse." I sighed.

"Your feet are connected even if the rest of you isn't." Her laughter sparkled throughout the tall space. "Let's go get lunch. I'll buy. I just sold a big piece that will keep me warm this winter. Remember the Sky Goddess? She's at a fancy resort up in Montana in the land of big sky. A perfect place for her."

"Lunch out two days in a row? I'm not usually a social butterfly."

∞

Nirvana and I had lox and bagels at the little deli around the corner from the Firehouse. She peppered her coffee that day. Crazy artist Nirvana. "Nirvana, use some salt," I joked, "it's better that way."

My earrings brushed my neck and I brought my fingers to them twirling the tiny chimes. Lips speak words, eyes speak more. I couldn't trust either with Zip. Why does my mind keep going back to that asshole?

"So, what's really going on with you?" Nirvana probed as we shared a piece of homemade blueberry pie.

"I don't know," I said. "Talia took care of my body and Harrie took care of a bunch of other stuff with homeopathic remedies. I even have my cranium aligned. You're my best friend and I'll never be able to thank you enough. Still I'm just in this weird space." I picked at the pie crust.

"Are you afraid of Zip?" Nirvana asked, and took a bite of pie.

"Hardly. I'm so pissed at him. I fear my lack of good judgment more than anything."

Nirvana nodded.

"Jeez, of course, I am afraid of him. He's on the loose. Even if he did go to California, he could show up at any time." My throat tightened. I took a drink of water and looked around.

"Yes, he could. A guard dog would be nice. Even if you hate Zip, you loved him once," she said.

"Or thought I did." I closed my eyes and leaned into my hands. Maybe Nirvana was right. A big dog—but Half Moon would never allow it. Besides I didn't have any space. Even so, a big German shepherd would be nice. Or a tiger. I could think of all kinds of crazy ways to protect myself from Zip. I envisioned a moat, a blue green dragon lurking in shadows...

"Whenever I'm crazy, I grab my welding torch and head for some metal." Nirvana leaned back and signaled the waitress for a check.

"Wait a minute." I opened my eyes. "I haven't been able to paint but what if I could do what you do."

"What? Learn to weld?" She grinned.

"No, no. Paint, put it all on canvas, work it out in color. I have some stretched canvas at the Coop, twenty four by thirty six."

"Dannah, how about a big canvas? Really big. Let it all out. No interruptions."

"I'm going home right now and..." I wanted to touch my brushes, mix paint. I pushed the pie plate away as Nirvana slid her credit card into the black folder holding the bill.

"What if you stay with me at the Firehouse again? There's a huge canvas in the back room—remember when I used to paint backdrops for the Fondis Fools Production Company? I still have some of those massive panels. And I have every paint color they make. If you're at the Firehouse, you won't be tempted to wash the dishes or play with the cat."

We stepped out of the deli into a brisk wind. A bright flare of Colorado sunshine cut through the clouds as we walked.

Panther greeted us with a yowl when Nirvana unlocked the door. She leaned down to scratch behind his ears. "I have a pot of soup simmering in the crock pot so we have dinner covered."

"You're sure it's okay? You've already..."

"Of course I'm sure." She put her arm around my waist.

I followed her to the back room, small by comparison to the rest of her studio. It had been a storage room with high windows that let in perfect light even if clouds smothered the sun now. I looked around the room, nodding. It was perfect.

"Here's the canvas backdrop," she said and closed the door. "It's kind of weird. I took it out of the frame and glued boards on the top and bottom so it would be easier to store." She pointed to the ceiling high canvas hanging against the wall, attached by pulleys. "It may move around a bit. Do whatever you want. Just make it work for you." She kissed my cheek. "You have all the power now. Speak it out through color." We stood looking at the stark blank canvas, I tilted my head against her shoulder. I had the power now.

"But first, I have to go back and pick up the Subaru, and check on Moonie and ..."

"I'll pick it up when I go to the post office. Where did you leave the car?" she said. I had to think. Then I remembered and told her where it was. I fished the key from my jacket pocket. "But what about Moonie? She'll feel abandoned again. But she can't go back to the Colonel's. Did I tell you he had a cat now?"

"No problem. I'll take a brisk walk, feed that rambunctious Half Moon and be back in a flash with your car. Moonie will keep the home fires burning. You settle in here. See the closet over there?" She pointed. "You'll find buckets of paint, rollers, brushes, anything you might need if you want to do big slashing work. But first I need to work on the Goddess for about an hour and then I'm outta here. I had an idea at lunch that I can't wait to execute. I won't bother you. Come out whenever you're hungry. *Mi casa es su casa.*"

"Thanks, Nirvana." She gave me a hug and headed back to the scaffold.

19 /

I've never been intimidated by a canvas. Usually they call me and I fall right into them. But this one confronted my normal response. It overwhelmed me. I usually see the image in my mind before it unfolds. Then I don't even know what I'm doing; the brush is an extension of my hand and I'm surprised by the result. And then there are the dream paintings, the ones that wake me up at night and I rush to find a blank canvas and begin painting like a crazed person.

Now, here I was not knowing what to do. I pushed art and sculpture magazines aside and sat on a cot beneath the high windows.

I sat there for some time, growing more and more angry. I was so pissed off that it seemed futile to attempt anything creative. I thought I should go home to bed. Instead, I stretched out, hands behind my head and stared out one of the windows seeing past slow, new snowflakes. Nirvana was right. I had the power now.

Finally I knew I'd either get up and walk out of the room and head home—or I'd walk up to the canvas and go for it. I tilted my chin up and squinted. Then I stepped back against the opposite wall. I didn't have any idea how I'd work this large. I inspected the brushes, the cans of paint, the color choices, and walked in small circles again, pondering the beginning point.

"Whose bright idea was this anyway?" I asked the darkening windows.

Finally I slammed out of the room—I was going to tell Nirvana I couldn't do it. She was welding a large hoop earring on the left side of the Goddess' head, all fire and focus. I shrugged on my coat, opened the door and stalked out into the alley. I just needed to move, to figure out my resistance. I pulled the hood up around my head, trying to ignore the dark clouds and the biting wind. Light snow fell faster.

One foot in front of the other, I trudged along, ignoring anyone passing on the sidewalk. I didn't know which streets I crossed or in what direction I walked. Mindless but full of mind. Scattered images tumbled in my brain. Angry thoughts muffled with a yearning to be free of the fear, the angst, the limitations. The black shroud wove itself between images, taunting me much like the threatening clouds and heavy flakes stinging my cheeks.

Snow continued to fall and I realized I was nearly to downtown Fondis. And it was dark. I could go rescue the Subaru and have a hopefully warm drive back to Nirvana's. I rounded the corner and stopped under a street light. The car wasn't in the parking lot. There was only one other car around. That was the pits. Borrowing a car and losing it, or worse yet, having it stolen.

"Damn," I shouted.

"Hey," a voice shouted out behind me. A male voice. Shit. Had I been so mindless Zip had followed me? No. It wasn't Zip's voice but it wasn't anyone I knew, either.

I whirled, aware I was alone in an isolated parking lot. Furtively I glanced around, looking for lights and a place to run.

The scrawny figure headed toward me. I patted my pockets, trying to find my cell phone. The man moved closer.

"No. No, I'm fine," I said. He drew nearer. "Keep your distance," I yelled. A car rounded the corner, its headlights striking his face. A narrow face with scars and matted hair. Was he a friend of Zip's? He stopped where he was. I ran as fast as I could, slipping on snow, skidding almost into the car with its passenger window rolled down.

"Need some help?" Another man, another problem.

"No. No help. Never mind. It's okay." I pushed off the car and sprinted down the alley to the Main Street where there were people, maybe a cop, lights. Street lights where I'd be seen or should I dodge down an alley behind the grocery store so I could hide in the dark? The snow had stopped and a full moon made jagged shadows in the alleys. I just kept running, sweat chilling on my brow, fingers icy cold, bruises aching. I was afraid he was following me and I was afraid to look back. I was panting by the time I reached the Firehouse. Only then did I remember that Nirvana had promised to pick up the car. Forgetfulness could get me in big trouble. I needed to paint. I'd never painted on this much adrenaline. My hands were shaking as I picked up a brush.

My need to paint was dampened only by the massive size of the canvas. White surface, whiter than over-bleached teeth. It needed paint. I wished Nirvana were here. Shit. I haven't been that scared since...Just paint, I told myself. No interruptions, no excuses. I went back to check the lock on the door. If I had the power, it was gone now.

Shit. How stupid could I be, walking back into that dark parking lot? My anger at myself layered with my boiling rage at Zip. I faced the humongous canvas. It was almost the length of the wall and hung from the ceiling on a bar. Pulleys attached to the bar. Nirvana had sawed the frame apart for easy storage. I remembered the first time I met Nirvana. We painted a backdrop together for the production of Wild Woman Meets the Cowboy, a melodrama, a Fondis favorite.

Pulling open the closet door, I reached for the string and tugged on the light. I'd start with big swathes of ink black. I was feeling black and blue. Damn. I shuffled around amidst paint cans, rollers and paint trays until I found what I wanted and began to lug everything out before the canvas.

The canvas, already sized, was a fitting bird poop white. The safety latch in my brain was ajar, that deep dark part that growled a scolding at me for running out in the dark night. I had to pay attention, keep myself safe. Keep out of shit.

Scolding myself made me angry, which took me back to all the old issues of being hurt. I turned on all the lamps that Nirvana had clipped around the room, poured a can of black paint into a battered old tray, grabbed a roller and swung with random slashes of paint crisscrossing the surface. The floor was already well initiated with color. I didn't worry about being sloppy. I felt a nervous, wild abandon. I'd stepped off the cliff into the void, falling into the blackness—flailing a brush in one hand, roller in the other.

I sloshed buckets of paint, one after the other into the tray, using a roller to cut the black with blue, gray and red. I was building up a sweat and tossed off my tee shirt, working in bra and jeans. I kicked off my shoes and tugged off my socks never taking my eyes from the canvas.

Once I felt sorry for Zip; even in the beginning, I thought I could help him. Well, what kind of a stupid control trip was I on, anyway? He was out of control from the very beginning. The more I tried to make it work, to help him out of his mess, the worse my life got.

Grabbing a rag mop from the back of the closet, I dunked it in a gallon of blood red paint and slapped it across the canvas. I thought I was being nice, helping Zip better himself. I reached for a broom and dunked it in mustard yellow paint, spiking flares around. I dipped my hands up to my elbows in a bucket of midnight rage paint. I waved my arms against the surface like a windshield wiper. I thought I was loving, but, instead, I was controlling. I wept. It was my fault, not just Zip's.

I grabbed a rope on the pulley and released one side of the canvas. It sagged half way down the wall until I did the same thing on the other side. Then it rumpled to the floor, folding over on itself and blocking the doorway. I jumped up and down on it until my feet were covered in paint and hurt. Then I tugged and pulled, and worked back and forth to spread it across the cement floor. My bruises were lost in smears of paint.

I could no longer see the painting through the blur of tears. I pulled off all my clothing and grabbed a sponge. Banging the sponge into yucca green and petunia pink paint, I swiped it over my heart. Again, I slogged the sponge into hibiscus orange paint and smeared my belly. With morning glory blue paint covering my legs, broccoli green dripping from my arms, I plunged onto the canvas, squirming, rolling, twisting, letting it come out of me. Let me be free of my own madness. What was my problem? Buying into it all? I would go to the psychiatrist. I would do whatever it took to stabilize myself. That was my job. Even if it changed my artistic passion? Exhausted, I sank into the wet canvas, crying. Even.

I am now here, I thought, letting it bleed out, bleed until I am beyond the pain of wounded flesh, let it all go. I can sew my bones into a bag of body ready to be refilled with rainbows and music. Even rain and icy snow will clean me and dissolve my past.

I stretched my painted body flat into the colors and sobbed onto the canvas. I am beyond the limitations of others now. I am birthing myself and who can know who I am but me? As I heal in my own womb and rebirth myself, I need clean new bright canvases to paint on and I need my skeleton fleshed out with health so I can bound freely into being.

20 /

"Dannah, honey, you're cold," Nirvana said.

I tried to open eyes, move my neck, wiggle my fingers. New baby Dannah, angel dreams born of light. I eased up. Dried paint in the creases of my body. Skin pulled and paint cracked with each movement. I shivered and even my hair quaked but I felt light in my being.

"I filled the tub with hot water for you," she said. "Lavender and bubbles." I'd cleaned up my mind's clutter, now I needed to clean my aching body.

Even my fingernails were chilled to the bone. As I started to move, I stuck to myself. The creases at my elbow broke open as I unfolded myself. Gradually, it came back to me, the painting, the craziness and finally, birthing myself. Nirvana helped me stand up. "Yes. Bath," I murmured. My throat felt like I'd been yelling. I don't remember. Nirvana supported me as we headed toward the bathroom. Bright sunlight shone through the windows, into my puffy, tender eyes. It was morning already? I must have slept all night on the floor.

Mounds of bubbles foamed on the surface of the old fashioned claw footed tub. I eased one foot in, sighed and gingerly climbed in, sinking down so just my chin rested above water.

Yes. Clean water and bubbles. Nirvana hummed sweetly. I smiled at her, a soft new smile. "New. I am new, Nirvana."

"I know, you are Woman of Courage, new and free."

"I am, I am. Thank you," my voice sounded rusty like an unused tool in the wood shed. "Thank you," I said again, stronger now.

"Thank you," she said, clear as a harp string plucked by an angel. "We always heal together. How do you feel?"

"Exhausted. And better."

"I checked on you during the night, just to make sure you were all right. I left food for you. You didn't touch it. I was a little worried." She handed me a bottle of water. "Drink. You're probably dehydrated. You were so focused. I know how that feels. I've done it myself plenty of times."

"Thanks, Nirvana. Crazy artists, eh?" We laughed.

"Here's a soft scrub brush. I think you'll need it."

"Thanks." I began to scrub paint off. My skin tingled. "Good thing it's water soluble paint."

"You created a masterpiece," Nirvana said.

"It's pure emotion. I've never painted like that before. I was so free in your room."

"That's where I used to work when I first took over the Firehouse. Then I started making bigger, larger sculptures. Finally, I claimed the space out here. Good vibes all over this ol' building." She smiled.

"Thanks for understanding what I needed," I said. I slid my head underwater and popped back up.

"Here, let me help you. You've missed a few spots on your back." Nirvana took the brush and scrubbed gently at my shoulder blades, down my back and across my buttocks. I looked down at my body, realizing that the bruises had almost faded. I was no longer so tender to the touch. Finally, she handed me a towel. When I stepped out, she began to pat my back with another towel. I searched for errant paint smudges.

"While you were working, Harrie came by and Talia called. They were both glad to hear you were painting. Here are some of your clothes from the Coop. Are you ready for food?"

"I'm not sure. I feel relaxed like I haven't been in a long time," I said. Then I felt this craving. "Do you have any apples?"

"I do." Nirvana said. "While you dress I'll cut some up and make a pot of tea."

I finished drying slowly and rummaged in the bag of clothes, pulling out bra, panties, a clean pair of jeans and a turtleneck. I found a pair of socks that Talia had hand knit for me a few years ago and pulled them on. My jeans hung baggy. I hardly registered that I'd lost weight in the past weeks or was it months?

Padding through the Firehouse to the kitchen area, I smiled, appreciating my friends' attentions. I slipped into a chair, pulled my feet up and hugged my knees.

"Tea," Nirvana said. "Take a look at the Goddess."

I turned. Sunlight shimmered through the southern loft windows, illuminating a slab of red stone at the base of the Goddess spine.

"Wow. I see. You were working, too. She's beautiful."

"We both worked around the clock. I just finished first. Amazing when sunlight strikes her chakras, she lights up like the mother of the rainbow. I wonder if I'll have to rig up some kind of lighting system to really enhance the beauty of the stones. I have a call in to my brother. You know he's a computer lighting wizard. I hope it can be done with minimal intrusion. I'm wondering about some kind of microchip that would produce light."

"You think in a completely different way about art than I do. I always like listening to you. It expands my expectations of myself," I said.

"Well, you certainly expanded your possibilities with the piece in the next room. I thought you might need a ladder or to put it on the floor out here. Looks like you worked out both issues. It's amazing. Are you ready to see it?"

"No." I took a chunk of cheese and an apple slice. "I think I want to go home and see Moonie first."

I wanted to be back home more than anything. I jumped up from the table and grabbed my coat. "Thanks again for everything, Nirvana." We hugged.

"Are you okay to drive?" She pressed her lips together, worried I think.

"Oh, yeah. The car." I told her about the parking lot incident.

Nirvana shook her head and frowned. "Please take care." She didn't scold me.

I hurried outside to the borrowed Subaru. When I tried to start it, nothing happened. Damn. I tried several times to get it to start but not a spark.

It was futile to open the hood. I don't know a thing about cars. I'd have to take Nirvana's offer for a ride home after all. A blue vehicle drove up and parked as I got out of the car.

"Good morning," the man said with an accent as he stepped out of the car. I knew that deep brogue but couldn't place it. I turned, squinting into the sunlight.

"Hi." I frowned. Where did I know him from? He looked familiar.

"Harriet introduced us. I'm Lachlan MacGregor. Most people call me Mac. Nice to see you again. I'm here for a viewing of Nirvana's sculptures," he said, "I'm buying a house in the Old District."

Harrie pulled up in her SUV and got out. "Small world. Hey, Mac. Hi, Dannah. I just came by to check on you."

"I'm going home but the Subaru won't start."

"Hop in. I'll take you," she said.

"Thanks."

"Nice to see you again, Dannah," I could see the mystery man now as he shifted away from the sun. I remembered him from the restaurant before but not really seen him.

"Bye, Mac," I waved as I pulled the SUV door closed. "That's the guy from the café?"

21 /

I stretched out on the bed. Moonie curled close to my shoulder and purred. I loved Panther but Moonie knew me better than any person. I didn't want to do anything. Just be here with the door locked and my cat. My cell phone rang. I'd let it go to voice mail. I scooted around and pulled it out of my pocket to see who it was. Fondis Dept. of—the rest of the readout wasn't visible. "Hello?"

"Miss Davidson, sorry to interrupt you. Deputy Scott with the Fondis Police." Wasn't that Loren's mystery man?

"Please call me Dannah," I said.

"Would you mind stopping by the station?" He words sounded ominous, his voice, kind.

"I guess so. I don't have a car right now." I started to shiver. What if they'd found Zip? "Well, I have a car but it's broken and I've borrowed..."

"Miss Davidson." He broke in my ramblings. "We'd just like you to come to the station now. I can pick you up."

I nodded and mumbled okay. I had no idea if it was okay at all. In fact, it sucked. It was bad, really bad. The only time I'd been in the police station was to bail out Zip. More than once. Not this time. Not anymore. I pulled on my sneakers and tied them. Moonie tried to play with the laces. I grabbed my down jacket from a kitchen chair and stood at the window. I wonder why he didn't tell me what this was about. I bit at a hang nail. Moonie gave her hungry meow. I hurried to the kitchen and scooped out a serving of dry food and put it in her dish. She walked away. The Colonel had been feeding tuna from a can, real human food. "Sorry, Moonie. You're back at home now and we're on a budget, remember?"

Deputy Scott pulled into my parking space. I opened the door before he knocked. He introduced himself and said he was sorry I had to ride in the back seat. It was protocol. I studied his profile through the grid. I could see how Loren was attracted to him. We were both silent as we drove to the station. He parked in the back lot, a place I'd never seen. He slid a plastic card across a digital code thing and the door to the building opened.

I followed him down several hallways to a room with a conference table and a mirror window. "Please wait here, Miss Davidson," he said.

"Dannah. Please call me Dannah." I glanced at the dull gray walls, nondescript linoleum floor, the scratched table and the lack of windows.

"Yes, ma'am," he said and left the room. I fidgeted and rubbed at paint stains on my cuticles. The deputy returned with Sgt. Reiner, a roar of a man with a sagging white mustache and keen eyes. He carried something under his arm. I knew right away what the roll of brown wrapping paper was. He laid it on the table.

"Oh, my God." My hands flew to my mouth. The airplane painting had been sliced into strips.

"You do recognize this?" the Sergeant asked, standing back, his arms crossed over his chest.

I nodded, a lump hardening in my throat as I stared at my painting. Despite my dream, I'd been hoping it would turn up. Intact. I hoped the potential buyer would love it. And I was looking forward to having some cash in my pocket.

"I'm sorry, Dannah." Deputy Marshall Scott said.
I sighed, holding back tears. "Do you know where he is?"

"Robinson Caruso Smith is back in town, spotted in the alley behind the Legion Hall on Elm. Gone by the time patrol arrived," the

Sergeant said briskly. "You may take the remains of the painting after we've prosecuted. It's got his prints all over it. We'll need it for evidence."

Shit. My mind bounced from anger at the destroyed painting and terror of meeting up with Zip. I just nodded. Maybe I could fix it. The painting. Maybe. The Sergeant rolled up the paper and shredded canvas and left, closing the door behind him. Deputy Scott and I stood there for a moment.

"I'm sorry, Dannah. How can I help?" he asked. "I mean, do you need anything, is there anything I can do?"

I shook my head, not trusting my voice. I twisted my fingers together but could not stop the shaking.

"Dannah, be careful. Keep your eyes open. Notice where you're going."

I was startled back to the moment. The painting was important. My life was more important. "Thanks."

"I'll give you a ride home."

I don't remember the ride back, just the dark clouds gathering outside and rumbling into my brain. "Uh, thanks, Deputy Scott," I said as I got out of the police car. I turned and ran toward the Coop. Snowflakes drifted to my cheeks. I caught my breath in uneven sobs, thinking I'd left all my dismay on the canvas on Nirvana's floor. Obviously I was wrong. As I unlocked the door, I looked around. The Coop was midafternoon dark and early winter cold. I flipped on the light. Locked the door and tested it twice.

"Moonie, where are you?"

Half Moon stretched and rolled over on the sleeping bag. I flopped down next to her and curled her against my belly. I closed my eyes and drifted, soon sound asleep.

When I woke up, I could hear the wind howling. I found my cell phone still charging and retrieved half a dozen messages. I returned Loren's call.

"Hi, Honey," he said. "Don't have time to talk. Come for dinner tonight. Harrie will be here. I have so much to tell you." He hung up before I could say, "I'm not so sure."

My cell sang its song. "Yes?"

"Hey, Dannah. Sam, here. I'm at Nirvana's. That old Subaru had a bad wire. I've checked out everything else and it seems to be running fine. I'll come pick you up. You still live at the Coop?"

"No. That's okay. I'll walk over. I need the exercise, Sam. Thanks so much."

"Are you sure? Snow's letting up but the forecast says more to come."

"Yes, I'm fine."

"I'll leave the key under the mat."

"Thanks."

22 /

I picked up the car and drove home. I didn't go to Loren's but slept most of the next two days. Heavy clouds hung over Fondis and spit snow. On the third morning, I forced myself to go for a walk—to get outside in the fresh air. I headed down across the familiar alley behind the Coop. A bare branch shivered with the weight of a black squirrel. The alley was clean and tidy until I got to Mr. Oxford's house. He'd let the place go since his wife died. I stepped around stacks of soggy newspapers, tin cans, old tires and an overturned trash can.

A biting wind hit me as I turned into the next street. I pulled down my stocking cap and ducked my chin into a sunset orange scarf. Snow bit my cheeks. Bijou Park was crispy white with layers of several storms. Kids squealed as they sledded down the hill. Studded snow tires crunched slowly along Main Street. Chains rattled and thumped on an old truck. I waited for traffic to clear before crossing the icy street. I looked across at the Fondis Library. For a while, I thought I would never read again. Now, I just don't think I'll ever read Shakespeare again. Snow stuck to the north side of the library columns. I hated that he'd ruined all the works of a great writer for me. I swallowed hard but tears still blurred my vision. I had to return that book on Leonardo da Vinci., my favorite structural artist. At Halloween, I'd thought I might paint an angel skeleton but I didn't. I hurried on two blocks and turned down the tight, narrow lane to the Firehouse. My feet were cold. I needed a new pair of snow boots. I hoped Nirvana would be in because I was feeling really out of it. I wanted to find a space where I didn't feel crazy. Nirvana's crazy. In the same way I am, so she listens to me and makes me feel sane. Harrie would listen but I always felt her reprimand: don't do that, Dannah.

I don't mean to screw up. But I do forget and keep thinking some man will be nice to me. The pavement was slippery. My sneakers were soaked. I rummaged in my down jacket pocket for a tissue and wiped my nose.

I meet some guy, a nice guy, or a guy I think is nice. Oh, yes, he might have potential. And I'll respond to the potential. But he'll probably just be another guy who will take advantage of me. I'm scared because I don't want to be so stupid about men. I don't want to keep thinking, oh, what a nice guy, he just needs somebody to listen to him, and, of course, that person would be me. Oh, yes, I can help him. Of course he'll listen to me too.

Please let Nirvana be home. I should have called. But I wasn't sure I was ready. Now I am. Ready to look at my painting, that grotesque regurgitation of trapped emotions. My fist thumped the door, tingling with each pound on the oversized entrance. No answer. I'd just look at it and then we'd roll it up and trash it. I had a key to Nirvana's place but couldn't remember where it was. I thought she hid one outside. I looked under a flower pot with withered and brown geraniums. No key. Maybe on the ledge of that high window. But no. Nirvana wouldn't be able to reach it either. I'd just have to wait.

I walked around the corner to wait inside The Fondis Deli. It always made me feel as if I were in New York City, but comfortable. Warm. Familiar. Maybe someday when I actually have an art show in New York City, I'll be comfortable there too. I took off my soggy, down jacket and hung it on a coat rack and sat at a table, my body thawing in the warmth. I wiped my nose on a paper napkin.

"Hi. My name is David. I'll be your server today. How can I help you?"

I looked up and smiled sheepishly. Jeez, he saw me sniffling into a napkin. How pitiful and he's cute too—those green eyes and his attentiveness. Of course, he gets paid to pay attention to me. "Something hot, please. Tea."

"Earl Grey, Mango Ginger, Oolong, Red Zinger, chai?" He continued to run off a litany of options. "You look cold. Still snowing, huh?"

"Uh huh. I'm freezing. Uh, make it Earl Grey. Thanks."

"Move to that booth," he said, pointing to the back of the deli. "Heat's best there. I'll put your jacket over here by the heater."

"Thanks," I said and moved to the back booth, sliding my back pack unto the dark green naugahyde seat.   It was warmer. David returned shortly and I couldn't help looking at his tight jeans.

"Here's your tea. I put a lemon wedge on the side," he said, placing it in front of me. "Or would you like cream?"

I shook my head. "Thank you. Are you new to Fondis?" I didn't want him to leave.

"Yeah. Just got in from California."

I imagined him surfing, his taut body on a board dancing with the sea.

"I transferred to Fondis University, got a job here for the time being."

A student. Definitely too young. I'd purged Zip from my mind, and now here I was, inviting a younger man's company. I must be tired, lonely or crazy. And even thinking of Zip meant I really hadn't gotten rid of him. Knowing he is back is town is creepy.

The bell hanging on the top of the deli door jingled.

"I've got to get back to work," David said and stood up.
I leaned out of the booth, just checking to see if it were Zip. A tall man was hanging his overcoat on a rack and turned.

It was Mac, that friend of Nirvana's.

Before I could pull back, he caught my eye and smiled that comfortable smile I'd noticed before. He headed in my direction. "Do you mind if I join you, Dannah?" He looked directly into my eyes. Soft blue eyes, trustworthy eyes. He had the kind of face I'd want to paint if I were still doing portraits.

"You look cold, Mac. Sit down. It's bitter out there," I said. "I'm warming up and waiting for Nirvana to get home."

He folded himself into the booth. "You'd think I'd be used to the cold," he said, "being from Scotland." He had a deep rumbling laugh. I liked a man who could laugh. I can't remember the last time I'd heard one. "I'm going to see Nirvana too."

"Hey, Mac. Good to see you again," David said, smiled and handed Mac a menu.

I didn't really know either of these guys but they made me feel safe. If Zip were to walk in now, I'd...well, I don't know what I'd do. I want to be able to stand up for myself, not have to depend on knights in shining armor. I felt crazy. I stared into my teacup, thinking of Grannie reading the tea leaves. I didn't really know either of these guys and my cup held no tea leaves.

David, so nice, younger, open.   Mac, mysterious, with that wonderful accent and those dreamy lapis eyes. I knew in my heart I was not ready for a relationship with anybody but I was ready for some friends, male friends. That was hard to admit. Not long ago I didn't want to ever see another man. Yes, David could be a friend and an easy person to talk to. Tight jeans don't diminish friendship, do they?

Mac was another story. I don't know what it was but I'd like to know him better. I wanted to fling paint on a canvas again. Dannah Davidson, you thought you'd never give a second thought to another guy, and here you are, thinking about two men on a snowy afternoon.

My cell rang. Nirvana was caught in traffic on the other side of town. I told her where I was, that I'd been waiting to see her but now I was on my way home to paint. I told Mac that Nirvana was on her way. He offered me a ride home and I declined. I wasn't ready. Besides, I was warm now. I pulled on my stocking cap and wrapped my scarf around my neck and retrieved my warm down jacket. When I left, Mac and David were talking.

23 /

A blue Mustang with a dented front end careened down the street, loud music blasting out an open window. I ignored it, and walked briskly, the wind at my back. My neck had been warmer when I had long hair. The Mustang squealed to a stop. I kept walking, but from my peripheral vision, I saw Zip stumble out the back door of the Mustang. "Holy shit." I turned to run.

"Dannah, baby," Zip slurred, staggering across the snowy sidewalk. "Got a coupla bucks?"

He smelled rotten like an alley. He lunged and tried to grab my back pack. I pulled away and bolted back toward the Firehouse, cutting behind Mrs. Morrissey's back garden and through another alley. I saw Loren's car moving slowly down the next street and was about to wave him down—but I couldn't move anything but my feet. My vocal cords were frozen. Wait. Zip would go to the Firehouse first, or the Coop, and then the Firehouse. I ran in the other direction.

Even though I'm short, my stride is long. I took the least visible route, heading along the trail toward the lake at a fast pace. My lungs were burning. Instinct must have moved my feet, kept me running, because I wasn't known for speed. I was bone cold and couldn't feel my feet. I slowed a little, turned, and peered into swirling snow. No Zip. Just keep moving, I told myself. I scanned the shoreline. Ice formed around a small, white call duck in the reeds but no people to call out to. No one was out on that bitter day. Fear bound and held flesh to my bones and kept me moving until I reached the pines. At last I was hidden from Zip. I walked on, moving quickly into the wind, my heart still racing. I thought I heard something and stepped between mountain mahogany branches and yucca spikes to hide behind a Ponderosa pine. I stumbled in a hole and went down hard. Shit. Breath taking pain like flash paper. I'd twisted my ankle.

Eyes closed, I clutched my leg, cursing and sobbing with the shooting lightning bolt that blazed from my ankle. Shit. What if I broke it? I looked around. I was close to the steep back trail leading to Deirdre's yurt. Zip would never find me up there. There was no sound but the wind crashing through the trees, knocking pinecones and branches to the ground.

I tried to stand but the pain seared up my leg and reminded me of bruises I'd suffered. God, for how long had I been lost in denial? "It takes a long time to heal," the counselor had said.

I scooted to my knees. Pain shot up my leg. Zip was always so mean. I could never please him, the macho dude in charge of an insane world. I half crawled to the nearest pine, dragging my injured leg, eased myself up and balanced on one foot. I hopped toward the next tree and went down again, my face in the snow. A cactus spine stabbed my knee through my jeans. I dragged myself to a rock and sat down. I couldn't remember where my cell phone was. I eased my frozen fingers into one coat pocket after another. My fingers were too numb to undo the zipper to check inside pockets. Tears froze on my eyelashes.

"Dannah, are you okay?" a muffled voice called. Not Zip. "Honey, it's Deirdre. I called 911 and Nirvana. You'll be okay. Can you open your eyes?"

I couldn't.

"I followed your foot prints in the snow," she said. "You've got more troubles than there were sand hill cranes flying over last week, sweetie. Look at me, Dannah. Can you say your name? C'mon, honey. Talk to me. Here, let me get my coat off, tuck it around you. You're sopping wet, girl."

24 /

I woke up in a warm hospital bed. Warm blankets, warm air—and an IV in my arm. I looked at blinking monitors. Despite the flower vases filling the window sill, it still smelled like a hospital. I heard high heels clicking down the hallway and into my room.

"Hi, Dannah. I'm glad you're awake. How do you feel?" Talia said.

"Warmer. What happened?" My throat was like matted felt and my voice, tinny.

Harrie, Nirvana and that new cute guy from Scotland came in the room. "I'm so glad you're awake, Dannah," Harrie said and hurried to her black valise of homeopathy vials that lay on a corner chair.

"Harrie, you just gave her something," Talia looked at her watch, "fifteen minutes ago."

Nirvana held my hand, the one without the IV. No kilts on the Scotsman who stood at the end of my bed.

"I was worried about you, Dannah. Mac and I were talking at the deli..." Nirvana began.

That was his name. Mac. I wondered what he was doing here.

"That's when I called Nirvana," Harrie continued, "to tell her Zip was back in town. I couldn't get you on your cell."

My eyes darted to the door.

"No, you're safe, Dannah," the man named Mac said. How would he know?

"You don't remember, do you?" Nirvana lifted a strand of hair off my forehead.

"I don't know what I remember."

"You were in the ambulance with the EMTs and me and you insisted on having my phone. I kept telling you, I'd call whoever you needed to talk to. You dialed 911 and reported Zip."

"I did? Good." I smiled.

"So, Mac and I took the short cut when Deirdre called me. You remember Deirdre found you?"

I shrugged. "I was on my way to Deirdre's yurt up on the bluff. I remember that."

"Mac picked you up like you were a rag doll. You were so cold. We were afraid..." Nirvana paused.

"The emergency medics arrived and took over," Mac said and seemed to frown at Nirvana.

"They had to carry their equipment around the lake trail. I'm glad they did," Nirvana said. "Deirdre said she'd check in with you later. Lucky thing she had a sick donkey or she wouldn't have come into town for medication. Not lucky for the donkey but because Deirdre found you."

"Zip will probably be in jail," Harrie said.

"Where he belongs." I closed my eyes.

I must have dozed off. I opened my eyes when the blonde nurse with a zillion earrings shooed everybody from the room. "Where's Talia?" I said.

"Dr. Master is seeing other patients. She'll be back to check on you." Her voice was clipped but her touch was gentle. She probed and prodded, took my temperature, blood pressure, pulse rate, wrote stuff on a chart and left.

Harrie and Mac returned. "Nirvana went to the gift shop," Harrie said. "What do you want to eat?"

"Pizza," I said. They laughed.

"I'll see if they have any at the cafeteria," Harrie said.

"World's Best Pizza would be good," I joked. It was part of the old town renovation. I tried to shift my body to a more comfortable position. My foot ached. "Harrie, I'm sorry. Whatever. I don't even know if I can eat."

"Don't worry, Sweetie. They'll deliver but I have to go outside the hospital to use my cell. I'll be right back." Harrie grabbed her coat and headed out the door.

Mac sat in the chair at the side of the hospital bed. I felt uncomfortable and turned my head away. It hurt.

I closed my eyes and sighed before opening them. "I guess I should thank you, Mac," I said. "No. I don't mean should. I mean it. I do thank you for helping me." I fidgeted with the tape covering the IV entry. "I just can't talk to you right now. It's not about you. It's me." Mac seemed like a nice guy. I hoped I wouldn't hurt his feelings.

"I understand," he said.

"No, you don't." I felt angry—and then sorry I'd said it. I wanted to cry. I bit my lower lip.

Mac stood up. I looked at him. He wasn't upset. He just seemed to accept what I said. "Be well, little friend," he said and turned to pick up his coat. I was glad I didn't have a male doctor. I'd make him go away too.

Nirvana came back with her hands behind her back. "Close your eyes, Dannah Banana." She laughed. "And open your hands."

I did as she said and felt something soft. I peeked and my eyes flew open. The softest, cuddliest red dragon stared at me.

"Your new protector, Dannah," she said.

I laughed and then stilled. "Nirvana, I want to be my own protector. I don't even know what that means. I just know I'm tired of being afraid."

She held my hand and I pulled the dragon tight and rubbed my chin on the soft fur. Soft and fire breathing. That's what I wanted to be.

Harrie returned. "Mission accomplished. Pizza's on its way."

25 /

After a day in the hospital, I was glad to be back at the Coop. I gimped around for a while on my sprained ankle. Between Talia's meds and the soft cast she'd wrapped around my ankle and Harrie's homeopathy, I was healing fast. I painted a lot of small pieces, my foot propped on a cushion, leaning against the red dragon as a pillow.

What a nuisance, I thought as I hopped around on crutches. I couldn't drive and I couldn't walk. At least I had the use of my hands. Nirvana stayed with me the first two nights. She wanted to do a tarot reading but I declined. I just wanted to get better, paint and figure out how to be stronger. Harrie dropped by every day. Talia called and came by when she got off work. Sari was in and out and the Colonel visited several times and read to me.

The following weekend, sunbeams slanted through the south window. I scooted the phone book from under the bed with a crutch and flipped through the Yellow Pages until I found "Martial Arts."

∞

I was still in bed when Nirvana unlocked the Coop door the following morning. "Coffee and doughnuts? Really?" I stretched, yawned, and scooted Moonie off my shoulder.

"Time for you to get over the Crutches Blues. I thought a decadent breakfast might help." Nirvana balanced the coffee holder on top of the pastry box. We both laughed. I crutch hopped across the room.

"I don't really have the blues. I'm just edgy and want to get back to really painting. Plus I called the Dragon and Pearls Martial Arts Academy. I think the little red dragon is giving me some hints. I can't start until I'm off the crutches and out of the soft cast," I said and picked up a chocolate cake doughnut.

"Really, you're going through with that? Good for you, Dannah." She reached out and squeezed my hand.

"Wanna come with me? It would be fun."

"I'll think about it. Depends on this next sculpture and what the deadline is for the New York juried show. Hey, you should apply too," she said.

"I'm not ready for that scene, Nirvana. You're the pro. I'm just happy to be in a couple of galleries up in Denver and Vail." I looked at my sketch of a dragon and angel from last night's dream. I'd love to be in a New York show.

"Dannah, you've got great perspective on canvas but not in real life. You're ready. Besides, it's been over two years." Nirvana reminded me of the divorce. I knew it had been two plus years, all the seasons circling around twice in a swirl of colors. Two years of finding myself, painting from my dream heart, moving into the art world, dreaming of bigger shows. I'd been so bogged down during the divorce. I'd found myself and it was good until Zip knocked at my door that night. And then the rape. The rape. I was trying not to claim it in a personal way. My rape. No. When he raped me.

124

Matter of fact. A statement. I don't want it to define my life or to find people casting that overly sympathetic look.

I washed and dried the dishes after Nirvana and I had tea. I wondered what it would really be like to leave Fondis. I imagined traveling with my oils and huge canvases in my old truck. Impossible. The idea seemed ridiculous. If I traveled to New York City, the cultural mecca of the United States, that would be a big deal. I thought of gallery openings and big hotels and selling my paintings.

I remember Mama had a St. Christopher when she went away to seek her fortune. Those were her exact words—seek her fortune—like we were in some black and white movie. Mama was a day booker, went to school at night to become a parrot legal. Whatever that was. That's my little girl memory. Later I learned she was a day hooker until she became a paralegal. Mama sent money to me and Grannie'd helped me set up a checking account at the local bank. Mama said she wanted me to learn how to balance a checkbook and I did. I was always afraid I'd be overdrawn and I never knew when Mama would send more money so I lived frugally, ate dinner at friends sometimes. I suppose it would be called abandonment today. I didn't think that. Besides, I lived with Grannie after a while.

Daddy abandoned us when I was four but Mama didn't; she was making our fortune. When she came back the following summer, she had a friend with her. Ronald drank a lot, had bad breath and a scruffy beard and wanted to touch me. I really hated him but I couldn't tell anybody, especially not Mama. Then one morning he was gone. I was so relieved. They'd had a big fight that woke me up in the middle of the night. Mama had caught him coming into my room. Her cursing woke me. I knew she loved me even if she never said it. I really knew it when he was gone and never came back. She loved me more than him.

When Grannie died, Mama said we were going to move away from Fondis. Someone was going to buy Grannie's old house and everything would be fine.

I was afraid to live in another town. Then something happened and Mama decided to stay here. It was a good time and Mama and I were as close as we'd ever be. She got a job at the airport and started dating pilots. I was a teenager by then. I didn't miss Mom when she was away and I certainly didn't want to talk about her boyfriends. Or mine.

Then one of the pilots retired and Mama moved to Germany with him. Sometimes I get a post card from her. I'd married Zip but lost the house Mama had left me. Grannie's house. My home. Just because Zip needed drug money.

26 /

That night I slept like a bear, deep and long. When I woke up in the morning, I realized my recent dreams had verged on nightmares. Now they melted into angels in the sky, hovering and protective. My angels were back. I didn't dream of Zip—or Mac. However, I wouldn't have minded dreaming of Mac's sea blue eyes. In the bright light of day, I didn't know what to think. Just because I found him attractive didn't mean it would work the other way. Or that I ever wanted another relationship. I climbed out of bed and stretched toward the slanted roof. Mac sparked my curiosity. I needed to stop thinking about him, focus on my ankle healing.

First things first. I straightened up the Coop and fixed a nice pot of old fashioned oatmeal with a splash of nonfat milk and a good glob of honey. I rummaged in a drawer and found one of the packets of vitamins Harrie had given me. As I ate, I thought about exercise. I needed to add that to the list. Maybe get back in Robin's yoga class if she's willing to do a trade for a painting again. My body always felt good after yoga. Plus, I thought I was ready to start martial arts. With dragons.

In my tiny, turnstile bathroom where I climb-over-the-toilet-or-scrunch-under-the sink, I studied my face in the mirror. I looked more relaxed. It was time to take charge of my life. I had a zillion things to do: see if I could get the slashed painting back, call Nirvana to see when I could go for a visit, try to call Zip's latest girlfriend, what's-her-name, paint Mac's eyes and call the Colonel and see how things were going, write a thank you note to Talia. Schedule with a new counselor.

I thought about stretching into the child's pose and saw the angel from last night's dream in my mind. She was different than previous dreams. She hovered over a blank canvas. She showed me how to reconstruct the Airplane Angel when I got the slashed strips back from the police. I pulled aside the bed and examined the canvases I'd already stretched. Nothing large enough. I'd have to build a frame from scratch. I pushed everything I owned to the sides of the room to make enough workspace on the floor.

In timeless no-time, I'd stretched a forty eight by sixty canvas and sized it with gesso. Now I had to wait until it dried. I called Nirvana. She said it was fine to come over. The Goddess was finished and the Womyn's Centre was going to display her in the lobby of their new building. They'd be loading her out that morning but it was fine for me to confront the painting in the small studio room.

I literally hopped into the shower on one foot with a smile on my face, feeling good about the Airplane Angel and happy for Nirvana. I dried, dressed, applied makeup and slipped on a dangly pair of earrings. I sprayed perfume behind my ears—just in case I ran into Mac. No, I said to myself, I'm not going to do that anymore. I'll wear perfume because I want to please myself. If someone else happened to be pleased with the results, cool.

∞

As I locked up, Sari Thompson waved at me from the back steps of the Colonel's house. I walked up the path to greet her.

"How're you doing, Sari?" I asked, giving her a hug.

"I'm fine." A look flashed across her face that worried me.

"And the Colonel?"

"It's not your fault, ya know," she began.

Shit. "What?"

"Well, you know it all started when he took on the care of your Moonie. Now I'd say he is moon crazed for that new cat of his. When it's too cold to go out for a walk, he warms up that old Army jeep and takes the cat for a ride, mind you." She huffed in exasperation.

"And the Colonel? He's okay? His health is good?"

"Fit as a fiddle and I'm fit to be tied. Cat hair all over the house and..."

I laughed. "Thanks, Sari. You give the Colonel my regards, okay? I've got to run. Take care and don't let that cat get the best of you." I smiled, touched her creased old face and headed to the alley, and the Subaru.

The sun shone in an azure blue sky. It was a perfect day to walk. "Soon," I said out loud. I missed walking and rolled down the window, enjoying the winter brisk air in my lungs. I wanted to enjoy the good feeling as long as I could. Somehow, I didn't look forward to the prospect of viewing the painting. It had become a monster in my mind, a mongrel of colors, an albatross, a waded mess of canvas and paint.

I drove around to the back of the Firehouse and parked. The garage-type door on the south wall was open and a crew loaded the Chakra Goddess unto a flatbed truck. Nirvana was running around, pointing and giving directions. I stood back, watching. I wondered if she worried about the stone slabs breaking. Maybe the Goddess's body was welded so securely nothing could damage it.

Once the goddess was secured with ropes, the truck pulled out, driving slowly down the street. I walked toward Nirvana.

"What a headache," she said. "Loading big pieces makes me a nervous wreck."

"Looks like they managed all right."

"I'm going over to supervise the unloading at the Womyn's Centre. Wanna come along?" She pressed the button on the door remote and it slowly grumbled to the ground.

"I think I'll stay here and deal with my inner demons while you dance with the goddess." I laughed to cover my discomfort. I did need to be alone for this encounter.

Inside, I shed my coat and hat and dropped them on a kitchen chair. Nirvana's workspace looked empty without the Chakra Goddess. Maybe the emptiness would inspire her to work on another piece. Panther cat jumped onto to my down jacket and sniffed. He probably smelled Moonie. Hesitantly I walked to the door where the painting waited.

I fumbled with the door knob and decided I needed a drink of water first. Sunshine streamed through the windows in slices of light. I turned on the faucet at the sink, filled a glass of water and held it to the light, squinting to see shadow from window panes against the bright of the sun. I'd like to paint that feeling I experienced. Light and shadow and prisms and openness. Instead, I tipped the glass and drank until it was empty.

Fortified, I turned and walked directly to the door and opened it. Dim light entered the room from the upper windows. I closed the door behind me without looking toward the painting and headed for the cot where I knew I'd get the best perspective. Sitting on the cot, I leaned back against the wall and sighed.

"Damn, why is this so hard?" I said and sank my face into my hand.

Finally I lifted my chin and looked toward the piece, determined to accept what I had released. It was no longer wadded up. Nirvana had untangled the battered canvas, nailed boards on each end and re-hung it with pulleys. I studied the painting for a long time, seeing the beauty of the past, the hope of a relationship, the demise of expectation, the anger, the pain, the hurt, and the elevation of my spirit to survive. It was too much. The emotions of those hours of creation rose again and lumped in my throat. Tears ran down my cheeks. "Dammit," I said, standing.

I tried to release the pulleys but they were jammed so I hauled out the ladder and climbed up to probe and nudge the knotted rope. Once I'd loosened it, I almost fell when it collapsed. I kicked the painting and stomped and screamed at it. I yanked the nails out with a hammer. Then tackled it, pulling the ends toward each other, wrestling it into a ball, rolling on it to pack it down, end it, get rid of it.

Exhausted, I finally collapsed backward over the mounded canvas and laughed.

27 /

I slipped into the Subaru and headed toward downtown Fondis feeling some sort of catharsis. I should be jubilant but I just felt quiet now. The laughter had been close to hysteria. I took a deep breath. Some part of my life had ended and a new way was opening. I nodded absently at acquaintances as I drove past. I needed a treat. Chocolate. The ever dependable pick-me-upper. I parked near Choco-Latte, searched my pockets for quarters and found two dimes and a nickel to slide into the meter. I locked the car and moved around two kids playing. As I stepped inside, I felt the warm aroma of coffee and chocolate surround me. I ordered a double espresso and three chocolate truffles with raspberry filling. My cell rang. I answered and licked raspberry off my upper lip.

"Dannah, Sam here. I think I've worked something out for a permanent car for you. When you have time, can you come by the shop?"

"Sure," I looked at the large wall clock. "I can be there in about fifteen minutes." I hung up, pushed the cell back in my jeans pocket and sipped the espresso. I smiled. But a permanent car sounded expensive. Still, I smiled. I really wanted to have a big gallery show and make lots of money. I've been told that it's an unrealistic dream. But I know dreams. Shouldn't they help me? And why not in New York City? As I stepped out on the sidewalk, a bitter wind gusted down the street. I pulled my purple knit scarf to my ears and ducked my chin.

"Hey, Dannah, look where you're going, Sweetie." It was Harrie in her red wool cape, her hand tucked at Mac's elbow.

"Sorry, I wasn't looking. The espresso will kick in any minute." I laughed and they did too. I looked at Mac and his eyes really were as blue as a summer sky. He had long eyelashes. He looked pretty cozy with Harrie. Of course. Beautiful, stylishly attired Harrie.

"Nice to see you, Dannah," he said as Harrie answered her earpiece cell phone and stepped away.

"Yes. We keep bumping into each other," I said. I had to lift my chin up to look at him.

"Perhaps we should do better than that. How about dinner some time?"

My eyes flicked toward Harrie and back to Mac. Then I smiled but before I could say yes or no, Harrie clicked off and looked at Mac. "We've got to hurry or we'll miss him. Business, Dannah, always something," she said and pulled on Mac's arm.

"I'll call you," he said and they hurried off into the wind. I got back in the Subaru feeling confused as I drove back roads to Sam's Garage. Mac didn't have my cell number. What if we did go out to dinner? What would we talk about? Besides, I wouldn't even think about it if Harrie were interested in him. And how could she not be?

Sam's office was dusty and filled with automobile books, engine belts, miscellaneous parts and a desolate, grease-smeared old computer.

"Have a seat, Dannah." He pointed to a chair. I pushed aside an auto manual and greasy jacket and sat on the edge.

"Well, here's my idea. You need a vehicle." He rolled a pencil back and forth.

"I know I can't borrow your loaner Subaru forever. Still no chance to fix the truck?" I already knew the answer.

"It's not worth it. There's more wrong than right with that old heap. So, like I was saying, you need wheels."

I nodded. No wheels sucked.

"I just finished fixing up a VW bug; not one of the old ones, mind you. A newer Beetle. They had a few problems but I've corrected them. This one is better than new. I can let you have it very reasonably. It was a payment from another client who didn't have cash so I took the bug as payment. Basically I just have parts and labor in it. So..."

"Sam, you know I don't have that kind of money. Even for parts and labor. I was going to have to make payments on the truck repair." I sighed. Everything seemed to be about money...or the lack of it.

"That's where my proposition comes in. I'll trade you the VW straight across for one of your paintings."

My mouth opened but nothing came out.

"And maybe a special one? Do you still have that one called Angel Helpers? Sally—you know my wife, yes? She really liked it when she went to your show up in Denver. She talks about it all the time. If you think it's a fair trade, I'd like to give her the painting. Beggars can't be choosers. I know she'd like any one of them."

"Sam, I hardly know what to say. I'm the one in the beggar's place. And yes, I do have Angel Helpers still. I just sent it to a new gallery up in Breckenridge but it hasn't sold. I can get it back here in a couple of days. It's one of my dream paintings, Sam. Do you know that I sometimes wake up with pictures in my head and then I paint them? Often they come with the title, like that one. I just saw this family at the dining table with an angel in attendance to each person. So I painted it."

"So, we have a deal?"

"Just like that?" I shook my head.

"Yup. If you're willing." He grinned.

"I'm sure I'll still owe you some money. Let me call the gallery first to make sure. You think about what else I'd owe you."

I tapped the gallery number and they agreed reluctantly to release it before the time. I promised to send two more paintings in its place as a compromise. They'd ship it out the next day. I hung up.

"The painting will be on its way to Fondis tomorrow. Now what?"

Sam steered me out to the back of the shop.

"Dannah, you get the car. I get the painting. Straight across. Got it?" He pointed to a shiny stellar jay blue VW beetle.

"Sam, are you sure this is a fair trade?"

"I'm sure. Let's shake on it," he said and then laughed as he looked down at his grease smeared hands. "Never mind," he said. "Here're the keys. If you have any trouble, it's guaranteed. There's the pink slip and all the repair records," he said, pointing to a file folder on the passenger seat. "You'll have to go to the court house to register it and get plates. Then it's all yours."

"I don't know what to say, Sam. You're the greatest. Thank you," I hugged him, despite his greasy mechanic's garb. He backed away, seeming embarrassed. I handed him the Subaru keys and eased into the Blue Dragon—that would be her name—and drove off in a daze. It was all too much. I needed to be back at the Coop. I'd take care of the paperwork tomorrow. I drove home. A car for a painting was too good to be true. Maybe I just needed to remember that everything can work out even if it's not the way I expect it.

∞

Half Moon had left paw prints in the gesso. I laughed. It would be a design factor, if it showed at all. The canvas was too big to fit on any easel, so I propped it up against the wall, got out my palette and started to mix colors. Most of the surface was sky and clouds with an elongated angel on top, stretched out like a Modigliani.

By the time I finished that phase of the painting, it was dark. I put on the tea kettle and turned to study the painting. I needed to find two replacements to send off to Breckenridge tomorrow.

A knock at the door pulled my attention back to the present. I pushed a hand through my tangled locks to make myself presentable and then stopped cold.

"Who is it?" I tried to keep my voice calm as I called through the locked door. I couldn't understand the answer. I eased the door open a few inches, glad of the new safety latch.

Mac stood there.

"Dannah, am I intruding?" He smiled.

"No," I said and glanced over my shoulder at what must look like the remains of a tornado swirl. "No, you're not interrupting. Wait. Yes." I took a deep breath. "Yes, I am in the middle of something. I'm sorry." I wanted to say "Come in." That's what I would have done before, stepped back and let someone else's interest

132

come before mine. I avoided looking at his eyes. His face was clean shaven, strong jawbone, high cheeks.

"No. I'm sorry. Dannah. I should have called first." He looked uncomfortable.

I shook my head. Was I missing the only chance I've have at beginning to know this guy? "I should be finished", I glanced down and was surprised to watch Moonie rub against his ankle. "If you'd like to give me a ring around midnight, that would be great." I couldn't believe I was saying that. I was actually beginning to take charge of my life. I wondered what would happen now. I looked up as he bent down to stroke Moonie's arched spine.

Mac smiled up at me. "That would be great. Again, my apologies." He rose, smiled again and turned.

I can't remember how the hours passed. I'd focus on one project and then another, always looking at my cell. I cleaned the kitchen. Found the paintings to send off, brushed Moonie. I was afraid to take a shower in case I missed his call. Maybe I should just have had him come in and then I wouldn't feel so crazy. Finally, it all became clear. I was standing on a glistening pond of ice and I wouldn't be able to skate if I didn't talk to Harrie. That's why I'd been nervous.

I punched her number. She picked up on the first ring. "Hi, Dannah."

"Harrie, sorry to call so late."

"Not to worry. I'm just giving myself a facial so I may sound a bit tight." She laughed. "Are you okay, Sweet Pea?"

"I'm fine. But, Harrie, I don't know how to ask this. You and Mac seem close and I'm confused..."

"Dannah, did he finally call you? Mac and I have a professional friendship. You should know he's not my type. How do you feel about him?"

"Relieved right now. I've just been frustrated and confused at my own confusion and yes, curious about him." I let out a deep breath that had been hiding in my belly.

"Dannah, you've come a long way. Follow your true heart. And thank you, for thinking that I might be interested in Mac. I'm not. Wait a minute. Is that your incoming call or mine?"

"Mine. I think it's Mac."

"Good. Night night, sweetie. Call me tomorrow."

"Hello?"

"Hi, Dannah. Mac here. Hope I'm not too late calling. I was talking to Mum in Scotland."

"Perfect timing." A guy who talks to his mother?

"Again my apologies for arriving unannounced." He had a deep voice I could concentrate on without being distracted by his features.

"Thanks. I'm probably best with making plans and not being surprised. I'll tell you about it sometime." I smiled to myself. Moonie jumped into my lap, circled and settled into a deep purr.

We talked, surface chatter like people do when they don't know what to say. Moonie pushed against my cell. "Can you hear Half Moon purr?"

"I can." He had a great laugh.

Before we hung up, I invited him to stop by on Friday night. I talked cat nonsense to Moonie for a while and slid into my sleeping bag. It was a long time before I fell asleep.

28 /

"Dannah, good to see you," Hubert said as I walked into the Pack & Send Shop. "Got some paintings going out? How's that ankle doing?"

"Fine, thanks, Hubert." I handed him one of the paintings. "I'll be right back with the other one," I said.

"Don't worry. Charlie," he yelled over his shoulder, "Get a painting out of Ms. Davidson's car, will ya? And be careful."

"Maybe I should get it," I said as the lanky teenager with spiked orange hair headed for the VW.

"Not to worry, Dannah... Charlie is an artist himself. I guess I just give him a bad time. This is a good job for him right now. But you wait. He'll be an up and coming artist with a known name soon enough."

Hubert was right. Charlie handled the painting with utmost care and respect.

"Thanks," I said.

Charlie mumbled something and headed to the back of the shop.

"Got yerself a new car, I see. Good for you." Hubert nodded as he rang up my bill.

"I can write a check for this but don't cash it today. I'm on my way to the bank."

"No problem." He rubbed his mustache. "Nice work here, Dannah. Glad you're doing so well. These go to the same gallery in Breckenridge, huh?" he said, scanning the computer screen.

"Thanks, Hubert. I should be receiving a painting back from them." I always had them shipped back here if they didn't sell. Hubert took good care of them until I could pick them up. "The only problem I'll have with my new little car is not being able to carry big paintings."

"We'll come over and pick them up or deliver them for you; don't worry," Hubert reassured me.

"Great. See ya soon."

I picked up a copy of The Fondis Magazine on my way out and drove home. The art review about my work was very flattering. Recently a journalist interviewed me for an article in a national magazine on angels.

Back home, the Coop was cold. I turned on the space heater, regretting lack of insulation. I draped a chenille blanket over the electric heater. Cat-cat pushed under heat tent. Purr. Cats purr warmth. I pulled the blanket up and wrapped it around me. Cozy warm. Snow and cold reigned this winter in Fondis. It would hatch a late spring. I layered wool socks on the heater and waited for them to warm. Cold feet stop my creativity—I can't paint. I have been known to paint with my feet. It was fun and gooey.

Days and nights passed with winter and sudden Colorado sunshine dancing the days and moonlight on snow pulling me into dreamtime and painting. I was still losing track of time but it didn't matter anymore. I thought on and off about Mac. One angel painting wore his midnight blue eyes.

29 /

I glanced out the window and saw Loren get out of the officer's car. I grinned and opened the door to the two of them.

135

"I'm just off duty, ma'am," said Marshall.

"Please, call me Dannah. Come in."

He hesitated but I saw Loren touch the back of his waist. "It's been released to you," he said, his voice officer-formal.

"Dannah," said Loren. "I know how happy you'll be to get this back. We can't stay. We're on our way to the Fondis Art Museum. Soon enough we'll find your work there."

When I closed the door, I watched them out the window, heads together and then could see they were laughing. I was happy for them both. Now, to get to work.

When I saw the Colonel marching down the path toward the Coop I'd figured out it was Thursday morning. I pulled on my old scruffy boots and walked outside in my old down jacket. The Colonel with his chest stuck out like a turkey almost made me laugh but he was so stern looking I thought I should salute him instead.

"Morning, Colonel," I called out.

"Glad to see you, Dannah. Wondered if that Moon Cat would like to take a walk with us." I saw he had Private Pusskin on a leash.

"I don't know. She was asleep the last time I saw her. Let me see." I opened the door and called Moonie. She stretched, blinking.

"Rise and shine," the Colonel called out. "Time to get a few miles in before lunch, you lazy good for nothin' critter."

Half Moon ran to the Colonel to be scratched under the chin. The Colonel produced a leash, snapped it on and the trio headed off down the alley.

"Good. Now I can work uninterrupted," I said, wishing I could leave the door open to catch the winter sun. I still marvel at my keekat's new behaviors.

I took the oversized canvas with the elongated hovering angel off the wall and placed it on the floor, unrolled the strips of the Airplane Angel and arranged them in order like a puzzle. The edges were razor cut with no fraying. Carefully I placed them on the larger canvas, each piece an inch apart so the sky shone through, the Modigliani angel overlooking all. I stood back to survey the effect. It felt like Magritte now. The masters of the past helping me like the angel helped the travelers.

I stirred up a batch of glue, water and another new adhesive and carefully brushed the back of each strip and applied it to the canvas, pressing firmly to see that it held without bubbles or glitches on the edge. Time passed as it does when I'm deep in the process of creation.

I sat back on my knees, realizing they hurt and my ankle tingled and ached. The painting looked exactly as I expected and better than the original. Slowly I stood, rubbing my legs. I had to wait for it to dry before I hung it back on the wall for inspection.

I heard a tune in the distance. I shook my head. I didn't remember turning on the radio. I couldn't take my eyes off the work. It gave me ideas for other paintings. Collage technique, oil on oil, maybe strips interwoven, one panel being a different image than the cross panel.

The music was closer now, familiar but I couldn't place it. I walked to the door, wondering if I'd left the radio on in the car and was running down the battery.

I recognized his dark red hair first, catching beams of glowing sunlight. Then I saw his outfit, the kilts and white cabled socks, a dirk tucked properly to the right side. His cheeks puffed out as he played, walking slowly toward me. There was no way I could stop smiling, nor halt the tears that rose to my eyes. This was one special man.

He paused several yards away and ended the tune. The pipes wheezed on their own.

"Mac, you're a wonder," I managed. "I didn't know you played the pipes."

"Ye liked it then? I didna know what to play for ye, there are so many tunes but I wanted one ye might know. Scotland the Brave is always a favorite."

"I loved it. Whatever you'd play, I'd love. Thank you." I saw the Colonel returning down the alley. I turned and closed the door behind me, not wanting Half Moon's help at this stage of the painting.

"Oh, Mac, would you mind playing some military tune for the Colonel? He's just heading up the alley now. I know it would make his day."

Mac elbowed the bag, put the chanter in his mouth and fiddled with the longer pipes. I watched in fascination as he blew and I recognized the tune. He turned toward the alley.

The Colonel and the cats came to an abrupt stop. The old man shifted a leash to his left hand so it now held two. Then he drew himself more erect if that were possible, and saluted with his right.

Mac was off to practice with the pipe band. The Colonel took both cats up to his house, scolding them like they were wayward reserves.

As the sun set, I edged around the painting on the floor and stretched out on the bed with my cell phone. I'd found the number of Amethyst Green and dialed.

"Hello, Amethyst," I said hesitantly, not really wanting to go through with this conversation at all.

"Amethyst isn't here right now. May I take a message?"

"Uh, well, yes, maybe. This is Dannah Davidson and I'm trying to get ahold of her. Do you know when she'll be back?"

"No. This is her sister Citrine. Not for a while."

"What does that mean? A few hours? A few days?"

"I don't know. Maybe longer. Who are you?"

"Dannah. I just wanted to talk to her."

"After she got out of the hospital, she was pretty riled up and just took off."

"Oh. I didn't know she'd been in the hospital. Why'd she go in? Is she okay now?" I was afraid of the answer.

"She had a scum bag boyfriend beat her up pretty bad. She's okay physically but she was plenty angry with him. Every time the phone rings, I hope to hear her voice. I was afraid she was going to kill him."

"What was his name?" Like I didn't know.

"Tip or Hip or something. Can't remember the last name if I ever heard it. She met him out there at Burning Man. That shoulda given her a clue to start with." She sighed into the phone.

"Zip. Was it Zip?" I persisted.

"Yea, that was it. I remember now. Like a zip code. Goddamn bastard."

Or a zipper he kept pulling down.

"Citrine, I'm sorry to hear about Amethyst. I was calling to tell her she didn't have to worry about Zip right now because he should be back in jail."

"It won't be good news until he's dead. Then I might think there must be a god after all." I heard her cigarette cough.

"Yes. I understand. I'll let you know what happens. Look, if you hear from Amethyst and she wants to talk, give her my number, okay? Do you have a pencil?"

I hung up, feeling rather depressed. How many other women had Zip hurt? If only he'd taken his meds and stayed straight. But, "if-onlys" never got you anywhere.

My cell phone rang.

"Hi, Harrie," I said after checking the caller ID.

"Dannah, darling. How are you? You can tell I'm fabulous, can't you? But first, you. Are you okay?"

"Yea, I'm okay. So, did Mr. Marvelous ask you out again?" I'd almost forgotten that Harrie finally had a date with Tad.

"Yes, yes, yes. And he's coming with me to Talia's on Christmas. AND I just talked to Loren and Marshall Scott is his Christmas date." Sophisticated Harrie almost squealed.

Talia's annual Christmas party. I don't even know where Thanksgiving went. I wondered if Mac MacGregor would go with me. That would mean I'd have to ask him. That was better than waiting for a call. Guess it would be pro-active. Part of the new me.

"Are you there, Dannah? Isn't that wonderful?"

"Um hmm. Yes, Harrie."

"He prefers Harriet. You want to call me whatever you want. I'll answer," she said and laughed.

"Okay, Hairy Harrie," I teased with an old name we laughed over long ago. "You called at the perfect time. I was a little down in the dumps after my last call." I told her about Citrine and Amethyst. I also told her about Mac and the Colonel. I felt better. Pulling an afghan up, I took a nap.

∞

The cell phone rang. I didn't know what time it was.

"Hello?" I tried to sound awake.

"Dannah, am I calling too late?" Mac didn't have to identify himself. I'd recognize that deep brogue anywhere.

"No. I just took a nap. What time is it?"

"After nine. We've just finished practice. Would you like some company?"

"You're bringing the pipe band here? I don't think they'll fit." I laughed.

"No. Just me. I already know I fit."

It seemed like an accidental double entendre but we both paused for an awkward moment.

"Yes, I'd like to see you. See you when you get here. Have you had dinner?" I thought I had a box of soup in the cupboard. Shopping hadn't been a high priority lately.

"No. We can order something if that's alright."

"Great." I clicked off and jumped to my feet, avoiding the painting on the floor as I inched my way into the bathroom. No time for a shower. I washed my face, brushed my teeth and put on fresh make up. A splash of perfume. Tugging a wide toothed comb through my hair, I glanced in the mirror, thinking it was as good as it was going to get tonight.

I tested the painting. The strips felt dry. Next I'd overlay a varnish that would hold it all together—but that would be tomorrow. I hung the resurrected Airplane Angel on the wall nails and studied it. Yes. It would do.

I straightened the bed covering, cleaned off the counters and the table and put on one of my favorite Celtic CDs. By the time Mac knocked, the Coop was tidy, or as tidy as a tiny space could get when one had lots of art supplies.

I stepped back and Mac ducked through my shorter than normal door, handing me a bouquet of iris. Moonie flashed through the door as Mac shrugged out of his overcoat—it looked like cashmere—and looked for a place to hang it. There wasn't one. As I closed the door, I waved to the Colonel. I set the flowers on the kitchen table, took his coat and laid it on the bed. I felt buzzy and confused. Moonie jumped onto coat, sniffing, and kneading and purring. "Oh, no, Cat-cat," I said and turned to shoo her away.

"Not to worry, Dannah. I miss having a cat and am glad for the sound of a purr." He squatted down and his long fingers stroked her back. He turned the back of his hand to her and let her sniff. She pushed her head against his knuckles.

I filled an old mayonnaise jar with water and arranged the iris, setting them on the kitchen counter. I was a little nervous. Should I feel angry that he just came by? No 'shoulds', Dannah.

Mac dwarfed the kitchen chair as he sat down. He flashed that brilliant smile. "I'm sorry to just drop in like this. I'd hoped to talk to you downtown today but Harriet was in such a hurry and ...well, here I am."

"If I'd been painting, it would be a disturbance. I get into a space and everything else disappears and I'm in the painting as much as creating it. I am the brush, the colors. Probably sounds weird.

140

However, I'm not painting right now. This has been such a yoyo day and I feel open to new experiences and I love the iris. Is it iris or irises? Sorry, I'm rambling." You don't have to say you're sorry, I told myself.

"I'm glad you were here, first of all. And that you weren't working. The iris, is it singular or plural? I don't know. I'll google it. Anyway, I had a dream of a beautiful woman walking in a meadow of iris with an angel flying above her," he said, his eyes on mine. Blue as Lake Fondis in August.

I stopped moving around the kitchen, turned and stared at him. "No way. I had the same dream. That painting is going to Vail tomorrow. How can that be?" A shiver ran over my body. This was too uncanny or creepy.

"Mum didn't believe in coincidences. She said it, the coincidence, was meant to be." His Scottish brogue deepened. "Especially if the dream portends the event."

"I'm not sure what that all means." I shook my head. "I'll show you the painting." I moved toward the stack of paintings by the door.

"What would you like delivered for dinner?" He sounded quite formal but, sitting like a giant in a doll house, he made me grin.

"I couldn't deal with a restaurant. Delivery is good." I looked at his face. No negative reaction. He didn't frown. "Let's call and get Mexican or Chinese." I turned back to look for the painting.

"Your choice, my treat," he said and stood to pull his cell from his right pocket.

"Mexican." Whenever had I become so decisive? I used to say well-what-do-you-want?

"Mamacita's, Gordo's or Playa Fresca?"

"They're all good. Let's go with Mama."

"I was in a dilemma when I was first offered this job in Fondis last year," he said. "I had another job offer in England. I was very divided about which job to take. I went on holiday back to Scotland. I talked it over with Mum. Da's been gone a good while now and I try to go back as often as I can." He was looking off into the distance as if he could see his childhood home.

"She told me to sleep on it. I guess I took it to heart. I had the iris dream that night. The next night I had another dream," he pulled his eyes from memory and looked directly at me. "I dreamed of a woman. I saw her energy, if you understand that."

141

I nodded, understanding that he was speaking like my airy-fairy friends spoke. But I did understand the energy of my angel dreams.

"The shape of her head, the bounce of her hair, the dimple that creased her cheek when she smiled. Do you think I'm crazy?" He looked nervous.

"No. I'm glad to find another dreamer. Oh, everybody dreams, but not everyone remembers them," I said, not wanting to focus on his interest in some dream girl.

"The next morning I called Mum and told her I was moving back to the States and taking the job here in Fondis, Colorado. She'd never heard of Fondis."

"So, who is your dream girl?" I looked down at my stained hands, not wanting to know.

"That day Harrie introduced us, I felt like I recognized you. I stared at you. I'm sorry if I made you uncomfortable."

I blushed. Jeez, I'd been so out of it that day. I frowned. "You mean, I was in your dream?"

"Yes. You were in the field of iris and your energy was in the second dream, too. I don't exactly understand it all but I'd like to get to know you, Dannah."

We sat in silence for a few minutes. I wanted to grin and dance about and I wanted to go hide and talk to Nirvana about it. I suppose I had to figure out how to tell him who I was—all the bad things I'd been through. Maybe he'd take his burritos and run.

"The other official reason I came to this town was to head up the Fondis Pipe & Drum Corp. They're a grade four band. When they heard I might be moving here, they asked me to join them. I accepted. I'm a grade one piper." He eased his chair back and stretched his long legs.

"You've been playing the bagpipes here for a year?" How could I have missed him?

"I have, lassie," he said.

"I love bagpipes. You look great in a kilt." I grinned, imagining his soft skin beneath his clothing. I think I blushed, brushed my hand through my hair and looked around for another stack of paintings.

"I hope you'll come to the Fondis Holiday Parade and hear the band then." He returned my grin. "What shall I order?" he said, tapping his cell.

"I'll have a bean burrito with guacamole," I said and fingered through more paintings until I remembered it would be in the framed stack. I was feeling all mixed up and crazy and happy. There it was. I eased the framed painting out, careful not to scratch the frame.

He turned and stared at the iris painting, silent. I was afraid he didn't like it. He stood, took the painting and moved toward the kitchen light. I busied myself in the kitchen, wiped the already clean counter. A knock at the door pulled me back to the present. Mac glanced at me as if wanting my permission to answer it. I liked that and nodded. It was the delivery man. I noticed that Mac gave him a good tip. Good, very good.

After dinner, I tidied up and put the plates in the sink. Mac moved to the bed—which was really just a sofa—and Moonie rubbed his elbow, nudged his hand and ended up in the middle of Mac's lap. I sat down, very conscious of his body heat and a subtle aroma that wasn't cologne, maybe just a special Mac smell. We talked and I showed him sketchbooks and pointed out paintings on the walls and told their stories. He always complimented my work.

Finally he turned back to the iris-angel-lady and asked if he could buy her, if I were willing not to send her off to Vail. He paid full price and wrote a check right then.

31 /

I slept fitfully that night, dreaming of angels rising from fields of yellow, peach and purple irises and switching on the light to sketch them. Nirvana knew someone who reproduced art cards and distributed them. She'd urged me to work on a series but I hadn't been inspired until now. The sketches of angels and flowers could inspire a series.

I tossed and turned on the narrow bed, thinking of Mac MacGregor and our obvious attraction. We hadn't "done" anything. He hadn't even kissed me except for the quick brush of his lips on my cheek when he left.. But the heat that rose between us was palpable. Or was that my imagination? Maybe it didn't mean anything. Maybe it was a casual Scottish gesture. I touched my cheek.

I wanted a clean slate with this man and I wanted to be fair to him. I wanted him to understand me, to know that things had been rough and I was healing. And I was afraid. Afraid of losing him when he did learn the truth. Afraid of how my body might react as we became more intimate. Afraid of intimacy. Afraid of not being able to be intimate. Afraid I'd be closed and dry with fear rather than open and moist with desire.

We'd sat at my tiny kitchen table eating burritos and he told me stories of Scotland and places he'd traveled. After dinner he told me how bagpipes were cleaned and it was so gross sounding that I laughed. He said he didn't talk about it during a meal. I was so at ease with him, not anxious or afraid. I missed him now that he was gone.

I worried about how he expressed anger. That was the truth of a relationship. Not how you could be sweet and lovey dovey. What happened when he was pissed off? I wanted to talk about it before it happened, maybe set some ground rules.

I got up and eased my way through the dark to get a drink of water and climbed back into bed, finally sleeping as a gray dawn lit the windows.

The phone rang a few hours later. I don't know why I worry that someone will know they woke me up. I always try to sound bright and cheery like I've been up for hours. Well, I had, hours of the night.

"Hello," I couldn't read the caller ID in the dim light.

"Good Morning, Dannah." His voice made my heart ache it sounded so good.

"I was thinking about you." All night long.

"As I was of you," he replied.

"Are you up for taking a walk? I'd like to talk." I was always better when I was walking and I really had to address these issues with him. I wanted to touch him, to hear him speak my name in an intimate way, to...

"Yes. Exactly. I wanted to talk also. Where would you like to walk?"

"Meet me at Lake Fondis in an hour. There's a parking lot by the Bait & Tackle Shop," I said.

"Would you like me to pick you up?"

"No. I'll just meet you." I didn't want to explain that he may not want anything to do with me after he'd heard my story.

"I'll see you in an hour than, Dannah." I could hear disappointment in his voice. There was a lot more disappointment to come, I feared.

I had time to fix oatmeal but I wasn't hungry. I made a cup of chai and headed for the shower. Hot water revived me. I was willing to pretend I'd had a good night's sleep.

Towel drying my hair, I wondered how to start the conversation with him. I couldn't just say I was raped by my ex-husband who I'd been stupid enough to marry in the first place. And stupid enough to let back in my life.

I pulled jeans on over a pair of black lace undies. I could feel sexy underneath, at least. A black turtleneck with a Celtic knot work silver pendant Harrie had given me. I liked the design of the piece and added a pair of silver earrings.

I put on my makeup carefully and smiled at my image in the mirror. Not bad. A dab of perfume. The day looked cold. I pulled my old Doc Martin boots over woolen socks.

I slipped on my black leather jacket. It fit nicely at the waist. Grabbed a black beret. Good. I liked the look. I looked hot. But I had cold feet. Well, I'd know what to say when we started walking. I did my best thinking then and I'd just share with him. It sounded easy.

I wrapped a red, wild wooly scarf around my neck and headed for the blue VW. The Blue Dragon. It was a miracle I was driving her. Not that I believe in dragons or miracles. I just paint what I see and people like them. Maybe I'd paint her, this lovely little car and yes, she had a blue angel flying over her. I acknowledged the imagined presence and pulled out into the alley, heading toward Lake Fondis.

The cell rang and I answered, wishing I had an ear piece to talk while I was driving.

"Yes?" I tucked it under my ear to my shoulder and shifted.

"Dannah, this is Hubert. We received the painting from Breckenridge today. It won't fit in that little bug of yours. Shall I have Charlie drop it off?"

"Hi, Hubert. That would be great. Could you have him take it to My Brother's Auto Shop? He'll need to be surreptitious about it, make sure Sam's wife isn't there because it's a surprise for her."

"Can do."

"Put the cost on my bill, okay?"

"No charge today, Dannah. Holiday."

"It isn't Christmas yet, Hubert."

"Close enough."

"Thank you. Happy Christmas to you too." I clicked off, thinking about the holiday. I'd missed Thanksgiving and now it was almost the end of the year. I had to check my calendar. I think I go to see the psychiatrist tomorrow. Might as well get all this out of the way and then I can be thankful it's over.

I pulled in next to Mac's car, unbuckled and got out. He was standing by a Ponderosa pine gazing at the lake, his hair flying askew in the wind. He turned as I walked up, a beam of sunlight striking his fierce auburn red hair for a brief moment.

I looped my scarf a second time around my neck. My impulse was to hug him but I refrained, as did he.

"Lachlan MacGregor," I said, looking up into his somber face. "Did I say it right?"

"You did, Dannah Davidson," he responded, a twitch of a smile at the corner of his mouth.

I indicated the path heading west with my chin and we turned in unison, walking easily together. I wasn't quite sure how it happened, his long legs and my short ones, strides matching as one. I concentrated on our rhythm, left foot to his left, no...I stumbled and did a skip, trying to pretend it didn't happen. I had to stop this. I didn't want to pretend anything anymore. I just wanted to be me, to be honest, and to work out what didn't seem to work. It didn't seem such a hard request.

Glancing up at his handsome profile, I was once again tongue tied. I really didn't know what to say. I'd let him start. He said he had something he wanted to talk about. Maybe it was over already. As if feeling my gaze, he turned, a question in his eyes.

I looked forward and dropped my gaze to the paved bike path, shivering. The wind rushed through the pine boughs along the lake's edge, moaning a sad song. My leather jacket may look hot but it's not. I should have worn my shabby old down jacket. Shoulda woulda coulda ...

We kept pace for some time and then I saw a bench facing the lake and headed toward it. I sat, wrapping my arms around myself. He sat close but not touching. Whose bright idea was this, I asked part of my brain that wasn't paying attention. I was freezing my ass off and I didn't have a word to say to this guy.

He put his arm along the back of the bench, but still our bodies didn't touch. I wanted to climb in his lap and cuddle up and weep. Or seduce him. I really had to clear the air so I could follow my impulses. I'd never felt this way about a guy before, never felt like we had to start out up front, without any hidden barriers that would block our way.

Why didn't he start? He said he had something to say to me. No. I should start. Get it all out and over with and then see if he had anything left to say.

We turned toward each other at the same moment, our eyes locked.

"This isn't working," I said.

"Let's go someplace warm," he said.

"Yes."

We headed back to the cars, silent.

32 /

I shivered even after the heat revved up in his car. I'd be glad to get into a warm building. I'd never been to the Fondis Fish House but it was the closest place to the lake. What was I thinking—trying to look good and not paying attention to the weather. Tiny snippets of snow gradually gave way to larger, more persistent flakes. I was freezing. I tucked my chin as we walked against the wind to the weathered diner.

Mac, ever the gentleman, opened the door and I entered the small, crowded restaurant. Mac spoke to a waiter who pointed toward a small booth in the back and we headed in that direction. I slipped into the faded navy blue seat, my body gradually responding to the heat of the room.

"Drinks?" the waiter asked as he slid two glasses of water across the wooden surface.

"Hot chocolate," I said between chattering teeth.

"I'd like the same," Mac said and the waiter turned into the crowd.

Mac reached his hands out and I put my icicles into his warm palm.

"Why is this difficult for you? What is it?" Concern creased the edges of his eyes.

"Oh, I don't know. I thought it would be easy if we walked and talked. I like to walk. I thought it was a good idea. It wasn't."

"Maybe walking when there isn't a blizzard on the rise would be very pleasant, Dannah. What do you want to talk to me about?"

I dropped my gaze and then raised my eyes to him. "Me."

"I always want to hear more about you. I take pleasure in getting to know you." His hands shifted on mine, covering them and warming me to the heart.

"I'm not so sure you'll want to know more after what I have to tell you." I sighed.

"Dannah, just start at the beginning. Then it will be easy." He smiled softly.

I did start at the beginning, telling him about my mom and my disappearing dad, about grade school. About Grannie. About Mom's second marriage and divorce and how she's now traveling the world with her French lover who is dying of cancer.

The waiter delivered two steaming mugs of hot chocolate with a mountain of whipped cream on top. I slipped my hands out of his and held the mug, sipping the hot liquid through the cool whipped cream.

I continued to talk, told him about high school and art classes and finally about going to art school. And about meeting Zip, who I didn't even like the first time I met him. But Zip was persistent and handsome in a bad boy kind of way and all my friends at college thought he was hot. Our marriage was brief. His returns predictable.

Zip expected special treatment and he got what he expected. I gave it to him, not noticing that I gave up myself in the doing. Special Zip soon lost his shine. It was always about him and I should just get used to it.

If Grannie were still alive, she'd tell me and I'd close my eyes and think of her pulling me into her soft lap and rocking me and cooing and then, and only then, when I was relaxed, we would talk.

I was so close to her that I could feel her heart beat and I didn't have to look at her face to see a shadow cross it when she worried for me. She never used that word "worry."

Instead, she said, "Well, how are we going to fix it?"

We.

She said "we", not "you." Grannie long time gone, can you hear me now? No. How am I going to fix it now and I know I have to solve my own problems now.

With Zip I was afraid to leave because he'd hunt me down and hurt me and …everyone in town knew he had a brutal streak and I'd see their faces pull tight and sympathy flood their eyes. "How are you, Dannah?" OK. I'm okay. And I'd pull my clothing tighter over my bruised body. Why worry them? I'd have to figure this out.

No Grannie now to help and when I finally left, my body bare and empty as my womb, I said it over and over—never again, never, never, never and then…

Yes, I did open the door a year later even though I had a premonition about who it was, I opened that door to Zip.

There's not enough concealer or foundation to adequately cover deep purple blue bruises. I ached all over and I was so tired, my eyes felt heavy. I couldn't concentrate. I looked at Mac now and his eyes were serious and he was listening. I noticed my legs were clenched tight and my arms were crossed to armor my breasts. I still felt too vulnerable.

I'd told this all to Hawk Nose so it should be easier now but it wasn't. I get along with a little help from my friends. The song skitters through my brain. My friends and my shrink and maybe him, maybe Mac.

A tear splashed from my cheek unto the table. I brushed it away wildly. I didn't want it to be like this. I knew my eyes would be bloodshot, rimmed in scarlet. I have to let him see me at my worst, with all the skeletons clanking out of my closet. Still I didn't like anyone to see me cry. Here in a crowded public space especially.

Even if I have a wounded vagina, I am learning to be whole again. My wild emotions will not stay strapped in the dungeon of distrust anymore. They must come out in a healthy way so I can be free of them, not bound by the fear.

Then, maybe then, I can love. I want to love myself first but does that mean I have to love the wound? I will love my total self, all the parts, bright and light and deep and dark.

"A gentleman," Grannie would have called Mac. Yes, Grannie, I think he is. But will he be a gentle man in bed?

We were quiet for a while. He handed me an ironed handkerchief. I blew my nose and sniffled. Gazed down at his initialed monogram and back to the depths of his sky blue eyes.

149

"When did he come back last?" Mac's eyes never left mine.

I told him. Everything. Every detail. How I'd felt, how I'd been responsible for letting him in, how I should have known better, how Talia thought he was bi-polar, and Nirvana said that just meant creepy. And I told him about the rape—and Zip's critical condition in the hospital and now maybe being in jail. I could no longer look him in the eye and stared hard at a water mark on the table.

The waiter stopped briefly at our table. "Order for two?"

Mac nodded.

"So, you can see why you might not think I'm acceptable." I forced myself to look up. "I feel a very strong connection with you, Mac. I like you. But if you go away and don't want to see me, I'll understand."

"We'll do much better if you don't try to make up my mind for me," his voice was firm but soft.

Startled, I began to protest. He shook his head.

"I have a story to tell also. Then together we will decide where we are right now and where we'd like to go. If that works for you." He was so serious.

"I'm sorry. I don't mean to be controlling or making up your mind about anything. Tell me your story," I said.

"Only if you're finished. I think there's more."

"Yes. I go to the psychiatrist tomorrow. I've been depressed. My body was injured and has healed now but I don't know about my mind. I think it will be okay." I shrugged.

"What are you still afraid of?"

Tears welled, unwanted. I willed them not to fall. "I'm afraid that I'll freeze up when I want to be intimate with you." I spoke so softly that he leaned forward to hear. It was the hardest thing I've ever said but I felt like a vice had been released on my chest. I looked at him through blurry eyes.

"Sweet One, know that I do not readily promise anything to anyone. To you I promise, I will never hurt you or force you to anything you do not desire. That is a promise. Should you still wish to continue our relationship."

"Why wouldn't I want to continue if you can handle who I truly am?"

"You are so much more than even you know, Dannah. My story is short but not simple. I married in my twenties and had a son. Before he was ten, he and his mother were killed in an auto wreck." He paused and drank some cocoa. I was stunned into silence, not wanting to break the intimacy.

"We all have skeletons in our closets, Dannah. My son wasn't mine. He was the offspring of a relative, an unfortunate occurrence on a rowdy New Year's Eve that left my wife pregnant. I raised him as my own and loved him all the more. After they died, I withdrew from everything but work and have been a workaholic until I had the iris dream. The bagpipes kept me alive. My dreams finally gave me hope. If you'll take another step with me on hope...?"

The waiter served two large baskets filled with fish and chips, the house specialty and only item on the menu.

Mac and I stared long into each other's eyes. It was never what it seemed on the surface. We all came with our garbage and grief.

"I'm willing," I said.

"As am I, my Iris of Hope."

We ate with gusto—perhaps both of us trying to fill the void of our pasts.

∞

"Dannah, let me drive you home. We can get your car tomorrow," Mac said.

"But I have an early appointment with the psychiatrist."

"I'll drive you in the morning—to your car or to your appointment, if you wish."

I gazed at the falling snow, four inches deep now, and realized how exhausted I was. I'd spent all that time worrying, and now it was all out in the open. He'd been married—and widowed. The tragedies of our lives overwhelmed me.

"Thank you," I said simply, leaning back on the head rest. "I'm liking getting to know you, Lachlan MacGregor." I closed my eyes while he drove.

"Gentle, Sweet Lassie," I heard his brogue from a deep sleep and realized he was lifting me out of the car and carrying me to the Coop. I snuggled against the soft cashmere coat and sighed.

"Dannah, what time do you need to get up?"

I opened my eyes in surprise to hear the deep brogue and realized that Mac had spent the night. On the floor, having found a cushion for his head and his overcoat for warmth, lay the man I was learning to trust, curled up with Half Moon. Moonie never liked Zip and I had worried that Zip would kill her. I trusted Moonie more than most people in deciding the worth of a human being. I smiled.

"Probably seven. I need to be there at nine." I yawned. "What time is it?"

"Six thirty."

"Plenty of time. Come cuddle," I said and scooted over and lifted the edge of the sleeping bag, wondering whose voice was so forward. Mac eased in and I turned on my side as he spooned against me, both of us still clothed. We lay quiet and drifting until Moonie jumped on my shoulder with a meowrl.

"The perfect alarm clock," Mac murmured in my ear. "Cat time. It is now seven o'clock."

We bumbled and bumped, getting ready. I wasn't used to having another person in the Coop and he wasn't used to such a small space I was certain. We laughed a lot and took turns showering.

"I'll buy breakfast," he said as I opened cupboards to ask if he wanted oatmeal, hoping I had enough to make up two bowls.

"Do you want to get your car or shall I drive you to your appointment?" he asked.

"Listen. Snow plows. If you can drive, we can get my car afterwards. I hate being late. We'd better go if we're going to eat breakfast first."

"I'll start the engine and get the car warmed up," Mac said, opening the door.

I was looking for my car keys in my backpack.

"Good morning, sir," I heard Mac say.

"That's Colonel to you, boy. Now just what are your intentions with my girl Dannah?"

"Most honorable, Colonel. It was very snowy and I gave her a ride home and stayed to make sure she had a ride this morning." He paused. "I slept on the floor, sir. With the cat."

"Now, then, that's a man. Good place for you. On the floor. Surprised the cat would put up with you. Mind you, I'll be keeping my eye on you."

I smiled—and found my keys, shoving them in the right hand pocket of my jeans. I heard the car start.

Things were going to be just fine.

∞

I'd only picked at breakfast, being anxious. Mac asked if I wanted him to go in with me. Certainly not. I was stressed enough that I'd even shared with him all these private details of my life. He said he'd pick me up in an hour.

Whispering Pines Mental Health was located in a tall, old brick building behind the new Justice Center. I'd been there before to teach art to a rehab program.

"Good Morning, Dannah," Sally, the receptionist said. I knew her slightly from my work here previously. "Dr. Redwood will be with you in a moment." Gentrified, even the lobby looked like you really might get mentally healthy there. An atrium with a forest of tropical plants, a fountain with a gurgling stream and one of Nirvana's sculptures of a woman's face with water falling over it like healing tears.

A door opened and a tall, slender woman in a flowing red dress walked toward me. Her gray hair was tucked up in a bun, wisps already slipping down her neck. "Ms. Davidson?"

"Dannah, please."

"I'm Dr. Redwood. I'm pleased to meet you." She took my outstretched hand in both of hers.

Blue eyes twinkled between dancing lines on her face as she expressed greetings. I liked her instantly.

Her office was soft and warm, pinks and reds with silver accents, bookshelves overflowing. She didn't have a standard desk, just a TV tray kind of thing with a laptop. I sank into an overstuffed chair, slipped off my shoes and tucked my feet under me.

"This will be a get acquainted session. I'm sorry I'll have to record all this on a computer. I hope it won't be too disconcerting," she said.

I thought of the hawk nosed guy and how distancing it felt when he looked only at the desk top computer. I was committed to being honest. Might as well start now. I told her about my last session.

"So, I'll let you know how I'm feeling," I said.

153

"Good. If you do that all the way through, no matter what we're discussing, it will be very helpful." She smiled and I took a deep breath.

She slid the tray thing into her lap, but her eyes never left mine as she began to ask questions. Occasionally she'd glance down, perhaps to check the next section to fill out but I felt her full, undivided attention. I told her my story, my disparate moods, my inability to know when I was going to feel the blues or ecstatic with unexpected turn of events. I told her about the truck, the slashed painting and I finally told her about Zip. In minute detail.

"We've run over by fifteen minutes," she said glancing at her watch. "I allowed for that. The first visit can often be very full, trying to get an overview."

"One more thing?"

She nodded.

I told her about Mac, about my attraction to him, about my fear of sexual intimacy if we progressed that far.

"Dannah, I appreciate how open you've been today. I'd like to schedule another appointment in a week. Your current situation may take the whole hour. Sally will put you in the computer." She smiled. "And I will prescribe something that should help you temporarily." She slid the computer table aside and stood up. She smelled good and I almost felt like hugging her. Her dress was soft silk, not some manmade fabric. I looked forward to coming back.

34 /

Mac picked me up. I was quiet as he drove me to my car parked at the lake. "Are you coming to the parade today?" Mac asked, as he walked me to the VW.

"I have to work," I said, unlocking the car and sliding behind the wheel. "I want to put a final coat on the Airplane Angel and then some other images are nagging for expression." I smiled at him. "But I wouldn't miss the parade. What time is it?" I'd almost forgotten.

"I'm on my way over to the rehearsal hall now. The parade starts at three. Are you coming?"

"Wild angels wouldn't keep me away. I'll get in a few hours' work and then go downtown."

"Would you like to meet me at Finn's Pub afterward? All of the pipers will be going there. Then you and I can slip out for a quiet meal if you'd like." His blue eyes sparkled.

"I'd like."

After inviting Half Moon to visit the Colonel, I once again placed the Airplane Angel on the floor and applied a final coat of varnish. I wouldn't have time to even start the painting that dominated all other images in my mind. Mac's profile, back lit by a table lamp that night I'd seen him in the café. My cell rang.

"Hi, Talia," I said, reading the caller ID.

"First, tell me how you're doing? Healing?" Her voice was soft and musical.

"I am better every day, thanks to you and all my friends. And yes, before you ask, I went to my first counseling session. I was ready."

"I'm glad to hear it. You're coming tomorrow, aren't you? I haven't talked to you in ages, it seems."

"Yes. I'll be there. Is it still okay if I bring someone?"

"Of course. I heard on the grapevine that you might bring a guest." I could hear the smile in her voice.

"Thanks, Talia. Is William here yet?"

"No. And don't change the subject. Who is the mystery man?"

"His name is Mac. He's the pipe band leader. I'm just getting ready to go to the parade and catch the bagpipes. Are you at work? Can you come to the parade? He'll be the tall, red haired one in kilts." I smiled just thinking about him.

"No, I'm at home. I'm helping Regina cook for tomorrow so I'll have to miss the parade. Do you think he might play the pipes here tomorrow?"

"I don't know. I'll ask him. Now, when does William come in?"

"He called from Alaska this morning. He should fly into Fondis International Airport tomorrow by 9:00 a.m. I can't wait to see him," she said.

"I'll bet. Do you want me to come early and help? Can I bring anything?"

"No. Regina has it all under control. I'm just pretending to help. This is an important time of year for her. She and Leonardo arrived here on Christmas day. They were so happy to leave the situation in Guatemala that it has become a special celebration for all of us, almost as important as the day they became citizens."

"I've got to run if I'm going to get to the parade on time. See you tomorrow, Talia."

"Bye, Dannah."

I edged toward a box of clothes in the corner and found a bright red turtleneck sweater. I liked wearing red even though I'd always been told redheads should avoid it. I've got red hair; he's got red hair. Is that weird? Well, his is dark auburn red with penny highlights and mine is...just red, somewhere between strawberry blonde and ripe peaches. Looking in the bathroom mirror, I brushed on fresh blush and some glossy lipstick.

The day was bright but in the twenties. I knew it would be freezing later so reluctantly I pulled on the shabby old down jacket and slipped on my old Sorrels. Outside a breeze out of the north made me glad of my choice. Form follows function. Be warm rather than pretty. I laughed at myself and headed down the alley to cut across streets to downtown. It was useless to drive. I wouldn't be able to park close so I might as well walk.

Fondis is well known for its parades and people come from all over the state, especially for the Christmas parade when out-of-towners flock to stay with relatives. I often had a problem seeing the floats and bands because I was so short. That problem had been solved by friends a few years ago. I avoided the crowds already gathering on Main Street and took the back alley to the Fire Station Museum.

"Dannah, I wondered if you might be along. Come on up, now, half the crew is already on the roof. The others are lining up for parade duty," the fire chief called out from the metal fire escape stairs that ran up the outside of the building. The lower part of the building was the Fondis Fire Museum, with old trucks and lots of photos of historic fires from the past. Parade days some of the firemen would march in the parade or ride on one of the trucks. Others watched from the roof, partially on duty. A skeleton crew stayed on call at the new fire station.

I could hear the bagpipes before I could see the beginning of the parade from where I stood at the brick wall, peering down the street.

"Here ya go, Dannah," said Ralph, handing me a pair of binoculars.

I took them even though I knew I'd spot that wavy red hair at a great distance. I focused the lenses and strained to see any sign of activity at the end of the street. Nothing. I lowered the binoculars and watched people shift and settle into a place.

"Hi, Dannah."

I turned to see the familiar face of Epona Maris, the poet of the plains, a sometimes member of the Womyn's Group. Epona was a fire fighter and allegedly a follower of Cerridwen, that old crone who does ceremonies out in the Ponderosas east of Fondis. I never saw Epona following anyone though. She had the stature and charisma of a born leader but she didn't seek followers. I always think of her streaking across the open spaces on a horse under a full moon

We hugged. I handed her the binoculars.

Across the street I saw Loren, bundled in a new overcoat and straining to see through the crowd. He was probably looking for Marshall. Hubert, in a baseball cap and plaid jacket, and Charlie, his Mohawk spiked red and purple, shivering in jeans and a Bronco orange jacket, made an interesting pair, seated in chairs down the street. Children dashed out into the street and were called back by adults.

"Dannah, I hate to tell you this..." Epona pushed the binoculars my way. "Zip is in the crowd. Over there under the sign for Curly's Bar."

"Shit." I grabbed the binoculars and looked through the wrong end. "Shit." Turning them, I scanned the crowd and finally came to rest on his troubled face. He'd always said he was Irish any day a pub was open. He was really Cherokee and Italian. "Shit."

"You already said that."

"He should he be in jail." Damn. He's as slippery as an eel and smart too. Smart enough to hide that surly face and con someone into trusting him.

I ignored Epona and wondered what to do. Lifting the binoculars I saw him turn and go into the pub. I took a deep breath, let all the energy of my release painting straighten my spine. That man will no longer ruin my life.

The Fondis Pipe & Drum Corp came around the corner and there he was: Mac in all his glory. Talk about opposites.

God, Mac looked good in kilts. I raised the binoculars. His cheeks were puffed and he was one with the bagpipe and the other musicians. The sound sent a tingle up my spine. I ran the binoculars down his body, he wore fingerless gloves, a sporran over his private parts. I grinned. I wondered if that was what it was initially intended for. I mean, what is it to wear a skirt without any protection there? His well-developed calves wore cabled socks. He was a fine looking man. I was still rather amazed that he seemed truly interested in me. The dream we'd shared nagged at my sense of possibilities.

"Don't hog the binoculars, Dannah," another fireman said. Reluctantly, I pulled my gaze and handed them over, my eyes staying on Mac.

I watched the band pass and turn off at the town square where I knew they would disassemble.

"Thanks, guys," I said, heading toward the stairs.

"It just started, Dannah. You can't leave now," someone said.

"I'm going to meet someone," I hedged, not wanting to say too much.

"Chasin' skirts just like us, huh?" one of them teased.

"I do like a kilt," I said and they all laughed.

"Good luck, Dannah."

I scurried down the old fire escape, and headed up the alley where I knew I'd eventually come to the parade end, intending to evade any contact with Zip and meet up with Mac.

35 /

I spotted Mac in the madness of the crowd and twisted and turned until I was near enough to shout out his name. He grabbed me and swung me around, laughing. He kissed my cheek as he set me down. We were surrounded by kilted men and women, whooping it up. They all seemed to pause in their celebration to turn and watch us. Suddenly, I felt like an intruder.

"Fine playing," Mac called out in the sudden silence. "Each of you played truer than any rehearsal. Good work, lads and lassies," his voice rang out.

"Hip, hip, hurrah for Mac," someone shouted and soon the chant surrounded him. He grinned.

"To Finn's Pub, I say. First round is on me."

The clamor now exceeded any before and I laughed as the band members headed off to the bar on a side street. Mac grabbed my hand and nodded in the direction the band had taken.

"I'll show you a short cut," I said. He nodded, picked up his pipe and ritually took it apart, setting each piece orderly in a black leather case. I liked how he took care of his parts. That made me laugh aloud. He looked up with a question.

"You were wonderful," I said and led him back down the alley, cutting across a side alley two streets and to the back door of Finn's Pub.

"I like getting to know the real city with you, Dannah," he said.

Mordred O'Leary beamed as we passed the kitchen. "Glad to have ye aboard, Mr. MacGregor. You're the talk of the town, lad," the owner said.

"Thanks. First round of drinks for the band is on me," he looked down at me, "and my lady and I would like a quiet spot if ye have one." He laughed as if he knew that would be impossible. I didn't know if I liked being called "his lady."

We settled in a booth near the back and he ordered a single malt scotch by a name I didn't know. He looked questioningly at me.

I shrugged.

"The same." Why not? I was trying to expand my horizons— and my taste buds. "And a glass of water."

"Make it two."

"You're very handsome in your kilt." I blurted before thinking I might be too forward with that compliment. Well, it was true and I was trying to shoot for truth in our communication.

"And without it, I'm not?" he teased.

"Stop fishing for compliments, lad," I said, picking up his brogue for a phrase. Besides, I hadn't seen him in the altogether. Yet.

He laughed, as did I. The waiter served us two shot glasses, two glasses of water. I watched Mac down his shot in one gulp. His eyes squeezed closed and then he let out a breath before he smiled.

159

My eyes scanned the crowd briefly, hoping not to see Zip. Satisfied I turned my attention to the jigger of scotch.

Sniffing, I shivered. I took a small sip, the burn raging though my mouth, snaking to my belly. Tears leaked out of my eyes and I coughed. "You like this stuff?" I asked in amazement. A sense of contentment began to ease through my body. He watched me, a small grin playing at his lips. It was a good thing I'd decided to try the new meds tonight when I could determine my body's reaction, if any. I don't think anything would be compatible with this single malt fire water. I gulped down the entire glass of water.

Various members of the band came up to the table to compliment him but he turned each one around, mentioning a special skill that the person had improved. I was impressed with how he handled people.

"I'll be right back." I nodded to him as I slipped out of the booth and into the crowd. The revelers tipped their steins in greeting to me and I inched toward the women's room. Scotch was nasty stuff and water didn't calm the after taste. I pushed the door open with my shoulder and eased in to the bathroom about the size of mine. I latched the door, pulled a paper seat cover, centered it, and sat to relieve myself.

The auto hand dryer still roared as I stepped back into the packed hallway. I slipped under an elbow here, an arm there. A face leaned down to mine. With breath reeking, Zip pinned me to the wall, pressed his body to mine. "Miss me, bitch?" He belched

"Let me go." I struggled.

"Just give me a few bucks and you won't see me for a while." He sneered.

"I thought you were in jail."

"I'm out. Innocent."

I took a deep breath; as I exhaled, I jammed my fist below his windpipe. "I do not ever want to see you again. You will never ask me for anything or come near me." My voice was low and fierce and true. My hand hurt.

"Who's gonna stop me, bitch?"

"A restraining order. If I even see you, I will dial 911." My voice was a growl.

I turned to leave. He jammed harder against me. I bent my knee, twisted, lifted an elbow hard into his sternum and left him bent over and panting.

"You look flushed, Dannah," Mac said as I slid into the booth.

"That firewater is more than I can take. I do think I need a breath of fresh air."

"Of course. I should have warned you." He reached for my unfinished glass, whisked it to his lips and drank it down. He signed the credit card slip, put the card back in his sporran and lifted an eyebrow. "Ready?"

"Jimmy, put the first round for the band on my tab," he called to the bartender.

"W'a' about me?" a dingy old man called from the corner.

"Can ye play the pipes, lad?" Mac asked. The group guffawed.

"Sure to certain." The old drunk straightened up a bit, pulled in his cheeks and began to whistle, fingering his windpipe in a strange tune. The laughter died.

"And a double for the king of pipes in the corner," Mac called to the bartender.

∞

We went to his house where he put his bagpipe away in a closet and showered while I studied the sparse furnishings of his home.

I stretched out on his bed, smelling Mac as I closed my eyes. When I opened them again, he was sitting on the edge of the bed wearing a plaid cotton shirt, weskit and pleated trousers. His hair was still damp, a darker red.

"I love watching you sleep," he said, and touched my cheek with a finger.

I rolled on my side, curling around him. "I'd rather be awake," I murmured as he rubbed my back.

"Would you like to have dinner at the bistro on the corner?" he asked.

"You are always treating me. Why don't we go to the Coop and I'll fix dinner," I said on impulse, then wondered if he'd like my cooking. "Besides, it will be crowded everywhere tonight with post-parade revelers."

"So, let's go shopping and I'll buy the food and you do the cooking."

"That will still be you treating me."

"No. It will be my sharing the dinner requirements. You don't know how I long for a home cooked meal. You are more than treating me."

161

He drove and I gave him directions to the Bijou Grocery, a long time establishment within Fuller's Mercantile. It was just hanging on since the arrival of the newer shopping chains. I liked coming here. The produce was fresh, the meat cuts generous.

"Hi, there, Dannah. Go to the parade?" the old man dusting shelves turned and asked.

"It was great. I'd like you to meet Mac, the new band leader. He was in the parade. Mac, this is Mr. Salamone." I noticed that I was proud of Mac. It was a new sensation.

"I've heard about you, Mac. Good words. Glad you're in Fondis, young man. Take good care of our girl, here," he said, nodding at me.

They shook hands and then we wandered the aisles. I headed for the produce department and found a perfect head of romaine lettuce and put it in the small shopping cart.

"Do you like artichokes?" I asked.

"Never had one. I'd love to try."

I selected several, squeezing and testing them before I found two that I thought fresh enough and put them in a paper bag.

"What kind of meat do you like? Or should I ask first if you eat meat?"

"I eat meat, everything from lamb to beef and me mum makes a great haggis." He grinned.

"I won't be makin' ye haggis, Mr. MacGregor," I said in an imitation of his brogue. "But lamb chops sound great. Let's see what Mr. Salamone has today."

I'd planned on a simple meal but Mac kept adding things to the cart, more vegetables and fruits, crackers and cheese and a tub of oatmeal.

"Did you see the fresh breads?" Mr. Salamone asked as we were checking out. "Mrs. Salamone baked them fresh this morning. Her French bread is the best." He pointed and Mac went to fetch the bread and came back with a pound of butter. My small refrigerator was going to be overflowing.

I told him about Zip as we drove back to the Coop.

"Damnit, Dannah. I wish you'd told me before. I would have had a few words with the bloke."

"No. It's over. I don't want to talk about it anymore tonight. You can't fight my battles. There is a restraining order out on him. I finally stood up to him for the first time."

"Still..." and his eyes turned dark as a midnight ocean.

36

I hung the Airplane Angel back on the wall though the varnish was still tacky. Mac eased down into a kitchen chair and made the salad while I trimmed the artichoke claws with scissors and put them on to cook. I rinsed the four lamb chops, diced garlic and rubbed over the surfaces and cut up fresh rosemary, sprinkling pieces on top of the chops.

Mac opened the bottle of wine and poured two jelly glasses as I sat in the opposite kitchen chair. Whatever was I doing here with this handsome man? Why was he even interested in me? What if Zip came by? The shroud started to appear, tighten and blind me, to shorten my breath. I ripped it aside. This was my house and my guest and he was just about the nicest person, well, the nicest man I'd ever met. Be in the moment. Who said that? Nirvana or Harrie? Whatever. The shroud is in the past. I am here now.

"Here's to you, Mac," I said, raising my glass.

"Here's to us, Dannah Davidson." We smiled, clinked our glasses and sipped.

"Oh, my gosh. I didn't talk to you about Christmas dinner, did I?" I blushed. I'd assumed he'd go with me but hadn't actually asked him.

"What about it? I really enjoyed the big celebration today."

"Silly me. Christmas is tomorrow. I'm been so out of it and just trying to get myself centered that I haven't noticed the holidays. Or maybe I don't want to.

"I don't know how you celebrate in Scotland. Or even if you celebrate Christmas. Or if you have plans already. I'm rambling. Anyway, I'm going to Talia's for dinner and you're invited too. If you'd like to come along?" I was nervous as he took a swallow of wine.

"May we go together? I could pick you up?" His voice was deep and warm.

"You'll go then? Yes, we will go together. Talia is a wonderful hostess. I don't know who all will be there. William is flying in from...where was he? Alaska, I think. That's Talia's husband. And Harrie will be there with Tad and Loren with Marshall. I don't know if you've met everyone or not but we'll have a great time. Thank you." I relaxed and got up to check the artichokes.

"Thank you, Dannah. You are gracious to welcome me into your life."

I stopped, thinking what it must be like to be in another country, even if they do speak English, and to not be familiar with the customs, the traditions that vary, the need to make friends and...

I reached out and grabbed his hand and squeezed. "You're welcome."

I lit a candle and set it in the center of the table, turning to slip the lamb chops under the toaster-oven broiler. I pulled a chopping board from under the sink and a knife from the utensil drawer and started to chop the zucchini and onions. I glanced at Mac. He was watching me, a sweet smile on his face.

"Do you wish you could go home for Christmas?"

"I went last year to see Mum and the family. There was too much to do this year." I thought there was a sadness in his eyes. My eyes watered from onion assault.

I served dinner on two of my three dinner plates while Mac filled our wine glasses. I had to teach him how to eat artichokes and we laughed as he experimented. I served both mayonnaise, my favorite, and a ramekin (really one of Moonie's cat bowls) of melted butter.

"It takes a lot of work for a little taste," he said, studying a leaf.

"Unlike a sip of scotch fire," I said.

He laughed.

"Wait until you get to the heart. It is so delicious."

"The heart is always delicious," he said, casting those eyes at me. "The lamb chops remind me of home." He changed the subject and cut into his second chop.

"Good. It's good to feel at home," I said.

"I do feel at home with you, Dannah." His face and tone of voice turned serious. And that made me uneasy. It wasn't him but negative images pushing from my past, yelling warnings that had nothing to do with the current situation. But they sat heavy in my brain. I decided not to have any more wine and to remember to take my new medication before I went to bed.

"Dannah, I have my laptop in the car. I'll get it and show you photos of home. I know, Fondis is home now but in many ways, Scotland will always be home. Plus, Mum lives there," he said, reminding me how different our lives were.

"Great. After dessert, you can get it."

We smiled at each other as I cleared the plates and served mango sorbet.

∞

The short length of me stretched along the long length of him as we sat side by side on the couch looking at the computer screen. I didn't smile with my lips but my heart was grinning wildly.

"Here is Edinburgh and oh, look, this is my favorite shot of heather above Loch Lomond. Do you know its history? Well, not now, lass. It is a sad tale. Ah, now here we are in London. I kept my flat there, not knowing if I'd be staying in the States. Have you ever been there? I'd love to take you there sometime." His arm was around my shoulder and he squeezed gently.

There were so many hinted possibilities of a future together. I was afraid to respond to them, to look at them, to want them as much as I did deep inside.

"I'd love to go to London one day," I said, as generically as I could. I'd love to go with him, to be comfortable traveling with him, to trust him to guide me in a city that big.

"I'd like that." He turned off the computer and slid it back into the carrying case. "I should be off. What time shall I pick you up for Talia's celebration?"

"She said to be there at two. Come by around one, okay?"
We stayed there, quiet, our bodies still touching but without the distraction of the computer. I was burning with the touch of him next to me and dared not look at him. He'd see everything on my face.

He lifted me into his lap, his hand gently turning my head toward him. I looked into his eyes and saw desire reflected there. He ran a thumb along my cheek and leaned forward, ever so gently kissing me, his lips soft, giving, wanting. I leaned into the hardness of his body, the sweetness of his mouth. How long can a kiss last? It was timeless and I was breathless as was he. Moonie meowed.

"I'll see you tomorrow," Mac said, his voice husky.

I slipped out of his lap, nodded and watched him go out the door. I needed a bigger bed. I wanted him to stay the night. Not on the floor. But with me, truly with me. So far, I wasn't afraid.

37

I awoke in a panic. I'd forgotten that I had to take my paintings to the gallery on Friday. I'd promised –what, something. And I'd forgotten to take my new medication. That man put me in a dither. I had to think straight but my thoughts kept boomeranging back to him.

I put a moss green clay mask on my face, fixed a cup of tea while it dried and then showered, removing the mud chips. Shampooed my unruly locks and shaved my legs. I felt better. I made a piece of toast, took my vitamins and the prescription. Moonie yowled at the door and I let her out.

I pulled on black panty hose and slipped into my slinky black woolen dress. The neckline plunged in a "V", the waist was snug and the skirt flared and moved easily when I walked. I loved wearing it and twirled around. I put on Grannie's double strand of pearls, a pair of pearl earrings and slipped into black heels.

I'd been advised by some makeup expert to put on makeup first, but then it can smudge as you pull the dress over your head. It's a brief moment of conflict, do it the way someone else told me to or do it my way. I preferred my way. I draped a towel around my shoulders, secured it with a clothespin and put on my makeup, dusky frappe eye shadow, shimmering black eyeliner, midnight black mascara, ivory lilt foundation, spring pink blush.

The holiday season is not always the best for me. In fact, it usually sucks. This year would be different. I could feel it in the air. Life was going to be better after all. I glanced at the clock and it was only noon. I'd have to wait another hour for Mac. Not enough time to do much of anything. I could read. I'd started a mystery novel but forgot what it was about so that wouldn't distract me enough.

The cell rang.

"Good Mornin', Dannah. Am I interrupting?" Mac asked.

"No, I was just thinking what a long time it would be before you got here." I laughed. Was it really smart to be this honest?

"So, might I come earlier?"

"Indeed."

"Good."

"Hold on a minute," I said when I heard a knock on the door.

I opened it to find Mac with his cell to his ear. We both laughed.

"You look beautiful, Dannah," he said. The words every woman wants to hear. And believe.

"Thank you. You look very handsome," I looked him up and down, the black trousers, the blue shirt and red tie. And his black cashmere overcoat. He looked delicious.

I pulled on the old winter jacket, hoping he wouldn't notice the poof of down that slipped out of a growing hole on the sleeve. I should mend it but it's low on my priority list.

"Would you like to drive around a bit before we go to your friend's house?" he asked.

"Tomorrow I need to drop some paintings off at the Gallery in the Square." I had totally forgotten about it, two days late but with the Christmas holiday, I hoped it would work out.

"I'd love to go with you. May I?" Moonie slipped inside and purred against Mac's leg. Mac took my hand as I closed the door.

I looked out the window to see the size of his car. "Neither of our vehicles is large enough. I'll have to ask Hubert to pick them up for me. Oh. Yes. You can go over to the gallery with me." I smiled up at him.

"I knew I was waiting to buy a new car for a reason. I need one big enough to carry paintings." He smiled but I had that weird feeling of how much his words created that future with me in it—and I didn't trust it yet.

"Can I watch you paint?"

"What?" My thoughts were flying toward his profile, the softness of his lips, and now I was lost, tangled in his question.

"When you paint, may I watch?"

I got an image and giggled. Watch like a voyeur. "Watching me paint is ...I don't know. It is my soul time." Would I be distracted if he watched me? Maybe it would be good to find out how we do together.

"Well, I paint when I am inspired. I don't know."

"Dannah, I'm sorry. I don't wish to intrude."

I could still see oil stains on my cuticles. Would it be an intrusion? "Yes, Mac. Sometime. Let's start as an experiment. You watch me paint and then we'll talk about it, how it was for each of us, okay?" I need alone time. We'll experiment.

"Tell me what she was like," I finally spoke.

"Who?" he asked, glancing at me, puzzled.

"Your wife."

"Ah, Jenny. We never thought we'd be with anyone else. We grew up together and so it was natural for us to become a couple. She was tall and blonde." He stopped and I wished I hadn't asked but I had to know.

"It must have been hard," I didn't know what to say.

"I didn't think I'd ever get over it. We had the easy kind of relationship one has with someone you've known all your life. She often was more like a sister than a wife. Sometimes we'd argue like we were still ten years old." He smiled, wistfully.

"I'm sorry to have asked but..."

"You deserve to know. Ask anything you want, anytime, Dannah. I'll show you photographs if you like. And Dannah," he paused, "I'm not looking for a replacement. I'm looking for a new relationship. I didn't think I'd ever say that ...until I met you."

∞

A valet took Mac's car to park it and Mac followed me around to the back entrance. We slipped into the kitchen filled with aromas of roasting turkey, baking ham and other enticing treats.

Regina looked up and scolded me in rapid Spanish, shooing us out of the kitchen, past a table full of pies. She didn't give me time to introduce Mac so we walked down the hall and I heard voices from several rooms.

Mac lifted my coat from my shoulders and slid off his own to give it to the hat check person near the main entrance. Yes, Grannie, he's a gentleman. Mac took the plastic numbers that identified our coats and put them in his pocket.

The living room was filled with people, some I knew and others I didn't. An old couple sat by the fireplace talking. Loren looked fabulous in a green velvet gown as he clung to Marshall's arm. In the corner near the grand piano, a harpist played background music.

Children were running around and a nanny rounded them up and ushered them into the little theatre for a puppet show.

"Dannah," Harrie called out, hurrying toward us with Tad Duncan in tow. "I want you to meet Tad."

"Tad. I'm Dannah. I think we met before when the bank funded an art project for seniors a few years ago."

"Of course. Pleased to see you again," he said and I liked his voice and was happy for Harrie.

"This is Mac MacGregor," I said turning to watch his handsome profile as he greeted both Harrie and Tad.

"We'll have to talk later, Mac," Tad said. "The bank is willing to set up a matching grant for the pipe band. It's been in the works for a couple of years and it looks like it will finally come together." Tad took out his business card and gave it to Mac.

"I look forward to our conversation, Tad." Mac flashed a smile that melted me even when it was directed elsewhere.

"Harriet, didn't you promise me shrimp?" Tad looked at my beautiful friend and she guided him toward a table of food.

"Are you hungry? Thirsty? Shall I find us something to drink?" Mac asked.

"Not hungry. I've decided not to drink alcohol until I get used to this new medication," I said.

"You are a wise woman. Would you like sparkling water?"

"With lime."

A waiter passed and he ordered two.

I waved at Hubert and his round wife Rosie across the room. They were engaged in conversation with Mr. and Mrs. Salamone. Waiters and waitresses were circulating with hors d'oeuvres. More people had arrived. I turned and noticed Charlie had just entered, his towering mohawk a chartreuse green, the edges, red.

∞

Everyone turned at the trumpeted fanfare. I grinned as I saw the impish jester proudly set the instrument aside and bow. He was dressed in satins of every color. His smile was magic and his eyes twinkled. He winked at me. I giggled as he did forward flips across the carpet. Circling Mac and me, he suddenly rolled between Mac's legs and grabbed my hand and kissed it.

"Me Lady," he said formally.

"Joseph," I whispered, and curtsied.

With his hands above his head like he was ready to make a great pronouncement, Joseph walked several yards away. Our eyes locked. I turned and pushed Mac back several feet. "Be ready," I said. "To catch." Slipping out of my heels, I bent and set them aside, faced Joseph and parted my legs and steadied my hands on my knees, my chin tucked.

Joseph skipped and danced and whooped and somersaulted across my back into Mac's arms. The audience applauded wildly. Mac looked somewhat astonished but his grin was true. If he wanted

169

to be around me, he'd have to take my spontaneous moments and friends. I laughed as he sat Joseph down. I bent down to hug Joseph.

"We'll talk later," he said and turned to lead everyone in to dinner.

"Talia certainly knows how to throw a party," Mac said, slipping his arm around my waist. "I hope you'll tell me later about your tumbling friend."

I slipped into the chair he held back and nodded. He sat to my right.

"Joseph the Jester," I said, nodding toward the head of the table where my longtime friend stood on the chair. "One summer I worked at the Fondis Renaissance Faire painting back drops. I stayed on, filling in wherever needed. I met Joseph there and he taught me a few routines. You'll see him around Fondis. He's actually CEO of Chipdom, a microchip factory over in the industrial area. But he loves jesting and does gigs occasionally."

"Ladies and Gentlemen," Joseph shouted, calming the group. "May I present my Lord and Lady."

Everyone turned to the double-doored entry as Talia and William entered, beaming and holding hands. Instead of taking their places at opposite ends of the table they sat together at the far end of the table from Joseph.

Regina and Leonardo orchestrated the serving of three turkeys, three hams and an abundant array of side dishes. It was a Christmas I'd always remember.

"Everything's right with the world," I said as Mac reached for my hand.

38 /

"Dannah, I'm so sorry to wake ye, my love," Mac said in my dream. I smiled. He'd said, "My love." I liked that. An angel floated over his shoulder. He touched my face with a finger.

"Dannah," he said again, slowly I opened an eye, realizing the dream was in real time.

How did he get in? Oh, yes. I'd given him Nirvana's key to pick something up and hadn't gotten it back. All I saw now was his eyes aching with a pain I didn't understand.

I eased up on an elbow. "What is it, Mac?"

"Me mum. I'm flying to Scotland now. I just had a call from my brother. Mum's in hospital. A heart attack. I leave from Fondis International within two hours. I had to tell ye." Lines creased his forehead, his eyes were bloodshot from crying.

"What can I do?" I asked.

He shook his head, unable to speak.

I sat up, running my fingers through my hair and staring without seeing at my easel where my necklaces hung.

"I'm so sorry to hear about your mother.." I pushed out of bed and took a crystal amulet from the easel. "Mac, here. This is for protection." I slipped it over his head. He grabbed me, holding onto me. I felt his body quiver with repressed tears.

"Come back to me, Mr. MacGregor," I said, pulling away, touching his cheek, feeling my own throat tighten.

"I'll be back as soon as possible, my love." He backed away from me and headed toward the door.

"Dannah," he said turning back. "I was waiting for the right time to give this to you. Now is not the best time." He reaching into his pocket and pulled out a small velvet covered box. I frowned.

"What?"

"Open it," he said, placing it in my hand.

I lifted the cover and gazed at a ring with foreign words written about the band. I looked up. "What?" I lifted it out, not knowing what to think, not wanting to guess, excited and fearful all in the same moment. He slid the band on my left ring finger. It fit perfectly.

"Mac..." I faltered. Seeing a tiny scroll in the box, I pulled it out and unrolled it. I could feel his eyes on me, intense.

"I am my Beloved's and my Beloved is mine," I read aloud as he recited the words in unison.

Collapsing on the bed, I dropped my head into my hands. How could this be? This wonderful man who I was just beginning to know and maybe even beginning to love, this man who seemed ideal, whose faults I had not learned—I had not known how deep his looks of love were rooted. I swallowed hard but couldn't push back the lump in my throat. My chest heaved a sob and I was crying. Angry tears. Why did he have to rush this? I wasn't ready. It felt all

171

wrong. My body quivered. He knelt to put an arm around my shoulders. I shook it off, sniffled and caught my breath.

Slowly I lifted my head, eyes on the ring that looked so comfortable on my hand and shook my head. "Mac, dearest Mac. I don't know how to say this. You were right. It is not the right time." I slid the ring off my finger. "I can't accept this." Tears floated the image of his face before mine.

"Dannah, please, dear one, I am leaving and want to know that you are mine."

"I can never be yours," I choked.

He pulled his hands from mine, a shadow of doubt crossing his face. "Why? Is there someone else?"

"No. It is the words. I cannot be yours, nor you, mine. It is just a romantic notion. I've fallen through those cracks before and been lost. I must be myself as I want you to be yourself. No belonging like a possession. I do not want to possess or be possessed. I love the ring but not the words, the idea of your gift, but I cannot wear it. Thank you."

"Oh, dear God. I did not see that, think that." He placed the ring back in the box and looked around like he didn't know what to do with it, finally placing it back in his coat. "I must go but I wish not to leave on this note." His hand stroked my cheek.

"Go. Go with your angel. Call me." I pressed my cheek to his. His lips were on mine and our passion didn't have a deadline at the airport. Finally I pulled away. "Go, Mac," I said softly.

He stood, pulling me up and off my feet and wrapping his arms around me for one last hug before going to the door. Moonie rubbed on his ankle and I had to pick up the silly cat so Mac could leave. We needed the comic relief and he left laughing.

"An angel flies with every airplane," I said. And he was gone.

Gone. A wind blew through my heart. I didn't know if his cell phone would work from Scotland. I didn't have his mother's name or address. I didn't know how to get ahold of his brother. Climbing back into bed, I held Moonie until she protested. I didn't get the airline or the flight number or if he changed planes or…I was afraid. Afraid for him, afraid for his mother and afraid for me. Afraid he'd stay in Scotland and I'd never see him again. Afraid I'd said the wrong thing when I returned his ring. My true self knew it was right but my sappy, lusty self thought I was an idiot. I tossed and turned until dawn.

39

At the gallery the owner was already placing my paintings on the wall. I felt hollow.

Nirvana danced up to me. "This is a great day—but you look down in the dumps," she said, hugging me.

"I'm okay," I lied.

"Harrie and Talia should be here soon," she bubbled.

"They're coming now? I thought maybe they'd come to the opening reception tonight."

"There they are," Nirvana pointed and dragged me to the lobby. She grabbed Harrie's hand, still holding mine. "Now that I have you all together." She laughed. "We're going to take a little tour of some of the finer art in the city. Who's driving?"

I frowned. I wasn't in the mood for a girlie outing. My paintings were here. I'd show up tonight. I was worried about Mac. I wanted to tell them but not here. I'd tried to call Nirvana last night but couldn't get through.

"Come, Dannah," Talia said. She put her arm around my shoulder. "Are you alright?" she whispered.

I shook my head.

"This will make you feel better. Let's go with Nirvana."

We all climbed into Harrie's SUV and drove over to the Museum of Modern Art. I hadn't been here for ages. It might be a distraction. I looked at my cell phone. No voice mail, no message, no text.. I wondered where he was now.

We walked up the hundred steps to the entrance. I lagged behind. I could still feel the ring on my finger. The ring I rejected. Maybe rejected the whole relationship.

I sighed as I entered the uniquely designed entry. It felt like hallowed ground. I needed to bring Mac here. Mac. I hoped he was safe and that his mother would be fine and that I could talk to him. I hoped he wasn't upset with me. Did he have an old girlfriend in Scotland? My mind ran in an endless circle of worry as I followed my friends. A curator hurried forward and was talking to them. I didn't feel like talking to anyone. Even my friends. I looked at an interesting Mondrian. I'd like to paint an angel in that style.

"Mizz Davidson, we are so honored to have you here. Your representatives have been most helpful," the curator said.

"What?" I took his extended hand.

He looked disconcerted.

"It's a surprise," Nirvana explained to him but I didn't know what she was talking about so I shrugged and tried to smile. Everyone was being so nice to me and I was being a twit. What surprise? I hated surprises. Surprises, unexpected things that made you crazy, like a man dropping his pants in your play room and Mama screaming. Nirvana said there were good surprises too. I doubted it.

"This way please," he headed down an oddly angled hall and opened a door into a huge gallery. We walked in quietly, almost in reverence. At the far end hung a massive painting by...my jaw dropped.

"Ta dah," announced Nirvana. "Isn't this fab? I figured you just hadn't had a chance to get around to re-mounting it. Everyone here loves it," she gushed.

"I..." I stared at my release painting, muted by the crackling of wadding and punching it. From this distance I could see different images and a sense of hope rising from the painting. I was furious and ecstatic at the same time. If that were possible.

"How could you?" I flared at Nirvana.

"Dannah, this is what you've always wanted," she stumbled over her words.

"Mademoiselle, we have already had several offers. I hesitate to mention the meager price so far. We must set a minimum and let the bidding war begin," he said.

"This is great, Dannah. Congratulations," Harrie said, hugging my shoulder.

"Dannah?" Talia said but I'd already turned.

"You know, temperamental artists," I heard Nirvana explain to the curator as I dashed out the door, running down corridors and getting lost. I never get lost. What was the matter with me? I stumbled into a women's room and leaned over the sink, breathing hard. Sinking to the floor, I sobbed until there were no more tears. My throat wheezed. My butt was cold. I was hopeless.

40

I don't know how much time passed. I ignored my cell phone. Finally, I washed my face with cold water. I looked horrid, puffy eyes, my skin pale and wan. Who cared? I didn't. My cell buzzed again and I sighed in resignation.

"Hello?" my voice caught.

"Dannah, is that you, honey?" The connection was poor.

"Mama?"

"Oh, honey, I was afraid you'd changed your number. How are you? You know I miss you."

"Where are you, Mama?"

"I just wanted you to know, I'm getting married. Oh, we're in Venice. We're going to India for a few months. Then I want to come back to Fondis so you can meet...Can you hear me, honey? I love you."

As much as she could or ever would.

"Mama? I love you too, Mama." The connection was gone.

I stumbled out into the empty hallway and began to wander through the maze of corridors, stopping to look at art but not seeing. A veil of shame constricted my throat, woven into the resurrected shroud.

I finally found the main entrance and saw my friends at the three exits. What? Like guards? I wouldn't be able to slip away quietly and walk. I stopped in the center of the solarium near the fountain. They came toward me, slowly, like I was a rabid dog. And then their arms were around me. We stayed that way a long time before Harrie led me back to her vehicle.

"We're going to Cerridwen's," Talia said quietly, holding my hand.

"Dannah, I'm so sorry. I thought you'd be pleased. I don't know what to say," Nirvana said, leaning her head onto my shoulder. "What do you want me to do about your painting?"

Harrie frowned in the rearview mirror like she didn't want Nirvana to talk.

"Whatever. You're in charge of it. I don't care. Whatever you want to do with it is fine. I'm done with it." I closed my eyes.

"You'll sign something to that effect?" She sat up straight and rummaged in her copious faux-leopard bag.

"Sure. Why not?"

"Not now, Nirvana," Harrie snapped from the driver's seat.

"Yes. Now. Or never," Nirvana returned the tone of voice.

"It's fine, Harrie. Nirvana can handle all the paperwork if she wants." My voice was lifeless. "Who is Cerridwen? I've heard you talk about her before but I can't remember." I didn't really care but I knew I needed to get out of this funk.

"She's an old Druidess who lives out in the forest on the east side of Fondis," Nirvana said, pushing a piece of paper with writing on it in front of me. I signed without looking at it. She pushed it over to Talia. "You're the witness."

Talia frowned but signed.

"Cerridwen is a wise woman," Talia said. "Some call her a medicine woman. A mystic. Others, a shaman. A Druid." Druids made me think of Mac. I needed to get over my distractions and pay attention to everything more.

"We've invited you to go out there with us many times," Harrie said, glancing into the rearview mirror. "Now we're just going to take you there." She smiled at me.

Sinking my forehead to my palm, I considered but couldn't come up with a protest. "Why?"

"Dannah, when do you have another appointment with the psychiatrist?" Talia asked.

"Next Tuesday. Why?"

"You need help now, girl," Nirvana said, tucking the paper into her bag and zipping it closed. "Right now. Did you notice you're pretty out of it?"

"Don't be so hard on her, Nirvana," Harrie said, turning onto a dirt road.

"Somebody's got to. And what happened to Lover Boy?"

"Mac? He flew out last night." My throat hurt when I talked. "No abandonment issues going on, huh?" I flinched at Nirvana's words. That was all that was going on beneath my fears. How many guys had said they'd take care of me and then split when things got intense? I didn't want Mac to take care of me but to be caring. I knew, logically, that Mac had to go. I would have wanted him to go, knowing the circumstances. Still my heart clutched with his absence. Would he be angry that I didn't take the ring? If he really cares about me, it won't matter. He'd have time on the plane to think about what I said. I can only belong to myself. That much I knew.

My fear of revealing who I really was through the painting was crushing me more. It was too raw, too personal, too un-nerving. It was the part of myself I hated. I'd planned to throw it away.

Even with the high tech suspension in Harrie's SUV, the vehicle bounced over ruts in the dirt road. We turned several times and I was lost. Again. In more ways than one. I slid against Talia and then Nirvana. What a metaphor for life. I had my friends to bounce off of, to stabilize me. I suddenly realized how grateful I was for their presence. That made me cry again—just when I thought I couldn't shed another tear. I guess my body is pretty good in the water works department.

Harrie parked under a Ponderosa pine. A wiry old woman with wild white hair stepped from the geodesic dome and hailed us.

"Cerridwen," the three others jumped from the car and yelled in return. I followed them. Nirvana turned back to me and slowed down. She put her arm around my waist. "You're going to be okay, Sweetie."

"Am I?"

So this was Cerridwen. I wondered what kind of airy fairy thing she was going to try to persuade me to believe. I wasn't buying. Life was too upside down for me now. I was just here to help my friends out. They wanted to help me so I guess I'd let them. But it wasn't going to work. I stepped through the entry.

"Come along, now, Dearie," Cerridwen said, grabbing both sides of my jaw with gnarled fingers, strong but caring. I felt a buzz of energy go through me. She led me to a table set for tea.

She served tea in bone china tea cups and homemade pastries on a silver platter. Any other time I would have been curious about the dome, about how the angles came together and how the space worked and was it comfortable and how did she heat it. Those thoughts drifted through my head but I didn't ask. I really didn't care. I just wanted to go back to the Coop and go to sleep and forget all this malarkey. They were talking hocus-pocus now, the alignment of the stars and the benefit of stones and healing energies. I sipped the tea. It was soothing.

"Time for some fresh air, Dannah," Cerridwen said.

I followed everyone out to the goat pen. A curly haired little white goat with the cutest face nibbled my shoelace. I laughed, bending down to scratch under her chin.

"That's Baby," Cerridwen said. "A little angora girl whose mama died and I took on the raising of her. She's very friendly. She'll sneak into the house if I don't keep the gate locked."

"She's so sweet," I said, looking back at the doeling.

"Sweet and spoiled." The old woman cackled. Did someone say she was a witch? She snapped a lead on the goat's collar, buried beneath beautiful white ringlets. Cerridwen handed me the rope.

"Time to walk out to the circle. The little one can keep you company."

She turned, heading out along a path near the pasture fence line. We all followed, single file. Baby and I brought up the rear. The pine trees felt nurturing. I started to relax as I paused while Baby nibbled at the tip of a yucca spike.

I was stunned to see massive standing stones in the middle of an open space. It reminded me of something I'd seen in a book about England. A stone circle. Stonehenge. Yes. It looked like that. The four women were already inside, standing in a circle, chanting. Baby and I entered. There was a space for me on the east side. Cerridwen took the lead and secured Baby. Then we all joined hands. I closed my eyes. My hands suddenly were alive with a jolt of energy. I opened my eyes to look at the other women. Their faces were calm, radiant, with eyes closed. They must be feeling it too.

The sparkling energy ran up my arms, through my head, down my torso and legs, connecting me to the earth. I felt it rise up again, as if the earth were giving it back, renewed, re-energized, returning a gift. The crown of my head tingled. I was lost in diffuse white light shimmering all around the circle.

Tilting my chin, even with my eyes closed, I saw an angel hovering above. A new angel of peace. Her face was sublime. I basked in her radiance. She looked right at me and I heard her voice. "Be at peace. All is well. Harmony starts within. All will turn out perfectly." I felt the muscles in my shoulders relax. The tension in my jaw disappeared. I opened my eyes and nothing changed. She was still there, casting a radiant light around the circle. Eyes shut, I inhaled a sweetness like roses and jasmine.

"Give me the shroud," she said. My eyes blinked open. Shroud? It was back, clung to my skin like dead flesh. I looked up at steady angel eyes. The shroud was hard to get off, sticky, attached. It came away in pieces as I clawed at my being, choking. I balled it up and pushed it to the center of the circle.

A chill passed over my body as the shroud burst into flames. My eyes burned as the vile substance vaporized.

"It is transformed. You are free, now. You are ready for the next step. There is no hindrance. When in doubt, think on me for I am always near."

I've painted angels for years because I see them in dreams. But they've never been alive, real. I've never heard an angel voice soft as a rainbow. Eyes open, eyes closed, there she was. Reality shifted. I didn't know what to think.

"Remember, call on me whenever you need me," she said. Gradually her form disappeared into the glowing light.

I opened my eyes again and felt tears rolling down my cheeks. Tears of peace. I didn't know they were possible. Soft tears, not gut wrenching sobs.

"You look radiant," Harrie said, smiling as deliriously as I felt.

"I am," I smiled back at each of them in turn.

"Thank you."

The goat bleated and we all turned, laughing. The curly haired kid pulled us back to earth.

41 /

The Coop was my refuge. I'd snuggled into bed, Moonie curled around my feet, and checked my cell. A message from Mac was garbled and full of static but at least I learned he was safe on ground.

I thought my friends all wanted to rescue me—or distract me. Nirvana invited me to the Loft. Talia had welcomed me to the Palace. Harrie insisted I come to her house. Wonderful invitations but I needed alone time to assimilate the happenings of the last few days. Reluctantly, Harrie had dropped me off at home.

My dreams had been filled with light. I awoke eagerly and set a canvas on the easel. I roughed in images but had a conflict with perspective. Suddenly I realized that two paintings were trying to get on one canvas. I pulled out my other easel and put another canvas on it.

One painting was from my perspective as I'd stood amongst the standing stones. The circle of women, the radiant angel above. However in my dream state, I saw that each woman had an angel and I began to paint the hovering images.

The other canvas was from my angel's perspective, high above looking down on the standing stones, radiating light to one person. Me.

I mixed and blended colors, turned from one painting to another, back and forth, working rapidly, putting in what I saw and felt. Time passed. The sun went down. I only stopped to let Moonie out and discovered snow falling.

My stomach growled. I went to the sink and drank two glasses of water, glugging them down.

I studied both paintings from the little distance allowed. Yes. They were done. I liked them. I felt refreshed.

I sank to a kitchen chair and peeled a tangerine and ate each section slowly, looking at first one painting and then the other.

Moonie meowed and pawed at the window. I let her in, locked the door and we crawled into the sleeping bag. Moonie purred at my ear. I slept. I woke at dawn, the dreamscape pressed hard in my brain. I stumbled into the bathroom to pee and hurried back into the room to look for another canvas.

Tears rolled down my cheeks as I painted the figure of a man in a black overcoat, kneeling at a grave. An angel touched his head. A second angel held the hand of the departed woman, both images fading into the distance.

Mac's call came as I finished the final stroke and signed it.

"Dannah, she just passed," he said. I could hear the lump in his throat.

"I know. I'm so sorry, Mac."

"I'll have to stay longer to help with things."

"I know. Be safe. Come home when you can."

"Dannah, I miss you."

"And I you. More than you can know," I said.

"I want to say more but not now. I have to go."

"Your angel is with you, Mac."

And he was gone.

The phone rang again. "Dannah, you didn't answer your phone all day yesterday. Are you okay?" Harrie asked.

"I'm good and bad but okay," I answered, knowing it was vague. I told her about the paintings, about Mac and his mom.

"Have you had lunch?" Harrie asked.

"No. I haven't had breakfast," I realized.

"Loren and I are coming to pick you up. Loren has a new place to try."

I showered, feeling sad for Mac. Inside me I carried a sense of ease. I could be there for Mac in whatever way he needed. So many people had helped me. I could help him and not lose myself in the process. I was sorry not to have met his mother.

Sunshine bounced off the snow, sparkling bright. I pulled on a turtleneck sweater and jeans, old boots and my trusty down jacket. I was glad to be going out. Grabbing a packet of vitamins, I shoved them in my pocket and jammed on sun glasses.

Harrie and Loren knocked and came in. The painting of the man at the graveside, head bowed, was on one easel. One stone circle painting was propped up against the wall on my bed. The angel view of the stone circle still sat on the second easel.

I was ready to be out in the sunshine but both of them stood frozen in place, staring at my work. I waited. They said nothing. I didn't know if that were good or bad. For once it didn't seem to matter.

"Honey, you've made a breakthrough of some kind," Loren said. "These are stunning."

"Dannah, is this why I didn't hear from you?" Harrie's voice caught with emotion. "All three of these are moving. Especially the man kneeling. Is it...?"

"Yes. Mac just called. His mom died. I painted this from my dream."

We all hugged before going out to Harrie's vehicle.

∞

The Unicorn Café was darling, everything in white with carnation pink trim and golden accents, like the unicorn logo over the counter—quaint but not over the edge. We sat at a table looking out on a courtyard that would be delightful in summer.

I had a green chili omelet but couldn't finish it. We chatted, Harrie telling me about Tad's invitation to spend New Year's with him in Hawaii. Loren urged her to go but Harrie had reservations.

"Why do you hesitate, Harrie?" I asked.

"I'm just not sure of the status of our relationship. I really like him but it may not be the perfect match I'd hoped for."

"What's up, honey?" Loren touched Harrie's hand.

"The Hawaii invitation is to the condo he still owns with his ex-wife. She'll be coming sometime while we're there. I just don't think I want to venture into that potential row. They had a very difficult divorce a few years ago."

"I don't blame you," I said.

"Come over to my house, Harrie. Marshall said he'd help me decorate. We're having a few other couples over. You know them all. That is, if you decide to stay here." Loren hugged Harrie who tried to smile.

"Couples? I don't want to be around couples," she groaned.

"You know everybody. Not to worry. They're all gay. And you know what I always say? I don't mind straight people as long as they act gay in public." Loren giggled. Harrie managed a smile.

New Year's. I hadn't even thought about it. I hoped Mac would be home but knew he wouldn't.

"What?" I said suddenly, realizing they were both looking at me.

"You're drifting, Dannah. Shall I guess who you were thinking about?" Harrie asked.

I grinned, sheepishly. "You know. You talked about New Year's and that made me think of Mac."

"I'm sorry, honey," Loren said, checking his manicure. "You and Harrie both come over for New Year's. It will be perfect."

"Don't you and Marshall want to be alone?"

His face became dreamy. "Oh, yes. We're doing something very special New Year's Day." His smile was suggestive. We all laughed.

Harrie paid for breakfast. Loren and I chipped in for the tip.

Sunshine bounced off the newly fallen snow and Harrie drove around the lake before dropping me off.

42 /

Several nights passed with no dreams. Nor any word from Mac during the day. I finished a landscape I'd set aside last summer and suddenly saw little angel beings hovering around the trees. It became a completely different painting.

On Tuesday morning I kept my appointment with the psychiatrist, blurting out everything that had happened in the past week. I even told her about the magic moment with the angel in the stone circle.

She wanted to know how the medication was working. I thought it was fine. I had no noticeable side effects and I was feeling more stable. Even if my week didn't look like it. She said it might take a little while to notice a continued effect. She asked me to keep a Feeling Journal, noting especially what went on when I heard from Mac or when I thought about him. We went overtime again. I scheduled for the following week.

The next night was Spa Night at Talia's. Harrie, Loren and I rode up together. Talia had invited Nirvana but she was off to a concert at the Lyceum.

Harrie had a new clay facial mask from Australia. Loren brought new nail polish in a shiny hot scarlet with sparkles. I offered naked toes and a clean face, ready for the event.

Loren was my partner and we exchanged mud applications. "Your skin is so smooth, Loren," I commented, spreading the mixture along his jaw line.

"I still have to get electrolysis upon occasional," he explained. "And I do take care of my skin." He shook his head as he began to apply mud to my face. "You need to moisturize more regularly, Dannah," he scolded.

"I know. I get distracted and forget. A week goes by, then a month." I shrugged as my face began to tighten.

I gave a capsule version of my angel in the Stone Circle.

"Do you realize what you're saying, Dannah?" Loren smiled.

"I think I'm free of my restrictions," I said.

"That and so much more. You believe in your angels now. Your belief system has changed. This is magical, girlfriend."

"Yeah." He was right. I hadn't put it in those words. This change was soul deep.

My cell jingled.

"Hello?" I knew my voice sounded funny as my face became immobilized.

"Dannah, how are you, Sweet One?"

"Fine. Especially now." I'd been soaking my feet in the hot tub and stepped out, walking to a chaise and stretching out. Loren dried my feet and began a pedicure. I smiled at him and turned my attention back to Mac.

"There are many details to work out since Mother's death. She didn't keep track of things very well. I've been helping my eldest brother Matthew straighten things out."

"When do you think you'll come home?" I had to ask. I wanted to hug and kiss him and get more intimate.

"We've been talking about that. I don't know for certain. It will be a while." I could hear the hesitation in his voice.

"Oh." I didn't know what to say. I'd assumed he'd be back soon. He had to do whatever needed to be done.

"Might you consider coming here?" he asked.

"What? To Scotland?" I was astonished. Loren looked up and nodded eagerly.

"Think about it, Dannah. I know you're busy with your artwork. Just say you'll think on it, lassie." There was a yearning in his voice that made me want to fly into his arms. Literally.

"Where can I call you?" The static increased in the phone line but I managed to write down a number with lipstick on a napkin. The phone cut out.

Talia and Harrie pulled chairs close to me. "Well?" they said in unison.

Loren trimmed my cuticles.

I told them what he said. "How can I afford to fly to Scotland?"

"Didn't he say he'd pick up the ticket?" Loren asked.

"I don't think so."

"Do you want to go?" asked Harrie, who still hadn't decided if she would to go to Hawaii.

"Yes and no. The Colonel would take care of Half Moon I'm sure. I just don't know where I'll get the money. I haven't heard from the gallery so I don't know if I sold my paintings." I chewed at a fingernail.

"Stop that," Loren commanded. "You'll make it hard to do the manicure."

"I need to talk to Nirvana. You know she applied to that gallery in New York for me?"

"Great," said Loren. Talia smiled. Regina served protein drinks with blended fruits.

"Dannah, I'm sure I have enough miles to give you a free round trip ticket," Talia said.

"Really?" The possibilities shifted. "Really?" I repeated, unnecessarily.

"Really." She laughed. "Do you have luggage?"

"No."

"I'll loan you a set," Loren said.

"Passport? Is your passport up to date?" Harrie asked.

"I don't know. How long are they good for?" I'd gotten one to chaperone a group of art students to Paris a few years ago.

"Ten years. I'm sure it's still valid. Do you know where it is?"

"Yes." I kept everything of value stashed in the back of my oil painting box.

"Call him back," said Loren as he began to massage my feet and calves.

I groaned. "I'm relaxed and excited all at the same time. Do you really think I should go?"

Again Harrie put it back on me. "Do you really want to go?"

I closed my eyes and saw my angel. She smiled but I couldn't hear her words.

"Yes. I do. I'm scared. But I want to go."

"We are your fairy godmothers," Loren said, and laughed. "If you want it, we'll make it happen."

"Go on. Call him," Harrie said.

Talia handed me a phone. "Use the ground line. You might get a clearer connection."

They politely walked over to the snack table that Regina had prepared while I dialed the number from the napkin.

"MacGregor residence." The voice had a brogue but not my Mac's.

"Oh. May I speak to Mac, please?" I waited while he called out. "Little brother, it's for you."

"Dannah, is that you?" Mac asked, catching his breath.

"Am I interrupting you?"

"Never. This is a much better connection. I'm glad you called back. Thank you."

"Mac. I'm coming. You did mean it, didn't you?"

"You're coming here? Oh, Dannah. Thank you. I'll pick you up at whatever time you fly in. Let me know what flight you arrange."

We chatted and talked about the possibilities. He did plan to pick up the cost of the flight so Talia could save her air miles. He said I could catch a flight to Heathrow. He could meet me there and we could drive or fly to Edinburgh depending on several factors. Whatever. As long as I were with him, I wouldn't care.

185

"When is the funeral?" I asked.

"Tomorrow."

"So, it's probably best for me to come after."

"I'll be waiting for you."

I closed my eyes and saw two angels smiling.

I handed the phone back to Talia who dialed immediately. I heard her say William's name. He'd flown out the day after Christmas to a meeting in Germany.

"Hold still," Loren said as he grabbed my little toe to apply polish. "You can't go anywhere right now and we have to get you fixed up for your big journey." He bent, concentrating on the polish.

"This is fabulous, Dannah," Harrie said.

"I know." I grinned. "Here I thought you would be the only one taking a big trip. Now look, it's me, too." I shook my head. "So, what's up with you and Tad anyway?"

"Traveling with someone is a good way to get to know who they really are. I thought it was an opportunity. However, his ex demands equal time at the condo. I can't deal with that." We laughed. "I don't think I'll be the traveler this time."

Talia walked over and sat back in the chair. "William will take care of it. He'll call back as soon as he has it figured out. He has three days in the Alps without any business. I may fly to see him." She smiled. Talia always said the two of them were on a perpetual honeymoon because he was never around long to be annoying. None of us referred to his indiscretion a few years back.

"But Talia, Mac said he'd pick up the ticket," I said. Then I'd owe Mac. Talia had already done so much for me. If I have the power, I want to make enough money so I don't always have to get help from friends.

"William can expedite things faster than anyone, Dannah. Let him handle it and use the money for something else."

I never knew how to thank my friends enough. I'd given them all paintings. It didn't seem enough. One of these days I might have enough in the bank not to worry about the cost of a flight.

"Remember your nails," Loren cautioned.

I blew Talia a kiss and then Loren.

Regina touched Talia's shoulder and spoke rapidly in Spanish. Talia responded and they both laughed.

"As soon as your nails are dry, we're going to the wardrobe. I have some clothes that Regina can alter so you have a few extra traveling items."

"Talia, thank you for everything." I had tears in my eyes. This was all going to work out. Loren put the final coat on my fingernails.

43 /

Nirvana flew to New York for the final gallery pitch. I was in a fever of excitement. Nirvana had taken all the paintings from the Coop and framed them. She'd beamed as she handed me my first ever credit card and told me not to worry about money while I was gone. Yeah, right. She was elusive about the amount because things were happening. Whatever that meant. When I fly back, I'm going to get organized about my funds.

I'd talked to Mac each day. He was pretty down after the funeral. I couldn't wait to see him, to hold him. To tell him more about the angel watching over his mother. To see what his home was like, to meet his family.

I stood at the huge plate glass windows looking out across the runway at Fondis International and watched planes take off. I could hardly believe it would soon be my turn. Flying to New York and then London. How could this all be happening?

I closed my eyes and saw my angel. This time I saw the incoming plane with its angel and then each passenger traveling had an angel or two in attendance. It was very crowded—it will make a huge painting. I pulled out my art bag, unzipped the front pocket and grabbed my sketch pad and a pencil.

My angel now fluttered on the other side of the glass pane. I saw her lips moving. I hadn't been able to hear her voice since the stone circle. I don't think angels are supposed to frown but she was frowning.

"What?" I said aloud and opened my eyes. The man next to me moved away. How could he tell I wasn't talking on my cell? Maybe he was just giving me space.

I looked back, eyes open, and she was still there. I pulled out my cell so the other passengers wouldn't think I was nuts. "You smiled when I said yes to Mac," I said defensively.

"Yes. You are making choices. Are you pleased with your choices?"

"Of course I am. I've changed. I know what I'm doing. And Mac loves me."

Oh my God. I heard her voice on the cell phone.

"Yes. This is more acceptable. Now, tell me how you have you changed?"

"I know, you want me to spell it out, say it out loud so I know it as well as you. I just have. Mentally, emotionally, spiritually. And I've changed how I think about men. You're with me all the time. Right? You know."

"Incoming call. I'll talk to you later." She shimmered out of my vision. The cell rang.

"Hi, Nirvana."

"Hi. Look this is all happening very fast. The gallery wants my work AND their sister gallery will do a New Year's show of your angels. This is unheard of with this short notice. Somebody cancelled this morning. You're in. I'm flying home tonight. Where are you?"

"Wow. I don't know what to say. I'm here at the airport. I was on my way to New York and then to see Mac in Scotland."

"Oh, God. This is not good timing. Shit, Dannah. Figure out what you want to do. This is a once in a lifetime opportunity. Call me back. I gotta go."

She hung up.

How could this be happening? Now? What would Mac think? Did my angel already know? What's my angel's name? Why haven't I asked? I am so self-centered. I paced back and forth, looking mindlessly toward the prairie. What kind of a crazy mess is this—be with Mac or get my work in a New York gallery? Who can I talk to? I can't even believe I might be in a New York gallery. Nirvana is a miracle worker. Fondis artists take New York. Or do they forget New York and follow their hearts?

My heart. What do I even know about my heart except it's been broken and inadequately mended. I dialed Nirvana's number.

"Talk to me. What should I do?" I asked.

"Your choice, Sweet Pea. But this time it has to be a quick choice."

"I don't know what I'll say to Mac."

"That's a pretty important revelation." I heard her sigh.

"How?" Why can't I just make up my own mind. Why am I in such a dither?

"Dannah, how is Mac like Zip?"

"Not at all. He's gorgeous and nice and..."

"What did you tell me about Zip when you first met him?"

"That ...that he was good looking and had beautiful eyes ... and he brought me flowers."

"See what I mean?"

"That I don't really know Mac any more than I knew Zip." I sank my head into my hand.

"How do you feel about going over there? What are you hoping for?"

"There's static in the line. I'm going to help him. His mother died. He needs me."

"You're not going for yourself?"

"Of course I am."

"You're familiar with the term 'enabling'?"

"Damn. So? Oh, no. You think I'm enabling him? Shit, Nirvana. Who's side are you on?"

"I'm always on your side. I just want you to be absolutely certain. I don't think anything. I'm just asking questions. Are you balanced within? Are your masculine and feminine balanced?"

"No." I was defiant. "What do you want from me?"

"Always the truth. Sometimes it's hard to find."

"What? The truth or the balance?"

"Aren't they both the same?"

"I don't know anything, anymore. I'm just afraid I can't have sex, that I'm 'broken', that I won't be able to let a man touch me again." I blinked, trying to hold back tears. I'd said it out loud, couldn't take the words back. Fortunately Nirvana didn't press. I looked over my shoulder. No one was close or listening.

"And Mac?"

"I want him but we haven't been intimate yet, so I don't know."

"It sounds like you may be getting to the bottom of this. What will happen if you don't go to Scotland?"

"I don't know. I guess I'll find out. You call just as I'm about to board the plane. What is your agenda? What do you get out of this?"

"No, agenda, Dannah. I just want you to be certain of your choices. I admire that you've come this far. Now I think there is another choice. An agent here in New York wants your work. It's your choice."

"You think I'm rescuing Mac?"

"No, not necessarily. You decide that. Tell me what is your experience with gallery owners?"

"Now or never. They grab you and hang you and or forget you."

"So, leaving now is giving up your long term goal of showing your work in a New York gallery...and going to help a man you may or may not love."

"I think I love him. What would you do, Nirvana?"

"Oh, no. You have to answer your own questions, Dannah. What would it look like if you didn't go?"

"Just cancel my reservation? I don't know. I haven't thought of it."

"How do you think Mac would feel?"

"I told him I'd come. Oh, damn, Nirvana. He is so dear to me. Kind. Considerate. He gave me a ring. Anyway, I think he would understand."

"He gave you a ring? What kind of a ring?" Her voice was quiet and I could imagine her eyes, hawk-like.

"I don't know. Certainly more than a friendship ring. I gave it back. The words said I belonged to him, him to me. I can't belong to anyone. Just myself. It was beautiful. Part of me wanted to take it."

"The choice is always yours. If you take care of yourself, he can take care of himself. You come together as equals. Not a one-upsmanship scenario."

"I don't even know where to begin."

I leaned back into the memory of him. Our bodies wanting to touch everywhere and our wanting put on hold by me, by his mother's death and would it, could it ever be the same and if they played that music once down at the café, could people see my memory desire when he was so far away now? My mind knowing Mac but I still didn't know and he was gone and I yearn for him but the shadow music plays on, luring me to desire, my belly, hot. The truth sometimes has been repackaged. What is the real truth without any frills?

Mac, so far away. If we are to be together, he will understand my change of plans. My choice. His love cannot be predicated on my doing only what he wishes. I need to show my paintings and now there is a chance.

Am I being selfish? Or will I deny my future as an artist?

It is like potential magic but I am standing on a cliff and there are two roads and I can only take one and if I misstep I will plummet into the abyss and then there will be nothing so I must choose now.

When Nirvana and Harrie conspired over the tarot and said I was on the Fool's journey and of course I was standing on the edge and I just needed a little encouragement from the dog but I don't have a dog. Moonie doesn't want to jump off any cliff.

Harrie says it's easy because no one depends on me and I can do what I want but she doesn't understand. It's not true because Harrie still gets alimony and Talia's husband is a trillionaire or something. Loren understands but forgets and then the angels tell me it is my choice and I finally jump because the choice is a man or my art and only in the middle of the abyss will I have true freedom.

I must find what the choice actually was and means and... I'm not falling. I'm floating so if I can float maybe I can fly and if I can fly what else can I do?

"What do you want to do?" Nirvana interrupts my spiraling thoughts.

I closed my eyes, looked for my angel. I couldn't see her but I felt wings surround me. I heard words in my head. It's your choice. I'm always with you. So, when the angel smiled at Talia's it wasn't an affirmation of the "right" thing to do, just that she would be with me. I opened my eyes.

"I want to cancel my reservation to London. Get my work to the gallery. If Mac and I have a future, this won't matter. I hope he will understand. I've spent my life working on my art. I've known Mac a couple of months. And, oh, Nirvana, I do like that man."

"I know you do. I'm happy you're taking care of yourself. It will all work out. I fly back on a red eye. See you in the morning with more details."

Now I had to call Mac. What time was it in Scotland? Probably morning so it would be okay. Am I being selfish? Will he be upset? Hubert and Charlie will have to ship out my paintings. My mind flipped all over the place.

I walked back to security, explained and waited while my luggage was retrieved. I could take a bus home but how cumbersome with these overstuffed bags. I looked up and saw a Green Cab. Yes, I hailed a cab. See, I have changed. I over tipped the cab driver who wanted to give me a tour of Fondis. I liked being on the generous end of life.

∞

"Time to get up, sleepy head," Nirvana called as she unlocked and pushed the Coop door open.

"Good morning. I couldn't get to sleep last night and had a headache and guess I slept in." Moonie cat purred. "And Mac in Scotland. Dear Mac. I called late last night trying to match his awake time." Sadness in his voice like a lost symphony.

How could I not go to him. Motherless now. He's a grown man. Get over it, my mean, inner teenage self muttered. Never would I utter those words out loud.

"Mac, are you okay?" I'd asked.

Static on the line, in the connection.

"Dannah, I miss you," his deep brogue sliding like his hand along my spine.

"Me too you. Mac, I'm..." Garbled sounds in the phone. His voice under water.

"Dannah, I can't wait to hold you in my arms."

I can't do this. "Mac, how are things going? Was the funeral yesterday?" And he told me of it, the pouring rain, the chill in his heart, of his toes, wet, and the sound of the earth clunking on the casket.

I should have been there. They buried her in the family cemetery and the dirt was mounded like a Druid monolith and his sister pushed daffodil bulbs into the soggy ground.

"Mac, I have to talk to you. We are..." And the cell fell dead. Looking at modern communication in the palm of my hand, I was frustrated. I couldn't connect. Technology does not promise heart relief. I need an antacid for love pain.

He called back. "Mac, Mac, I'm so sorry."

"I know little one. We are all sorry."

"No, Mac. Yes, I mean. Losing parents is sorrowful. I'm so sorry."

I didn't even know if my father were dead or alive so he was dead to me. Mama off in Europe or is she in India by now, with her new lover, companion she says, husband to be, and she's not dead but I can't remember how many years, three or four, since I saw her and she told me to leave Zip and like a bad daughter I didn't listen and—

"Mac, I'm not coming."

"What?"

"I'm not flying to London. I'm so sorry. I got a show in a gallery in New York City. A New Year's show. It's like a miracle. I'm so excited." My voice, fast, nervous.

"Oh, Dannah, I don't…congratulations. I'm happy for you."
And his voice so unhappy that I should change my mind.

"I'm sorry." I am and I'm not.

"Don't be sorry. It's fine, Dannah," he said. "I'm happy for you."

"My angels in New York, can you imagine?" I'm smiling and crying at the same time and then I hiccough. "Mac?"

"Dannah, I'll be here a while."

"I know." I pause and then my voice flies. "I need to get the paintings ready now. I really lucked out. I need to paint."

Should I tell him about his mother's angel? His angel? And there was fuzz in the phone. "Oh, my, the …Mac, are you there?" And he was gone. Am I abandoning him as I've been abandoned? Should I go to him? No wonder I didn't sleep well. Stay or go. Go or stay?

I have what I want and I don't know what I want and I don't know if Mac will ever come back to Fondis and if we can be the same.

"C'mon, dream girl. Let's get breakfast and organize the angels." Nirvana called over her shoulder again and I jumped up and headed for the shower, avoiding her questioning voice. Just get on with it. What I want is this.

∞

Nirvana sipped the black mud of espresso and looked hard at me. "Still on the fence?"

"Yes and no." The corner of her mouth lifted slightly. I knew she wouldn't let me off the hook and that I needed to be clear.

"I'm not your task master, Dannah, but if you're going to do this, you've got to go for it one hundred and fifty percent."

"I know. It was just the sadness in his voice that replays in my ear. Okay, I'll focus on myself here. I really have changed from the door mat I used to be. My body healed with western medicine and homeopathy, cranial sacral and Reiki. The painting release in your studio let me burst out of all that confined emotion. Counseling and psychiatrists helped my mental morass. The shroud burning in the stone circle and the angel coming with a voice really made me whole. So, my whole self made the choice to do the show."

"Good. Let's go."

44 /

Forget the Wright Brothers. Here comes Dannah Davidson and I'm on a ship and the sail is one of my paintings and we're skimming over clouds and it stops and I go to the angel's tea party.

It is wonderful, full of wonder and they're speaking in every language on earth and even the dead language Latin and ancient Anglo Saxon and I can understand them all and when I speak it is like a heavenly Esperanto and I wonder if I'm dead.

This was cool but I want to keep my body experiences going for a while and I sit up suddenly and I'm not in the Coop but in Nirvana's studio.

I pull out my sketch pad and draw the angel tea party, sketch details of faces and try to remember tidbits of conversation. "Silence is not golden; it is repressed," said a large red haired angel with a lemon pound cake. They all had tidbits of wisdom.

The possibilities are enormous. With this one gallery in New York and the next Fondis showing and then when Mac and I get together...and there the bubble bursts and what if I don't get back with him? Now he's hurting and I'm here basking in potential glory and maybe I just need to talk to my angel—whoever thought I'd say that?

Talk to an angel like some looney new age woo woo geek but I'm not like them. I'll just rest a bit. Close my eyes and let all these conflicting thoughts fly away with Fondis holiday traffic.

45 /

The first months of the year stuck together like a collage. Mac sent me a beautiful Scottish woolen coat. I sent the painting of the angels with his mother's passing. We talk on our cell phones almost every day.

The New York gallery wanted me to be there for the opening but they also wanted more paintings and I couldn't do both. I was going to stay cooped up at the Coop. The day before the opening, the gallery manager called with flight info. I took the red eye. Nirvana had a new red dress for me to wear to the opening. It was a crowded fantasy evening. I talked to art critics, buyers and other artists. I gave several interviews for newspapers and magazines. It wasn't just a dream. It was a dream come true.

When I flew back to Fondis, I painted day and night. Paintings were selling at the gallery here and in New York. It was an inward/outward time. Busy beyond memory, exciting, scary and again, so crazy busy.

Mac flew in for Valentine's Day. It wasn't really for Valentine's but for work. We met for dinner at ten that night. It wasn't the same as before but it wasn't over either. We sat for a long time just looking at each other. Sadness sat in the creases at his ocean deep eyes and behind that I saw what I hoped was love.

He was busy at work. I was crazy busy mounting another show at the Faerie Arts Gallery in Fondis and painting madly for another show in New York City. We managed to see each other for afternoon tea or a late dinner. It was not long enough to process. Someone was filling in for him at work but he was feeling the pressure of not being there. I was filled with the pressure of wanting more time to discover us. We were both too busy. We stood in the glaring sunlight at Fondis International a week after he'd arrived. I didn't trust my voice as we clung to each other. I did not walk him into the airport but hurried back to my car and wept.

On St. Patrick's Day I pulled away from the frenetic passion of painting and went to Nirvana's studio party. It was crowded with artists, friends and townspeople. Just before midnight, the call came. I guess they called me first. I didn't hear my cell phone. Nirvana answered her ground line amidst all the happy revelers, frowned, nodded. I watched her from across the room, only half listening to a gossipy woman. Nirvana hung up and beckoned me; then pulled me into the smaller studio where I'd done the release painting.

"What?" I felt it wasn't going to be good.

"I don't know how to tell you but straight out. Zip robbed a liquor store again tonight. This time there was an altercation. The police heard the alarm, arrived just as Zip shot the clerk. Just wounded him. Two of them shot at Zip. I'm sorry, Dannah."

"He's dead."

She nodded. We could hear the crowd celebrating, whooping it up. She held me, let me cry. Why would I cry? I remembered...remembering, I wanted to forget. Forgotten? Is it possible to erase the images, the pain from brain cells? Or does it just filter down into the sands of gray matter? And then you stub your toe on an angry old chunk? It all comes back, belching upward into your face. Grind it up. Blend it into the amorphous seas. Wash it away.

It is a new day. A new season. Or will the past cling like a barnacle? I want to be in the present. Not anchored by remembrances. Here. Expecting, hoping for a phone call from Mac—instead hearing about Zip. No expectations. Expectations throw me into the future. The future, a place the angels know. I don't want to know or hope. What is life without hope? But maybe it will be better than I hoped. Maybe hope is a restriction.

Zip...dead. How many times had I wished that? I can't believe it. How could it be true? Logic shakes his head and glares at me. Zip was asking for it. It was bound to happen. He'd brushed against the odds too often.

No tears rose now—but a massive sadness blanketed me. And a sense of release. I felt the earth beneath my shoes, the lake mist dewing my face but still, no more tears. Nirvana said I did not know Zip's life path. I do not. Somehow I think he lost the map to his path. It is not your problem, she said. It is not.

Fear evaporated from my cells like sweat drying.

Nirvana went to the funeral with me. I wore the old black dress Zip hated. Grannie's not-going-to-church hat. And my spiked heel boots. Nirvana wore a purple Sari. No one else is there but the Unitarian minister who tends to all the lost and disowned souls in town. Mac offered to fly back to Fondis and go with me. No. I didn't need him here. It was a completion, a closure I hadn't expected. Nirvana and I ended up at the pub where I'd last seen Zip. We drank margaritas and went to the Firehouse. She taught me how to heat and bend a metal rod.

A storm in Scotland took out the electricity, phones. No cell coverage, no email. My heart raced with delight when I received snail mail from Mac. He had lovely old fashioned handwriting. He said he was sad, sad about his mother's death, sad to be away from me. And he said he understood. He would wait and let his, our love, unfold. I still wasn't ready to use the "L" word unless it was for lust. And I wasn't ready to cope with that, either. The old crone in the woods, the one he'd trusted since childhood, had challenged him. Was he in love with me or the dream of me? He wrote that he was in love with me. He'd return to Fondis the following week. He wanted to court me as his father had taught him. He'd tried to be too American, too fast, afraid to lose me to another.

I re-read the letter several times. He thought he was in love me. No one had ever "courted" me. That would be different. I needed time and perhaps this was the best way for both of us.

46 /

Thank you...I can't say "Thank God" and I can't say "Thank Goddess" like Harrie or Nirvana but who can I thank? Like something outside myself needs to be thanked when things are good?

Which would mean I should scream and shout at something outside myself when life is screwed up but I don't think that makes sense either. I could thank my angel but I don't want to yell at her when things aren't good. Besides, I know what she'll say. She'll just smile that angelic beatific smile and say "It's your choice."

So why do I feel this great need to thank anyone? Okay. I thank myself for being willing to change. I thank myself for trying something new, for expanding my beliefs. I mean, what did I believe before the angels? Not much I guess. I believed I could trust Grannie and I believed Mama could make our fortune, funny I still say those words, but what about me making my fortune? I never even thought of it, let alone believed it so now I can believe in myself and then I can thank myself and there you are. What else?

No man is an island nor is any woman. I thank my friends who have been there even when I didn't know I needed a friend. I drifted off and a scintillating light filled the room. I saw my angel with a knowing smile and I reached to give her a hug, all feathers and light, she was as she embraced me and whispered in my ear, "The choice is always yours." The feather light kiss on my cheek lingers until I waken in the morning with a great sense of wellbeing.

I began to sketch the angel hug and know I can do portraits of people with their angel hugging them. If I can just sleep on it and I can feel light and energetic and know it is all as it should be.

I smiled at my winter pale freckles in the mirror. Yes, Dannah, you are a wonderful person, full of wonder, and you never said that before. Sure, my friends had said it but I didn't believe it so that's something I believe in: Myself and my friends and the angels. I want to start as a friend to Mac, not a lover.

The possibilities are endless and I believe in myself.

The mirror eyes check me out with a glint and the mirror lips smile and say "You've come a long way, Dannah Davidson. I love you."

My Brother's Keeper

William C. Thomas

1 /

But whatsoever hath a blemish, that shall ye not offer, for it shall not be acceptable to you. (Leviticus, XXII, 20)

Even now, I really can't blame my parents, who were two separate planets revolving around the same two suns: The Fondis Farmers and Mechanics Bank and my football superstar brother, Chuck Young.

Harold and Dorothy Young looked so settled and so happy that Dr. Brace, at one Country Club New Year's Eve Party, actually broke down and kept saying "If I had a marriage like that, think what I could do," which embarrassed Mr. Holmes, the lawyer, who maneuvered Dr. Brace out the door and into a taxi.

Of course Dr. Brace didn't know and it probably wouldn't have mattered anyway, just how distant my parents really were: they were the Banker and his wife, the leading socialites of Fondis, Colorado. She always made sure he had correct clothing, drove the correct grey conservative midsize sedan, lived in a correct and well-kept house and prompted him to remember the names of customer's wives. For his part, her bills were paid on time every month, including the doctor's bills and the medication bills; he supported her cooking classes; her art classes; her tennis and golf lessons and all the charities she was part of. He would always show up at a charitable dinner she or her committee hosted or a relay race for a disease or a hospital function where he would talk sports with the other men while she flitted from group to group.

Then they would come home and he would turn on the TV in his den, mindlessly watching the News and the ads: "THE RUNAWAY HIT, HERPETOLOGY AND YOU, STARRING FOUR DEDICATED BIOLOGISTS: TANNER SMITH, IAIN SANDERS, HAL JONES, AND ANH VU, TAKES YOU, EVERY THURSDAY,

TO THE MOST ENDANGERED PORTIONS OF THE WORLD WHERE MANKIND AND GLOBAL WARMING HAVE MADE SURVIVAL ALL BUT IMPOSSIBLE!" and she would go online or read a magazine until about 11:30 or midnight, turn out the lights, and go to sleep.

And I would probably be in bed by then, having gone to the Whispering Pines 4-H meeting, presided over by my best friend, Bonnie Lassiter and her mother, Barb, who was the club leader. Bonnie would drive me home most nights when we were studying together or working on our projects. She even made sure I had accommodations in the Lassiter trailer during Fair. I couldn't ask for a better or closer friend.

When a rabbit is threatened, he lays his ears back along his body and tenses his powerful hind legs, ready to spring, which I felt in a few seconds as I brushed Nebula, my prize Polish Rabbit, before he was grabbed by a pair of jaws, slobbering and huge fangs, closing on that small body, crushing it with a peanutshell sound underfoot and the body, screaming, writhing as I struggled against those fangs, pulling it free with a thud to my chest. Blood, warm and sticky, flowed from his mouth onto my white blouse and his black eyes, still unclouded and open, looked at me as I held him and I heard my brother laugh and saw the bored face of the Fair Princess during the afternoon's competition and my mother's screaming CLEAN IT UP when she saw the dead chickens and blood all over the carriage house and I heard a rushing in my ears and saw nothing but that dog, only a few feet from my face, his leash dragging on the cement floor.

I laid my rabbit's still bleeding body on the carpeted grooming table where he'd been, then grabbed the leash, its handle heavy in my hands, pulling the dog toward me with a jerk and jumped on the dog, kicking and tearing, my hands turning the leash around and around the dog's neck as I kept kicking, holding the dog up in the air as it yelped and cried to match my screaming. I forced it into a wall between two sets of rabbit cages and kept lunging at it, watching its nose scrape the wall and smear it with its blood and I heard it cough and wheeze and I knew I was killing it and I felt glad and triumphant that I was avenging something I had raised and protected and loved. Then a steel band wrapped itself around my waist and my arm was snapped into the side of a cage. I dropped the leash. I was lifted and hurriedly carried from the Rabbit Barn, my legs and arms still punching and lunging wildly.

"Lisa, calm down," a voice kept repeating. "Calm down. Calm down. Calm down."

Chuck? He'd said that. I shook my head. I was under the cottonwood tree at the white painted wood bench with the Rabbit Barn behind me.

"Calm down, Lisa. Calm down," the voice kept saying as the hoops of steel kept themselves around my arms and below my chest.

I suddenly went limp. My legs no longer kicked. My arms no longer jerked. "I just killed Barabbas," I said wonderingly. "I just killed Eddie Brace's dog." I said, hearing the Country Western music from the speakers above, feeling the afternoon sun, palpable in the unshade, and the sounds of confusion coming from the Rabbit Barn. .

"Hmm." I felt a cheek press itself into my back while the arms kept me in the air. "No trembling anymore, but that could mean you'll be weak—here—" I was carried to a bench under a tree and released. "Grab the bench, Lisa, and sit down," the voice ordered. I did so, breathing deeply after the constricting arms. The owner of the voice, Kevin Allen, in his plaid cattleman's shirt and blue jeans, his light cowboy hat only a little out of place, took the seat next to me.

I was in a car next to a little girl named Janie, who judged rabbits. I don't know how I knew that. I don't know how I knew the driver of the car was named Felicia and I don't know why I was on Road 17 headed for Kutch with them. I shook my head.

I began trembling again, shaking my head slowly. People who'd paused as he sat me on the bench, having watched me calm down, moved on, probably interested by the Sheriff's car that stopped in front of the Rabbit Barn and the purposeful stride of Sergeant Vern Lassiter, the older brother of Bonnie Lassiter, who went in, then stepped out, accompanied by an older man with large glasses, who had the dog by the leash. Vern pointed to the clump of trees a few steps away from where Kevin and I sat and the man led the dog to them. The dog, now subdued, wagged its tail as the man petted its neck. "How did you do that?" I almost murmured to Kevin, finding my voice was raw from screaming.

"What?" he asked, puzzled.

I swallowed and licked my lips. "Pick me up like that?"

He shrugged. "It gets people out of fights real quick."

"Oh," I answered, trying to figure out why he'd say that when Eddie Brace came pounding up.

"You seen my dog, Kevin?" he asked, panting, completely ignoring me, sweat matting his brown curly hair to his forehead and his breath behind his braces sour.

Kevin didn't say anything because Eddie saw the man with his dog under the trees. "What the hell?" Eddie yelled as he approached them. "There's blood on his ear!" Then he noticed the tender forefoot and the blood caked on the dog's nose.

I turned. Kevin was running after Eddie.

Eddie went right up to the man holding the dog, spitting at him, "You're gonna' pay for this, you old fucker! Get some kinda' pleasure outta beating a helpless animal? How'd you do it? Hit him with a baseball bat?" The dog, sensing Eddie's distress, began lunging at the leash as Kevin took Eddie down in a flying tackle, knocking the wind out of him just under a nearby tree. The old man was petting the dog and talking gently to him as if Eddie weren't there. Two additional police cars appeared, followed by an ambulance. A female officer stepped out, looked at Eddie, who was stunned, Kevin standing above him, and radioed. Two more uniforms came to stand next to Eddie. Kevin remained a moment, then returned to sit next to me.

"Do you know who I am?" Eddie demanded, yelling at the deputies, who helped him up, then shoved him into the backseat of the car. The door closed. An officer went over to the man, still holding the dog's leash, spoke a moment with him, then came over to where Kevin and I were sitting.

"Are you Lisa?" she asked. "Sergeant Lassiter asked if you would come in to the Rabbit Barn to make a statement—whenever you're ready..." she added.

"I guess I am," I said, standing and dusting my jeans. "Thanks, Kevin."

"Don't mention it," he said. "Um, bye." He rose and started to walk across the Fairgrounds toward the cattle barn.

I looked after his six foot five inch frame a moment as the officer remarked quietly, "He's a lot like his dad: real quiet but handles emergencies well."

"Hmm?"

"His dad—Undersheriff Mark Allen."

"Oh—yes," I answered as we entered the Rabbit Barn, wondering why she'd say something like that: so common. Then I realized why. It was to give my brain something to distract it from what I would see: a pile of food pellets in front of an open cage, an overturned table, and a pool of blood drying on the floor, beyond which was the spent body of Nebula, whose eye was clouded but still stared at me in silent accusation, like any helpless thing. I thought of an old lady who'd come to the bank to get a loan last summer and had been turned away. The hurt in her eyes matched Nebula's, I thought. The difference was that yellow tape was strung around the space where Nebula was and an officer was taking pictures while Vern Lassiter was at a table, writing down names and addresses. His radio crackled and he answered: "Edward Brace, Junior, sir." More crackling and Vern called out: "Deputy Forrester?"

The woman still standing with me answered.

"Please call the Sheriff on your cell phone."

"Lisa, I'd like to take a statement from you," Vern said after he wrote something down on an official-looking form. "Would you take a seat, please?"

"Where's Elizabeth?" I asked, wondering why the Rabbit Superintendent wasn't at the center of things, helping the younger ones comfort their rabbits, reassuring parents.

"Oh, just popped out a moment," Vern answered. "I'm sure she'll be back." He turned a notebook page. "I'd like you to tell me exactly what happened, Lisa. Take as long as you'd like."

His dark eyes were still hypnotic, I realized; as hypnotic as three years before when I really tried to dress for him whenever I went to Bonnie's: my hair just so; my glasses off and those contact lenses that hurt my eyes. Vern was only four years older than I was, and his dark hair was just wavy enough to curl above his right ear; his tanned face and arms strong and his square jaw showing determination.

I started my story and Vern took notes. He had me stop and repeat some sections, like when I attacked the dog and what I saw the dog do to Nebula, which made me start to tear up. He pulled a tissue out of the box on the table and told me to take my time. So I repeated it to him.

He nodded. "Did you know the dog belonged to Edward Brace, Junior?"

"Not until after I was carried out by Kevin," I think. "I mean—all I saw was the teeth and the black shape. I..." I couldn't answer.

He put the notes in front of me. "Read through these carefully and make sure I've gotten it all down as you remember it, but before you do, also realize you can press charges for the loss of your rabbit."

"Charges?"

"On this form, Lisa. If you feel it was Eddie Brace's fault that your rabbit died, you can check the box for the District Attorney's Office to press charges."

"Really?"

"Yes, ma'am. Now—Please read this statement and sign if it's correct."

I did, stood, and then sidled over to where the body of my rabbit still lay. Because the Rabbit Barn was a long, wide hallway with cages along one side, I could stand and not be in the way. Elizabeth came over and stood with me. She didn't hug me. I was grateful for that.

"We called your mom," she stated. "She'll be here in a few minutes. We can take care of Nebula's body for you, Lisa."
I nodded. I'd bought Nebula at a rabbit show a couple of years before. Elizabeth pointed him out to me, saying: "If I were to raise Polish Rabbits, I'd like to have that one, even though he's smaller than most."

I took her advice. Except for two of my thirteen rabbits, every one had been recommended by Elizabeth to me and the awards I received for them at Zebulon County and at the State Fair were pretty large. I'd taken her advice on a lot of things: she'd suggested I have a barn for my rabbits instead of cages in the garage or a hutch in the backyard. When I told my parents about wanting one, they looked at each other a moment and my mother asked why I wanted a "whole house for one rabbit when the garage would do," then stopped. My chickens had been in the garage. They died there.

"What sort of a barn were you thinking of, Lisa?" My father asked.

Elizabeth supplied the plans; my father hired a contractor to build the barn, which was up in two days, complete with windows that opened and shut, running water, heat and electricity.

Elizabeth, when she inspected the place, was impressed. "This will be a nice, secure place for rabbits," she told my father. He smiled his banker's smile: the one without teeth, that said It's all I can do to protect your funds, ma'am, and told her about how he'd arranged to have rabbit feed delivered every month: "All Lisa needs to do is open the hopper here"—he opened a door— "and get as much food as her rabbits need."

"It certainly is large," Elizabeth remarked. "Room for at least fifty cages in here with room to spare."

"Fifty cages?" My father asked.

"Oh," she answered airily, "some of the other rabbit judgers have at least thirty or so."

"Lisa won't need thirty rabbits, will she?"

"Oh no: just the number she thinks she'll need."

"Will you be able to help her with that?" he asked.

"Of course, Hal," Elizabeth promised.

From the back door, my mother called something about Chuck's basketball practice, which I heard, then didn't make sense of because she was saying, "I want to know where my daughter is right now!" and someone was saying "Right this way," and there she was, in her flowered skirt from Mrs. McDermott's garden party, reaching to hug me, right under the banner that hung from the rafters: Zebulon County Rabbit Judging Team Sponsored Solely by Farmers and Mechanics Bank of Fondis, which moved back and forth in the miniscule breezes that reached it. "What's happened? Elizabeth said your rabbit had been hurt—"

She saw the mess on the floor and stepped back involuntarily, right into Elizabeth, who steadied them both with a hand on my mother's shoulder. "Who did this?" my mother asked, pointing to the floor.

"Eddie Brace's dog," I answered.

"But dogs aren't allowed on the fairgrounds, are they?" she asked, looking at Elizabeth, who shook her head.

"Lisa—are you hurt?"

"Okay" was what I managed to say before she asked how it happened.

Elizabeth sketched it in a few sentences before my mother again asked if I were hurt. "There's blood on your shirt," she added.

"A little," I said.

"I'll take you home and get you changed," she said, "and have Dr. Eckert look you over. You never know," she added in a hopeful tone. I think she really wanted me to be sick or hurt right then so she could do something she'd noticed other mothers doing with their children.

"No," I replied. "I've got my clothes in the Lassiter's trailer. I'll change there."

"Let's get you in the car," she said. "I'm sure Dr. Eckert can see you today."

"Your mother wants you to see the doctor, Lisa," Elizabeth said in a tone that I knew not to cross. "We'll make sure your other rabbits are taken care of, okay?"

I nodded and followed my mother to her car as she speed dialed the doctor's number on her cell phone. "Of course I wouldn't be calling and asking if it were something simple," my mother said as she turned on the ignition and pulled away from the rail that said FIRE LANE NO PARKING, right next to the police car and maneuvered around the Wool Barn and into the parking lot, hitting the gas as soon as she reached Elm Street. She stopped at Main, angrily holding the wheel in one hand and the cell phone up to her ear with the other, looking, as I'd seen her in some fund-raising dinners, as if she were the last competent person on earth. Beyond her, at a construction site, a sign proclaimed THIS OFFICE COMPLEX FINANCED BY BRACE AND ASSOCIATES, LLC, WITH FUNDING FROM FARMERS AND MECHANICS BANK OF FONDIS.

I thought about Bonnie and her mom, Barb, probably still at the horse show where Bonnie was in the English Riding finals. I wondered if they knew about Nebula. Probably. Vern had probably called them. I knew that Elizabeth would make sure that whoever handled Nebula would do so gently, lay him in the plastic bag, and then make sure the body was taken care of.

"We just have a few errands to go," Felicia assured me from the driver's seat, suddenly appearing before my vision, *"then we'll get home, okay? I think we'll get another windchime from that new shop."*

2 /

Likewise...set thy face against the daughters...which prophesy out of their own heart... (Ezekiel:14,17)

"I saw Charles Holmes today," my father said as he cut into his Tandoori Chicken, one of those specialties from my mother's gourmet cooking classes.

"Anything wrong?" she asked quickly. Mr. Holmes was "the rich folks' attorney," according to locals because he represented Dr.

Brace, the Bank, and anyone else who could afford him, including my parents. Mr. Holmes had done something a couple of years before to help Chuck after he'd wrecked his car and lost his driver's license, reducing his community service to playing a couple of exhibition games with the Fondis Over Forties, the middle-aged athletic team, for charity.

"No; nothing wrong," my father answered. "Just a couple of housekeeping items for the Bank, and—" he pointed his fork toward me— "a matter of pressing charges against Edward Brace, Junior."

"Pressing charges?" My mother was intrigued. In her world, people did not press charges. They went to the Country Club and played tennis and golf and swam and they helped raise money for charities. "Who's pressing charges?"

"Lisa," My father answered, "swore in an affidavit taken by Vern Lassiter last Thursday that Eddie Brace killed her rabbit."

"His dog killed my rabbit," I said.

He looked right at me, his eyes steely. "I told Mr. Holmes that dropping the charges was the right thing to do."

"His dog killed my rabbit," I said, feeling stupid.

"That may be," my father replied, "but I'm not going to make that boy's life any more difficult by letting my daughter charge him for a dead rabbit. Pressing charges was not only irresponsible, Lisa; it was a violation of friendship. Do you understand?"

Friendship? I thought as I left the table and headed to my room: upstairs at the end of the house, across from my parents' room, where my mother had a constant play of birds twittering or a waterfall so she could sleep and not hear anything else that happened in the house, including rape, screaming or crying.
Friendship? Maybe between our fathers; nobody else.

"Eddie's got it tough," my father would say, and my mother would agree. "Eddie's got only one real friend," she'd observe for the umpteenth time, "that dog; and he never goes anywhere without him. Of course, last week, you know, was especially hard on him: His mother's getting remarried with no word after two years. Eddie was devastated and took a walk for half the night and no one could find him. They finally found that dog, standing outside a café on Elizabeth Street and there was Eddie, inside, eating breakfast."

Yeah: I knew all that. I'd heard her on the telephone while she prepared dinner for the past three nights. It was hard enough, my father would say, for Charles Holmes to get Eddie's dog out of impoundment for endangering the Fair; to have Lisa do this is just putting salt into the wound.

I had a cell phone. It sat, turned off, in its charger on my dresser most of the time because I really didn't have anybody to call and even though Bonnie texted from her phone all the time, I figured that I'd just say whatever I wanted to her when I saw her. This time, I had someone to call.

"This is the Prentices," the voicemail began. "Jeff, Jim, and Elizabeth are busy right now, but if you leave a message, we'll call you back as soon as we can." I recognized that voice: it was her son, Jim, the veterinarian now in Australia, who'd probably recorded it— what? Ten years ago? Wow.

"Elizabeth, this is Lisa. I want to talk to you about pressing charges. My father says I can't do it against Eddie Brace and I'd like to know what you think. If you want to call me around ten tomorrow

As I sat on the bed, I clearly saw an aluminum windchime being wrapped in newspapers and stuffed into a paper bag. "I sure thank you, Ms. Duncan," the proprietor said through his beard. "Can't hardly make a livin' without customers like you."
Elizabeth worked for Richard Calkins, who was "not the rich people's lawyer," by any means, she told me once. "We have a lot of clients who pay in monthly installments, Lisa, and sometimes clients who need help but can't pay at all, so we work something out. It's not quite the paycheck I bargained for, but it's comfortable enough."

No; she knew no way that I, at 17, could press charges, and why would I want to go against "your father's major business partner" when it was a matter of public record that she and the Fair Board had all pressed charges against Eddie? "Arthur Sanders was going to, initially, but he decided against it because of how much Eddie loved that dog. 'Heat of the moment,' I think he said."

"You pressed charges?"

"Yes, I did," she answered. "As Rabbit Superintendent, I expect anyone who violates the safety of the Rabbit Barn to be prosecuted."

"Oh. Is Arthur Sanders that man who got threatened by Eddie?"

"Yes. He's a reporter for The Divide-Review. He wrote that big story last year about you and Jenny and Kathy winning the State Rabbit Judging," which she had enlarged and framed on her office wall.

"Oh." I'd spoken with him on the phone. "What's the Fair Board charging Eddie with?"

"The same. Safety. Destruction of property."

"So when does it go to court?"

"There's a hearing scheduled for September 20th, Lisa."

"Could I come?"

"That's up to your parents."

"But Nebula was my rabbit," I protested, "and the reason I'd be at State right now! Isn't there anything I can do?"

"When you're eighteen," she said. "Not before. That includes pressing charges on your own. Lisa, if it makes you feel any better," she added, "I think this is something that Eddie won't get out of. I think he'll probably have so many hours of community service cleaning the Fairgrounds; probably a bunch of anger management classes; maybe he'll have to work off a fine."

But isn't that the way it works around here, Lisa? A voice asked inside me. Remember, when you were first raising rabbits, when Cookie wouldn't eat for two days and you asked for them to call a veterinarian, and they didn't? Remember that you had to call Elizabeth to ask them? That same day, Chuck cut his hand and they took him to the Emergency Room. Do you remember that you had to wait until they were sure he was all right before your father called the vet? Do you remember that Elizabeth loaned you a couple of books to teach you about rabbit sicknesses so you wouldn't bother your parents anymore? Remember how they acted, two years ago, when you went to feed the rabbits and all their cages were open? They didn't even bother to look; just told you to make sure you shut the door more tightly. Did they even notice when you put that padlock on the door? Not yet. It's been two years, right? Do you think they've noticed much? Do you think they really understood how you felt about Nebula?

The phone rang, shattering my thoughts.

"Is this Lisa?" a small voice asked. "I'm Sharon. Hi."

"Hi," I said. Who was this?

"I'm with Chuck," she said. "Have been for two months. I'm in Fondis at my sister's, and I'd like to meet you and maybe have lunch?"

"I'm busy," I said, feeling the old, creepy cold hands down my back feeling whenever Chuck's name was mentioned by other females.

"Can I give you my number?" she asked, "In case you have some time..."

"Sure." I took it down and tore the paper from the pad, stuffing it into my pocket. She'd be like all the rest, I figured: Chuck went out with a bunch of girls; had been doing so since he was 16, and the ones that looked like they were really serious suddenly stopped. My father always said that Chuck was just playing the field and wondered why the girls' parents sometimes stayed at the other end of the room during Booster Club functions and he really wondered when one father closed all his accounts at the Bank; but "some parents are convinced their daughters are always right."

You remember how guilty you felt about putting that padlock on the Rabbit House door? The voice continued. Just like when you wanted to put that hook on your bedroom door, remember? And your mother said it would put holes in the woodwork and when you did it anyway, after Chuck tore it out by banging his shoulder against the door. Then you had to fix it with glue and putty and sandpaper while Chuck watched, remember?

"It's funny, Lisa," Bonnie said casually as we were watching Herpetology and You a couple of nights later, "Most of the senior girls really like Tanner Smith: so muscular; almost dangerous looking, while you like Iain Sanders, who looks all right; but he's such a geek."

I shrugged and giggled. "I like brains," I answered simply.

"Well—that's the thing," she said, pointing a pretzel stick at the TV, where Hal Jones, "the awfully good-looking black guy," was explaining something about a gecko in Madagascar, "You were all over the place about Vern when he started the Police Academy, but when he started seriously working out and started to get buff, you weren't interested in him anymore."

"Hmm," I answered.

"Oh, look," she laughed. "Your geek's gone snorkeling!" The camera panned Iain Sanders, all 6' 4" of him, in red trunks and swim fins, stepping gingerly into the surf, then diving in. The camera followed the snorkel a moment, above a reef, then began to rise, taking in the immensity of the blue water and the lava floes and the white beaches and as it did so, a pair of red trunks floated to the surface without anyone in them.

"Where was I?" Bonnie asked. "Oh yeah. Do you have something against guys who have a body type like your brother?"

"I just like geeky guys," I answered after a pause, trying to sound nonchalant, hoping she wouldn't make the connection that was making my underarms moist right then: that a well-developed male body scared crap out of me.

When he was 15, Chuck was taking Body Building from a trainer my father had hired and what had been our basement playroom was turned into a weight room. I'd stood in the shadows, behind the wall where the washing machine was, listening to the man tell Chuck and my father: "Women love muscle. They find it irresistible because it's overpowering, but there's a lot more to it than that. You want to build until it's comfortable, then keep it trim; not turn into some sort of monster that has to work out five hours a day to keep from being flabby. That's discipline. That's what I'm training you to do."

My mother used to like to squeeze Chuck's sinewy biceps as he passed, and once, she playfully slapped his tight butt with a rolled-up newspaper and a lot of laughing as he chased her around the kitchen, grabbing the newspaper and swatting her with it.

Because of his weight training, I noticed, his hand on my arm was twice its size, sort of like a hand squeezing a toothpaste tube, and his movements, disciplined by the bodybuilding coach, made any wriggling away impossible. The hair that he'd started to grow on his chest and tight stomach was like sandpaper on my skin.

I shuddered, as the usual blurb came up:! NEXT WEEK: MOROCCO!"

"No, Bonnie," I answered, looking at the television, "I just like geeky guys."

"Like Kevin Allen?" she teased.

"I guess," I ventured. I'd never really thought of anybody I knew. I didn't feel especially ready to be interested, much less go out with them. Romance and all that was something I'd make time for when I made time for it.

"I think he's interested in you," she added. "I think he has been for a long time."

I chuckled, shaking my head.

"No—really, Lisa. Why did he show up suddenly in the Rabbit Barn when you needed him? Why was he the one who pulled you out?"

I shrugged. "Going to his truck or something?"

"When his truck was parked right outside the Cattle Barn? Awfully long way to go, halfway round the Fairgrounds, to get something from his truck if you ask me."

I'd never really thought about it, but Kevin was around a lot during Fair: looking at the scrapbooking exhibit when I was in the Open Crafts Show Building; talking with the Archery superintendent when I looked in at the Shooting Sports Booth; saying hi to me both morning and evening when I was taking care of my rabbits.

"Just another shy person looking for something to do between shows, I guess," I said dismissively.

She shot me a look under her dark hair as she gathered her car keys to drive me home. "You sure, Lisa?" she asked.

It took me awhile to get to sleep that night. I finally landed on something that just came: I was with a nine year old Rabbit Judge named Janie looking at preserves at BOONE'S ARTIFACTS, which had closed, I knew, about seven years ago.

"What do you think of this one?" I asked, looking critically at a peach marmalade.

She shook her head. "I like the ones with sugar," she said decisively, reaching for the boysenberry.

3 /

Shall the prey be taken from the mighty
or the lawful captive delivered? (Isaiah: 49.24)

February 2nd. Groundhog Day. My fourteenth birthday was a lot like my thirteenth birthday and a lot like my fifteenth birthday. We'd go someplace for dinner, then I opened presents afterwards at the house. I'd decide on what kind of food we'd eat and my mother would pick the restaurant based on what she'd heard someone say about it. When I was thirteen, I wanted spaghetti, which meant we went to Aldo's Trattoria, where they had fish, chicken, and lots of bread but no spaghetti; when I was fourteen, I wanted fish. So we went to Boston Chowder House, where they served every kind of fish soup but no fillets. When I was fifteen, I thought I'd play it safe and say I was in the mood for Mexican, but even then, what was served wasn't what I wanted. We ordered rice, beans, flat bread that wasn't tortillas, and fish and chicken at Playa Fresca. My father, who probably preferred going to a place where he could read the menu, usually put a good face on and let my mother order the house specialties, which sometimes involved talking to the chef. My father tried to look interested as they chattered over sauces or whether olive oil or butter should be used in a sauté. It must have looked a lot like her birthdays, I thought: Uncle Henry would treat her to a big dinner at Cunningham Chop House and invariably invite someone else to join them: a local widow; a couple of other farmers: people he'd talk with while his niece, Dorothy, quietly celebrated her birthday. The McDermotts had once joined us on my birthday at the Chowder House, and while Lydia talked with my mother and Mike talked with my father, I wondered if I'd do the same thing my mother had done to Uncle Henry: after so many years of being ignored, she just stopped going there. She ignored the end of Uncle Henry's life as he'd ignored the beginning of hers. Chuck, who wasn't in the least interested and who grumbled that my birthday dinner made him lose practice time, ate everything available at the table: crackers, vegetables, bread: he once even ate the side dish of jalapenos!

And I'd usually sit quietly, wondering what Bonnie was doing or think about homework while my mother gushed about the food or my parents talked adult talk.

"I saw Ed Brace today," my father said between spoonfuls of Oyster-Beer Soup. "He's still hurting."

My mother nodded. "Takes time to get over these things."

"But it was over a year ago, and he still wears that hangdog look and talks about how much she's milking him and whether or not he can send Eddie to Florida to visit her and how much therapy at Whispering Pines is costing for both him and Eddie."

"Whispering Pines?" I asked. That was the name of my 4-H Club.

"No, Lisa," my mother laid a hand on my arm. "Not your 4-H Club. It's a mental health center where people go for help." She looked at my father with a finger to her lips, which meant not in front of the children. "Hal, did you see the story in The Divide-Review about Sheriff Thompson?"

"About the same time the Feds did," he said, not smiling. "They called, then sent down an auditor. I'm glad it was just one. He stayed from nine til two, interviewed the cashiers, then told me he'd be in touch. Nothing out of place, thank goodness."

"They aren't going to arrest him?"

My father shook his head. "Long administrative leave. Undersheriff Allen will take over the job until the investigation's done."

"Do you think he really did it?"

"Used Homeland Security funds to buy a condo in Vail?" My father shrugged. "If he did, it was pretty stupid."

My mind went on to after the dinner. I'd probably get new clothes; a CD of tunes they thought I'd like; some books, perfume, jewelry: what they couldn't supply in time or attention, they supplied in things. That was fine by me. They could devote as much time as they wanted to watching or encouraging Chuck: I had activities that they either couldn't understand or were bored by.

The one Saturday that my mother endured my rabbit judging, she sat on the edge of a folding chair, smiling in a brittle way at anyone who approached her, taking calls on her cell phone that lasted hours, flipping through a magazine. Obviously, she had a great deal to do, and it wasn't with me. Her childhood with Uncle Henry was a lot like that. He never had time for her; just got her clothes and saw that she was fed. About halfway through the judging, Elizabeth spoke quietly with her and assured her I'd be driven home after the judging. My mother's relief was really kind of funny, even though I didn't think so. I'd asked her if she'd like to look at the Satins because their fur was so smooth: "Oh—later, Lisa—" she said, punching a number into her cell phone.

Elizabeth called my father that night. Instead of the obligatory attendance at Rabbit Judging Tournaments that most 4-H parents had to deal with, because he and his wife were busy, would he like to contribute some amount that would help the Rabbit Judging Team? Of course, Lisa would be picked up and dropped off by Elizabeth. My father agreed. That was about the time Elizabeth bought the Rabbit Judging van, which she picked up all ten or twelve of us on Friday afternoons in and drove to her house where we'd have pizza afterwards; then the van would take us to the Rabbit Judging Tournament the next day.

"Did you like your bisque?" my mother asked, seeing I was about to the bottom of the bowl. "It's made New England-style, with just a touch of Sherry."

Dinner was almost over and heaven knew what would happen after my parents had gone to bed, when my mother had her sound machine on and Chuck could prowl freely.

He did that night after they'd gone to bed. I had my presents: boxes of clothes, a few small boxes of jewelry, a couple of CDs, all over my bed and was just going to stack them near the closet when he came in. I froze. Funny, I still froze when we were at the SAC game against Notre Dame and Chuck came to hug me, some three years later. I froze that night, too.

He smiled that smile that everyone loved: that smile that I hated because I knew it meant I had to pay. "No, Lisa; I've found something else now," he said, putting a jewelry box on my dresser, then kissing me on the cheek before he quietly shut the door behind him. "Happy Birthday," he'd said as he left.

That was the last time.

I opened the box. In it was a heart-shaped locket with his picture inside. I wore it all the rest of the year, its thin chain and small heart between my breasts: a reminder of tenderness that I sometimes felt for Chuck—immediately followed by revulsion. I'd pull on the chain in Math class; just a small tug; and I'd be back in the thought of the house we'd share together: a large Victorian place full of antiques where I'd have my home office and he'd come home after playing football for a professional team. Everything would smell like lemon oil and pine and I'd make him some wonderful dinners! Then I'd remember his laugh when he said he'd kill my chickens and the memory was replaced by sleepless nights where I'd soak the sheets in perspiration.

4 /

...when I begin, I will also make an end. (I Samuel:3.12)

So the summer collapsed into the third Monday in August, when students returned to Fondis High School.

Dorothea Harris, head cashier at Fuller's Mercantile, looked funny at me as I paid for my donut and Italian Ice from Bijou Grocery that morning. "Won't be seeing much of you next year, Lisa—" she left the suggestion hanging in the air.

"I won't be here," I said lightly, opening my wallet. "Going somewhere far away."

"Hmmph," she shrugged as she rang my purchase. "You know Mrs. Carey's dead?"

Mrs. Rowena Carey was my English teacher: had been ever since ninth grade; she and Mrs. Pierson, who'd traded off schedules every year. This year, she was supposed to be my Advanced Placement Literature teacher.

"Died of a heart attack in the middle of her kitchen last night," Dorothea observed, "and she was only fifty two years old."

I held my doughnut in its napkin, crushing it slightly while my chocolate teetered. "Dead," I repeated.

"Only three years away from retirement. Don't know what Frank's going to do."

I left for the front hall of Fondis High: a place of marble and glass, "like a tomb," someone once remarked, taking in the refrigerated atmosphere that pervaded it with its huge stairwells and long frosted windows: a monument from the outside; a cold and prepossessing place on the inside, where I entered alone and sat on the stairs: the only senior without a group to be part of, I realized, watching groups talk, playfight; polyglot masses forming and re-forming.

"Mind if I join you?" Kevin Allen looked even taller than he was. He had a wispy cowlick that didn't sit right on his parted hair: problems of wearing a cowboy hat, I guess.

I shrugged. "Heard about Mrs. Carey?"

He nodded as he sat down beside me. "Haven't seen you much since Fair," he observed. "Didn't see you at State Fair, either."

I shook my head. "Didn't have a rabbit to show there. The Lassiters said I could come and help Bonnie in her horse events, but I didn't want to this year."

"Sorry," he said quietly. "Forgot." He paused a minute. "They let Eddie plead out of his hearing."

"They didn't make him stand in front of a judge?"

He shook his head. "For a minute he had to. That's all. Mr. Holmes talked to the District Attorney and I guess wore him down because Eddie has to pay some damages—" (Dr. Brace does, you mean) "and write a couple of letters of apology."

"That's it?"

"That's it."

"YOUR ATTENTION, PLEASE!" the loudspeaker boomed. "INSTEAD OF GOING TO YOUR FIRST HOUR TODAY AS PLANNED, DR. HOEPPNER WOULD LIKE TO MAKE A SHORT ANNOUNCEMENT IN THE AUDITORIUM."

I normally wanted to sit as far back as I could in that auditorium and held back while everyone trooped ·in, including Bonnie and all the fashionable people she knew. She gave me a wave as she passed by, looking puzzled until she saw Kevin standing beside me. Then she gave me a smile, which meant that in her mind Kevin and I were an item.

Eddie Brace came up behind Kevin and slapped him on the back, hard. "Helluva pass you threw at practice last night," he said loudly, in the same voice he used around Chuck. As usual, he ignored me. "Probably beat Dysart by at least ten Friday!"

Kevin nodded as Eddie found another football player to cozy up to in the swirl. "You going in?" he asked.

I nodded. We took our seats in the back row. "This way we can get out quickly," I said. His shoulder touched mine as we sat and I smelled hay. I let my shoulder stay where it was.

I looked over the heads before us as they descended toward the stage. There were Dr. Hoeppner and his assistant principals and the faculty in double rows of folding chairs on the stage and I looked just at them; not above them. Above them is a wall of glory, which I'd memorized by my second time in that auditorium: Harold Holbein, track: 1926; Joseph Liebowitz, All American Footballer: 1932; Clem Clemson, All State Baseballer: 1941; and so on, to the center of the stage. There, above the proscenium, is the record of Chuck Young: All American Footballer three years in a row; All American Baseballer two years in a row; All American Basketballer two years in a row: the school's greatest athlete.

Dr. Hoeppner cleared his throat and thanked everyone for coming. "Students," he finally said, "Last night, we lost a dear and special friend, Mrs. Rowena Carey, who passed away, quite unexpectedly, of a heart attack. Mrs. Carey was well-known throughout Zebulon County for her sponsorship of spelling bees and her belief in the promise of youth."

There was a buzzing among the students. Most of them knew who she was: she'd been a fixture at Fondis High School ever since they or their older brothers or sisters could remember. She'd even taught some of their parents.

"I'd like to have a moment of silence, please," he continued. It wasn't a moment. I counted to 26 as I looked down where I couldn't see my shoes.

"We will put a card in the Main Office for her husband if you want to sign it," he said. "She served both Fondis High School and Zebulon County with distinction."

He paused, probably thinking of some of the crap students would write on the card, then said, "But I do have good news, students: We have found someone just as qualified to fill in this year:

217

a retired English teacher from Kutch who now writes for The Divide-Review newspaper, Mr. Arthur Sanders."

"That guy looks familiar," Kevin said, peering closely at the man standing with Dr. Hoeppner.

"That's the guy who held Eddie's dog," I answered, hoping idly that the applause would tear the awards from the wall above the proscenium.

"What Janie finds wonderful about Rabbit Judging, Lisa," Felicia said confidentially, leaning in to me as she extended her credit card to the clerk, *"is the fact that it's timeless and only limited by your abilities or experience."*

I shook my head, wondering if I were going crazy.

5 /

...Yet shall not thy teachers be removed into a corner anymore, but thine eyes shall see thy teachers. (Isaiah: 30.20)

Mrs. Carey's room still had her name on the door. The bulletin boards, which she always prepared a couple of days before school began, were decorated in fall colors of orange and yellow. Black letters were arranged on the tables in front of each: ANNOUNCEMENTS and GOOD WORK. Her photos of her husband and her daughter and grandchildren were still on her desk and her dictionary, thesaurus, her Milestones of English Literature and Bartlett's Familiar Quotations showed their bindings to us between the sleepy gnome bookends. Her sachets were still up, too, adorning each corner of the bulletin boards.

Mr. Sanders, carrying roll sheets, strode in, and carefully sat down at the desk, laying aside a sheaf of papers as he did so, looking curiously at the top page, torn from a magazine. He set it aside after a moment and I saw that it was the cast of "Herpetology and You:" probably a page Mrs. Carey had torn from a fan magazine to try and be relevant, knowing that a lot of tenth grade girls had their photos in lockers or on the covers of their notebooks. Did Roweena Carey's perfume exhale from those pages? I thought I smelled lilac.

As he took roll, the Lood twins, Cheryl and Tracy, giggled; Wendy Simpson smiled attractively, I looked at the floor, Eddie Brace looked hatefully at the teacher, Kevin Allen stared at his desk, and Meg Chambers rubbed her glasses furiously. I didn't know about anyone else in class; I was remembering how easy roll taking had been for Mrs. Carey, who traded with Mrs. Pierson every year, so we'd had Mrs. Carey as sophomores, learning American Literature, then Mrs. Pierson, learning World Literature. Now, AP Literature, where we were expected to take all those books and all that poetry and make sense of it. I looked up as he cleared his throat.

"Here's what you need to know about me," he began. "I'm not Mrs. Carey; I'm Mr. Sanders. I'm sixty years old and have lived in Zebulon County for the past thirty six years; thirty of which I taught at Kutch. I never anticipated that I'd return to teaching because I've made a new career out of reporting for The Divide-Review, but when Dr. Hoeppner called me last night, I couldn't refuse. I plan on being here until they find a suitable replacement."

He stood up and wrote on the board: ADVANCED PLACEMENT LITERATURE. "This is a college class," he continued, "and its purpose is to prepare you for whatever career you choose, because no matter what you end up doing, you'll be writing and analyzing. I expect papers in on time; I expect you to do the homework: reading, mainly. You will be prepared to discuss the works of literature we read and to write papers on them. I expect you to honestly approach your studies and work hard."

That was quick. Mrs. Carey usually showed us a notebook and divided it into sections for us. "Oh—you'll need a notebook for this class," he said as an afterthought, "divided into two sections: one is your literature notebook, where you'll take notes on the works we read. The second section is your grammar, or rhetoric, portion, where you will take notes for your papers and keep the finished ones for future reference, like your final papers."

"Will you be looking at them?" Meg asked.
He shook his head. "You're too old for that," he answered. "I expect you'll be using the information for your final exam at semester's end, so take good notes."

Eddie Brace raised his hand. "Were you in the papers once for being a drunk?"

Mr. Sanders looked at him quizzically. "What papers?" he asked quietly.

"The Fondis Daily," Eddie replied, suddenly looking busy with his notebook on which his dog's photo had been placed. He stood the notebook on the desk so we could all see it.

"I might have been in there," Mr. Sanders replied, "Reporting. I've been in another newspaper for the past six years, almost exclusively—a monthly."

"No—" Eddie's eyes grew steely. "I mean, a story about you as a drunk."

Meg looked bored. Kevin looked at his paper. Both Wendy and I looked at Eddie, disgusted. Why he was in this class was just because he could; not because he deserved to be here; same as part of the football team—because nobody wanted to cross Dr. Brace, the most powerful man in town. Teachers who graded Eddie like he should be were dismissed; even a lunch lady, when we were in third grade, who made Eddie clean up his spilled tray...

Mr. Sanders shrugged, looking back at Eddie. "I don't know. Do you know of such a story?"

Eddie nodded. "I'll bring a copy to class tomorrow," he announced.

"That's wonderful!" Mr. Sanders replied. "It'll help us with our first assignment—DETERMINING BIAS" he wrote on the board. "I want you all to get a copy of The Divide-Review from Fuller's Mercantile tonight, and look through the following columns:" He wrote ROGER RURAL, DEIRDRE MOON, and EPONA MARIS on the board, "for evidence of bias. Bring them in tomorrow and be prepared to defend your viewpoints." He smiled at Eddie. "I appreciate that. When I wrote about Sheriff Thompson two years ago, I had to make sure I wasn't ruled by bias, even though it was clear he'd misused government funds. Due Friday," Sanders said, addressing the class again, "is an essay entitled "An Event That Changed My Life," which he quickly put on the board. "Most college scholarships and admissions essays ask for something similar, if not this very topic, so I'm presuming it will be useful to you. Double-spaced, typed, with your name, date and class on the upper left hand corner. Three pages maximum." He paused and suggested, "If you haven't already obtained a copy, Deirdre Moon's Column, 'Fondis Nights,' in this month's Divide-Review discusses this very topic. If you need inspiration or some time to see how this can be done, pick it up. There are usually a lot of copies at Fuller's."

"Fondis Nights," I wrote in my notebook as the bell rang.

"Your new English teacher has made this newspaper real popular today," Dorothea greeted me, waving a copy. It's on page thirteen, if you want to read it." She slapped the paper on the counter before her. How come you're so late?"

"School just got out," I said, puzzled.

"Oh—you got a full load this year, huh? Help for scholarships later, I bet."

I hadn't thought about it that way, but she was probably right. I was taking Art and Physical Education as my extras. Art was an extra; PE was required. I'd avoided it ever since ninth grade because I didn't want anyone to see me in the shower. Briefly I wondered if she knew that, too. There was a lot of mystery about Dorothea. She'd been said once to have made Eddie Brace crap his pants when she caught him shoplifting, but I didn't know if that was true or not. She'd looked at me when I was twelve at the checkout counter the first Saturday of Chuck's high school football season, when everyone was congratulating him on the two runs and four passes, smiled, reached for a candy bar and handed it to me. Shouldn't I pay for it? I wondered. No, she was sure. Ever since then, she'd seemed interested in what I was doing. "Big article about the Rabbit Judging Team taking second at State," she'd say, handing me whatever newspaper covered it, or she'd ask if I were interested in something they had on sale, like pieces of jewelry.

"Haven't seen a run like this on Divide-Reviews since two years ago, when Sheriff Thompson embezzled all that money. I had to call Roger Rural to send a bunch more copies over; and those were gone within two days. Made Arthur's reputation as a writer, I can tell you. He coulda' walked right out of Fondis and into a really big paper like The New York Times. Instead, he's teaching you guys." She shook her head. "Doesn't need the money. It's 'cause he and Mike Hoeppner go way back. Mike was one of Arthur's first students."

"Dr. Hoeppner went to school in Kutch?"

"Didn't know that?" She shrugged. "Old timers in the county: Hoeppners, Dr. Brace's family, the Holmes, even Elizabeth Prentice's family—the Wrights. Mine, too. Some of 'em feel as though the county owes them something, though: 'specially those in elected office around here. Roy Thompson was that way. His daddy was sheriff, too. Dr. Brace—his daddy was county commissioner for years. They just sort of feel it's their right."

I started thumbing through the paper. "Thanks, Mrs. Harris," I smiled.

"Take a little of the Country Club posh off them by a generation," she promised, "and you'll see the dirt. Bye now."

"Found anything yet?" Kevin Allen stood in front of me, a copy of the paper in his hand. "I saw you as I parked my truck and figured you'd know what Mr. Sanders was talking about."

"About a girl named Nocturne who's a concert violinist," I answered.

He sat down beside me and started reading as well. The story went along predictably until Nocturne gave a concert at the Fondis Lyceum, had a late night with Deirdre and Epona Maris, then stopped playing altogether. "Now, Nocturne teaches music each semester."

"So this is change?" Kevin snorted. "She just stopped playing for concerts and teaches. So what?"

"Take a look a couple paragraphs from the bottom."

"It was the magic of letting go. She knew when."

Kevin listened thoughtfully. "How old's this Nocturne, anyway?"

I shrugged. "Maybe forty." Time of menopause; time of change. When my mother turned forty-something, she stopped cooking at home regularly—about the time Chuck went to SAC.

"So we're supposed to write about something like that?"

I smiled. He knew. "Goin' to the 4-H meeting tomorrow night?" I asked.

"Sure. You gonna' be an officer again?"

"Whatever they need." I'd been secretary, reporter, historian; Leader's Council Liaison—whatever nobody else wanted. Barb Lassiter, Bonnie's mother, who ran the meetings, usually insinuated me in those spots, knowing I'd do the job. "How come you haven't run for anything, Kevin?"

"Don't wanna," he responded shortly, getting up and slapping his folded paper on the bench. "I got a bunch of cattle to feed, Lisa. See you around."

What changed me. What changed me? That'll be nineteen cents in change, ma'am. What changed me? Change of life. Had one of those already. Not like that, but involving the same section. I wondered if Kevin had any clue what I was thinking about as I watched him get into his truck. I thought of how grateful I was when I got my period every month for those first two years and felt cold inside. What changed me.

It felt good to walk the eight blocks from Fuller's up the hill to my parent's house: the place I wanted to leave as soon as possible. "So large! So beautiful!" I could still hear the guides from the

Garden Club waxing enthusiastic during the House Tour last year, looking at my father's den with all its matching bindings on the oak shelves, then moving to the dining room with its matching walnut sideboard, chairs and table; the "true chef's kitchen" with its grill, range, cured marble counter space and preparation area; its two refrigerators and "cozy, old fashioned breakfast nook, perfect for a busy mom with a star football player to feed." If they'd looked in those refrigerators, they would have found milk, yogurt, butter; maybe eggs, bacon, and cheese: little else. If they'd looked in the freezers, they would've found stacks of frozen microwave meals.

My mother hadn't done too much cooking that year so my father and I just ate whatever appealed to us from the red box or the green box or the yellow box. I once did some idle figuring when I warmed some up one dinner time: ten boxes a week for each of us: 520 microwave meals over a year's time. Weekends, though, my mother was in the kitchen, cooking just enough for the three of us. She hated leftovers, even though my father was sure that he'd be very happy to have some of the chicken or ham or salmon for a midday meal at work when he wasn't at a restaurant with a client.

What changed me. The grandfather clock in the front hall was chiming four as I opened the back door and there was the usual splash of mail and magazines on the polished oak hall floor where the mailman had pushed them through the slot in the front door. I absently picked it up, flipping through the brochures, finding my copy of Domestic Rabbits, then looked through the letters. One was addressed to me. What changed me. It was one of those cute envelopes with a light blue border and written in a penmanship that I remember liking when I was ten. Hi! I had some time on my hands after class and I thought we should get to know each other since I've been with your brother for three months and I've never met his family...I crumpled it up and tossed it in the kitchen wastebasket.

What changed me.

"What am I supposed to do with you?" I demanded in my mind as I was suddenly whisked on that car trip with Felicia and Janie. "Are you telling me I'm crazy?" No reply. Instead, Felicia looked at me significantly. "You'll see soon, Lisa. Meantime, just look at what we've bought for the house!" She had stopped on the street and pulled the items from the bag: a windchime; a couple of scented candles and a heart-shaped wooden box.

As usual, the rabbits were all in their cages. Nebula's was vacant. A couple of times before I put the padlock on the outside door, the cages had been opened and a couple of the rabbits were scooting about on the floor, which was pretty uncomfortable on concrete for a rabbit. I checked their water: a matter of making sure the spigot was on and the bowls were filled from the automatic waterer. Their food was delivered the same way. All I had to do was make sure there wasn't anything blocking the bowls from the automatic feeder. Along the wall opposite the cages were shelves holding the cups, plaques, trophies and ribbons my rabbits had won over the years, plus all the stuff I'd won in judging over the years. It was all in the rabbit house. What changed me. I sometimes spent hours after school here, a room that was always sixty degrees Fahrenheit, with three different levels of lighting, brushing a rabbit, or doing homework, or reading. It was clean here; the usual waste of the rabbits taken care of by a drainage system, and it was sterile; not like Elizabeth Prentice's barn, where cleaning was done with shovel and wheelbarrow; feeding was a matter of filling a bunch of bowls: thirty three of them daily. "You'll like the routine," she assured me when I began with my two Polish rabbits, housed in the garage, filling their water bottles and their bowls with feed pellets every night.

That was when my parents believed my rabbit fancy was a passing fad—like my chickens, they believed. After the chickens died, I didn't want to go back to raising poultry, even though I'd won first place with a bantam rooster that year and the Round Robin as well. When they realized I was serious about rabbits, however, my father, who I'd hoped would build a hutch or a small shed with me, hired a contractor. I was allowed to watch them pour the concrete, frame and build the shed, painted and sided so that it would match the house and garage, then landscaping was added to make it look as if it had always been in the yard. What changed me.

Wilt thou not from this time cry unto me, My father,
thou art the guide of my youth? (Jeremiah: 3.4)

It was the third day of school and we'd just finished our discussion of writer's bias and motivation, when the teacher pulled out a box from behind his desk. Mr. Sanders had asked Eddie for the news story concerning him, but so far, Eddie had not produced it.

"Put your paper in the box," Mr. Sanders announced, "And I will give you something in return." Kevin Allen looked amused at the box, which used to hold bourbon, and put his paper in it.

"Have a book." Sanders handed him a tattered copy of Homer's Odyssey. "Get started reading the Introduction." He did the same for the Math nerd, Meg Chambers, who giggled as she received her book.

"Our printer broke," Tracy Lood said quickly. "Can we turn it in tomorrow?" Her twin nodded.

"How true is that?" Mr. Sanders asked, looking intently at Tracy.

"Uh—"

"When are you going to turn in the paper, Tracy?" he asked quietly.

She and Beth hesitated together as he walked past slowly, getting another paper and giving another copy. Wendy Simpson was the same way. He did not give her a copy of the book, either. I handed him my paper, got my book, opened it, and pretended to read as he approached Eddie Brace. I knew Eddie did not have a paper. Correction: he had a paper. He tore a blank page from his notebook, crumpled it up, tossed it in the box, and held out his hand contemptuously. "You almost got my dog destroyed," he announced.

The room was interested.

"Really?" Mr. Sanders asked. "You might want to check with the Fair Board on that one, Eddie. Why are you making baseless claims about me? It could be called slander." He moved down the row.

Eddie was surprised. Here was a teacher who held his ground; not one like Mrs. Carey, who'd give him a book and pat him on the shoulder, ignoring his remarks, even though some of them, like "fat cow" were heard by the whole class. "You bastard," Eddie said quietly, grabbing his backpack and striding out of the room.

Mr. Sanders shrugged and continued to distribute books. "Read pages one through twenty tonight," he said. "Those of you who haven't turned in your papers, please see me right after school here to make arrangements."

Wendy and the Loods sat quietly. I imagined Eddie Brace was in the Office, complaining to Dr. Hoeppner and phoning his father.

7 /

Defile not therefore the land which ye shall inhabit,
wherein I dwell... (Numbers:34)

Bonnie and I didn't have many classes together. Ever since high school began, we'd started going different directions. I'd take Advanced Biology; she'd take Biology. "If they had Advanced Lunch, you'd take that, too," she once joked. That was when we met: Lunch. Then she'd tell me who was dating what person; what clothes people were wearing; what was hot. It usually made me laugh. It wasn't that Bonnie was dumb; far from it: she just didn't want to clog up her life with Advanced classes because she was a cheerleader and in the Student Senate. She also didn't have the goal of leaving completely, as I did. She'd go to SAC, major in Agriculture, and come back to run the horse farm. I would do something completely different.

"What happened in your English class this morning?" she asked, wide-eyed. "Eddie Brace came in to Dr. Hoeppner's Office crying."

"Really? How'd you find out?"

Bonnie shrugged. "You know." That meant one of the males who constantly tried to impress her. Bonnie got a lot of information that way. "Then his dad came in." She imitated Dr. Hoeppner, who usually slumped in his chair, sitting up straight. "I'll get right on it,

Dr. Brace. Then Mr. Sanders came in. They spent half an hour in there and Dr. Brace got madder and madder. A bunch of people saw it through the conference room window."

"Was Mr. Sanders fired?"

"Don't know. Looks like he was."

I finished my sandwich and drank my milk. Mr. Sanders fired? I'd only known the guy three days—three class hours—but I liked him. He was willing to stand up to Eddie Brace.

In Gym, Coach Quintana issued our uniforms, talked about sports bras and lycra. My mother talked about those things, too. A sports bra wasn't a problem: I had a couple she'd bought me. Lycra? I didn't like how close it felt there. I raised my hand.

"Could I just wear my regular stuff under the gym shorts? I get a rash."

That was a lie, but Coach Quintana didn't know that.

She nodded. "Yeah. Yeah," she responded. "You can do that. Anybody else have that problem?"

To my relief, five other girls raised their hands. I was the only senior in a class of fifty five; mainly sophomores and freshmen.

What changed me. I left the gym just as the last bell rang and lockers slammed and headed up to Mrs. Carey's; I mean, Mr. Sanders' room, where the Loods and Wendy were standing around the teacher's desk.

"Do you guys remember that big spread about two years ago on the Plains Horse Exhibition that your father did?" he asked telling the Loods. "I got to know your dad pretty well then. Do you really want me to give him a call?"

They shook their heads.

"Here are the books. I want the essays tomorrow, without fail. Understand? Do you understand, Wendy? I talk to your grandma pretty often."

They dispersed like dust motes in a sudden breeze.

"Yes, Lisa?" He looked at me over Mrs. Carey's desk, his eyes scrutinizing me through the large glasses; his grey hair at the temples shining with the afternoon sun through the windows.

"Are you fired?" I asked.

He laughed. It was a genuine laugh, from the heart. He shook his head. "Wonderful!" he said, and smiled. "What do you think?"

"You were in Dr. Hoeppner's Office—"

"With Dr. Brace," he answered, "during my planning period." He smiled and settled back in his chair. "Trust the students to see too much and understand none of it," he mused. "No, Lisa. I've not been fired. I've had a parent conference with Dr. Brace; that's all."

He seemed unwilling to continue. I figured it was that distance between adult and child or teacher and student. "So you're not going to leave us?" I asked.

"Not until they find a replacement," he answered. "They might; during Christmas break, but it's doubtful. They'll probably find someone in the summer because teachers don't change jobs once they've found one for a year."

"That's good," I breathed. I again realized that I liked him. Then, "I wonder if you've noticed that Mrs. Carey's stuff is all over this room," I said.

He nodded. "I've tried to put most of it in a box—" he indicated another liquor box behind the desk— "for her husband to pick up, but I've probably missed a lot of it."

"Could I help put that stuff away?" I asked. "I liked Mrs. Carey and I feel really bad coming in to a place where I remember her every day."

He stopped smiling and sat up. "Would you, Lisa? I don't notice a lot of these things, and I don't think Frank—her husband—would notice them, either."

"Like the sprigs of bouquet on the bulletin boards," I answered.

"The what?"

I stepped up, pulled one of the stapled sprigs from the corner. "These," I said, waving it a second and carefully putting it on the table in front of the board.

Mr. Sanders pulled an ancient looking cell phone from his pocket, and punched a number: "Frank: If you're available, we've got a box of stuff to put in your truck." He paused a few seconds, then asked, "Meet you in the parking lot?"

"Huh," he breathed, looking at the phone's screen. "I've got two new messages." He clumsily punched a number and listened, hastily writing a message: "Iain," it read, as he scrawled a number under it, I saw as I bent to pick up the box behind his desk. "My son," he said. The other message I didn't see.

"You've got a son?"

"He has a Doctorate in Biology. Graduated from Kutch almost ten years ago."

"Was he in 4-H?"

"Until he was fourteen. Then he lost interest. Not like my daughter. She loved it, especially Rabbit Judging."

"Your daughter?"

"Janie judged rabbits a few years before you started, Lisa."

"What's she doing now?" *My name's Janie and I'm a Rabbit Judge,"* the girl in the seat beside me had said.

He shook his head. "I believe Frank Carey'll be in the parking lot by now, if not just turning in. Let's get the box and anything else that was Mrs. Carey's."

Mr. Frank Carey quietly shook my hand and thanked us both for helping him. "Kids'll be coming in tonight," he added. "Funeral's on Saturday at Saint Aloysius. Two o'clock."

"I'll be there, Frank."

"Can you spread the word?"

Mr. Sanders nodded. "I'll make sure the school knows."

"She'd like that." He blew his nose loudly and put his handkerchief away. "She'd been here twenty-five years. Was gonna' retire in three years—once she'd hit fifty five. This place was her life."

I thought of all the years and years she'd put into grading papers, calling parents, tracking down lost books, telling students to pay attention. I thought of my mother's outrage when she received a note in the mail about Chuck's failing his junior year: "After all he's done for Fondis High! To fail English class when all his other teachers understand! What's wrong with that woman? Maybe he doesn't turn in a paper—that's no reason to fail him!" And she visited Dr. Hoeppner the next day, waving the failure notice like a flag. I wondered how much Chuck's undeserved passing grade, "it's still a D," my mother sniffed, "but at least it's passing," caused Roweena Carey's death. There were probably a lot of those. Eddie Brace certainly hadn't done her any favors recently; nor had the Lood twins or Wendy. How many other kids skated past? I could only imagine.

Mr. Sanders and I returned to his classroom after we'd watched Mr. Carey leave the parking lot. No: it didn't feel like Mrs. Carey's room anymore. It didn't feel like anybody's room.

"Um—I have some posters I can bring for your room," I volunteered.

He smiled. "I kind of like the empty look; but I know what you mean, and you're most kind, Lisa. No—I'll bring some things tomorrow for you to put up—that is, if you're interested in doing that?"

I nodded. I didn't have a great deal to do other than homework after school. Fifteen minutes in Mr. Sanders' room putting up posters wasn't difficult with a schedule like that.

"Now—can I offer you a ride home?"

I was surprised. The last time I'd been driven home was by my eighth grade Science Teacher on a Saturday. "Yeah, sure," I answered.

"Good," he answered. "I need to get these papers—" he pulled the AP Literature papers from the bourbon box— "Into my briefcase. I can't stick around here most afternoons, Lisa, because I have two goats to milk, chickens and pigs to feed."

"Nice way of life," I remarked as I picked up my backpack and started toward the door.

"Yeah, I guess it is," he answered. "Keeps me grounded. As long as you've got someone else or something else to take care of, you never grow old."

He asked for directions and the car scooted from the empty parking lot onto Elm Street, past Fuller's and the Library and City Hall and toward what was known as "Establishment Fondis," according to guidebooks, because it was full of prominent families and those who wanted to look prominent, with two-and three-storey houses set back on a couple acres each; "enough to raise a horse, if we wanted to; not that we would," My mother had sniffed, knowing that zoning laws had allowed raising animals in Establishment Fondis, which Mr. Grubber, down the street, did. He had a couple of highland sheep. She felt the only two important families on our block were us and the Braces. "The rest are all nouveau riche," she explained. "There are the Clarkes, who can't hide their auto part store roots; the Stevens, who married big oil and now think that they're entitled—"

My father made a grumbling noise. They were clients of the bank.

"Nothing against how they use their money, Harold," she said as she passed the salmon to him. "They're just so common. Lydia Brace and I, remember, both come of good homes where fathers don't wear overalls to work!"

Even though her uncle Henry was a farmer who probably wore overalls to work, my mother had this story, ever since she got to SAC, that her father was a professional of some kind, who wore a tie. She said it often in the interviews she did when she was in the Miss Colorado Pageant, hoping that the dust of eastern Colorado hadn't stuck to her, and she made sure it hadn't by marrying my father.

"I was in your house once," Mr. Sanders remarked as he pulled to the curb. "The Garden and Home tour. Your dad had quite a library, if I recall."

"Doesn't mean he's read those books," I answered, realizing that my father's good intentions in buying a home library was in part to help my mother decorate.

"Maybe he'll read them someday," Mr. Sanders replied.

"Maybe," I answered. "Anyway, thanks for the ride, Mr. Sanders," I said, grabbing my backpack and opening the passenger door.

8 /

The meek will he guide in judgment: and the meek will he teach his way. (Psalms: 25.9)

It was Thursday night, a week after I'd helped Mr. Sanders decorate his classroom with posters- art prints, like the one of the Airplane Angel by Dannah Davidson: modern and subtle. It was the last week of August, and I was watching Herpetology and You on the widescreen TV in my father's den with all Chuck's trophies on the shelves surrounding it. Unlike all the rest of the women in Zebulon County who were snuggled in watching these shirtless athletic geeks, Bonnie had a horse practice to go to, which irritated her to no end. "I just don't understand it," she'd said at lunch, "Everybody else has moved meetings to Tuesday or Wednesday, but once a month, I still have to go to horse practice. I won't get to see Tanner without his shirt!"

"You can see anyone without his shirt," I observed slyly, giggling. Bonnie had no end of guys wanting to take her out.
"But this is different," she said, smiling. "I could talk to Tanner."

"And you couldn't talk to—say—Frank Fillmore? He's in all my advanced classes. He's also athletic."

"And Eddie Brace is his groupie," she said, frowning. "No—I've just got to get Mrs. Davis to change the horse meeting night."

"Hal Jones: 26. BA Pennsylvania; MS and PhD Florida State. Specialist in Fish. Anh Vu: 27. BA Caltech; MS MIT; PhD Columbia. Specialist in Hydroelectric Technology and Environmental Design. Tanner Smith: 28. BS University of Wisconsin; MS University of Illinois; PhD Oxford University, England. Herpetology Specialist. Iain Sanders: 27. BA Cornell; MS University of Vermont; PhD Columbia. Specialist in Riparian Habitat worldwide." I watched the trailer at the bottom of the screen, moving on the couch to get more comfortable, thinking of how alike my father smelled at fifty to Mr. Sanders at sixty—sort of dusty—I'd just seen the name. Sanders. And there was Iain, somewhere in Malawi, I think, holding a four inch-long turtle in his hand, explaining how a power plant upriver was going to "destroy this little guy and the thousands of years his species has survived here" because of "water discharge in cooling the plant." There was something about his rimless glasses or maybe his expression that made me think of Mr. Sanders telling us: "There is no great man in The Odyssey, unless you believe Odysseus is great, which is a subject of speculation and conjecture, which is part of Homer's art." Flick of the wrist, maybe? Maybe holding his head to one side when he said something profound? I suddenly knew that Iain Sanders had to be related to Arthur Sanders and I thought of the tenth grade girls whose notebooks had the Herpetology and You cast on their outsides looking right at Mr. Sanders while he taught. His son? I remembered the phone message from last week: Iain. The name was spelled differently than most people I knew did it.

The episode ended and I popped the DVD from the recorder, popped it into its case, and put it into my backpack on the coat hook in the mud room outside the kitchen to give to Bonnie next day as my father, looking tired, came in.

"Seven thirty already?" he asked. " 'Been a long day, Lisa." He went to the kitchen chair that was his and sat down. "This damn golf course," he muttered, taking off his glasses and wiping his eyes. He shook his head as if to clear it then looked up. "Why don't we have the yellow box for dinner?"

"Sure," I said, going to the freezer and pulling two yellow boxes from it. I popped one into the microwave oven, set it on 333 and waited as he flipped through the day's mail, which I'd set on the table that afternoon.

"Everything all right in your English class?" he asked, idly studying a bill from Hamilton Eckert, my mother's doctor, who seemed to send a bill once a month for something.

The microwave oven timer went off and I stirred the sauce around the burrito, setting another 111, and starting it. "Yeah. Fine. We're reading The Odyssey."

"Any problems between Arthur Sanders and Eddie Brace?"

None that I could think of. Eddie came in every day and sat in his seat like a gargoyle. Even though he'd finally been issued a book, it was obvious he hadn't read it, so he just sat. I shrugged.

He frowned as he opened Dr. Eckert's bill. "It's just an uncomfortable situation: Eddie's never been quite right since his mother left, then having to face his new English teacher after that misunderstanding—"

Misunderstanding?

The microwave oven timer went off, startling me and I picked up the steaming plate, not worrying about hurting my hands. I put it in front of him. "You'll find a fork in the drawer," I said. "I'm not hungry."

I went upstairs to do homework, slamming my door behind me.

" A point in the universe is far different than a point on Earth," the Physics book told me at about eleven that night as I struggled to keep my eyes open, "and we can see the infinitude of that point..."

It was snowing all around a little cabin in the mountains, where I lived, with a bed not far off from a small table and a couple of chairs, one of which was next to a window, where I sat, in a long calico dress, embroidering on a small frame as I awaited the arrival of my husband? No; friend? No; not quite; but I depended on him a lot and even got the feeling that I knew his smell close: the smell of dust. Was I excited? No: but I knew that smell and I awaited it because it was good and that smell came in the room as the plank door opened to a broad-brimmed hat covered with snow and large eyebrows iced behind rimless glasses and I knew what I'd been waiting for had returned: He took off his hat, hung his coat on a door peg, and warmed his hands before the cheery cookstove where stew was bubbling before turning to me: Arthur Sanders, who smiled at me and really appreciated me for me. I was no longer Bonnie's friend or Chuck Young's Younger Sister or the Bank President's daughter: I was me.

It was three in the morning. I picked my head off the Physics text and felt a prickling down there. Something was coming. I headed for the bathroom. When I bleed, I bleed heavily.

9 /

I will be his father, and he shall be my son... (II Samuel:7.14)

September first was a Saturday and a game against Louisiana for SAC. "If they get this one, they'll be first toward the Houston Bowl," my father remarked as he reviewed the schedule on the laptop computer in the kitchen.

"They've only played three games," my mother answered, neatly folding the dishtowel and hanging it on the rack. As usual, the dishwasher was loaded and everything cleared away within ten minutes of the meal. "Have any plans today, Lisa?"

I shrugged from where I was sitting at the kitchen table. "Bonnie's," I answered quietly.

"You'll take your bike?" It was more a statement than a question. "I wonder when you'll get your driver's license."

I shrugged. We'd had this conversation before. Why I didn't just sign up for courses at Fondis Driving Academy and why I didn't want to: I wanted, plain and simple, to get taught by my parents, as Chuck had; but my mother was always too busy, and my father, after one lesson in a parking lot, got red in the face and drove us both home.

Fortunately, her cell phone went off with its characteristic ring tone: "When Irish Eyes Are Smiling," and as she answered it, I headed toward the stairs. "Lydia," she said absently as she put the phone to her ear.

"Hmm? Really?" I heard her asking as I mounted the stairs, then paused as her tone changed. "Today? At Fuller's? Oh—"

I went up and closed my door. I'd probably finish Oedipus the King for Mr. Sanders' class by noon. After that, I'd call Bonnie. If she wasn't out, I'd go on over. It was only a couple of miles on Road 17, behind a faded sign: LASSITER RANCH: BEST

HORSEFLESH ANYWHERE! Every now and then, they'd manage to sell a horse; most of the time, though, I knew that what kept the place going was Vern's deputy's salary and Eric's job as waiter and groundsman at the Country Club. Bonnie's father had died of cancer a few years before.

My mother knocked on my door. "I'm just going to Fuller's," she announced, opening it. "Anything you need?"

"I'll go with you," I answered.

Dorothea looked quizzically at us in the checkout line. "What brings you out on a Saturday?" she asked conversationally. "I usually see you Tuesdays, Mrs. Young."

"Couldn't wait," my mother murmured. "Big party Sunday."

"Hmm," Dorothy murmured as she rang up the two salmon steaks and the breast of chicken.

"Oh—Lisa—could you find a copy of The Divide-Review over there?" My mother nodded at the magazine rack.

"Cover story," Dorothea said, winking at me as she bagged the groceries.

I pulled three copies from the stack.

PAR ONE MILLION? PAR TWO BILLION?
Experts Have Little or No Idea As To How Much the New Golf Course Will Cost
By Arthur Sanders
"It's likely that the investors of Fondis, lured by a quick profit guaranteed by the Farmers and Mechanics Bank on the new Brace Memorial Golf Course, haven't read the fine print of their contracts, which specify the cost of upkeep..."

Calls were made from my father's den: "Yes, I understand, Ed, but we can't stop now; not with so many of our friends backing us; it would look like he was right. I don't know, Ed; I don't know if he's got it in for you or not. Sure looks like it, doesn't it, what with that mess at Fair and Eddie's English class. No, you can't exactly get him fired. How would that look, so soon after this article? The paper? Remember when we asked advertisers to put pressure on after that hospital article? No, we've just got to ride through it. His past? Ed, you can't bring up anything nobody knows already. Five years ago, he was a drunk; ten or eleven years ago, he lost his wife and his little girl. What else is there? He doesn't drink anymore, as far as I know, and anything else—well, most people would wonder why Dr.

235

Brace was calling the kettle black. Yeah, Ed, I know: Gloria left you because she was selfish and didn't want to be a good mother to your child; but a lot of people around here see it differently; you know that. Yeah, they're sonsofbitches, but we can't do anything about that. They're the same sonsofbitches who didn't vote for you when the school board election was held last year." He paused. I knew it was the closing of a deal: I'd watched him over the years, especially with some of the ranchers who came in while I was on Summer Break: He'd always casually mention something about their finances, like "Mr. Holstein, your calves were selling for less this year than last year because you haven't brought them to proper weight," and wait for a response, which was usually truthful. In this case, Dr. Brace said he'd just hold tight. "Yeah:" my father answered. "You just hold tight, Ed. We'll get this settled." He paused and added, "And we'll get this sonofabitch figured out as well."

"Lisa," he called after a moment, fortunately not moving to see me at the top of the stairs, listening, "Lisa," he called again.

I counted to ten, rose, and stepped onto the creaking second stair. "Yes?"

"Could I see any of your papers from Mr. Sanders' class, please?"

What Changed Me and *A Major Theme in The Odyssey.* "Sure. I think they're in my notebook."

"Also, any comments by Mr. Sanders, please."
I headed down the hall to get my papers, pulled out my notebook then stopped. Why would I want to help him?

"Couldn't find them," I called from the top of the stairs. "I guess they're in my locker."

I went back to read Oedipus The King until my mother called me down for lunch an hour later. The pre-game analysis was on the television in my father's study: "Well, Jim—think SAC has a chance against the unstoppable Moose?"

"Dunno, Bill. With that hamstring, Tyson Cleavis, their best back, is benched. I think SAC might just pull it out..."
"Lisa, what sort of man is Mr. Sanders?" my father asked as he cut into his salmon steak, keeping one ear for the television. His statistics notebook would be on the arm of the couch and his playbook would be on the coffee table in front of it. He looked at Chuck's games more intently, I realized a few years ago, than I studied Biology.

I shrugged, a puzzled expression on my face.

"I mean, does he pick on anyone in class?"

I took a bite and nodded, taking a long time to swallow my food. "Yeah. A couple of days ago we were talking about the perfect woman and this boy said that Penelope wasn't as exciting as Calypso or Circe or even Helen, and Mr. Sanders kept asking him to explain. The boy couldn't, after a while, and got pissed off."

"Was it Eddie?" My father asked.

"Kevin Allen," I answered sweetly, "And then Mr. Sanders said he was exactly right and that Odysseus had to mature in order to meet Penelope as an equal."

My father was unimpressed. "What about Eddie?" he asked. "Does Mr. Sanders make an exception for him?"

I shrugged. "About the same as Mrs. Carey did. Just lets him sleep."

"Sleep?"

"Most of the time, we don't even know Eddie's there. Like when it was Mrs. Carey's class."

"But Eddie passed Mrs. Carey's class," my mother observed.

"Well, Bill, it looks like we've only got a few minutes before the game: the SAC Wolverines versus the Thundering Moose of Oregon, played at the beautiful Oregon Woodsy Field, so we need to break for these messages..." the television announced.

"So'd Chuck," I answered, spearing the last of my salmon steak and eating it quickly, "and Mrs. Carey's dead."

I wiped my mouth and left the table. My bike, which I'd had since seventh grade, was ready and I glided down the driveway, hearing a confused repetition of my name as I headed down Schley Street, passing Eddie Brace walking his big black dog and slid onto Road 17 from Elm, just past the Fairgrounds where I put it into top gear, racing down the hill past the gravel quarry, past the fields of alfalfa ready for their last cutting and into the rutted driveway, past the faded sign: LASSITER HORSES: BEST HORSEFLESH ANYWHERE!, and pulled in behind the house, where I fully expected to see Vern tinkering on their old truck, or Bonnie exercising Trigger, her show horse; but nothing. Deserted. From the pasture, a couple of horses whinnied, and Sam, the Lassiters' cattle dog, came out and greeted me.

Puzzled and not wanting to return to my parents' house, I scratched Sam a few times behind the ears, which he always seemed to enjoy, then mounted my bike again, going away from Fondis on Road 17 to where it joined the Kutch Road. Sooner than I thought, I was at the back door of Elizabeth Prentice's, flushed and windblown and out of breath.

Elizabeth opened the door, surprised to see me, then asked me in. "Everything all right?" she asked.

I nodded. "It's just that I hadn't come over in so long; not since Chuck—" I stopped, noticing the two figures seated at the kitchen table in the cool semi-darkness created by the curtains pulled over the windows.

"Lisa, I believe you know at least one of these gentlemen. Arthur—"

Mr. Sanders smiled and pulled a chair out.

"—And his son, Iain."

So it really is true, I thought. They are father and son. I shook hands with Iain, who was a tall gentle smile, wire-rimmed glasses and wavy brown hair.

"Iced tea, Lisa?"

I stammered something then listened to Elizabeth talk about a family that had hired a law firm just so two brothers could start talking to each other. There was some inheritance involved, and the dispute over it had gone on for years while the inheritance just whittled away because it wasn't being properly looked after.

"In the end, it just came down to pride," she concluded.
Mr. Sanders nodded. "Lisa's class is studying Oedipus the King," he remarked, looking at her; not Iain, "which, as you recall, is about a man with all the answers who cannot see the truth until he blinds himself. I think a number of fathers are like that—even me."

"Sometimes," Iain added, "their heirs are just as belligerent. You're going to teach Antigone, too, I imagine." Without waiting for a reply, he went on, "I was always struck by Creon falling right into Oedipus' mistakes in that play and not realizing how stupid he was until it was too late."

"Yeah." Mr. Sanders nodded, smiling at Iain. He took a sip of his tea. "Just how much time do you have before you have to get back?"

"I can spend the night. Then I'm on for forty eight hours, looking for the Mormon Toad."

Mr. Sanders raised his eyebrows.

"Oh—cute little bugger; no bigger than a quarter. Pioneers used to stew them when they appeared around fall during the nineteenth century—loved 'em in soups, I understand."

I probably looked kind of sick. Iain noticed it. "We don't eat them anymore, Lisa." Then without changing a beat, he asked, "You're one of the top rabbit judgers, aren't you?"

"I do my best," I answered.

"Lisa, why don't you show Iain the rabbits in the barn?" Elizabeth suggested. "It's been years since he was there last. And if you get really ambitious, there's a shovel and wheelbarrow by the door. Take your drinks."

I suddenly found myself in the company of somebody I'd only seen on TV and in a dream or two and on the notebook covers of a lot of my classmates, headed toward Elizabeth's barn, which used to house a couple of horses and pigs but was now lined with cages at eye level of all kinds of breeds of rabbit, which Elizabeth would quiz the Rabbit Judging Team on before a tournament. We'd learn the weights, sizes, colors, feeling of the fur, various disqualifications, eye colors and toenail sizes. "This is why Breed Identification is such a snap for all of you," Elizabeth told us. "You actually can feel and see the difference between a Himalayan and a Californian, which often trips up less experienced judges."

"Show me what you do to judge a rabbit, Lisa," Iain suggested as I closed the barn door behind us. One of the first rules of rabbit judging is to make sure the area is safe for the rabbits, Elizabeth had always told us, so close the door.

"Okay." I took a gentle Polish from its cage and carried it to the carpet covered table in the middle of the barn, explaining the steps of bunching the body, checking its fur, determining ear length, then flipping it on its back so I could examine its paws and underside markings. "This female has recently given birth," I pointed out, "because the hairs are sparse on its underside. They always pull hair out of their undersides to line the nest for their kits."

"Really?" he asked.

"In any show, it would be disqualified."

He nodded. "Yeah. Now what about a larger rabbit? Would you like me to put this one back in its cage?"

I nodded and as he put the Polish in its cage, I chose a Satin and explained why it was an excellent meat breed, pointing out the loin and the shape of the back. Was he genuinely interested or was he just taking up some time with me?

He listened to the points I made, including my notation of the miscolored toenail on its left rear foot, then asked for me to show him a medium-sized rabbit. He seemed genuinely interested and even imitated my movements in checking the fur and the legs, looking carefully as I pointed out irregularities.

"Anything else you want to see?" I asked as we put the rabbit back in its cage.

He chuckled, shaking his head. "Not really, Lisa. I just wanted to see it again. It was about fourteen years ago that my sister was rabbit judging and going through all these points—and my mom was busy and there wasn't anyone else to show so she showed me, over and over again so she'd get it right. Janie had about twelve rabbits—mainly Polish—and she was going to show a couple at Fair. She told me all about it: everything her eight year-old brain could conceive of: why her rabbits would win above everyone else's; why she took such care grooming them; why she wanted to do so well in Rabbit Judging." He smiled at the memory. "It sounds silly. It was silly, then, too; but she left so suddenly—it was all I had of her. That and the rabbits I kept feeding and watering after she was gone."

Elizabeth had a stool she kept by the carpet covered table where she sat as we identified the various breeds; I sat on it and pointed to one of the folding chairs she kept in the corner. "Do you want to sit down?" I asked. Then I remembered we'd put our iced tea glasses on one of the cages near the door. I hurried to get them and put them on the table.

He awkwardly flipped the folding chair into position. "It's funny how you go all over the world, then wind up back where you started..." He took a sip of iced tea and I watched his tanned Adam's apple move above his collar. The afternoon sunlight in the barn was a dusty golden color which fell in stripes across us both. "This barn—" he looked around him. "Jim and I used to play in here when we were little; we even got drunk in here and tried cigarettes." He closed his eyes a moment.

"You've known the Prentices a long time?"

"My dad's place—our place—" he corrected himself, "is next door." He smiled. Elizabeth had known him all this time and I never knew. "Do you want to see the place? I think I still know my way around, even though I haven't been there in almost ten years."

The car, a compact station wagon, pulled alongside me as I walked along Road 17, toward Elizabeth's, and Felicia told me to hop in. I settled alongside Janie, who, after looking me over, announced, "You're a rabbit judge, aren't you?"

I nodded and pulled my seatbelt on. Felicia put the car in gear and we were in Kutch, buying things.

I thought of that image again and again as I thought of Iain.

Curiously, Elizabeth did not mention to my parents that I'd spent the afternoon with Iain Sanders or that I'd helped his father and him with their afternoon chores. She also did not mention that I'd fainted when I'd found that dead hen on her roost and that I'd been put into a rocking chair in Mr. Sanders' living room until I'd recovered. No: she merely told them that we'd had a nice afternoon together and she was looking forward to seeing me again when I dropped by another Saturday, which she hoped would be soon. We unloaded my bike from her van; she waved and was gone.

"If you e-mail me, make sure you use some kind of code, Lisa," Iain had urged, "like—here you go—Antigone. Nobody uses that one and I can find it easily enough. Just put 'Antigone' in the subject line, okay?"

I nodded. Of course, I had e-mail but I never used it. Like my cell phone, it was one of those things that didn't seem to matter. Now, all of a sudden, it did.

"I'm asking you to keep all this secret," Iain had told me in the barn. "Can I trust you?"

OF COURSE! I wanted to shout. I'd never been so happy. I wanted to take Iain Sanders and hold him until the world ended.

I nodded, solemnly, wishing I could tell Bonnie, but I couldn't. It was in that area she never told me about but sometimes hinted at: that part not honorable or generous: the senior who gave her a necklace when she was a sophomore and who still looked at her with cow eyes from the counter of the grocery store two years later; the law enforcement classmate of Vern's who decided to move two states away after graduation just to get over Bonnie. I suddenly had a closet, too.

It's funny how easy you are to talk to, Iain wrote. I've usually found that most people are vapid or into some form of hero worship or just don't really respond beyond themselves. You're different that way, Lisa. You're genuinely interested in who I am…

Not hard to be interested; especially since he brought up all kinds of topics to talk about: books, music, animals; stories about where he'd been and who he'd talked to and what treaties the show had managed to get signed. It was fascinating. You'd told me a little about what it was like at home for you, Iain. If you could, tell me about your mother. My mother is a socialite who spends a lot of time raising funds for the hospital and plays tennis and golf at the Country Club. She's also a gourmet cook.

241

He told me about Felicia Duncan: his mother who ran the Whispering Pines Mental Health Center on Elm Street; how he was able to talk to her about anything that came to mind: including boy/girl issues, he added. Maybe she wasn't always available, he pointed out, but she always tried to understand what he was going through. Her death was a fluke: she and Janie were coming home from shopping in Kutch on Road 17 and were overtaken by an earthmover whose driver was asleep at the wheel.

Iain was fourteen when it happened: a freshman at Kutch, having difficulties with Algebra and not really performing at grade level. My grades, after their deaths, plummeted, and my father, gentle man that he is, proved little help: he was probably trying to deal with it himself. He finally took me to some of my mother's former colleagues at Whispering Pines and I spent six months, every Wednesday afternoon, just talking to Janet, who cried with me. I started to study more and got better grades. By the time I was midway through tenth grade, I was cruising. It meant that my father didn't do much besides asking how I was doing, then went back to whatever he was doing, which meant burying himself in his work.

10 /

A friend loveth at all times, and a brother is born for adversity.
(Proverbs: 17,17)

Those days, probably because of the warm cocoon I was in, e-mailing Iain Sanders and seeing his father after gym, were like a dream. I'd shower quickly, smiling at how dumb I was earlier about someone suspecting something because I was naked, then, hair still wet, I went to Mr. Sanders' room, where I'd sometimes sort papers or put grades in the computer for him while he read papers or talked with my classmates. The Loods were there a lot: each of them trying to figure out how to write an effective paper; Wendy Simpson showed up occasionally to get work when she knew she'd be out;

even Eddie Brace showed up sometimes; usually to ask some question that was more spat out than a question.

"You said that Oedipus the King was a tragedy," he began.

"I did," Mr. Sanders replied.

"So why did you tell me my story wasn't a tragedy?" he asked.

"Because your story doesn't reveal hubris, Eddie. You wrote about two reasonable people having dinner together, then one jumps up and leaves, cursing the other. That's not hubris. That's not tragedy. Go more deeply and you'll find your tragic hero."

"It's personal, okay?"

"I had the feeling it was," Mr. Sanders replied. "Here's a personal story, Eddie: Let's say you had a son, but because of circumstances, you ignored him. Don't worry about the circumstances, except that they made you feel you were much more important to others and so you ignored your son. What would the son do?"

"Hate his father."

"Exactly. Show some hubris in one of the characters. You have a couple of days to rewrite it."

"Where'd you go to University?" Eddie asked.

"Didn't we go over that before?" Sanders replied.

Eddie left.

One who was rather a surprise was Kevin Allen, who breezed in with a copy of the September Divide-Review in his hand. "Do you really think that the Mellons' farm is going to last?" The Mellons were a continual topic among the 4-H Leaders' Council because they were the only farm in the county that practiced "organic agriculture."

"If the weather cooperates; yes," Mr. Sanders replied. "They're raising high-end beef, poultry, and swine and have a demand list from top groceries and restaurants."

"But it's so slow!" Kevin said. "A turkey shouldn't take more than a few months to gain weight; a pig shouldn't take more than six months. How do they survive?"

Mr. Sanders shook his head. "By the seat of their pants, Kevin: but when they sell, they sell high, and to people willing to pay for it."

"But it's crazy, Mr. Sanders. You've raised animals: you know: If you don't get it out in a year, you have to pay for it."

"Yeah." Mr. Sanders sighed. "Which leads to artificial feeds and all kinds of toxins in what we eat, Kevin."

"I can't agree with you," Kevin said.

"Then let's leave it at that, shall we?"

Kevin nodded and left. I thought of the prize steers he showed and the premiums he'd won: I could understand why Kevin would be concerned about what he fed his cattle, especially if his English teacher had just pronounced it fake. Boy, I thought, Mrs. Carey hadn't managed to provoke as many people in her umpteen million years at Fondis High as Arthur Sanders had managed in only four weeks!

"He sends me a copy of the paper in the mail every month," Iain wrote, "usually care of the studio, because he never knows what part of the world I'll be in, and sometimes I read what he has to say. I read all the stuff about Sheriff Thompson because it was so incredibly funny: imagine a guy who'd been thrifty all his life suddenly having a half million dollar condo at Vail all paid for! I'd always thought Sheriff Thompson was a pompous ass anyway: he'd come to Kutch High School to present a trophy during a Science Fair and didn't even know the name of the recipient; didn't even bother to learn it.

"Is my dad really writing articles about Brace and Associates? It's about time. I sort of remember that some of old downtown Fondis was going to be turned into high-end condominiums, displacing a bunch of poor people, and Brace and Associates was behind that..."

I also found out, from Iain, just what his mother had meant: not only to him, but to her co-workers and a bunch of clients of Whispering Pines Mental Health Center some fourteen years before: "If you're ever in the neighborhood of Second and Elm, stop in at Whispering Pines, which is a big metal and glass building with a huge atrium. That's my mother's. She loved plants and growing things and there was enough money to landscape it and hire an artist to design a water sculpture..."

I sat in a copse of trees in a sunlit building, beside a sculpture of bronze over which water trickled from some unknown source. Behind the water was a woman's face, changing its looks as the water ran over it unevenly and cried for Iain and his dead mother, for Mr. Sanders and his dead wife and I felt, watching it, that I could trust Iain with anything.

11 /

*He that hasteth to be rich hath an evil eye, and considereth not that
poverty shall come upon him. (Proverbs: 28.22)*

Sometimes, depending on how she was feeling, Bonnie and I
would go get lunch then we'd share a table under a tree in the
Courthouse Park and watch the ducks in the pond or people passing
by. She'd use those lunch hours as a "pressure valve, because I just
need to get away."

"Who is it this time?" I asked, teasingly as we climbed into
her car, "Robbie or Eric?" I found it didn't take much attention to
know what was bothering her. But this time it was different.

"No;" she said as she pulled out of the parking lot. "We're
going to Adobadas, okay?" She hit the gas and then began: "It's your
dad."

All thoughts of thinking about Iain as I nodded while she
talked disappeared. "My father?"

"His bank, actually. Mom was telling me about it last night
and said not to tell you, but I figured—" She turned into the drive-
thru and we ordered. "I think it's your turn, Lisa," Bonnie observed.
I knew it wasn't: the ratio of meals I'd paid for was five to one, but I
paid anyway, wondering if I was helping her financially somehow.

"Okay, here's how it worked." Bonnie looked contemplatively
at her taco. "My family took out a line of credit three years ago; you
remember when we bought Trigger?"

Bonnie's show horse. I nodded.

"And he cost more than we thought and so we used part of
that line of credit for him and tack and repairs to the barn. We went
over the line of credit limit, which wasn't a big deal: a lot of ranchers
do that, then square it with the sale of a couple of steers or even a
new loan.

"But yesterday, my mom got a notice in the mail that said
we'd have to pay the whole thing within a month or they'd start to
foreclose." She chomped on her taco, spilling parts on the table.

I was stunned. "That means you'd have to sell Trigger—"

"The whole place!" she said. "In order to pay the line of
credit, we'd have to sell all the horses; then what's the use of having
a horsefarm without horses?"

I just listened as she went through different scenarios: how much money Vern and Eric contributed to the household income: "It's just not enough; and my mom couldn't understand why the Bank would be so heartless until we started asking around: the Bank wants to buy all the land for a mile around that new golf course so they could build developments there. We're right on the edge of all that."

I knew who I'd talk to, but I didn't want to tell Bonnie—yet. Just like that secret I kept from her—well; both secrets I kept from her.

"If someone wanted to take your land, and you owed a lot of money on it, could you go to somebody to help you keep it?" I asked, as the door whooshed behind me.

Mr. Sanders tilted his head in warning. Eddie Brace was sitting at his desk along the wall, writing something furiously as he scowled at the book. "Let's talk outside," he said quietly.

"A friend of mine—" I began. He held his hand up to stop me. "Our friend Elizabeth works for an attorney who's been doing a lot of that lately, Lisa. I suggest you talk with her about it and then talk to your friend."

"A lot of it?"

He nodded. "A lot of ranches around the golf course site are filing suit, Lisa, against Brace Developments."

"Really?"

He nodded. "Not a word where you got the information, understand? But if your friend wants to get in touch with Richard Calkins, I'd recommend it."

Eddie was suddenly there, between Mr. Sanders and me. Wordlessly, he handed Mr. Sanders his paper and walked away. Mr. Sanders, holding the paper, stood beside me, watching Eddie make his way hurriedly down the hall, probably late for football practice.

It was early October and early in the morning when I saw my counselor, Mrs. Grimes. "I wanted to know if you'd gotten the results of those tests I took last year: the ones for academic scholarships?"

She pulled my folder, sipped her coffee, and flipped through a few pages. "Some results are still missing, Lisa; but overall, it looks like you've got a good shot. See me in a month so we can apply for early admission. You could miss a semester, couldn't you?"

I shook my head. "Gym," I stated.

"That's all?"

At the meeting of Whispering Pines 4-H that night, Barb Lassiter gave me a hug. "Lisa, I haven't seen you to thank you these last couple of weeks, but I wanted you to know that your idea about consulting Richard Calkins was just great!"

I hugged her awkwardly, hoping nobody noticed. The Divide-Review cover story had been tossed angrily on the kitchen counter only a couple of days before:

DEVELOPER LOCKED IN BY RANCHER LAWSUITS

By Arthur Sanders

A series of "stop" orders have been issued, halting acquisition of local farms and ranches, all within two miles of the proposed new golf course, according to the District Attorney's Office. The District Attorney is responding to a petition filed by the office of Richard Calkins, representing a number of property owners whose mortgage terms have recently been called into question by the mortgage holders...

"You're coming with me to the Art Museum on Tuesday, aren't you, Lisa?" My mother knocked on my door before turning the knob and looking in. She was still in her tennis outfit from the Country Club, even though it was eight at night and the weather had started to get chilly.

"I guess so," I answered. Fund-raiser for the hospital. She never liked going alone, which meant that if my father wasn't available or Lydia McDermott had something else planned, I was her companion. I stood around, drank a soft drink, ate lots of olives, smiled a lot, and tried not to get pinched by a lecherous old man. Then my mother, around ten o'clock, would announce that the Museum was closing, thank everyone, tell them how wonderful they were for contributing so much for the hospital, and march to the car. How she managed never to wreck it, since she was slurring her words, really amazed me. "Can I get something for it?"

"Get something?"

"You know: a dress," I said quickly.

"But I don't have time to go shopping with you. Tuesday's only two days away and I have a million things—"

"I know my size. Is it all right?"

"You'll go to Wately's, won't you?"

I nodded.

"You wouldn't believe the dress I bought today," I e-mailed Iain. "It's red."

He asked how it looked.

"I love how it looks. I'd like to show it to you sometime." I'd like to show you a lot of things about me, I thought. I'd like to show you how I can be on a summer afternoon or how I've advanced in Biology or what I know about friendship or what I can do as a rabbit judge: doesn't compare to being a top TV star, I know; but it's solid. I'm the girl you'd come home to: 5' 11" and slim with dark brown hair; green eyes behind my glasses.

In a red dress, I might be quite different.

In my dreams now, I was either walking along the short graveled path of the Felicia Duncan Memorial, which seemed more lush and much larger, hand in hand with Iain, or was in some camp where I was aware of other people, but nothing seemed to matter as long as we were snuggled together in a tent: always with a sleeping bag between us, even though we were both naked. In one of the dreams, I tried to take the sleeping bag away and suddenly saw Chuck's face and heard his laugh.

"I'm kind of sick of this," I announced, setting the cardboard tray of chili rellenos in front of my father. My meal of choice was the plastic tray of mandarin duck and rice: both cooked "to perfection, ENJOY!" in the microwave oven: "One minute thirty: turn; One minute thirty: turn; Stir. Cook for three more minutes and add Golden Brand Sauce. Let sit for two minutes, then ENJOY!"

"Hmmf?" he asked, part of a chili relleno in his mouth.

"I'd like to cook a meal tomorrow night," I said. "Probably steak and potatoes. Sound all right?"

"Sounds wonderful," he answered. "Just tell Salamone to bill me. Buy whatever you want."

I threw my mandarin duck with rice and Golden Brand Sauce into the trashcan and went to do homework.

"Odd to see you doing the shopping," Dorothea remarked as she bagged my sirloin steak. "Approved?"

I nodded. "Maybe I'm going to do a lot more shopping from now on."

"Got butter and sour cream for the spuds? Might want chives, too. Steak sauce?"

"Where would I find those?"

"On Friday nights, when my dad would come home from his job at the factory, my mom would always serve him steak and potatoes," my father said, expertly cutting a bite-size piece and pointing it toward his mouth. "I never understood that ritual until years later, when I realized it was to make up for his not having a beer with the boys, like a lot of his co-workers did. She cooked what he liked and always followed it with a chocolate cake and he'd settle in for an evening of TV." He smiled at the memory. "I'd forgotten that, Lisa, until I bit into this steak. Your mother's cooking is different from what I remember." He smiled again, lost in a memory that he'd not indulged in, to my knowledge. I knew that his father, my grandfather, had died of a heart attack when my father was fifteen and my father had to work throughout high school, which made any participation in sports impossible. He'd gotten a small scholarship to SAC for good grades and worked when he was on vacations and breaks at jobs that nobody else wanted: mainly janitorial stuff. He'd majored in Economics, especially Finance, because he didn't want to have to do those menial jobs anymore, and he'd met my mother and she was glamorous.

"There's something to be said for a meal like this," he said as he finished it. "Could you cook it again sometime?"

I nodded. "Wednesday nights?"

"I certainly wouldn't object, Lisa." He looked around: at the grill pan, the dishes. "We'd better clean this stuff up. You know how your mother hates a mess." He unbuttoned his shirt sleeves and started the water in the sink. "Is there a place where your mother dumps grease? My mother always dumped it in a coffee can under the sink because she didn't want to clog the pipes. I've never thought about what your mother does."

I took the grill to the trash compactor as I'd seen her do it a few times and poured the grease out. Such a simple thing that my mother did and I'd never really thought about it.

We loaded the dishwasher together and he hummed the SAC Fight Song, then went into his den to watch television. I went upstairs to do homework.

"It's funny, Lisa," Iain wrote back, "I'd been thinking about that sort of stuff just today because I don't know just exactly when my father and I became distant after Mom's death. It must've been pretty soon after, though, because we were two people living in the same house but I couldn't talk to him about anything. He'd start showing up late after play rehearsal and get mad because I hadn't

249

bothered to feed or milk the goats and take care of my sister's rabbits. Well, he hadn't told me to. Then he offered me money to do it and that was okay but it wasn't the same as if he was there, doing the work with me. And the more I wanted him there, the more he was not. I finally just lived in my room and cooked my own meals. Except for some tax information that I got from him my senior year of high school, I really didn't deal with him. The first time I really saw him was that Saturday after Elizabeth told me to grow up and come see him."

"This is Hal Jones," the voice intoned over the credits at the end of Herpetology and You on that Tuesday night. "In January, we'll be presenting all new shows from many parts of the world: some right in your backyard! Make sure you stay tuned to see where we'll be and how you can help us protect endangered species in the United States."

"Good," I murmured to no one in particular. "Maybe they'll show some of the stuff they're doing in Rocky Mountain National Park right now."

"Hmm?" Bonnie asked. "Is that where they are now?"

"Yeah," I answered, trying to sound vague. "I heard that somewhere."

"Oh." Bonnie looked squarely at me. "Lisa, is there something you aren't telling me?"

I shrugged, trying to look defenseless. "What your mom said—"

"Oh—that—" she was almost going to apologize for Barb's telling all of us, over and over again that the lawsuit was going forward and the bank couldn't purchase any more land until a judge had looked at the mortgages and loans.

I nodded. "Yeah," I said. "You don't have to live with him, Bonnie." I thought of cooking for my father and how human he had become. He really didn't think about displacing people; he thought of buying land as a business decision. I wondered how he thought about marriage. Probably in about the same way. Herpetology and You that night was about the four scientists going to a lot of different bureaus in India and discussing the fate of a tiny reptile found on the bank of the Ganges. Since the show had been "recognized by the United Nations as a Scientific Unit," Hal Jones explained, "it's a whole lot easier to gain access to government ministers, but sometimes, the results are just as disappointing." No: the scientists didn't get government protection for the little reptile and they had to leave India midway through filming the show because the government asked them to leave. The final picture in the show was of a large ship leaving a harbor, a trailer with Herpetology and You painted on each side, chained to the deck, Anh Vu leaning on its front rail, looking out to sea.

REMEMBER: YOU CAN SEE US WHEN WE WEREN'T SUPERSTARS AND ADD TO IT!, the advertisement read, showing a photo of a really serious-looking, eight year-old Anh Vu holding a snake. JUST LOG ONTO HERPETOLOGYANDYOU.COM!

"I think I'm going to look at that," I told Bonnie.

"Just like every ninth grade girl in Zebulon County," she answered. "I thought you had a Physics test tomorrow."

"I went to your mother's memorial today," I lied to Iain. It had been yesterday, but I figured it didn't matter. "I'm still amazed that her co-workers and the community would have donated funds in her memory; and also to establish that greenery in the atrium! I looked on the website and found a couple of articles..."

"Yeah," he answered. "She was loved by a lot of people. I think that was why her death was so tough for my father: he'd always been quiet; just doing his work or helping her do her work when the occasion called for it. Then he didn't have any reason to deal with those people anymore. Sure: he was grateful that Fondis opened its heart to him: People still come up to him, when he's in the courthouse or at the fairgrounds, fourteen years later, and tell him how much she meant to them!"

"You've said how much your mother meant," I wrote back, "but what about your father? I know some students hate him, but most of us really like him because he tries to tell the truth."

"I've got to tell you the whole story in person, Lisa," Iain responded, "but there were a lot of students who really liked him: especially during his last eight years at Kutch, when he was running Yearbook, Newspaper, and both class plays; but after a couple of years, their lives had moved on. The talented ones were in college or doing something else; the ones who'd stayed behind were busy working on their farms or raising families or doing whatever people do. They didn't have time to call Arthur and ask him how it was going or to hang out with him. I sure didn't have much time for him at that point: I had to keep a 3.5 GPA and worked 20 hours a week in food service to keep myself in school. Besides, I really hadn't known him since Mom's death. I only started getting re-acquainted with him when I started getting copies of The Divide-Review in my mailbox when I was in graduate school and then at the studio."

251

It was a Wednesday, toward the end of October, and the air was chilly. The first fall snowstorm had lain wetly two weeks before and all the trees had lost their leaves, which lay sodden in the gutters and on the walks. The afternoon smelled of new snow when there was a sudden ringing of the doorbell and a Zebulon County Sheriff's Deputy greeted me as I opened it.

"Lisa Young?" he asked, consulting his notebook under the brim of his hat—one of those worn by Smokey the Bear. Behind him, across the street, I saw Eddie Brace standing, watching, that black dog of his straining on the leash to move. I turned my attention to the deputy and nodded.

"I need to know your whereabouts on Tuesday, October twentieth, between the hours of four and seven in the afternoon."

"My parents aren't home," I had the good sense to answer.

"Can you tell me if you saw anyone enter or exit the atrium at Whispering Pines Mental Health on Tuesday, October twentieth, between the hours of four and seven in the afternoon?"

"I wasn't even there," I answered.

"Um—" He flipped a couple of pages in his notebook. "According to my records, you had e-mailed an Iain Sanders that you had gone to the Felicia Duncan Memorial Fountain on that afternoon, Tuesday, October twentieth."

I felt cold in the pit of my stomach. I nodded. I had e-mailed Iain that.

"Did you see anyone else enter or exit the atrium when you were there?"

"My father will be home after eight o'clock," I answered. "Come back then."

I shut the front door, leaning my back against it. What could have happened? The house creaked. It always did that as cold weather approached, and used to scare me before my brother gave me a reason to be scared. My eyes examined the front hall with its Louis XIV table for the mail and the ornamental umbrella stand, then swept the lattice window of oak that separated my father's den and the television set. I ran in and turned on the local news.

"The Sheriff's Office is puzzled about vandalism at Whispering Pines Mental Health," the newscaster began, looking seriously at the camera. "The statue in memory of Felicia Duncan, which graces the green atrium of the building, was hit continually with a hammer or other blunt object, destroying the face of the statue and causing the water to flood into the first floor..."

Okay; that was what the deputy wanted to know. Now: what do I say when the deputy returns tonight? That I wasn't there? I took a deep breath. Yeah. I wasn't there. Well, I wasn't. I'd been there maybe on Thursday, last week. Would Iain look at that and call me a liar? Maybe. Maybe not. I shrugged. I didn't think the truth was so bitter.

"...Do you want to go shopping? I've been working all week and I want to do something fun. Climb in, Lisa." I found myself seated next to Janie, who was on the Rabbit Judging Team and enrolled in third grade at Kutch Elementary. Her daddy taught in the high school.

We went to Tenorio's, where Felicia bought two scented candles that the clerk wrapped carefully in newspaper; then to Freddy's, where Janie found a wooden box in the shape of a heart and Felicia found an aluminum windchime. The items were wrapped and we carefully placed them behind the backseat...

Was I dreaming? I was lying on the couch in my father's study.

There was the scrape of a key in the back door and my mother, looking flustered, came in, shrugging her coat off as she did so. "Lisa, why aren't you at school?"

She started the laptop computer on the counter, not waiting for my answer. "Now where is it?" she asked, looking among the addresses. "Lister. Lenox, Lexar, Lister, Preston!"

"Who?"

"Preston Lister," she said absently. "Manager at the Country Club.

"There was a deputy here," I said.

"Hmm?" She was busy punching a phone number. "That man will never—Oh. Sylvia? Dorothy Young. Is Preston there? Yes; I'll wait."

"There was a deputy here," I repeated.

"Preston? Dorothy Young. I'll make this short. There was a misunderstanding at lunch today, and if you value your job, you'll get rid of Ronald immediately, and—" she stopped. "I see." She paused, then added, "If you feel that way about Ronald, I can certainly understand, but I will never use your facilities again and I will recommend that my friends no longer use them, either. Please consider this carefully."

Replacing the phone in its cradle, she asked, "What was that, Lisa?"

"A Sheriff's Deputy came by this afternoon," I said.

"A what?"

I repeated myself. "He wanted to talk to me."

"Is this something to do with Eddie Brace?" Her eyes searched around the room for no reason. "Or what happened this afternoon?"

I was bewildered. "What happened this afternoon?"

"You haven't heard?" She sometimes didn't realize what happened to her was not immediately flashed to the press. "Oh—You were at school all day. Of course. Just something that happened with Ronald over a late lunch." She tried to laugh and sort of groaned. Ronald was the athletic trainer at the Country Club. Last summer, my mother was interested in my learning tennis from him. "You'll see how good he is," she'd promised. "So strong and gentle, with such a backhand!" So I'd signed up for a couple of lessons with him— "and just a few others," who turned out to be my mother's friends, all of whom demanded lots of attention from him. I spent both lessons lobbing a ball against a concrete wall, which I figured I could do at home.

"A deputy?" she asked quickly. Removing the phone from its cradle, she called the bank, pulling my father out of a meeting. He said he'd call Charles Holmes and have him meet us at home.

Vern Lassiter was dispatched to my father's den at six and he interviewed me in front of both my parents and Mr. Holmes; asking what I knew of the Felicia Duncan memorial and why I visited it. I explained that it was quiet there and I liked looking at the fountain. "Did you e-mail Iain Sanders that you'd been there on the day the vandalism happened?" he asked.

I nodded. "I couldn't remember if it was Tuesday or Wednesday."

He made a couple of notes while my mother asked, "Iain Sanders? Who's he, and why are you going to a mental institution, Lisa?"

Vern looked up quickly and caught my eye as I shrugged. "A friend," I said. "Felicia Duncan was his mother."

"And your English teacher is his dad," my mother concluded. "Why have you been e-mailing him? Have you been seeing him, Lisa?"

I shook my head. "It's not like that," I answered. "I met him when I went over to Elizabeth's in September and he gave me his e-mail."

"So you've known him a whole month," Mr. Holmes observed. "Where is he now?"

"I can answer that," Vern said, flipping his notebook closed. "He's staying with his dad this weekend. He wanted to see the damage for himself and came down from filming in Rocky Mountain National Park."

"Filming?"

"Well, that's concluded," he observed, standing up. "Mr. Holmes, is there anything you need me to convey to my boss?"

Mr. Holmes smiled. "Nothing, young man. Conducted in an entirely professional manner."

"Bonnie would like you to call her, Lisa," Vern said over his shoulder as he stepped out. "Good night."

"Why didn't you tell me?" was the same question from both Bonnie and my mother, although my mother was a little slower in figuring it out.

"He's just a friend," I told them both, adding to Bonnie that he'd asked that nobody else know about our friendship, but then he'd gone and told the Sheriff's Office about our e-mails and the TV news immediately picked up the connection between him and the ruined fountain and suddenly Arthur Sanders wasn't just my English teacher: he was the father of a celebrity. I was thought of by Bonnie and my mother as the girlfriend of a celebrity.

"Let's have them for dinner tomorrow night," my mother suggested. "It's high time we got to know your teacher anyway, Lisa."

"No," my father said quietly. He and Mr. Holmes had opened the scotch decanter and were sharing a drink together. "Dorothy, I believe the last thing that a television personality would want is to feel obligated to dine with us."

"But he's Lisa's friend," she began.

"So is Bonnie Lassiter and we don't invite her to dinner."
My mother said nothing; just took her drink and headed for the kitchen from where we could hear the clanking and rattle of pots and pans being mishandled.

"I don't think I should have seen that," Mr. Holmes observed, "and so I'll just let myself out—" He gulped the remains of his drink.

"No, Charles: I'd like you to remain a moment while I talk with Lisa," my father said, his banker's look replacing his concerned father look. He poured a splash into Mr. Holmes' glass, then settled back in his chair. "Lisa, how serious is this?"

I shrugged. "We're friends," I answered.

"And I'm friends with his father," he answered quietly, with just a hint of sarcasm, "and sometimes his father writes articles that are unfavorable to the business that keeps you fed and clothed."

"I know that."

"So has this Iain Sanders asked you for any information regarding me or the bank?"

I shook my head. "We e-mail about books, usually. He told me about his mother."

"Felicia Duncan was probably the finest director of Whispering Pines that we've ever had," Mr. Holmes observed, swirling the scotch in his glass. "Took it from a second-class facility in a trailer, loaded with debt; ten years later, an office building on Second Street, with the finest counseling programs available. Quite an accomplishment."

My father looked at him, puzzled as Mr. Holmes finished his drink for the second time.

"Lisa," Mr. Holmes said, standing up, "this relationship—friendship," he corrected himself, "hasn't affected your grade in Mr. Sanders' Literature class, has it?"

"No: he doesn't even know about it," I said. "Or didn't know about it until today," I added.

"Do you think it will?"

I shook my head.

"Good," he replied. "Arthur Sanders was Haley's teacher, back in the day, and I've never known him to be anything but impartial." Haley was Mr. Holmes' son, now an attorney in Denver. "I don't think you have anything to worry about, Hal."

Dinner was quiet that evening as my mother glared at my father.

"But you never even hinted that you knew Iain Sanders!" Bonnie told me. "And I'm your best friend, remember?"

"It's because he didn't want anyone else to know; not even his father, Bonnie. Besides," I added archly, "Do you tell me everything?"

"Only the good parts," she retorted, giggling.

"Okay—you win, Lisa. But there was something else. Eric told me about it. It happened this afternoon, while he was serving lunch: that late one they have after all the old ladies are done swimming, and Ronald, the trainer, who was sitting with your mother, started saying stuff about her."

"Stuff?"

"He called her a high class whore, Lisa. Everybody could hear it. He was drunk. Really drunk. Then he told Mrs. McDermott the same thing. Everybody in the dining room could hear him, Eric said, and then he broke his chair on the floor and passed out."

"Really?"

"Everybody knows Ronald's been sleeping with all these women ever since he was hired, two years ago—maybe not sleeping with them, but having sex with them—"

"Who knows about this?" I asked.

"All of Fondis," she answered. "Of course, Ronald's been fired, but everybody's going to remember what he said."

My mother had taken a couple of sleeping pills, I noticed, from the cabinet in the kitchen that had her vitamin supplements and other pills and medicines. She hadn't done that in a couple of years—not since Chuck had crashed the sports car.

12 /

They that trust in their own wealth, and boast themselves in the multitude of their riches, None of them can by any means redeem his brother... (Psalms: 49.6,7.)

"Can I talk to you?" Kevin passed a note to me in Chemistry, which was weird, because as lab partners, we were constantly together in that class, but I figured it was important, so I wrote him back: "Meet me at Fuller's after school?"

I didn't go as often to Mr. Sanders' room as I had before: in some ways, I felt a chill from him; that he wasn't quite as open as before, and the e-mails I had from Iain were very, very short. What had I done and what did they think I'd done?

The biggest change I saw after that weekend was how both Mr. Sanders and I were perceived: Mr. Sanders was no longer just an old English teacher hauled in to fill a vacancy: he was the father of a superstar, and every sophomore and senior girl in his classes suddenly paid attention. I was no longer the rabbit nerd who quietly did her work and wanted to get out: "It's so nice to see you bloom, Lisa," Mrs. Grimes, my counselor, told me as she consulted my scores on the tests. "I imagine that being with Iain Sanders is a part of it."

I demurred, hoping she wouldn't ask me about going on moonlight walks with him or some other interesting but misinformed speculation that I'd already heard in the gym locker room.

"Well," she puffed, "the scores show that you can get a tuition waiver to Miscatonic if you're willing to pay room and board; Boarshead, if you're willing to work for full tuition; and—" she obviously wanted to save the best for last— "Siwash, which will subsidize most of your room and board and all of your tuition if you agree to a work study plan. But why not right here, at Fondis University? You can get all of it waived."

I shook my head in such a way to make her withdraw. "Siwash?"

She nodded. "Small college in the Midwest. Are you interested?"

"Yes."

"Be far away from here," she observed. "You'll miss the mountains. You'll miss your family."

"Maybe," I answered, "but I'd like to take that risk."

She looked over her half glasses at me. "They're willing to take you on for fall next year. Even though your transcripts say that all you need is gym to graduate, Coach Quintana is going to hold you to two semesters, so there's no way you can enroll early."

Goddamn Coach Quintana.

Mrs. Grimes handed me an e-mail address and told me to tell them I was interested. "They'll send information to me and to your house. Your parents need to be informed since you're under age. That reminds me—" she tapped her pencil against her teeth a second— "just my own curiosity: how do they handle your having a boyfriend who's ten years older than you are? When my daughter, Kristin, was fifteen, she went out with a twenty one year-old, and it scared me to death."

I shrugged. So Mrs. Grimes thought I was going out with Iain? Everybody else seemed to think so, too.

Although my mother was once again cooking during the week, having stopped going to the country club, I still was in charge of steak and potatoes on Wednesdays, which I always bought at Bijou Grocery in Fuller's, adding greens for a salad and a couple of slices of chocolate cake from the bakery as my knowledge of the meal improved. Even though she was invited, my mother would not join my father and me; preferring to eat before I cooked, then asking about how much money I'd spent on the cut of beef; which, she indicated, she could have gotten for half the price. Even though it was a Monday, I figured I could get the shopping done early: so I did, sailing through the vegetables and the butcher counter, to arrive at Dorothea Harris' checkstand with my purchases.

"Charge again?"
I nodded as she put the groceries through the scanner and bagged them. "Young man waiting for you outside," she remarked. " Not good to keep a young man waiting, Lisa. They don't wait for very long."

"I think that Eddie Brace destroyed that statue, Lisa," Kevin said, buried in the folds of his parka and hood.

"Why?"

"For one, he can't stand Mr. Sanders. Is there anything else?"

"I guess not."

"I like Mr. Sanders," he observed, kicking some ice that stuck to the bench stubbornly. "I think I've learned more about writing from him than I ever did from Mrs. Carey. I'd hate to see him leave before we do."

"Yeah," I answered. Even though I hadn't really hung around after school for the past couple of weeks, "I know what you mean. I think we'd lose something."

He kicked at the ice again.

."Okay," I said, shivering in the wind that whipped over the bench: "So how are you going to prove Eddie broke the statue?"

"What's the one thing besides that dog that he always has?" He stretched his long legs out and looked like a scarecrow. "Want a ride home?" he asked.

"Sure. In that backpack? Probably his camera. He's taken more pictures of Barabbas..."

We climbed into his truck and he drove slowly toward my parents' house. "So how do we get that camera?"

"Somebody could go through the backpack," I answered.

"But he never puts the backpack down."

"Maybe somebody could open the backpack when he wasn't looking. Be a big spill all over the floor."

He handed me the two bags of meat and potatoes and salad and chocolate cake slices. "Say—" he stopped me. "Did you ever see Eddie carrying a hammer around?"

"He could have anything in that backpack, Kevin," I observed.

"That's true. Sure as hell not a copy of King Lear."

There was a letter lying beside the computer on the kitchen countertop, on Country Club stationery, telling my mother that there had been changes in management and personnel and that she could return any time she liked, with or without her friends. I wondered if Eric Lassiter was one of the "changes," but I didn't think so: he wasn't senior enough to get in trouble with my mother and her friends; but now, as I looked at the last paragraphs, maybe he was: he'd been made assistant manager of grounds and the restaurant. It meant longer hours for him and better pay for him, I guessed, but he'd have to deal with a lot of spoiled rich people.

"What are you doing, Lisa," my mother asked, breezing into the kitchen, "reading my mail?" She checked on a chicken piece, grilling on the stove and opened the oven to check on something tomato in a casserole. "That's not what I wanted the Country Club to do," she remarked as she stirred the casserole. "I wanted them to completely refund our dues for the hurt caused by that man."

"That's a lot of money," I observed.

She shut the oven door with greater force than it needed. "A lot of money they'll never receive again," she said smartly. "Your father and I are going to Europe," she announced, "for at least six weeks."

Although I was surprised, I kept it to myself as she went on, "with the McDermotts. Since Mike lost the election as District Attorney, he's had some time on his hands; and your father—he hasn't taken a holiday in years!"

That was true, I reflected. Although we had gone on vacation, it was always my mother, Chuck, and me. The last time we'd gone, I remembered, was when Chuck was still in high school, some five years before—before Chuck started filling up his summers with football camps. Even though she and I'd had the time, she'd never taken me on vacation.

"Don't you have rabbits to feed?" she asked, pulling the chicken off the grill and throwing the pan into the sink. She'd settle down to e-mail at the counter while munching her dinner then go to her room where she'd slip the "SOFT SOUNDS OF NATURE" into the CD player and read a book or a magazine until bedtime.

"How was class with Mr. Sanders?" my father rubbed his eyes as he sat down. I was busy grilling the steak, wondering why he'd ask. When I didn't reply, he went on: "Mark Allen came into the Bank today to refinance his loan and was telling me how interested Kevin was in his English class, which I think is the first time Kevin's ever expressed any interest in his teachers; and a couple of days ago, I saw Margaret Simpson and Hank Lood, who told me the same thing. The only parent I haven't heard positive things from among the Bank customers is Ed Brace." My father looked puzzled. "Is Eddie really that bad a student?"

I nodded, smiling a moment. It was a rare moment when my father let down his guard and really tried to understand something that went against his Bank's best interests. "I mashed the potatoes tonight," I said, turning off the burner under the pot. I hope you like them as much as baked."

"Homemade mashed potatoes?" he smiled tiredly. "Haven't had those in years."

"You want to know what Eddie's like?" I asked vaguely, pulling down a couple of plates and putting the butter dish on the table. As he nodded, I took a deep breath and exhaled the words: "I think Mrs. Carey passed him because she wanted to keep her job, and I think most of the other teachers do, too, because I've never seen him take homework home until this year, and only in Mr. Sanders' class."

"But it's all set that he's going to Princeton," my father observed. "If what you're saying is true, he won't last a week there."

I shrugged as I served the plates and sat down.

"So he's not a good student—" my father began.

"No; he's not a good student," I replied, cutting a small piece of my steak and chewing it before adding, "and he has called teachers names, broken desks, torn books, thrown things, and probably made a lot of teachers quit. Mr. Flanders, the Science teacher in Junior High? The one who took Kevin and me to the Science Fairs in the winter?"

My father nodded.

"On the last day of eighth grade, I remember Mr. Holmes came to see him with Dr. Brace. Bonnie's brother, Vern, helped load Mr. Flanders' van the next week and Vern said that Mr. Flanders was told to make Eddie pass or lose his job. Mr. Flanders didn't and now he's gone. And Eddie went on to high school."

My father chewed his meal thoughtfully, nodding. "So Eddie could be the cause of a lot of his own misfortune."

I nodded.

"I believe I misspoke the other night, Lisa, in front of Mr. Holmes," he said quietly. "I don't want your interest in school or your teacher to be influenced by what goes on at the Bank."

"Thank you," I said, passing him the salad. I felt closer to him than I had in years and maybe would have said something else, but the telephone rang with Mike McDermott on the other end, wondering if they could get some golfing in at Saint Andrews during their trip.

I cleared away the dishes after a few minutes then headed up to my own room.

"You're hardly ever there anymore," I started my e-mail to Iain, hoping I'd get some kind of response other than "That's nice," "and I wonder why. What have I done to make you stop writing me? Tonight, my father and I had a talk about what a creep Eddie Brace is and I really was able to talk to him. I'd like to tell you about it, but can't if all I get from you is two words every now and then."

I received a reply later that evening: "Ask my father, Lisa."

I printed the e-mail and put it in my backpack, strolling into Mr. Sanders' room after school to toss it onto his desk, in the way of the papers he was mulling over.

He looked irritated, then smiled. Then he read the e-mail and scratched his head. "Would you like this back?" he asked, handing it toward me.

I took it quietly.

"How old are you, Lisa?" he asked.

"Seventeen."

"How old is Iain?"

I shrugged. "Twenty-seven."

He nodded. "How appropriate is it for the son of your English teacher to be carrying on a flirtation with you; or what may look like a flirtation; even though it's entirely innocent?"

"We're just friends—"

His eyes flashed. "Lisa, when you're graduated, you may e-mail Iain anything you like. Until that happens, however, I am not going to allow him to make a fool of himself or of you through a written record that could embarrass you both and could open me up to a lawsuit. Do you know how many people wonder where I get my information regarding the proposed golf course? Some think you go through your father's files and feed the information to me."

I drew back. I'd never seen Mr. Sanders so angry and the idea that I would betray my father—

"So does this mean that I can't see Iain?" I asked quietly.

He shook his head. "Half the town thinks you're his girlfriend, Lisa. When he comes to visit, of course you can see him. I just do not want any written or spoken record between you; do you understand?"

I shook my head. "You're doing this because you're a reporter, right? Because you don't care really about my feelings or Iain's or anyone's but your own stupid newspaper—"

"No," he said quietly. "Get some tissue and listen carefully, Lisa."

I pulled a tissue out of the box and blew my nose and started wiping my frustrated tears.

"It's hard to explain all of this to you, Lisa, but just hearing the talk in the faculty lounge a week ago, I knew I needed to stop it as quickly as I could. Your counselor, Mrs. Grimes, already had you married to Iain, and was laughing with Mrs. Pierson about what it would be like making a home on a windswept atoll in the Galapagos. They're just speculating, of course, because I know how cautious Iain is and I know how cautious you are: you're both smart as well; but I can't let any written record exist between you that can be hacked. Take a look here." He reached into his briefcase and pulled out a page from The Fondis Daily, dated a couple of days previous:

"Just where is Arthur Sanders, of The Divide-Review, getting his information? We suspect that it's from the lovely 17 year-old sister of Chuck Young and daughter of Hal Young, Lisa, who is a student in Mr. Sanders' AP Literature class and dating Arthur's delicious son, Iain, a star of Herpetology and You, although the connection was not made publicly until the Duncan Memorial was destroyed two weeks ago and Iain immediately reported that Lisa had e-mailed him that she'd visited it on the evening it was destroyed. Just what else is in those e-mails? We'd all love to know…"

I sat quietly, still mad. I knew he was right. That didn't stop the tears, though. He returned to his papers until I began to speak. "When is Iain coming back?" I asked quietly. I was irritated that my eyes were still welling and I dabbed them angrily.

"Thanksgiving," he replied. "The whole cast and crew has been invited to spend the weekend at our place—Iain's and mine."

"Really?" I blew my nose as I figured. That was ten days away.

"Really," he answered, smiling. "Elizabeth, God Bless Her, is coordinating the whole thing, figuring out where everyone will sleep;

how we're going to have meals; the whole lot of it: seven cast and crew of Herpetology and You." He chuckled at the rhyme.

I wondered if Elizabeth needed help.

13 /

...and there is a friend that sticketh closer than a brother. (Proverbs: 18,24)

That whole week was spent by my mother in packing and my father in frustration as he spent more hours at the Bank, tying up loose ends; then on the phone and the computer all hours, leaving orders for every little thing that came to mind, from a trust fund set aside years ago for an aged cat to a multi-million dollar loan for a building going up.

Except for Wednesday, when I cooked, and Thursday, when I was with Bonnie, I just waited for the call from downstairs, around 6:30, that dinner was served, and then I spent fifteen minutes listening to my mother as I shoveled food into my mouth. "Now you'll be able to watch any of Chuck's games, Hal," she assured my father, who was grousing about the league championship against Idaho, "as long as you've got your laptop plugged in. Lydia and I talked to the travel agent and she assured us that everywhere we go, we'll be able to check in. And of course, there's the telephone, if Lisa runs into trouble. I've got all the numbers you'll need in my directory on the kitchen laptop," she added. "I also put our entire itinerary there, so you'll be able to know where we are on any given day."

I smiled. I knew they'd be gone a month and a half: that was all I needed to know. "Will Chuck be back while I'm gone?"
She frowned. "No; I don't think so, Lisa. He said something about spending Christmas with the team. They were all going to Florida, I think. Yes: I'm fairly sure it was Florida."

"Good," I thought.

"But what are you going to do with yourself while we're gone?"

Glad you noticed, Mother. "Oh—I thought I'd have Thanksgiving dinner with Elizabeth," I answered, "And Bonnie's open for Christmas," I added.

"But you won't have any presents to bring—"

"She can charge what she needs at Fuller's," my father cut in. "Lisa's a big girl, Dorothy; she'll figure out what to do."

They left on Saturday morning, each giving me an obligatory kiss at the door before they descended to the car, driven by Karl, one of the tellers, who looked like he couldn't wait to get rid of them. He smiled wanly at me and waved. He'd take them to the airport, check their baggage, make certain my father had his passport and steer them both toward the gate. I didn't envy him one bit.

As I'd promised Mr. Sanders, I kept only a minimal correspondence on e-mail with Iain, telling him I looked forward to seeing him on Thanksgiving and asking if there were any particular places he and the rest of the cast would like to go.

"I asked the others and everyone agreed that we'd just like to sleep in beds for once and do the things normal people do," he responded. "Nothing out-of-the way, nothing different. Tanner told me he just wanted to go shopping for his kid sister's birthday; Hal said he'd like to go dancing."

"Lisa, I don't know what I'm going to do," Elizabeth was on the phone the Sunday before Thanksgiving. "Arthur is going to host this television crew, and when I offered to help, I hadn't realized that there'd be so many. Besides the four stars, they've got a wardrobe person, a director and two film editors!"

"Aren't they going to live with Mr. Sanders?"

"Oh—" she caught herself. "I've been thinking so much about this, I'd forgotten that you don't know—I offered to serve Thanksgiving dinner and possibly lunch the next day. Arthur just called and said they'd have everything catered; paid for by the producer; and could they just use my home for eating and sleep at his?"

"It sounds very nice, Elizabeth," I said. "You don't have to do any of the cooking."

"No; I don't suppose I do," she answered hollowly. Then, after a pause, she asked, "Would you mind living here over Thanksgiving and while they're here? You know where everything is and—"

"When do you want me?"

It felt good cleaning Elizabeth's house that afternoon: making sure that all the linens were in the right drawers and all the china and silver were in place and clean and polished. We pulled apart her already massive dining room table and added all the leaves while she quickly figured the numbers then figured them again. The total number of guests, she figured, would be fifteen: Mr. Sanders, me, Mary and Caroline from the Library, Dorothea Harris, and her in addition to the cast and crew of Herpetology and You.

"I'm so used to cooking for myself," she said, puttering around her kitchen, "and I really don't know what you eat, Lisa, besides pizza."

"Just about anything," I answered.

"There are steaks in the garage freezer," she added, not really listening. "I always keep them there for Arthur, when he comes over..." she paused. "Do you want one of those?"

I shook my head. "Whatever you're eating is fine," I answered.

"Now, we're going to have to make sure you get to school these next two days. I suppose Arthur could drive you in. I need to call him."

"There's the bus..." I volunteered.

She shook her head. "All the children around here are middle school or elementary age. The bus doesn't go to Fondis High."

The telephone rang and Elizabeth brightened as she spoke. "Just salad and chicken," she said, "but you're welcome, if you want to come. Lisa's here, too. Okay." She hung up, then pulled two wine glasses from a cabinet and set another seat at the kitchen table. "Arthur's coming over for a few minutes," she remarked. She fixed a quick salad and placed it just as Sanders knocked.

"Hi," I said as I opened the door, feeling foolish. I hadn't really spoken to him for two weeks since he'd told me about the e-mails with Iain and I really did not know what to say to him.

"Lizzie," he announced in a broad voice, "I have news from the catering front that might be of interest to you!" He strode to the kitchen table, put his arm around her and kissed her on the forehead, then hung his coat on the kitchen chair and sat down. "The caterer is Candlelight Catering, and Mr. Steve Mitchell, its owner, will be coming by tomorrow night to figure out how many plates you'll need, how many servers will be required, and what kinds of food he'll be preparing."

Elizabeth nodded as he took a forkful of salad. "That's wonderful," she agreed. Then, "Are you interested in watching the film I ordered? It came in today." She pointed to the red and white envelope in the pile of mail on the counter.

He shook his head. "Papers to grade," he said, looking at me with a smile.

"So the caterer is going to be here tomorrow night?" Elizabeth looked relieved.

"Nothing to fear," Sanders answered quietly. "Just Iain and a few of his friends."

"Nothing to fear," she repeated. "The prodigal son—"

"Who was dead and is now alive," Sanders added, smiling. "Thanks to you, mostly."

She smiled back. "Coffee?"

He finished his salad, tipped his second glass of wine, and leaned back in his chair. "As usual, Elizabeth, it's just what I need."

She smiled to herself, washing the dishes in the sink. I could see them both, much younger, for just a second, then Sanders got to his feet. "Lisa," he told me, "I'll be leaving at six thirty. I'll meet you at the mailbox at the end of the drive to get you to school. All right?"

I nodded. "I'll be ready."

Coach Quintana called me out from the two basketball scrimmages at Gym that Monday afternoon after I'd run into the wall twice and my glasses had gone flying. "Enough, Lisa," she commanded, gesturing that I was to join her on the bleachers, right underneath the framed jersey, #7, that was my brother's. I felt kind of prickly, but I knew she didn't want to discuss my performance: even though I was a klutz, I was out there trying to do whatever it was that she ordered and I'd aced all the quizzes she gave on the muscular system.

"Ms. Grimes tells me that this is the only class you need to graduate," she said shortly, "And she was asking if I'd waive it for next semester."

"Yeah," I answered.

"What would you do with a semester off?"

I really hadn't thought about it. I could work at the Bank, I guessed; or maybe take a couple of courses at Zebulon County Community College. I shrugged.

"What's senior year like for you?" She asked, genuinely interested. She'd probably never spoken with a nerd about it; if she were like the athletes I knew, she'd never have to.

I shrugged. "It's okay, I guess."

"Hmm." She nodded, then blew her whistle to break up a tussle over the ball. Clearly, I reflected, Coach Quintana and I weren't going to bond very quickly. "I think this class is good for you," she said, resuming her seat. "It's teaching you things you don't get anywhere else."

I guess she expected me to say something; I didn't know what to say.

"Well, I'll think about it," she said.

"How come you didn't tell me you're living with Elizabeth Prentice now?" Bonnie asked me at lunch. "I called your house last night. Left a message. It's probably still there."

"Oh—" I smiled. "I didn't even think—Elizabeth was worried about entertaining all those people and asked me to help out; that's all. I spent yesterday cleaning."

"No ulterior motives?" She raised an eyebrow.

I giggled. "Maybe." It was fun joking with her at this level. I'd told her about not e-mailing Iain and she got predictably mad but then cooled off when she understood why I couldn't. "I did get an e-mail from Iain the other day," I added. "He says that the whole group just wants to do normal things during the four days they're here, like shopping and dancing."

"Really?" Bonnie was thinking aloud. "I could borrow the Suburban and take them anywhere they want to go. What do you think? There's also the dance at the Country Club on Saturday night: Eric could get them tickets."

"I like it. I'll e-mail Iain tonight."

Mr. Mitchell of Candlelight Catering had probably dealt with worse people than Elizabeth in his thirty years in business and he set her at ease immediately. All he needed, he told her, was a place to put his steam tables and a place to prepare. The steam tables would be set up on Wednesday and the chef and servers would arrive one hour prior to serving. No, she did not need to provide dishes, unless she wanted to. He would prefer that she did not. No, she did not need to provide silverware or tablecloths: he would take care of all that. No, it would not look like a cafeteria: the waiters would be in bowties and the china would be restaurant quality in a festive pattern, as would the tablecloths. The forks, knives and spoons would be polished silverplate. The centerpiece would be a small fountain. He would also provide glassware. Of course, the dining room table was perfect. Thanksgiving dinner would be served at six; breakfast at seven the following morning; lunch at eleven-thirty; dinner at six on Friday. Was that all right?

Elizabeth nodded happily. "And this is all being paid for?"

"We received a credit card order this morning from the network," she was told, "for everything from Thursday to dinner on Sunday night."

"What if they don't eat everything?"

"That's your option. If you want to, we can pack it for freezing or take it with us."

"C'n you swing by my parents' house, Bonnie?" I asked, climbing into her car as we left school. "I want to check on my rabbits."

So Bonnie got herself a drink in the kitchen and turned on the laptop on the counter while I spent five minutes making sure the water was flowing to the cages and the food was not clogged up.

"You might want to look at this," she said, pointing to a couple of exclamation marks.

"HAVING THANKSGIVING WITH MONICA BECAUSE TEAM NOT GOING TO FLORIDA. WISH ME LUCK IN NEW ORLEANS GAME ON XMAS. CHUCK."

"Thought you'd like to see it," Bonnie said. "Checked the telephone messages yet?"

I punched the numbers and erased Bonnie's message; saved a couple from the Art League for my mother, then paused as I heard the fourth one. It was Monica, so happy to get to meet me, if I could make it up to Northfort to meet her mother, she gushed. I erased it.

"All done?" Bonnie had been flipping through one of the gourmet magazines on the counter, humming to herself. Iain had responded almost immediately: yeah, the crew wanted to go to the country club dance; most of them hadn't been to a dance since college—and being driven around by Bonnie—well—they'd see. Anh wanted to see the Agricultural Building because of the solar panels and alternative energy; Hal wanted to tour the University museum because of its dinosaur exhibit; Tanner wanted to find a smoky jazz joint. Iain didn't tell me what he wanted. I liked that.

"Planning anything special?" Bonnie asked.

I shrugged. I really didn't know. The last time we'd been together, we climbed all over Elizabeth's barn, walked to the trees down by the creek at the bottom of her property, and looked at a rickety treehouse that Iain had played in with Jim Prentice. Then we did chores.

"How romantic," Bonnie giggled as she turned into the driveway.

Did it have to be romantic, with candles and holding hands? I didn't think so. When I was twelve, and didn't understand the whole thing completely, I made sure I had a couple of candles and some matches for when Chuck would come to see me and I made sure to have a lavender spray ready on my dresser. I'd thought that was romantic. No: Iain was romantic enough just being himself, I thought, remembering the thrill I had when he helped me up the ladder to the hay loft and the feeling I had when he'd told me about building that little platform on the branches high above. No: I couldn't think of it as romantic in the usual sense: I treasured it because it was very real; especially that afternoon in the hayloft, where we spent time while his father and Elizabeth sat in the kitchen far away. I thought of the cobweb I noticed in the corner: the sunlight on it like so many rainbows and how I felt.

Very real was also the arrival of Herpetology and You about two in the afternoon, Thanksgiving Day. The cable TV stars, looking ragged and unshaven, slowly got out of two large SUVs, one pulling a large trailer, and headed quietly into the Sanders house where they found their rooms, shut the doors, and slept for a couple of hours. We were in the kitchen to greet them: Only Iain stopped in the doorway, saying: "If you all don't mind, we'll just go to bed now." The others filed past him: a cameraman; a film editor; a middle-aged wardrobe specialist; a director; a producer. Anh, Hal, and Tanner briefly nodded at us.

"You'll find fresh towels in the bath—" Elizabeth called as doors upstairs were slammed, the occupants finding their names on cards we'd posted earlier. "I guess not," she observed. "Do you suppose there's enough room here, Arthur?" she turned to him. "There's room enough in my house."

"Maybe for the women," Mr. Sanders replied. "I imagine the women and men don't really care who's sleeping with whom right now."

"I counted exactly one woman," Elizabeth observed. "Their wardrobe lady, I gather. She'll feel a little more welcome with me than with the boys."

I couldn't quite get over the idea that he was sleeping with Elizabeth during his son's stay. It made sense, of course: he'd turned over his bedroom to three of the crew and he'd done the same with Iain's old room, as he'd done with Janie's.

"We'll arrange as we need to," he promised, giving her a quick kiss on the forehead. "I'm sure you'll find something else to worry about, Elizabeth." He turned to me. "Want to help me with the goats and chickens, Lisa?"

"Sure," I shrugged. Anything was better than following Elizabeth around, watching her obsess over a bathroom corner or a twice-dusted shelf.

He nodded toward a trashcan in the garage. "Grain's in there. Put it in the bucket beside. Remember where the chickens are?"

I nodded. As I filled the bucket, I wondered if following Elizabeth around was preferable to this. In the back of my mind, I heard Chuck's laugh.

"Funny," he observed as he led the first goat to the milking stand and fitted the stop so she couldn't move around, "I was looking at Fair results from about ten years ago. You had the champion chicken that year, but then the next year, I find you in rabbits. Why'd you give up on chickens?"

I shook my head. Since he covered Fair, he probably also knew that I'd won the Round Robin, where champions in one animal are given another to try and present for exhibition, because I was lucky enough to have the champion pullet, I remembered most of the characteristics and what to look for in a prize bird like that and beat everyone else soundly.

"Cat got your tongue?" he asked conversationally, settling down to milk, the bucket under the teats of the goat, who was happily eating grain from a tray in the milking stand.

"No," I answered politely. "I—something happened to my chickens a couple days after Fair that year. They were all dead."

"Oh," he said softly.

"I'll go feed," I said, pulling my jacket around me against the chill. There was more to it, of course: I'd told Chuck I'd tell and I did and he killed them. I told and my mother said it was a lie, just like when Bonnie Holstrom had called the house and said Chuck beat her because she wouldn't have sex with him— "How could you say that about your own brother, Lisa?" she demanded, and called Chuck downstairs to the kitchen and made me apologize. I came home the next day and found every one of my twelve chickens: Austrolorps and Rhode Island Reds, their necks broken and thrown against the wall of the carriage house, blood all over the ribbons I'd won and blood all over the pages of my poultry book, where I was reading about turkeys for the following year.

271

Mr. Sanders' chickens weren't very attractive, I realized as I broke the thin sheet of ice that lined their waterer; nothing show quality, but a mixed bunch: a flock that had been much bigger years before, who moved quietly into the henhouse, where I poured the feed into the feeder, then checked for eggs along the shelves behind. I found three, which I carefully put into the bucket. I turned, closed the henhouse door behind me, then closed the gate, making sure it was latched against predators.

"Back door's open, Lisa," Mr. Sanders called from the garage, where he must have heard me because he couldn't see me, "Just leave the eggs on the counter by the stove."

"What did you do?" My mother demanded when she saw the dead chickens. She'd just been awakened from her nap by my crying. "I want this mess cleaned up at once!"

Chuck stood in the doorway afterwards as my hands, covered with blood and feathers, stuffed chicken after chicken into a garbage bag, his arms folded; a grin on his face.

"I noticed something I missed last time I was here," I said, putting the bucket down next to the trashcan full of scratch grains, "there's a rabbit hutch next to the fence."

He smiled. "I just don't want to take it down yet," he murmured, "even though it's probably pretty rickety."

14 /

He hath uncovered his sister's nakedness;
he shall bear his iniquity. (Leviticus:20,17)

"Do you want to lie down, Lisa?" Elizabeth asked as we re-entered her house. "Still a few hours before the party, and you've been up the last two days nonstop."

I shook my head. "I'll be all right, Elizabeth. Is there still something that needs to be done?"

"Bathrooms, kitchen, hallway, spare rooms in case someone wants to move in—" she ticked the items off on her fingers. "I can't think of anything, Lisa."

"Oh—I can," I answered. "The barn needs work."
She shrugged. "If you want to—"

It gave me time to think. Shovel, fill wheelbarrow, take wheelbarrow to the top of the ridge out back, dump wheelbarrow, continue. Bonnie had told me that guys were strange. They seemed interested, then didn't seem interested, which drove her nuts the first couple of times, then she learned to back off. "I've learned to go where I want to go and if there's someone who wants to come along, I guess I'll let him," she'd said. "Kind of like Kevin Allen and you. He seems to want to come along wherever you're going. I think he's got a crush on you."

But I had a crush on Iain. No reason to deny it, I figured. It made me laugh. Of course: me and thirteen million other girls who watched Herpetology and You.

"Don't tell anyone," he'd warned me that afternoon, then he goes and tells the Sheriff's Office that we'd been e-mailing regularly since then. What did he mean? I'd kept a secret that did not need to be kept—except that he was a popular television figure—and I suddenly shared a certain fame with him. I didn't understand.

It was getting dark when the caterers arrived, their arms loaded with trays and supplies. "We'll have dinner in an hour," one promised as Elizabeth pointed him to the kitchen. If we need anything, we'll holler."

I looked down the stairs from Jim's room, watching the shadows on the floor, hearing the sounds of cutlery and dishes. Jim, who was the veterinarian in Australia, had left behind a few items from his childhood: a couple of Biology and Chemistry textbooks, a mobile of the solar system, and some glow-in-the-dark stars that he'd put all over his ceiling. They'd startled me when I first noticed them, then they became charming as my eyes adjusted to the dark with their pinpoints of light. His bed was long and narrow: I stretched out fully and still had a foot of mattress left. He also had a fair amount of closet space, where I had my red dress hanging. There was only a small mirror, though, and I had to move around to see how I looked. Half an hour to go. I sighed and read a few more chapters of The Adventures of Huckleberry Finn.

Six o'clock. I put on my dress, made sure I had the little pearl and gold necklace I was given last birthday round my neck, put on my heels, which I only wore to openings and art exhibitions, put the straps through the buckles, and stepped out to the second floor hallway, where I waited. The cast and crew, most still blinking from sleep and hasty showers, all wearing work shirts and jeans, started seating themselves around the table, some remarking at the place cards I'd made. Elizabeth was greeting her other guests at the door: Mary and Caroline from the Library and Dorothea Harris. I heard exclamations of the usual sort about how lovely the house looked; Dorothea Harris' a bit louder than the rest: "Well, Elizabeth, this place looks about the same as it did last year." Elizabeth laughed at that; I smiled. "You never let any dust settle, do you?"

"Part of it's because of Lisa—Lisa, where are you?" she called. "Lisa did a lot of the housework this year and even—" Elizabeth stopped as I came down the stairs. So did everybody else.

"Here's Lisa," she said.

"You don't look a thing like last year," Dorothea said.

Iain found his seat next to mine with Anh on the other side. Across the table was Dorothea. Mr. Sanders was at the foot of the table; Elizabeth was at the head.

"Wow," Dorothea remarked. "Dinner catered?"

Charles, the director, answered: "As many days as we're here: breakfast, lunch, and dinner."

"What happens when the ratings go down?"

"Then we get a jar of peanut butter and half a loaf of bread." He raised his newly-filled wine glass. "Mrs. Prentice, we're very grateful to you. Every one of us. We've been on the road for three years through Thanksgivings and Christmases doing the show and I know we all miss our families and get togethers like this, in a home, instead of a hotel somewhere or an embassy, and we also appreciate the chance to sleep in real beds once more, Mr. Sanders. For the past two months, we've been sleeping in tents or the trailer."

"Hear, hear!" Marla, the costume/makeup specialist added, taking a large drink of her wine.

"So: to two people who are willing to take in Iain Sanders and even admit they know him!" Charles clinked his glass against those closest to him and drank the wine in a gulp. Everybody else did, too. My raised glass was full and I followed suit. It made me cough and then filled me with a kind of warmth. My eyes filled with tears and I looked at my plate. I coughed again.

"Everything all right?" Iain leaned in close. "That wine can hit you kinda' hard if you're not used to it."

I cleared my throat, dabbed at my eyes with the napkin, relishing his closeness. It was as if every hair on my right side was standing on end and the left side wanted to stand on end, too. His cheek was right above me. I turned quickly and planted a kiss on it and said I was all right.

"Just take it easy," he advised like a big brother, which made me feel slightly sick, thinking of my own big brother.

I nodded as the wine was quickly replenished and the soup and salad were served. I toyed with the salad, ate part of a roll, and had half the soup as I listened to Iain tell Dorothea about his travels. "Antarctica was probably the worst," he said. "We were there in the midst of winter and a storm was blowing, cutting off all supplies for a week. I seriously wondered if we were going to starve to death, or wind up like Scott's Expedition. Nobody could get through on satellite phone; the computers couldn't get any speed, and then someone turned on the radio." He shook his head at the memory. "The radio," he repeated. "And in Morse Code, it was asking, 'Iain, how are you? It's your father.'" He turned to look at Arthur, who, interrupted from a conversation with the wardrobe/makeup specialist, looked at him curiously. "How you managed to patch a call from a bunch of ham radio operators to us in Antarctica still amazes me."

"What amazes me is that I still remembered Morse Code," Hal Jones added. "How did you do it, Mr. Sanders?"

"I wanted to wish you Merry Christmas," Mr. Sanders said. "I asked some of the ham radio operators around here to try and get the message to Antarctica. They were pretty happy to do so."

"And they wished us all Merry Christmas, then got hold of the Navy to come help us out."

"Glad to do it," Mr. Sanders replied.

"Probably saved our lives," Anh said. "A toast to Mr. Sanders and his ability to save our lives with ham radio!"

Everybody drained his glass again. I sipped mine. The bread and the soup had taken off the effects of the first glass. Mustn't lose control. I'd had wine before, of course, at the museum, the hospital opening, the VFW hall across from Whispering Pines Mental Health, where my father held the Bank's annual Christmas Party. But there I'd sipped it; not slammed it. I didn't want to slosh my way around like my mother did, saying stupid things to some people and hanging onto others, laughing hysterically. But this is different. You're among friends.

"A toast to Fondis!" someone yelled. I again sipped my wine. A couple of waiters not only charged the glasses; they skillfully began clearing the soup and salad and replaced it with turkey, gravy, and mashed potatoes.

"A toast to the small frog, whatever it's called!"

"A toast to the Swiss Navy!"

And on it went. "You've already had two glasses of wine, little sister," Anh observed, leaning in. "Take it easy, okay?"

"That's just what Chuck—I mean, Iain—has told me," I answered, laughing.

"Chuck?" Oh yeah; you're his sister, aren't you? The quarterback for SAC?"

"Yes, but—"

Anh's cellphone suddenly went off. "Damn! It's my mom, probably calling for the tenth time about whether I took a shower or not. Vietnamese mother," he said by way of explanation to the rest of the table.

Mr. Sanders was having a discussion with Marla; Charles, the Producer, was discussing something with Elizabeth. Tanner and Hal were entertaining the Librarians, Mary and Grace, both of whom were animatedly laughing.

"Oh yeah," Dorothea was telling Iain, "some folks in town already have you two pegged. The Fondis Daily has run pictures of you in your high school days and compared you to then, interviewing all kinds of people; or trying to—most said they weren't interested."

"Good," Iain answered. "Nobody made anything up?"

"Oh—Mrs. Sugarman, but she's senile anyway and nobody really believed her when she said you used to ride a white horse to her house and feed her spoonfuls of caviar."

"But that was the most fun part of my childhood!"

Anh sighed as he slapped the receiver of his cell phone shut. "My little sister wants to date a guy she met at Berkeley and Mom says no. My little sister is doing her residency in internal medicine. My little sister is twenty five years-old."

"So nothing's changed?" Tanner asked.

"Your brother's Chuck Young?" Anh asked, returning to the table. "I follow a lot of college ball out there: don't have much else to do sometimes. I love his moves, Lisa. He's everywhere. That game against Idaho—"

I nodded. I'd heard it all before: from my father, my mother, Dr. Hoeppner, who still had a photo of him and Chuck hugging after

Chuck's first touchdown. "I'd tried to find more information on him, like before college," Anh continued, "because I have this theory, you see, about great athletes: that they show their stuff between age six and twelve and I've been trying to find videos of Chuck from then. Parlamon Rex, Stacy Henderson, Rick Smith—I got the videos off YouTube. There anything like that of your brother? Maybe like Little League games, or something a parent filmed? I'd love to get hold of it."

My parents kept those DVDs and videotapes hidden away because my father did not want to show Chuck's promise "until it's time, Dorothy: then he'll burst onto the scene." He'd planned Chuck's first football game, knowing exactly how the team was doing; knowing exactly what Chuck would do to dazzle them. Did he pass some money to Coach Mecklinburg? I wondered. Wouldn't have surprised me: everything scripted, everything in place, and Chuck comes out of the wings to become the hero of Fondis: well! This was a time that the script wouldn't be followed.

I took a big gulp of wine, which surprised Iain. He put his hand on mine, which felt good. "My brother's a rapist," I said, quietly, "who talked me into my first fuck when I was twelve and went on, at least once a month, to screw me until he found somebody else. I could care less about his athletic ability or his football career. I could care less that Fondis thinks he's some sort of damn god who walks on water; I know what he is and I know what he does to women because he did it to me and I've felt like shit ever since!"

Dorothea stopped cutting her turkey and stared at me: her knife and fork in the same position. Anh looked as if I'd kicked him. Iain smiled, looking pained, picked up his napkin, dabbed at my mouth, and said, "You're drunk, Lisa."

Maybe it was the way he wiped my mouth; maybe it was the babysitter way he acted: I jumped up, knocking my chair to the side and spilling the wine, which soaked the front of my dress while a fork clattered to the floor. Couldn't he figure out that I was telling the truth; that I wasn't some child to be indulged?

"No I am not!" I answered him, fierce in my quiet. "I am not drunk. I am telling the truth! Do you want times and dates?" My voice cracked with that and my dress felt suddenly heavy. What had I done?

They sat motionless, forks and glasses poised. Then Anh's cell phone went off loudly.

I turned, suddenly unable to control my tears and the redness of my face matching the redness of my dress, and I ran to the stairs, tripped, grabbed the rail, pulled myself up, slammed the door to Jim's room behind me.

Somewhere, I'd read that the mind puts up defenses against unpleasantness, and "the female mind has been known for hysteria," which I guess I had as I threw myself on the bed. I began thinking, hearing and seeing words that made no sense together: Did Iain know I'd cleaned the barn? Wickedness Wretched Excess Watch the Mansion Fall Into the Tarn He'd found the Scarlet A in the Custom House and Louisa May became Bronson's spouse And Ishmael became denied of his friends. DID YOU FORGET IN CHURCH TO RECOUNT YOUR SINS?

My eyes focused on Dorothea Harris, who dabbed a cool washcloth on my forehead, then patted my cheeks. I was on my back. She must have turned me over.

"You know who I am?" she asked flatly.

You're the sacrificial angel of death, tied to a cash register and a warped cynicism. I still don't know if I was saying that or not. I knew the words. I thought I heard them and felt a weight on my neck because I'd suddenly arched my back. Dorothea unceremoniously pressed my shoulders and I lay on the bed again, panting. She wiped my forehead again. Elizabeth had told me that she'd come over when the boys were young, during Thanksgiving, helped her cook a real dinner, fed the boys, then helped Elizabeth kick Don out for good.

"Stain on your dress," she remarked. "It'll wash out."

Are your sins within or do they stick out?

"Look at my finger, Lisa." She moved it side to side. "Don't move your head. Just your eyes. Now up. Now down. Now move your right index finger. Just shake it. Good. Now your left index finger."

Does carnal knowledge disappear, or does it linger?

"When I was a girl, Lisa," she told me, examining my reactions as she spoke and bathed my brow with the washcloth almost rhythmically, ":my mother taught me a lot of old fashioned remedies for what ailed women on the prairie. It wasn't just chicory and sassafras for the monthly; it was all the other things that ailed women: the feeling of being left alone, vulnerable, unloved—"

So why is the virgin not shaped like a glove?

"—There were a lot of women would have killed themselves out here a hundred years ago if they didn't know this stuff." She held the washcloth to my nose a moment. It was sharp, then I recognized it.

"Peppermint," I said.

She smiled. "Busted up one of the candy canes from Elizabeth's pantry and warmed it in a pan until it dissolved," she said. "Your forehead and hair might be kinda' sticky, but it still does the trick. A girl needs some sweetness sometimes."

She wiped my forehead again, then opened the door. I heard the clink of glassware and cutlery from below and voices as she went down the hall to the bathroom, washed out the cloth, and returned to wipe off the sugar.

"Tell me the truth," she said as she not too gently applied the clean cloth. "I don't agree with my mother, who said that hysteria should be treated with a sharp slap to the cheeks, but I'm willing to if you keep talking nonsense. Do you understand, Lisa?"

I nodded.

"Tell me."

I was drunk. I was hallucinating. I wanted to impress Iain. I didn't like being treated like a little girl. I hated Iain patronizing me. "Watch out boys: she's a live one!"

"Then everything would go on as usual, wouldn't it? You'd still carry Chuck around in your brain and your heart, and be a walking timebomb and then explode somewhere else? Where, Lisa? When, Lisa? You're among friends here— Can you confide in these people, knowing that they'll drag the Sheriff's Office in; your parents will be told; Chuck will probably be accused?" It sent a shiver down my spine. Everybody would know. Everybody would know.

"The party?" I asked. "Where's Iain?"

"Crap," she answered. "The party's been going two hours so far," she added, glancing at the clock. "While I was bustling around looking for peppermint candy canes in the kitchen, Tanner was telling some story about how they had to sit at a state dinner like nothing happened after some riot started in the street outside. Because they were all so charming while the gunshots and yelling were going on, they impressed the Interior Minister to save some turtle. They're experts at ignoring stuff."

"Elizabeth?" I asked. "Mr. Sanders?"

She shook her head. "Doesn't mean they aren't concerned. Elizabeth has guests to attend to, like a good hostess; and Arthur should be there to help her. Now: what happened between you and your brother? And," she added, looking perfectly capable of it, "I need to warn you, if this is some stunt or hoax, I'll know. I once punched my sister Lavinia; gave her a shiner, when she pulled this crap."

I nodded. "It's true."

"What's true?"

"Chuck and I—" I felt tears coming on again, "had relations."

"What do you mean by 'relations?'

I nodded, choking through the tears. "When I was twelve and Chuck was fourteen, he would—" I was sobbing. "He would have sex. He would have sex with me." There. I said it.

"And how long did this go on?"

"Two years!" I shouted. "Do you understand me?"

She pursed her lips and began dabbing my eyes with some toilet paper. "You passed the acid test," she remarked.

I heard voices; the front door closed; the party was breaking up and Elizabeth knocked on the bedroom door. "Dorothea? Should Arthur call the Sheriff?"

Dorothea nodded. Elizabeth stepped out again, returning almost immediately. Below, I heard the efficient scrape of plates and cutlery and clink of glasses; the dishwasher and vacuum cleaner going simultaneously: the caterers were cleaning up.

Elizabeth sat beside me on the bed. "I'm glad they're gone," she sighed. "I wanted to be here so much, but I couldn't."

"You had guests to entertain, Elizabeth," Dorothea said primly. "You and Arthur were doing exactly what you should have done."

"I think they would have understood," Elizabeth answered.

"Well, Lisa," Elizabeth smoothed my forehead and patted the bed beside her. "I've known you for these six years and have always thought you were on a tight string. I never knew what it was until tonight. Tell me about it."

I began, telling her about how I'd thought it was natural at first; how I was going to marry Chuck and how we'd have a home—

There was a sudden noise of whooping and singing from the Sanders house.

"Thank goodness we let Marla move into Jeff's room," Elizabeth remarked. "I couldn't sleep through all that. Still going out. And we're supposed to see them again at six thirty tomorrow."

"You are," Dorothea rejoined. "I'm not going to be here tomorrow."

And I went on about how Chuck started acting toward me: how he kept his distance when we were together; how he stopped playing games with me that I understood and how he started playing games I couldn't understand.

"Go on," Elizabeth urged.

I just cried. "Every month; sometimes, twice a month, he'd come into my room, always after midnight—and I couldn't do anything—" And I just kept crying.

And finally, the sobs stopped. I heaved a sigh and threw myself on the bed, my face wet.

"You look like you were submerged," Dorothea remarked. "Now you've come up for air. We can do something. Are you hungry?"

15 /

...Fear ye not the reproach of men, neither be ye afraid of their revilings. (Isaiah: 51.7)

"I guess I already said there's leftovers in the 'fridge," Elizabeth said over her shoulder as we descended.

"Several times," Dorothea grumbled.

Elizabeth paused in the middle of the stairs. Marla, the wardrobe/make up specialist, was seated at the dining room table, talking with Mr. Sanders, a bag next to her. She looked up and sort of flushed, then stood as we continued down.

"I have just the thing for the stain on that dress," she announced, coming toward me. She hugged me while I stood. I still felt submerged.

"Arthur has been telling me all about you," Marla said, to Elizabeth, as she let go of me, "and about how good you've been to him and Iain."

"Really?" Elizabeth asked, raising an eyebrow, mainly toward Arthur.

"Really," she said sincerely, not noticing Elizabeth's sarcasm. "It must have been hard to raise two boys on your own. My Greg's graduated college now, thank goodness, and has a teaching job in California; but every day, at the shop, I wondered if I'd make enough money for both of us to live on. That's why I took this job: to get out of debt. I wanted to pay for our house and credit cards."

"Really?" Elizabeth continued. "Has it been hard?"

"I've liked the travelling," she confessed. "I've seen more things than anyone can see in a lifetime from all over the world; but I've paid for it in other ways."

"Other ways?" Dorothea asked.

"I've been lonely," Marla answered. "I've also had to put up with less than a lady should, I'll tell you."

"Like the cast?"

"Oh—they were princes in comparison to some fellas from Morocco, I can tell you—"

Dorothea drifted to the refrigerator and began pulling out food. "Turkey," she announced. "Two boxes of mashed potatoes. You want some, Lisa?"

I nodded, then said "Yes! Fix me a plate!"

"Lisa," Mr. Sanders called from the table. "Why don't you seat yourself?" As I did, he began, without ceremony, "I called the Sheriff shortly after you went upstairs. He's expecting us at nine tomorrow."

"At nine?" I asked. Dorothea set a steaming plate of turkey and mashed potatoes in front of me. "After they all" I tilted my head toward the Sanders house, "come over for breakfast? With Bonnie?"

Marla reached into her pocket and placed a small polished piece of white quartz on the table in front of my plate, then sat down next to me, across from Mr. Sanders. "I can help," she said simply. "I've spent five years travelling the world, Lisa, and I've found some things that can protect you. This is one of them."

I could imagine Dorothea's sarcasm and Elizabeth's irritation that this woman would intrude but there was something about her that interested me and I nodded.

"Go on, Lisa; hold the pebble in front of you and close your eyes," Marla urged. As I did so, she asked me to relax and feel its warmth. "It was blessed by the Pope himself in 1918, right after World War I, and scattered in his garden in Rome so that whosoever received it would be chosen. I was chosen because the quartz sparkled up at me even though it was a cloudy day. The bearer of that pebble will be granted peace. Do you feel it?"

I nodded, putting the rock back on the table and opening my eyes. Maybe it was my imagination, but the rock did feel warm.

"Just keep that on your person somewhere and you will always have peace," she promised.

"Anything else?" Dorothea had fixed herself a plate and sat down. Elizabeth joined her with a cup of coffee.

Marla smiled. "I know I sound presumptuous, but Arthur suggested it, since Lisa feels like hiding in her room right now—I can do your hair, your makeup—everything—for tomorrow's appearance."

"It's almost midnight," Dorothea observed. "I don't have time to listen to talk about makeup and hair right now."

"Hang on, Dottie," Mr. Sanders cautioned. "Marla has a point. Elizabeth, you can see that. We want Lisa to look her best, don't we?"

Elizabeth sipped her coffee. "Do you want to join us and the cast tomorrow for breakfast, Lisa?"

I shrugged. Then I shook my head.

"Very well. They'll be gone by seven thirty. Why don't we all go to bed?"

"I'm not leaving until I've finished these mashed potatoes," Dorothea said. "Got anymore coffee?"

"Remember what I said," Marla told me, scraping her chair and getting up. She patted me on the back.
Elizabeth walked with her to Jeff's old room, then returned, shaking her head. "I think she's crazy."

I held the rock again. I felt its warmth. "There might be something to this," I said.

"Yeah; there is. You're tired, you've been crying, you've said some things you've been keepin' in since you were little and you get a magic rock," Dorothea remarked, finishing her dinner and leaving her knife and fork clattering. "I'm going home to bed," she announced. "If you need to find me, you know where. In the Pope's Garden with Herpetology and You." She headed for the door where her coat was hanging alone on the hook opposite. "Oh—Elizabeth—" She paused, her hand on the doorknob. They spoke a few minutes and Dorothea once shot a significant look in my direction, then Elizabeth shrugged. Dorothea shrugged also and let herself out, shutting the door behind.

"I guess I'd better be moving also," Mr. Sanders said, putting down his cup of coffee. "That pebble was genuinely given, Liz; if it brings comfort—" He stood, kissed Elizabeth on the cheek, and headed for the stairs.

At six, when the caterers arrived, I let them in, then went upstairs again and tapped on Marla's door. She opened it almost immediately. "I knew you'd be up and I knew you'd be ready today," she said. "There's a tiger in you, Lisa."

283

They usually didn't refer to a rabbit judge that way, I thought; but maybe they should from now on. "I'm going to see the sheriff today." I looked at her. She understood and looked me over.

"The jeans are fine. Do you have a loose-fitting shirt or blouse? Something with a collar?"

"Let's do something with your hair real quick." She began brushing it, tied it in a loose bun, then began with the makeup. By the time she was finished, I looked discreet and confident. "Now get that blouse on and let's see the effect," she urged. At the back door, the cast and crew had started to file in quietly. "I'll bet they found the nightlife of Fondis. Did you hear them come in?"

"Let's get down there," she suggested. "I want to see if the rock works for you as well as it did for me."

"You really believe—"

"It got you up, didn't it?" she asked. "Just after I received it, I noticed that I could sit with those guys and not get irritated by what they said; especially the crude stuff. They might appear clean cut and wholesome on TV, but they're men, just like all the others. They'll have their conceptions of you and your job is to bust them."

"Do I look okay?" Bonnie asked as I answered the door at seven. She stepped in and examined herself in the mirror.

"With that sweater, you need to ask me?"

"Thanks," she answered as we stepped into the dining room. "Dinner okay last night?"

I started to say something, then stopped. She didn't need to know; she was going out with TV stars. Why ruin it?

"This is Bonnie," I announced. "Your tour guide today."

"Hi, Bonnie!" they yelled in unison.

She smiled, embarrassed, and sat down to toast and coffee as the rest returned to their eggs and bacon. The party had become animated since the first cup of coffee, and Hal began telling Mr. Sanders and Elizabeth about the problems of the leatherback turtle.

"They actually appear off the coast of British Columbia in late summer; thousands of them!" he marveled. "Possibly a tribute to global warming! We were gonna' break the story, but National Geographic scooped us."

"Your mother all set for the onslaught?" Tanner asked Bonnie, pointedly ignoring the lecture.

"So's Eric," she smiled. "The manager found out who he was inviting and asked about dinner; then, when he found out you all just wanted to dance, he reserved the center table for you. They haven't done that since—forever."

"We gonna' go to the Ag Building?" Anh asked, "See the solar panels?"

Iain nursed his coffee. He didn't seem to notice I was sitting right next to him.

"You coming?" Bonnie asked.

I shook my head. "Headache," I said.

They all trooped out soon enough, Marla giving me a thumbs-up sign as she stepped through the doorway, leaving the house to Mr. Sanders, Elizabeth and me while the caterers finished the dishes. Soon they left, too.

I settled on the couch and tried to read, grabbing the paper lying on the coffee table.

"Some things, if they're bottled up inside, can eat away at us.

"Lillian was fourteen when she saw something that made her blush, then turn to watch more, then run away, locking herself in her room at the top of the stairs, vowing to forget what she'd seen...Call it Victorian morality: a woman would always be discreet, no matter what it was she'd seen or done, even to death...Lillian was some eighty eight years old before all of Fondis found out why she'd bitterly walled herself behind her money, when they found her voluminous diary, describing her father's relations with a serving maid so many years before..."

"Found something to read in there?" Mr. Sanders walked in from the back.

"Um—'Poet of the High Plains,'" I answered, looking at the title.

"Oh yeah: about Miss Davis," he answered. "It really happened, you know. That secret just ate her up. She couldn't ever marry—just a sad life because of what happened when she was fourteen." He shook his head. "You can say times are different now, but—"

An officer greeted us at the door of The Zebulon County Sheriff's Office, leading us down a hallway marked OFFICIAL BUSINESS ONLY. Elizabeth and Mr. Sanders were pointed toward one room; I went in the one next to it.

"Lisa, I'm Evelyn Washburn, Social Services," a set of white teeth and black hair in jeans, addressed me as she shook my hand,

"and this is Investigator Tompkins, from the Sheriff's Office. Our purpose is to interview you and also to determine if your current home is safe for you. Everything we do in here will be videotaped and recorded."

"Why?"

"As evidence, of course," she answered, as if everyone knew that.

The Investigator cleared his throat. "Everything's taped in these interviewing rooms, Lisa," he said. He had horn-rimmed glasses and a pencil-thin moustache: more like an accountant than a policeman. "We'll start by asking you a few questions together, then I'm going to excuse myself for a while. Would you like a seat? There's some water over here and I think we can get a cup of coffee if you want one."

"Water," I answered, and was handed a bottle as I sat down at a table across from them both. They had pads of paper on which they took notes and laptop computers as well. I'd sat in on a college class the year before where the students were taking notes on their laptops and I started laughing at the similarity. "Am I going to lecture you both on Archaeology?"

Evelyn smiled. Mr. Tompkins began by pushing a button and saying the date, time, place, who was there, and stating that what I was "about to say was freely given, without coercion." He asked me my full name, where I lived, how old I was, where I went to high school, who my teachers were, what my favorite classes were, who my friends were, what I did for entertainment, if I was planning on going to college, where I was planning to go to college, what I was planning on majoring in. Did I have any jobs outside the home? What were my hobbies? Who were my parents? What did they do? Did I have any brothers or sisters? Who were they? What other relatives did I have? Were they alive or dead?

After all this, while occasionally taking notes, Mr. Tomkins then asked: "What happened at Thanksgiving dinner last night, Lisa?"

I drew a deep breath and began slowly telling both about drinking the wine, what was said, who said it and how I felt while it was happening. The Investigator asked a few more questions and suddenly, the whole story came roaring out: he was fourteen and I was twelve. The first few times, I said, with a lump in my throat, were fun; interesting. I felt glamorous and special—the girl in Chuck's life who knew him better than anyone—while he practiced his game, went out for basketball after football, went out for baseball

286

in the spring. Girls would call, e-mail him: No; my father said he was too young for all that. When he was sixteen. In the meantime, I was there. The sound machine was there. Our mother and father, both of whom were tracking Chuck's successes avidly, attending booster club meetings, athletic banquets, and doing fundraising for "Chuck's less fortunate teammates," were there—for Chuck.

"Please state the full name of the assailant," Investigator Tomkins told me. Then, "What is your relationship to him?"

He wrote down some notes and said, commandingly, "Investigator Tomkins is leaving the room at ten thirty-five. Lisa Young and Evelyn Washburn, of Social Services, remain." He smiled, pushed back his chair, and headed for the door.

"So is this more about neglect, Lisa?" Evelyn asked, "than molestation?"

I shook my head. My parents had always been distant. The closest I'd gotten to my parents—I realized was cooking for my father once a week during the last two months.

I'd sort of wept before then: moist, I guess. Then I really started crying: not because of Chuck; because of how senseless it was that everything important to me was not at home, but at school, Elizabeth's, Bonnie's, or the Fairgrounds: even the Science Fairs on Saturdays in Junior High! There was nothing besides my rabbits at 245 Schley Street. I tried to explain this, looking at the wall behind her as I did so.

"Exactly what was it that your brother did to you?" Evelyn asked, wanting dates, times, and places: most of which were a painful blur. After awhile, I learned to think of somewhere else while Chuck did things to me; then I went to the shower, where I'd spend hours; sometimes, I think, even sleeping there. Chuck never hit my face, but he bruised my shoulder; he bruised around my breasts and thighs; putting on underwear was sometimes painful. Did he use protection? I thought so. Yes; he did, or withdraw quickly. Did I seek help? Yes; no. I nodded, shook my head, nodded again.

"I once tried to tell my mother and she told me I was lying. My chickens were dead the next day, like Chuck said they'd be." Did I persist? No. There was no point. My mother brought up a girl who had a crush on Chuck who'd been saying all kinds of things about him that weren't true.

Did I try and notify someone else? Yes; the School Social Worker in junior high school when my period was a week late. There was a sign: "CONFIDENTIAL, CARING, QUICK!" posted outside her office and I walked in before Math class. The woman there told me to wait a couple of minutes while she spoke with someone else. Even though the door was closed, I could hear what was said over the partition: "We'll have to inform your mother, Desiree. If you're pregnant, we need to make some choices very quickly." Hearing that, I left after crossing my name out from the sign-in sheet.

I was worried, for a year afterward, that the Social Worker might recognize me and figured out different ways to get to class that weren't past her office. I'd even tried to tell Mr. Flanders once, but not very hard. He was monitoring scores from the Physics booth where Kevin and I figured out gravitational pull between the earth and the moon. Mr. Flanders had put his arm around me briefly in congratulation and I said something about how he was so much nicer than my brother. If he'd asked, I might have said something. Instead, he showed me the results. Kevin and I were ahead of a lot of kids from Denver.

Why didn't I tell Elizabeth? I shook my head. Because Elizabeth called parents to make sure everything was all right even when getting rides home from judging practice, I was afraid she'd talk with them and I didn't want to be thought a liar. The only time I'd not known Elizabeth to completely report what the Rabbit Judging Team had done to bored parents was the afternoon I'd taken off to her house and met Iain.

Why not tell Bonnie? Of course, Vern was a deputy and Barb would have fought for me against any suspicion. No: they owed money to the bank for a mortgage they could barely pay. Besides, even when it was going on, Bonnie couldn't believe what I told her once in eighth grade and I treated it as a bad joke afterwards. Since it had stopped when I was fourteen and Bonnie had started becoming fabulously social, I never felt I could talk about it, even when some circumstances between her and a boy mirrored just what I'd been through. I sometimes asked her questions, I admitted, that if she'd thought about where they'd come from, she'd realize I understood from experience, but she never did. She just talked and laughed about what happened.

Couldn't I have gone to someone else? Whispering Pines Mental Health, for instance? The Sheriff's Office? My counselor?

I smiled as I thought of Mrs. Grimes, who'd followed Chuck's career after helping him fill out the paperwork for SAC, trying to get her mind around the idea that he was a monster. "I'm seventeen," I told Evelyn. "I'm still a minor. The first people they'd call would be my parents."

"Now that Chuck's out of there and at SAC," she asked, "Do you feel safe?"

I thought of the weekends and evenings he'd suddenly appeared: he spent Sunday night during the Fondis Oktoberfest and was gone really early the next morning, but short of saying hello to him that evening, I saw little of him. Fear, perhaps? Yes. I couldn't stand to be in the same room with him.

"There was one time, when he still had a driver's license, when he came to the Rabbit Barn at the end of Fair and helped me carry my rabbits to the car," I shivered, remembering, "and I felt sick all the way—I felt sick when he took a cage from my hands. When he was somewhere in the house, like the kitchen, I used to go to my room. I didn't want to be anywhere near him."

"Is that still the case?"

I nodded.

"Do you feel he is a danger to you, Lisa?"

I nodded again.

"Please answer the question, Lisa. Do you feel he is a danger to you, Lisa?"

"Yes I do," I answered.

"In what way?"

"I still am scared that he will come to my room after my parents have gone to bed."

"Is this true?"

"I'm scared of him. He is strong. He did things to me that I'll never forgive him for."

She asked more questions about Chuck and my fear of him: how tall he was; how strong he was; what sort of temper he had. I remembered when he'd taken a CD in its case and broke the whole thing in his hands when I'd refused him; I remembered him ripping a blouse from the closet: it looked like a piece of paper in his hands.

"Do you feel safe at home?"

"No; I don't," I answered, thinking of Chuck suddenly appearing and then re-appearing.

She nodded a couple of times. "Would you feel safer living with Elizabeth?"

Evelyn produced a note from her tablet. I could see that it was in Elizabeth's handwriting, on her ivory colored paper: "She'll be happy to have you as her guest until you go to college," Evelyn said, scanning the note, "and she feels that your schooling will not suffer since Mr. Sanders, next door, will be able to drive you to school every morning."

289

"Um: I'd like that," I said haltingly. "I've been able to sleep," I said.

She took some more notes, then began talking about my parents. What were they like? When did I talk with my mother? When did I talk with my father? Did I ever tell them about Chuck?

I reiterated my story about trying to tell my mother about him and the dead chickens afterwards.

"Is there a time you could tell me about when you felt close to your parents, Lisa?"

I told her about cooking for my father Wednesday nights.

"That's all?"

I felt defensive at her words. I talked about the museum evenings; the fundraisers with my mother; the Bank Party every Christmas at the American Legion Hall; all the football games.

"So every time you've been with your parents, except cooking for your father, have been involved with Chuck or something to do with your father's work?"

I suddenly realized: "Yeah. Yes."

Did Iain realize that I'd cleaned out the barn before Thanksgiving? He'd said there was a smell that he didn't like when we were there in the fall. I'd gotten rid of that smell: I knew I'd gotten rid of it, shovelful after shovelful of rabbit waste: wheelbarrow full; push it to the ridge; dump; return. Do it again.

"Lisa," Evelyn declared, "I don't think you've been raised in a very safe environment. "You needn't say anything about it right now; I'll let you think about it."

16 /

...choose you this day whom ye will serve... (Joshua: 24.15)

"The less recent a crime is, the less likelihood it can be proven."

I understood the words and I understood, slowly, that they probably couldn't take Chuck and put him in jail or whatever they did with people like that. "But that's good, isn't it?" I asked, rising. "He won't go to jail and he won't have any problems in the future—"

Evelyn looked curiously at me as I continued.

"Chuck can be a major NFL player and make lots of money and people will cheer for him. That's good, isn't it?" I sank back into the chair. "Isn't it?"

"Depends on how you look at it, I guess," Evelyn answered noncommittally after a couple of minutes.

I started crying then. Had any other girls come forward, ever? I didn't know, but I didn't think so. They'd been savaged by Chuck, too: I knew it. They were the ones after me: Charlene Hauptman; Desiree Bainbridge; Nicole Salazar; Tony Urtl; Kristie Nicholson; Suzanne Lamphier; Karen Nguyen; Valerie Wilson were the ones I could remember. "I don't know who he's going out with now—someone named Monica, I think." It was odd: I wanted to know what he was putting them through but I did not want to know them. In May, when I was fourteen, I was leaning over the sink, washing my hands, the locket dangling below my neck, when I was pulled by it. I felt the chain snap and Charlene Hauptman was in front of my face, holding the chain and locket dangling from her right fist.

"You putting out for this?" she demanded. "You his fuckin' slut now?" She threw the locket and chain on the floor and ground it under her heel. The hinge snapped and the heart lay in two halves.

I washed my face and dried it. The broken locket was still on the floor.

It was three in the afternoon when I was ready to leave and I was exhausted. I'd given Evelyn names, dates, times, as nearly as I could remember, all of which she wrote down. I gave Inspector Tomkins the names of Chuck's former girlfriends.

"I've recommended a few things for you," Evelyn said, pushing a few buttons on her laptop computer. "First, I'd like you to continue living with Elizabeth. Second, I'd like to investigate your parents. There are some neglect issues here."

There was a knock at the door and in walked Mr. Holmes, followed by the Sheriff, who looked apologetic.

"You have no right to interview this minor without her parents' consent," Mr. Holmes began, "and whatever you have recorded is their property." He sat down next to me, opened his briefcase, and produced a sheaf of papers. "This is a cease and desist order for you to stop this immediately; the others enjoin Mrs. Prentice to stop putting suggestions into Lisa's head." He handed

291

copies to the Sheriff; he handed copies to the Investigator and to Evelyn.

"I have cause, Mr. Holmes, to believe that Lisa is in a dangerous situation," Evelyn was incredibly cool. "I believe she's in immediate harm from her brother if she stays in her parents' home. Her behavior, during the last five hours, has convinced me that she is afraid of her older brother and of the neglect of her parents."

The Sheriff looked at Mr. Holmes. "Because a caseworker from Social Services has given me recommendation, I need to act on that recommendation, Charles," he said.

Elizabeth and Mr. Sanders appeared in the doorway, then hastened to the table where Mr. Holmes and I were. They stood behind him, which made him noticeably uncomfortable.

"Do you mind?" Mr. Holmes asked irritably.

"Nowhere else to stand," Mr. Sanders answered.

"Can chairs be found for these people?" Mr. Holmes asked testily.

"Nope," Mr. Sanders answered. "Just have to do without." I noticed, as I glanced at him, that he was looking over Mr. Holmes' shoulder at the documents. "I'll bet that Elizabeth and I are in those documents, Charles; aren't we?"

Mr. Holmes nodded.

"Where are our copies?"

Sheriff Franklin smiled and handed Mr. Sanders one of the documents, which Mr. Sanders flipped through. "You're saying that Lisa can't exercise her First Amendment rights here, Charles? That she cannot tell anyone why she will live with Elizabeth instead of with her parents?" He flipped through another document. "You're saying that Lisa denies everything she said here?" He tossed the documents on the table. "You know, Charles, I've got a lot of respect for what you do; but this is really over the top."

"It's pretty damned over the top for a teacher to pretend he's a lawyer," Mr. Holmes answered. "What are you, a psychologist as well? Can you verify that Lisa was in her right mind when she made these accusations and can you tell me that you and Mrs. Prentice haven't railroaded her here?"

"I can tell you that I'm capable of reading," Mr. Sanders answered evenly. "I can also tell you that I am acting entirely on Lisa Young's behalf."

They both stood glaring at one another.

"I think it's time to go, Lisa," Elizabeth said.

"Lisa," Mr. Holmes turned to me. "If you go without talking with me, you will be divorcing your family. They will have nothing to do with you. Do you understand?" he asked quickly. "They're on their way from Austria; should be at home sometime tomorrow. They're concerned about this. Don't you want to consider what you're doing?"

I thought of the five hours I'd spent telling the investigators about Chuck; I thought of the years I'd spent at 245 Schley Street; I thought of my rabbits and chickens. There was nothing to hold me there. "There's nothing I want from them, except the rabbits," I answered. Something felt warm in my left hand and I realized I'd been holding the piece of quartz Marla had given me throughout the interview.

17 /

And I will deliver thee out of the hand of the wicked, and I will redeem thee out of the hand of the terrible. (Jeremiah:15,3)

"Not everyone is as brave as you are." Evelyn said to me as I left the courthouse.

"I agree completely," Elizabeth added as we clambered into the van, Mr. Sanders behind her. "How do you feel?"

"Like rubber," I answered. Then a thought struck me.

"Let's look at my parents' house," I suggested.

"What?"

"Let's stop in front of 245 Schley Street," I urged Elizabeth. "I want to see something."

"Check on your rabbits?"

"That—and has anything changed?" I asked aloud.

She signaled left and turned the van down Elm, then onto Schley. I got out and went to check my rabbits, then I just sat in the rabbit house, looking through the open door at the house. The basketball hoop was still in place; the garage hadn't changed: nothing had changed. How could something so momentous in my life not have changed a thing?

"So you'd lose your job at Fondis High School as a substitute teacher. So what?" Elizabeth was asking as I got back in the van.

He didn't reply for a while. He looked at me; then away. "So what?" he asked. He sighed. "You know, when it was my paycheck, I probably ignored some of the politics of the job—I did ignore some of the politics—or just played along. Most parents and students understood when a kid hadn't done his work and had to fail, but there were some—the Hollis kids, for instance—who probably should never have graduated, and I just passed them on because it was easier than standing up to Wallace Hollis and the Board of Education. I figured it out awhile back, Elizabeth: the job with the newspaper is great and has given me a status that nobody as old as I am deserves; but what if I really did some ethical teaching as well? Like failing Eddie Brace because he deserves it; not passing him like Roweena had to. Really telling the truth. Fighting those battles my paycheck couldn't afford before now. I know it's given Elmer Hoeppner some grey hairs but it's also made some teachers like Llwyn Morgan raise his head and really grade his students in Science once again: trying to prepare them for college.

"It probably doesn't rank with the stories about Sheriff Thomson, Elizabeth," he said, "But it's sort of a vindication and also cancels out those two years I was drinking. Sticking with this job all the way through means that I've sort of grown up."

"You grew up a long time ago," Elizabeth murmured. "Some people would think you're persecuting poor little Eddie Brace," she remarked, "because his dog killed Lisa's rabbit."

"Do you?"

"Of course not," she answered.

Elizabeth smiled at me. Seen enough, Lisa?"

"Nothing's changed," I said.

"It's inside here," Mr. Sanders said, touching his coat near the heart. He watched the street recede with me, then asked, "Are you ready to dance at the Country Club tonight?"

"Oh God," Elizabeth said. "I'd forgotten. Arthur, are you serious about Lisa going to the Country Club after what she's been through today? The boys and Bonnie will be back soon and they won't know a thing. Do you want to be downstairs when they arrive?" She turned into the driveway.

"I think I'll just go upstairs," I answered. "I don't want to go to the Country Club."

"That's wise," Elizabeth answered.

18 /

...therefore, she took a veil, and covered herself. (Genesis:24.65)

I saw it on the front page of the Fondis Daily the next day: CAST AND CREW OF HERPETOLOGY AND YOU FETED AT COUNTRY CLUB DANCE, with a photo of everyone: Marla, the two editing guys, Charles, Hal, Iain, Anh, and Tanner, with Bonnie on the side. The small article described how each of the cast and crew danced with "everyone present by way of a lottery system devised at the last minute by Assistant Manager Eric Lassiter."

I didn't appear from my room until about midnight. I was hungry and figured I'd get something from the refrigerator: some turkey or stuffing or mashed potato; maybe some gravy.

Instead, I encountered Iain Sanders, barefoot in tuxedo jacket, cummerbund, twisted tie and puffy starched shirt, trying to remove a hot plate form the microwave oven with his hands, which he couldn't do. I grabbed the dishtowel from the refrigerator door and threw it at him.

"God," he groaned, "I don't want to do that again," as he removed the plate from the microwave oven to the counter.

"Cook something?" I asked.

"Dance," he replied. "I never want to do that again. I was dancing with every woman in the room, all of whom had so little in common with me that I regarded them as specimens, but I still had to talk with them. I'd rather track alligators."

"So you had a good time, then?" I asked, looking into the refrigerator. There was some turkey, some mashed potatoes. I grabbed a plate from the cupboard above and began picking pieces.

"No; I didn't have a good time," he answered. "You weren't there."

That was sweet. "Do you know why I wasn't there?"

"Had to do with what you said at Thanksgiving, about your brother?"

So far, so good. "So what did I say?"

He took a bite of his still hot food. "I guess you got interviewed by the Sheriff's Office."

"Did your father tell you this?" I asked.

"He's asleep," Iain said. "He's in the chair over there." Iain indicated the darkened front room. "I wanted to grab something to eat and wake him up to go home. He waited up for me."

"That's nice."

He gestured to a spot across the table from him. "It's kinda' weird that he'd be waiting for me now," Iain continued, "because my father wasn't always waiting for me when I was coming home. As a matter of fact, he'd turned off the lights and gone to bed more times than I can recall when I was a junior and a senior at Kutch because he figured I was in my room, studying. He didn't check. He'd have Drama students over until ten to learn their lines, then he would grade papers until one in the morning—he didn't have time for me until about May or Christmas break, then it was usually connected with school somehow. June one year, he took me to Cincinnati where there just happened to be a teachers' conference. I spent the whole week walking around Cincinnati until he was free to sightsee, then it was with other teachers. It was like I wasn't there at all, so I stopped being there. I'd bring my books over here after dinner and study with Jim. If I fell asleep, Elizabeth would throw a blanket over me. By the time I graduated from Kutch, I'd gotten a job lined up at a ranch in Wyoming. I figured I'd never see this place, or him, again."

He'd e-mailed me some of it before, of course and I half listened to him as I microwaved the leftovers and brought them to the table. "Gonna' need your shoes on when you go home tonight," I observed.

"They pinched," he grinned.

All Felicia Duncan's clothes and shoes and purses were gone one day when Iain arrived home from school; "Even the dozen or so windchimes off the back and front porches, for Chrissakes, which she'd bought at various stores throughout my childhood—could never have enough of them, she always thought; just gone;" the same happened with his sister's things. No explanation. Iain's father had just loaded the truck one day and took it to the thrift store.

"The only stuff he saved were Mom's paintings and what she'd written; some decorations. He even gave away all her books—said it was too painful to look at them."

"He got rid of everything?" I asked. "What about the stuff that they'd bought before the accident from the shops? The wind chimes and the candles and the box?"

I guess he didn't hear me. "There was some stuff, he's said, that he shouldn't have given away, like her degrees, some pictures." Iain shrugged. "Fortunately, the folks at the thrift store knew enough to hang onto those items and give them to the Mental Health Center. Oh—I think Elizabeth has the windchimes and a birdfeeder packed up somewhere. It's just off the Atrium; it looks just like our living room used to: the same books, the photos, the paintings. It's named after her. Have you seen it?"

No: I'd not noticed when I went to the Memorial. Since the statue and fountain was destroyed, I'd stayed away. I wondered if he knew that. Probably not.

"Is there anything to remember your sister?
Iain shrugged. "He gave all her toys and clothes away. Nothing except for some schoolwork, some pictures, and all her rabbit ribbons. I stopped him from giving the rabbits to Elizabeth and I took care of them every day I was here. You've seen the hutch?"
I nodded.

"Dad put that together when Janie first started rabbits. He made sure she measured it all and drew the lines so he could cut it. There are still two cages that don't quite meet in that thing—There were two rabbits who hadn't died of old age when I graduated from Kutch. I made sure they went to Elizabeth. I brought them over a couple of hours before I was going to leave.

"About two years ago," he continued after a bite of mashed potato, "I got Janie's ribbons in the mail. My dad wrote that they would help me remember her. He also said he couldn't find her first ribbon: a third place at her first rabbit show. It was pretty weird." He scraped his plate. "I decided not to send them back. I think he was trying to tell me he was sorry he'd neglected me."

"What'd you do with them?"

"I asked Hal's parents to store them for me. I guess they're still in a garage in New Jersey."

"That's all that's left of your sister?"

"There's a picture she drew, and of course, she and my mom are buried in that atrium: just behind the fountain; that's where their ashes are; but that's about it. Not much footprint when you're nine years old."

"Guess not," I agreed.

"What about you?" he asked, a forkful of mashed potatoes poised above the plate.

I shrugged. "In the Sheriff's Office, where I was interviewed. Mr. Holmes was there—"

"Charles Holmes?" Iain seemed delighted. "How is he? I was a couple of classes behind Haley; but that didn't mean we weren't great friends! God! We used to sail his boat at Grand Lake during summers—even won a couple of the races; though God knows how! A couple of teenagers against a lot of really experienced older guys who just entered races because they looked like fun. He'd call me really early on Saturday and tell me to get ready, and there he'd be a few minutes later, boat behind his Jeep, and we'd go. Sometimes, his dad would come along. Not like mine," he finished soberly, taking a few last bites of turkey.

"No; not like yours," I repeated. Then it hit me. "How come you didn't stick around this morning?"

"Oh—" he waved his hand dismissively. "I figured I'd just be in the way. Elizabeth was with you, wasn't she?"

"So was your dad. He was at the Sheriff's Office, too."

"Well then;" he finished his meal. "Looks like everything was handled." He yawned.

Yes. I guess it was, I thought. All handled without my boyfriend or whatever he was. "Did you know I cleaned the barn right before you came?" I asked.

"You did?" he asked, puzzled.

"Yes," I answered. "That smell you complained about—remember?"

"I don't remember, Lisa."

"Oh."

"What were they asking you in the Sheriff's Office?" He yawned again, deeply.

"Oh—About—"

There was a cough from the other room.

"Dad's awake," Iain said automatically. "Let's have this conversation later, okay?" he said, rising and putting his dish in the sink. "I'll just carry my shoes."

I still sat at the table. I wanted him to touch my hand or—something. Instead, there was a murmur, a snort, and his father stood in the doorway.

"I'm going home, Dad," Iain said.

I sat in the kitchen a long time after he'd gone. I had the feeling that I was like the specimens he'd danced with: somebody who was interesting and no more.

19 /

Therefore, behold, I will hedge up thy way with thorns, and make a wall, that she shall not find her paths. (Hosea: 3.6)

Her vacation, even though it was cut short, had helped my mother. She didn't have that sort of fidgetiness that put her in constant motion anymore: jumping up to cut an apple, moving along the counter to check her e-mail, refer to a recipe, twirl around to open the refrigerator, answer the telephone: none of that was there when I saw her a few days later, seated at a long table in the Justice Center Family Courtroom. She appeared slightly distracted between Mr. Holmes and my father. My father looked angry. He'd suddenly appeared at work that morning, I later found out, looking over mortgages of places around the proposed golf course, and hadn't even taken lunch. Mr. Holmes smiled and stood as we arrived, shaking hands with Mr. Calkins, whom he greeted warmly. He nodded at Mr. Sanders and greeted Elizabeth without much emotion. We took our places at another long table parallel to it.

Investigator Tomkins and Evelyn Washburn sat in front, where everyone could see them, across from where the judge, a Mr. Williams, sat. Evelyn had her laptop computer open; no doubt, I thought, to the DVD of my interview. I hoped it wouldn't be needed. There was another man, a Mr. Hazlitt, from the District Attorney's office, who was representing "the People."

"Judging by Lisa Young's statement," Mr. Hazlitt said, "it appears she no longer wishes to live at home. Investigator Tomkins and Ms. Washburn, who took the statement, and the Sheriff, who has seen the DVD, have all concluded, from Miss Young's words, that she is more comfortable living with Mrs. Elizabeth Prentice."

Mr. Hazlitt passed a paper to Mr. Williams and handed a copy to Mr. Holmes. "This is confirmation," he said. "Miss Young feels endangered…"

My father's hand moved over my mother's. She moved her head slightly toward him. He whispered something to her and she brightened.

It went on for what seemed like hours, even though only fifteen minutes had passed, Mr. Hazlitt producing paper after paper and talking about me. Was Elizabeth a fit guardian? Yes; she'd raised two boys. Where were they now? Jeff was in Iowa, Jim was in Australia. Yes, Lisa would have her own room. Yes, there was a lock on the door. Did Mrs. Prentice earn enough money to support another person? Yes, with some exceptions. That's why Mr. Calkins had drafted a financial contract for Lisa, payable each month to Elizabeth.

"Could we have a moment to review this contract?" Mr. Holmes asked the judge, who ordered a fifteen minute recess. Mr. Holmes pushed back his chair and my father did the same. They took a copy of what Mr. Calkins had drafted to another room.

"Isn't this always the case, Elizabeth?" my mother asked brightly. "You have a perfect child and then she does something to assert her independence. This happened with Chuck when he smashed that sports car and now it's happening with Lisa. I really don't mind, dear," she turned to me, "if you spend the rest of the year with Elizabeth: after all, she's a dear friend, but why did you have to tell lies about your brother to do it?"

"Mrs. Young, perhaps you'd like to freshen up a bit?" Mr. Hazlitt asked suddenly. "Ms. Washburn can take you there."

"Oh no; I'm fine," my mother answered. "I just want Lisa to tell me why she's wasting your time and everybody else's and why she doesn't just come home. You did this, didn't you?" she asked, turning to Mr. Sanders. "You're still bitter over your daughter's death and you write such lies about Harold's business! What better way to destroy him than by poisoning his daughter's mind?" She gulped for air a second as Evelyn approached her, then continued, a bit more loudly: "Did your son seduce my daughter and in her guilt you coached her to tell this tale?" Then, really loudly, taking the entire room in her gaze, "Did you know we're being investigated?"

Evelyn pulled my mother up out of her chair, said something quietly to her, and began leading her toward the door.

"And do you realize, Elizabeth, what you're doing to my family?" my mother demanded. "That you sleep with this man is quite enough, but taking an innocent child and—" Evelyn Washburn pulled her through the doorway.

I found myself crying: not at what she'd said, which stung; but at the fact that she really did not know me at all. Seventeen years under the same roof and she really thought I could be brainwashed?

Elizabeth pulled the facial tissues toward me and put her arm around me. I shook my head, frustrated that I couldn't stop. The harder I tried, the more the tears flowed. Just like Sunday morning, when the crew loaded up their trucks and vans and Bonnie kept giggling as she took pictures with a digital camera that she must've paid for with money the Lassiters didn't have, and Iain, probably to show how big a player he was, tried to kiss me goodbye. I was like a mannequin: my arms were crossed in front and I complained about being cold as he tried—well, all he got was a kiss on my cheek.

"If Lisa is to live with Mrs. Prentice, we need to modify this document," Mr. Holmes stated when court resumed. "First, all medical decisions, owing to the immediate availability of the parents, should be left in their hands, including the acquisition of prescription medication; second, that spending money be reduced by seventy-five percent. Miss Young can enroll in the school lunch program. Third, that Miss Young can support herself financially after the end of the school year since she will be eighteen; fourth, that any psychiatric evaluation or counseling, which we consider superfluous, be conducted at the least possible expense; therefore, at a public mental health center..."

At the end of an hour, as the clock at the end of the room turned 9:45, they'd agreed that I would not have any spending money, that all my stuff from my parents' house, including the rabbits and anything associated with them, would be delivered to Elizabeth's; that I'd not say anything against my brother as long as the investigation was going on, and that I wouldn't receive anything financial from my parents unless they willingly gave it to me as a present. The document also said that as long as I lived with Elizabeth, Mr. Sanders and she could not "cohabit" until after I had turned eighteen. I noticed Mr. Sanders was going to say something at that, but he just nodded instead.

My mother had returned, her eyes red from crying. She sat stiffly next to my father.

"Is Lisa going to college?" she asked.

"Scholarship to Siwash," Mr. Holmes answered.

"What's that?" she asked.

Mr. Calkins and Mr. Holmes shook hands.

"I could come over on Wednesday nights," I suddenly offered, looking at my father, "and cook you dinner."

There was a flutter and a shushing sound from Mr. Calkins and Mr. Holmes.

My father looked at me then with a steely gaze, the kind he used with people he would never loan money to: "As far as I'm concerned, Lisa," he said, "You've never existed."

20 /

And Esau said unto his father, Hast thou but one blessing, my father? Bless me, even me also... (Genesis: 27.34)

The contents of my room and the small impact they made was apparent when the movers showed up, two days later, and left ten boxes, all labeled, SOCKS, SHIRTS, CLOSET, DESK, BOOKSHELVES, NIGHTSTAND, COMPUTER, from my bedroom; all the way to my bulletin board and my photograph of Iain, taken off a webpage and framed by me. Nothing was soiled, torn, or trampled. "Just sign here, Lady," the mover told Elizabeth as I poked through the boxes. My books, 17 notebooks, extra paper: "It's all there."

"What about the rabbits?" Elizabeth asked, signing the inventory after looking questioningly at me. I'd nodded.

The mover shook his head. "We don't move live animals."

So there we were: Mr. Sanders, Elizabeth, and I, turning the van into the driveway that next Saturday morning. "I'd figured a couple extra cages wouldn't go amiss," she'd remarked as she loaded them into the van. "I don't know how much your parents own and how much you own of those things."

Mr. Holmes met us with a clipboard on which the contents of the rabbit house were listed. It turned out that Elizabeth needn't have worried: all the cages, ribbons, books, manuals; even the currying equipment and the folding show table, plus any food, were listed. "I was surprised at the number of notebooks you've kept,

Lisa," Mr. Holmes said pleasantly, noting my expression at once. "Oh no—I didn't look in them—that's your business—but you are quite prolific! You'll find everything in order. Here's a box you can start with while Elizabeth and I go through the cages."

I smiled and carried the box to the van. Those notebooks—it suddenly struck me—those notebooks were a record of what Chuck had done, more or less—and I leaned against the van frame a moment, thinking what that meant.

"Decided to rest so early?" Mr. Sanders came up behind me with another box.

"Just thinking," I answered. "If you had evidence of something, would you turn it over to the Police?"

"What kind of question is that? Of course I would. Do you have evidence of something?"

"I think I do and it's at Elizabeth's."

It's a funny thing about a neighborhood like Schley Street: people sense when there's some ripple in the air, and as I was helping haul my rabbits, all the folded cages, the boxes and the folding table into Elizabeth's van, I noticed several neighbors at their windows or outside, doing something. YES! I'M LEAVING! I wanted to shout. Instead, like Mr. Holmes, I ignored the looks.

"What's going on, Lisa?" Eddie Brace's voice piped up behind me.

"Eddie—Is that dog on the leash?" Mr. Sanders asked quickly.

"Yeah, yeah." He held up the handle, wagging if from side to side, like a trough of water. "There's something like sand in the handle," he remarked, "which makes it a perfect weapon in places like Central Park. My mom bought it for me so I'd be able to control Barr-"

I saw the dog lunge, felt my feet slipping under me on the ice, felt the back of my head hit something hard and just saw darkness.

"Who was on the rabbit judging team that won state with Melinda Theiss?" A voice demanded above the darkness. "Lisa Young, you've seen the banners all around the Ag Building Arena; don't pretend you haven't. Who was on the rabbit judging team that won state?" I saw a light like an oncoming train and closed my eyes. "Good; your eyes are starting to work again," the voice, not unpleasant, but insistent, continued, "now let's see if your memory works. Who was on the state champion rabbit judging team with Melinda Theiss?"

303

Melinda Theiss. I started going over the banners in my memory: big, green and white ones with the 4-H clover on them, all coached by ELIZABETH PRENTICE. Melinda Theiss: "She's a veterinarian, now," I remarked. "Left Rabbit Judging a couple years after I'd joined."

"Good," the voice continued. "Now, who was on that team?"

I concentrated. It hurt. "Oh—Melanie Davis and Rachel Rural."

"Good!" the voice announced. "Short stuff for long term memory, but I'll bet it's all right." The light no longer shone at my eyelids and I tentatively opened them. The room was full of medical equipment.

"Well, you got my sister right," a man with whiskers and glasses remarked, grinning, "and if I'm not mistaken, she's on the golf course in San Diego at the moment while her brother practices Emergency Medicine."

Rural. "You're Raul Rural?" I'd read his father's columns about him in The Divide-Review. I didn't know he really existed. "Did you really once make a shadow velociraptor in a picture of your sister's soccer team?"

He laughed. "You've really read my father's columns, haven't you?" Then, checking my pulse, he added, "Most of it's true."

"Elizabeth?"

"She's in the waiting area. She'll be up to see you when we get done here."

"Mr. Sanders?"

"Don't know," he answered. "I guess you weren't aware of it: Arthur Sanders got bitten by that dog of Eddie Brace's. Not major, but enough to be looked at."

"Is he okay?"

"Already released. Arm's in a sling from the bite, but he's still full of piss and vinegar. Do you wear glasses?" Dr. Rural asked, shining a light in my eyes. He turned it off as I blinked and nodded at the same time. Something hurt in the back of my head and I grimaced.

"Got a bang on the occipital," he remarked. "Now: can you see this?"

"I see a piece of paper."

He came closer. "What does it say?"

He came closer as I read: "To be healthy, a rabbit needs a quiet place away from danger..."

"Good," he remarked. "Do you have a headache?"

"No; but I feel—" I pointed to my head.

"Understandable," he said. "I'll put a bandage around it and give you something so it won't hurt."

I was in the hospital for three hours: enough time for Bonnie and Barb Lassiter to show up and wait; enough time for Kevin Allen to show up and wait; evidently not enough time for my parents to show up.

"That's crap," Dr. Rural remarked as he walked me to a couch in the waiting area. He stepped behind the receptionist's desk and started working on a form while Bonnie came up and hugged me gently.

"Eddie's dog was impounded," she said. "Probably for good." She stepped back. "Elizabeth has been telling me about why you're living with her now. I didn't know, Lisa."

"And no reason you should," Barb chided.

"But we're best friends!"

"With something like this, Bonnie..." Barb began.

"But—"

"Heyuh—" Dr. Rural appeared with some paperwork in his hand. "You're released, Lisa, and the visit's paid for." He looked significantly at Elizabeth. "The Bank's Insurance is covering it, plus your prescription, plus some visits to the Mental Health Center."

Mr. Sanders, his arm in a sling, took the paperwork from Dr. Rural. "How'd you do it?" he asked.

Dr. Rural shrugged and winked at me. Then he turned and walked back into the Emergency Room.

*But if he thrust him of hatred, or hurl at him by laying of wait, that
he die... (Numbers: 35.20)*

"I didn't want to say anything," I answered. "It's all so new.
Really—I'm numb.   It's only December, only a week after
Thanksgiving, Bonnie."

"Two," Barb corrected.

"Okay: two," I answered. "But it's too soon.   My stuff just
came last Thursday and I still haven't unpacked it. I saw my parents
on Tuesday before and that was awful.   I just—lawyers and
everything."

I'd gone with Bonnie after being released from the hospital
and we stood in the kitchen, where Barb was bustling around, fixing
dinner for Vern and Eric. Bonnie busied herself with the TV remote
control, eventually turning on the local news station: "In other local
news," the announcer intoned, "SAC Football Star Chuck Young is
addressing groups of junior high and senior high school students
about inspiration gained from the gridiron and plans an inspirational
DVD: "My Inspiration," which he's mixed with Mike Landres,
former SAC quarterback who now owns his own recording studio..."

"I want to throw up," I announced.

"You know what my greatest inspiration is?" Chuck asked us
all a few days later after telling some stories about struggle on the
gridiron and how they'd made him "more respectful and more loving
toward those who are weaker,"

'NO!" the audience yelled, 'WHO?"

"A man who's been an inspiration to just about everybody
who's ever been through Fondis High School; A man whose learning
and experience have shaped this school and made it what it is; a man
whose work has made you what you are and me what I am: Doctor
Elmer Hoeppner!" And Dr. Hoeppner came out from behind the
wings and Chuck hugged him while everyone around, students and
teachers, rose from their seats. I thought of what I was going to cook
for dinner that night for Elizabeth and me. I had learned to boil
water and wanted to try spaghetti.

"Did you notice the phone message?" Elizabeth asked.
"Kevin Allen called."

"What did he want?"

"I think he was concerned for you," she answered. "You pretty well ignored him when you were in the hospital, going off with Bonnie like you did—"

I called Kevin. He was awkward. Then he asked me if he could come over. I guessed so, but I wasn't in much shape for company.

"It's okay," he said. "We'll just watch TV."

And that's what we did. Elizabeth made some popcorn and we watched a show about some woman who'd lost her identity. Kevin left at ten. He was still awkward.

"I noticed you'd been using that lip gloss I got you: peach dream," Elizabeth said as his truck fired up.

"Yeah; it's nice," I said.

"Probably made him come over."

I laughed. "Don't know why he came over."

She shook her head. "Maybe he likes you, Lisa."

22 /

Thy first father hath sinned, and thy teachers have transgressed against me. (Isaiah: 43.27)

"Is there anyone we'll study who is good?" Kevin asked, laying aside the copy of Huckleberry Finn on the desk beside him. "Everybody who is interesting is always bad: Oedipus; Creon, Antigone; Odysseus; Regan; Goneril: they're all bad."

"The folks in these books who are really good are all worth looking at," Mr. Sanders replied, "Because they're good. What makes them good? They're much more complicated than the bad characters. Look at Mary Jane Wilkes in Huckleberry Finn; Cordelia in King Lear; the relatives of Jane Eyre: they're all extremely complicated because of their goodness. What can you learn from them?"

I thought about that as Mr. Sanders dropped me off in front of Whispering Pines Mental Health Center: the first of a number of appointments that were being paid for by my father, who'd told the insurance company that I needed someone to prove I was a liar. The good people are more complicated than the bad ones.

They'd built a plywood wall around the fountain, like somebody's shed in the middle of a forest. It was still a crime scene and they were doing forensic tests to catch the culprit. Would they find him or her?

I doubted it. Whoever had done it was careful not to be noticed.

I hesitated before the glass door that read ROBERTA ROBINSON MEMORIAL, then pushed it open, quietly giving my name to the receptionist, who I'd seen somewhere before. I looked at the receptionist again, trying to place her.

"You're looking at me," she stated flatly.

I felt myself go red.

"Do I know you?"

"I don't think so, but did you work at the Farmer's and Mechanic's Bank? Or do you have a son or daughter in 4-H, maybe?"

She laughed. "Try again," she teased.

" A restaurant or Fuller's, maybe?"

"I like all of those," she answered merrily, holding up a sketch of a girl who looked a little bit like me. "Please don't be offended," she offered. "I sometimes find a subject that I really like."

"Oh—" I remembered where I'd seen her face: she was on the Wall of Fame above Fuller's magazine rack, where he had photographs of all the Fondis citizens who'd "made it" beyond Fondis: a pretty impressive list, really. The Calfbranders were up there after their third platinum disc; Senator and Secretary of State Chauncey Haney was up there; even my brother was up there, after the Iowa game, when he'd been voted best college player by the press in his freshman year. But this was remarkable: "You're Dannah Davidson," I said. They published articles about her in Art magazines and she'd won a bunch of awards. "What're you doing here?"

She laughed again. "You mean working as a receptionist for Victims' Services? I volunteer every Tuesday."

"Do you live in Fondis?"

"Yup. Still do."

"I remember seeing your paintings at the Art Museum last spring," I said, "during the hospital fund-raiser—"

She nodded. "The 'drink till you drop' for alcohol research?" She put out her hand. I got the feeling I was going to enjoy coming here on Tuesdays.

"Could you drive past my parents' house, please?" I asked Elizabeth, who'd come to pick me up that afternoon. "I don't want to go in;" I added quickly, "I just want to see it."

Elizabeth looked at me quizzically. "What's your therapist's name?" she asked as she put the van in gear.

"Nancy," I answered. "I met—do you know who Dannah Davidson is?"

Elizabeth eased the van down Schley after negotiating the streets around the town square. The Ripleys already had their Christmas lights up; as did the Smiths. My parents' house was quietly imposing, as usual, behind the hedges. There were a few lights on and the back floodlight shone in the cold on the outline of my rabbit house and the carriage house.

"All there?" Elizabeth asked.

"Nothing's changed," I answered. "Nothing."

"Should we go?"

I nodded. "Nancy gave me some homework," I announced as Elizabeth pulled away from the curb. "I need to write about what I was like when I was twelve."

"I remember you were very serious. You wanted to succeed; not only in school, but with rabbits, too. You still are.

"Let's do some shopping, Lisa," she continued, pointing the van toward downtown once more. "I need to figure out my Christmas list and I guess you'd like to figure out something for Bonnie and anyone else who's on your list—I don't know who that would be—"

Neither did I. In the past, I really didn't do any shopping. I saw something at Wately's, where I bought my red dress, and charged it to my father, then gave it to Bonnie or my mother. One year, I bought Chuck a sweater that I thought looked really nice, and it was ten sizes too small. My parents laughed about that a long time. I'd sometimes buy something for a favorite teacher: I bought a lavender incense packet for Mrs. Carey; I bought a pound of coffee for Mr. Flanders. I'd always bought something for Elizabeth: a bud vase or a set of glassware or a barometer. I'd always appreciated seeing those things when the Rabbit Judging Team spent its Friday nights with her: she kept them on a shelf in the living room, next to other gifts from Rabbit Judgers: a photo of a Himalayan Rabbit on a tray; a mug that said BOTTOMS UP NIAGARA with a Satin Rabbit above the Falls on it, upside down; a large metal ashtray in the shape of a rabbit; and several china representations.

"We'll shop, then do dinner somewhere," Elizabeth promised, parking in front of the craft store.

We purchased a bunch of baskets, some wrapping paper, and ribbons; then went to Fuller's, where Elizabeth bought cans of ethnic food, canned salmon, spreads, soup mixes, and staples such as cornmeal and dried beans: all off a list she consulted that was yellow with age.

"Getting a start on Christmas?" Dorothea greeted us as we checked out. "I don't want those soaps ever again, Elizabeth," she said. "Fill mine with liquor next time."
Elizabeth smiled. "Who says I'm going to give you anything?"

"I do," was the tart reply, "For putting up with your tired wallpaper on Thanksgiving." Then she turned serious. "Have you seen The Daily today? There's an article about your brother, Lisa. Picked up for bothering a girl."

I went to the magazine rack, above which a smiling VICTOR GORDON, GOVERNOR, beamed, and tossed a copy onto the counter. The article was small: Chuck Young, this weekend, was warned by officers of the Sheriff's Department, to stay away from Charlene Hauptman, 21, who complained of harassment and suggestive remarks. Miss Hauptman, who was once one of Young's girlfriends, told The Fondis Daily that she was no longer interested and that she'd press charges against him if he pursued her again..."

"Hardly worth the fifty cents it cost," Elizabeth sniffed.

"Don't know why he'd bother with Charlene," Dorothea observed as she processed Elizabeth's credit card. "She's studying to be a preacher in the Methodist Church. Maybe she wants to know what sinning is—"

"Stop it," I found myself saying. "Just stop it." I grabbed a couple of bags and threw them into the cart. Dorothea busied herself bagging; Elizabeth, after a moment, signed the receipt and helped me load the cart quietly. Dorothea hadn't charged us for the newspaper. She picked it up, re-folded it, and put it back in the rack.

"You're going to have some moments that you can't explain," Nancy had told me earlier that afternoon, and you'll just have to live through them. As you explore yourself, you'll find a lot of unresolved stuff."

Elizabeth pulled into the parking lot of Pho #1, the Vietnamese Restaurant, saying, "I'd like something spicy tonight, Lisa. It gets my blood going. I need it," she added, "because of something between Arthur and Iain."

"Hmm?"

"You know I'd e-mailed him and called him and he promised to call me back. Well, he did, but it wasn't what I'd expected. When he called my cell phone, he said he was too busy to come to Fondis for just one night when he knew his father was okay."

We ordered: vegetables and shrimp for me; pork and peppers for her.

Elizabeth continued: "I think he wouldn't come down and at least spend the night with his father because of you."

I looked at her.

"I think—" she said deliberately— "that he's led you on and doesn't know what to do about it."

"I know he's led me on," I answered. "I know he's a selfish bastard." I smiled at her. "And you're thinking he hurt me?" I shook my head.

She smiled back. "Enough about Iain." And that was that. "Could I have Barb Lassiter's phone number? I figure, if I'm your parent, or surrogate, or whatever, the least I can do is show up at 4-H meetings with you."

"They're the fourth Wednesday of every month," I said automatically. "Usually, I catch a ride with the Lassiters."

"Well; this time, I'm going with."

I realized, as the food was served, that it would feel weird to have a parent with me: mine hadn't attended since I was seven or eight, then Barb took over. "Had a good 4-H meeting?" my mother would ask after I'd been dropped off. Then I'd show her the meeting agenda and the list of projects we needed to do and she'd smile and go off to read. "That's nice, dear," I think she said. Had my parents paid Barb, too? Usually, the parents would help with some sort of community service or fund raising for the club: driving the truck for recycling or road clean up, for instance. My parents had never done that. After awhile, I just popped my head in where they were watching TV, announced I was home, and headed up to my room. For Community Service or Fundraising, I just worked with Bonnie, handling the rake or the shovel as we shoveled manure for the Community Garden compost heap.

"You've served with great distinction, Lisa," Barb announced at the awards ceremony in November, "working well beyond anyone at the Community Garden this year." That was because the Lassiters had dropped me off there one Saturday morning to weed the garden with volunteers, two of whom showed up; and then a horse buyer interrupted the Lassiters' schedule and they spent most of lunch and four hours of the afternoon trying to sell a mare. They didn't arrive to pick me up until the Community Garden had been completely weeded and fertilized at five o'clock. "You should've brought your phone," Bonnie told me as I climbed into the truck. "I could've called you and—"

"No," I answered. "I liked it. "Even when Greg and John left, there was still so much to do."

They gave me a bronze pin for that. I wondered if it was out of guilt.

23 /

This heap be witness, and this pillar be witness, that I will not pass over this heap to thee... (Genesis: 31.52)

Of course I'd done my homework, Nancy. I really tried to figure out what I was like at twelve and couldn't figure out what I was like, short of what Elizabeth told me. Well, what made me attractive to a predator? Was it just that I was around? No; it was something else. What was it? Oh yeah: I'd slipped on the floor for some reason and Chuck was right behind me to catch my fall. And he caught me gracefully in his strong arms. But what does that mean?

"What did your fall into his arms mean, Lisa?" Nancy asked me. "Did it tell him that you were vulnerable?

"What did you say? What did you do?"

I didn't know. Certainly, sex wasn't on my mind. "I probably crumpled up like a paper doll. I did that then. I thought it was funny."

"What about closeness? Protection?"

Closeness when I didn't particularly feel close to the folks who were supposed to be close to me. Closeness: How close was my father to me?

When I fixed dinner for us on Wednesday nights; maybe five times in the fall. That was how close we were.

"Did you ever think of your father affectionately?"

Plied with all these questions and Nancy's homework, which was to draw my father and mother and brother, then write an essay about my interactions with each of them, I almost looked forward to Gym, where I didn't have to think or worry: just run around.

"You're sluggish, Lisa," she observed, having called me out from volleyball. "You couldn't have missed that unless you were sluggish. Late night?"

I shook my head. "Got a lot on my mind."

"I heard about that," she answered. "I guess you do." She was about to say something, then paused. "I heard about that," she repeated. "Why don't you go on in—back to the game?"

She'd coached Chuck in weight training, I remembered; helped him in his moves in tennis as well. If she'd heard what really happened, how much would she believe? I played a mean game of volleyball the rest of that class hour: spiked the ball twice into another girl's breasts, which was probably painful.

"You're fighting back," Coach Quintana said as I went in to shower. "Good job, Lisa."

24 /

And they shall not profane the holy things... (Leviticus: 22.15)

Of course I'd baked before: I trotted out my mother's Baking Cookbook last summer and followed one of the bread recipes to the letter, removing a brown loaf from the oven. I wanted to add it to that night's meal, which was the yellow box, but forgot, then offered it to my father the next night. He wasn't hungry. Neither was I. The bread sat in the refrigerator for a while, then my mother, who didn't like leftovers, threw it away.

"Tell me about your mother's dislike of leftovers," Nancy had begun our session. "Why do you think that is?"

Like so many other things, I'd never really thought about it. Elizabeth's refrigerator still had remnants of Thanksgiving dinner in it and they were starting to turn different colors. When she noticed, she threw them into the trash, then asked me to tie the bag and set it in the garage. "We should have frozen some of it," she observed. "When the boys were growing up, I'd never let something like that go to waste."

"Maybe you're more prosperous now," I said, suddenly struck by the fact that the fruit baskets and the fruitcake and the brownies that had come in during Christmas at my parents' house never remained. My mother would always take those gifts and give them to the Food Bank after taking off the cards. Of course, my mother would always write a nice thank-you note, but I did not remember ever eating any of the food.

"Uncle Ralph was a farmer," I told Nancy, "who took care of my mother but wasn't close to her. Everything I've learned about farmers through 4-H is that they try to save everything they can and give away what they don't need. That's not always the way, but a lot of them, if they don't need something, they give it to the silent auction or the Thrift Store so someone else can get the use of it."

"So was your mother in the habit of giving your old clothes to charity?"

I'd never thought about that, either. "She probably did," I answered, "but I never knew what happened to those clothes. I had a favorite t-shirt when I was seven that I'd outgrown and I know I looked and looked through the laundry for a week at least for it until she finally told me that she'd given it away."

"Are farmers like that?"

"Not all of them. Bonnie has a bunch of old shirts and pants she's loved that sit on her closet shelf even though they're too small for her. Kevin's family, though—"

The Allens gave away all kinds of things all the time. Old shoes; galoshes; teddy bears: anything they didn't need. When Whispering Pines 4-H had its annual Garage Sale, the Allens could always be counted on to donate tons of stuff.

"Why is that?"

"Because they feel they can give away everything and still have something left?"

314

"When your mother gave things away, did she give them away with your consent?"

"No." The Allens all knew what was going to the garage sale and frequently joked about it; Bonnie's family always had a box in the barn for old clothes to which they all contributed. "My mother never asked me."

Elizabeth wrapped the cookies and the bread in waxed paper to line the sides of the box to which she carefully added bottles of hot sauce, cans of oysters, cans of beans, cans of soup; cans of broth. "This'll probably take care of the Carters for a month, if they're careful," she said, covering the box with bright red paper. "Doreen isn't too skillful in the kitchen; but Helen is. That's why I addressed this just to Helen." She smiled as she affixed the tag. "Helen reads and writes, thank God. Careful with the box, Lisa: we'll deliver it tomorrow first thing if I can get up the Carter's driveway. It's so rutty and there's been so much snow: I don't know if the van'll take it." That Saturday, we went to the Carters;' the Thompsons;' the Schippers;' the Schwabbs:' all homesteads from years ago, where they welcomed Elizabeth, Mr. Sanders, and me and our Christmas boxes. They were all poor families, just making a bare living off the land or raising animals that sold for another year's mortgage payment. "Ye're Lisa Young!" Robert Schipper announced, "Ye're the daughter of the banker. Why're you here?"

"Lisa lives with me," Elizabeth quietly explained. "She's not with the bank."

"So why's she here?" he asked.

"Because she can carry your box, Robert; for me."

"Young young Lisa Young:
She carries boxes for you:
She carries boxes for me, too,
But I'm no foo
I make Lisa Young carry boxes for Elizabeth, too," Arthur Sanders suddenly recited, standing in front of Robert Schipper. "Good rhyme, eh?" he asked.

Robert Schipper suddenly relaxed. "Yeah. Good," he said.

"Your father didn't renew the loan on their land a few years back," Mr. Sanders explained, "and Robert went south on it, as you can see; even though the other bank took it over. That's true of a lot of hardscrabble farmers around here, Lisa."

"Le's get you a cup a coffee," Robert Schipper said. "I read that article you wrote about hog prices bein' down, Artur, and it didn't surprise me, 'cuz I feel it, but yur prediction fer next year?"

Mr. Sanders nodded. "Looks grim," he answered, "Unless you can sell high-end organic to restaurants."

"An spend more money?" Robert Schipper paused in mid-pour. "An have some govmint fella trampin round here?"

Mr. Sanders shrugged. "Works for the folks down the road."

"Shit. Oh—'scuse me, ladies—but they were starving! Mizz Prentice, d'you take milk?"

Robert Schipper directed most of his remarks to Mr. Sanders as Elizabeth and I listened. There didn't seem to be anyone else on the place and I wondered how Robert Schipper lived. The house was clean enough: filled with the smells of bacon and woodsmoke; the wood floors were swept and the furniture, though battered, was dusted. At the kitchen table where we sat a Bible lay open to First Corinthians.

"So Lydia and the girls are all right?" Mr. Sanders was asking.

"Alwus have been," was the reply. "Jest in a different state: North Carolina, where her folks live. But Social Services has left us in peace now. They cud care less wad I feed meself; but they wuz all over us wen the girls wuz little; well: you remember. You wrote the story."

"They going to be back for Christmas?"

"If Lydie gets the money they will."

Mr. Sanders nodded his head in sympathy. "Must be lonely around here."

Robert Schipper nodded and sipped his coffee. "I got the pigs and chickens," he answered.

...thou shalt surely give them a possession of an inheritance among their father's brethren... (Numbers: 27;7)

How Chuck was able to sell his DVD during finals week at SAC was a mystery because he should have been on campus, studying. Some of the sportscasts on TV focused on Brian Williams, the Pre-Vet Basketball Player, who was in the library, day and night, studying, even though there was a crucial game against Idaho that weekend. "This is a dedicated student," remarked the sportscaster wonderingly, "who wants to succeed in the classroom and on the court."

Not like Chuck Young, I added. Chuck's major was Education "because I want to give back to students what was given to me," he'd announced time and again, "through coaching and teaching."

The woman who'd conducted the tour of SAC that I'd attended during my sophomore year had stated matter-of-factly that studies were intense in many of the majors: Pre-Vet; Poli-Sci; English; Music; Psychology; Engineering; Geology: I'd listened for "Education" to be announced. It wasn't. Dr. Hoeppner had a degree in Education, I remembered.

I baked a loaf of banana bread for Kevin; zucchini bread for Barb and Bonnie; a dill bread for Mr. Sanders. I thought of baking a loaf of bread for Iain. Then I decided to bake a loaf of banana bread for Nancy instead. It seemed strange to be making Christmas presents instead of just going to a store, selecting, and watching them wrap it, then giving it. I'd bought cufflinks for my father which he never used; a knit scarf for Chuck that I never saw again; a large cast iron pan for my mother that she gave to charity a week after opening the box.

I wrapped the bread in tinfoil and wasted some ribbon because I couldn't measure it properly to put round the package. "No problem;" Elizabeth assured me, smoothing the wrinkles. "We'll put this on a plate of cookies."

"Don't know if you've noticed," Dorothea said as she rang up our groceries, "but there are a couple of articles about your brother in the paper."

317

Elizabeth looked at me. I looked away. She threw a copy of The Fondis Daily on the counter.

"DA's Office Seeking Information on Chuck Young," it read, "in investigation regarding alleged molestation and rape..." and the article continued with quotes from a County Attorney, someone from the Sheriff's Office, and "an unidentified victim," all of whom were interested in Chuck's activities in high school.

"This is probably the result of the investigation," Elizabeth declared after reading the article aloud over dinner. "They saw something in what your parents said; in what Coach Mecklinburg said; in the attitude of your brother toward girls and started wondering."

"What does it mean?"

She shrugged. "Depends on what they're looking for. My guess is that they aren't sure what they'll uncover, but there's enough of a question for them to pursue it." She flipped a couple of pages. "Letter from Dr. Brace in here about government intrusion into private lives. Want me to read it to you? It's about Eddie's dog."

26 /

So shall we come upon him in some place
where he shall be found, and we will light upon him
as the dew falleth upon the ground... (II Samuel: 17.12)

"I don't know what could be keeping him," Elizabeth mused for the sixth time that evening. It was the Friday before Winter Break and Final Exams had been given, which meant that grading had to be done and the grades entered on the computer. I was expecting all As with a question mark in Gym because part of it was proficiency on the basketball court, and I'd missed the ball a couple of times. I knew I'd passed, at least, with a C, and I didn't figure it would matter much anyway. A in Chemistry; A in American History; A in Art; A in Advanced Placement Literature; A in Calculus; C in Gym: oh, the possibilities! Mr. Sanders had been invited to dinner because "he won't eat if someone doesn't remind him, and he's spent far too much time working at school and his articles." She sighed as she looked over to the Sanders house; still dark. She'd kept the potatoes in the oven and had set the roast beef aside so it wouldn't dry out an hour before. As usual, I'd taken care of the rabbits, then sort of occupied the couch or the kitchen table: helping where I could, but just sitting, mostly, my copy of Things Fall Apart opened to the first part, splayed on the table. I couldn't read while Elizabeth tried to busy herself by sweeping the floor, loading the dishwasher, loading the laundry machine—just waiting for Mr. Sanders.

The evening news was on the TV and idly I watched it as Elizabeth, leaning against the counter above the roast beef, listened.

"Finally, in our breaking news segment tonight, long time Fondis attorney, Charles Holmes, has filed suit against Fondis High School Principal Elmer Hoeppner and the Fondis School Board for hiring Arthur Sanders as a substitute teacher because of 'significant improprieties regarding his conduct as a teacher; particularly in regard to the children of two prominent citizens.'" The newscaster hesitated. I knew exactly why. How much could she say? She looked up briefly above her coiffed hair, then straight at the camera. "Mr. Holmes' lawsuit concerns the children of prominent Urologist Dr. Edward Brace and Banker Harold Young and their relations with Mr. Sanders, which Mr. Holmes' lawsuit deems 'inappropriate and misleading and ultimately slanderous and dangerous.' We'll have details as they are revealed."

We'd been too invested in the story to notice Mr. Sanders had come into the kitchen, letting himself in quietly. He stood in the doorway until the story was over, then cleared his throat, making us jump. "I turned in my keys and grades to Dr. Hoeppner tonight," he said without greeting. "I have a backseat full of certificates that Lisa helped me put up as decoration and a few books that didn't belong to the school. I left a pile of newspapers behind and after I saved my records on flashdrive, I wiped out the computer completely." He smiled. "I've never been fired from a teaching job before.

"Oh—there's something here for you, as well," he added, pulling an envelope from his pocket, and holding it before him, looking directly at me.

I went to him and pulled the envelope, followed closely by Elizabeth, who locked her arms around him tightly. Holding the envelope in one hand, I set the oven, timed it for ten minutes, and put the roast beef in.

TO LISA YOUNG:
YOU HAVE RECEIVED AN A IN GYM, WHICH IS
YOUR ONE REQUIRED COURSE THIS CREDIT
YEAR. IF YOU CHOOSE TO WAIVE THE NEXT
SEMESTER IN GYM, WE WILL ACCEPT YOUR
CHOICE. YOU WILL RECEIVE A PASS FOR YOUR
REMAINING CREDITS.
 PLEASE USE THE ENCLOSED ENVELOPE BY
DECEMBER 28TH TO LET US KNOW YOUR
DECISION.

27 /

...A woman slew him. (Judges:10.54)

I'd only seen Nancy for three weeks, but I'd learned quickly.
She'd said that some people receive opportunities; some people have
to strive for them. I was facing an opportunity. Should I take it? I
could kiss Coach Quintana goodbye; I could kiss the locker room
goodbye; I could kiss everything goodbye. I could get on with my
life.

"There are also times when we need to face those things we
don't want to," Nancy continued, "and sometimes, we become better
because of them."

"Your parents are paying for all of it," Dr. Rural had told me,
"and you should take full advantage of it. It'll make you a better
person."

"Just have dinner," Elizabeth urged. "Sleep in tomorrow.
Decide tomorrow, Arthur."

"But what about facing that false charge?" Mr. Sanders cut a
piece of beef precisely and poised it before him. "I've been fired
over the charge of Socrates: corrupting youth. I want to fight it.

"I want an apology," Mr. Sanders continued. "I was doing
what was right; I was honestly grading the students; not just going
along so I could keep my job."

"They'll have it documented, Arthur; especially since it involves Eddie Brace." Elizabeth passed round the salad and poured water from the pitcher for all three of us. Although alcohol wasn't mentioned in the papers drawn up regarding my custody, she felt it was safer not to drink anything stronger. "He's passed everything else. Won't you just be seen as unfair; especially since you filed charges to have that dog put down? "

"That dog's a menace," he muttered.

"So what are you going to do?"

"In a way, I've already done it," Mr. Sanders replied as he helped himself to more roast beef. "They passed me a paper to sign that was a resignation, admitting that I'd prejudiced the students and had engaged in questionable moral practices. It looked like something Charles Holmes would draw up—and when I refused to sign it, Dr. Hoeppner fired me and handed me a copy of why he did so." He shook his head.

"Oh—Lisa, what was your letter about?"

I'd already made up my mind. I was going to spend the next semester of my senior year at Fondis High School, even though it was only for Gym.

28 /

And I charged your judges...saying, Hear the causes between your
brethren and judge righteously between every man and his brother,
and the stranger that is with him. (Deut:1.16)

"You ready?" Elizabeth asked from the bottom of the stairs. It was the Saturday night before Christmas week, when Whispering Pines 4-H had its annual Christmas Party.

I should be, I thought, having helped decorate since nine that morning and setting up tables and chairs. I'd figured out who was each Secret Santa and Bonnie phoned various families to fill in main dishes or desserts for the potluck. Bonnie had just dropped me off to shower and here was Elizabeth, who'd had to go in to work that morning, getting ready to take me to the party. My parents had never done that. They'd just drop me off and pick me up when the party was over.

Elizabeth was humming to herself as she drove down Road 17, but she wouldn't tell me why, short of "You'll see."
Kevin was wearing a coat and tie as were a couple other seniors hoping to receive the two SAC Agricultural Scholarships allotted to the County and awarded at the Club Christmas Party. This year, there were twelve seniors vying for it and nobody knew who would receive the scholarship until the Extension Agent, who was always invited to speak, made the announcement. Bonnie was in a western skirt and boots, a blue plaid blouse, hoping for one of the scholarships, too.

"Your new mom," Kevin nodded toward Elizabeth, who was talking seriously with Barb in a corner. "You did well on finals?"

I nodded. "Mr. Sanders got fired."
It was his turn to nod. "I got a call from Wendy last night about it. The Loods called her, then they called Meg. The whole AP class was buzzing about it last night. Wendy talked about a petition; Meg likes the idea of a Letter to the Editor."

"I like the idea of a Letter to the Editor, too," I answered. "I'll sign it."

Barb spontaneously hugged Elizabeth, then gestured to Bonnie to join them. Bonnie hugged Elizabeth, too.

"Your new mom's making friends pretty quickly," Kevin observed. "Can I get you something?"

"She's not my new mom, Kevin," I said sharply. I walked away, angry, stopping right in front of the desserts, fuming.

"If you're a little raw now and then, just keep remembering that you're healing…"

I'd only seen Nancy three times and already I was shaky, uncertain; just not myself, sometimes at least.

"Let's get started," Barb announced. "Secret Santa is in that corner. Get the package with your name on it, then open your package. There's a card or a note inside that tells you who it is." Since I was close by, I grabbed the present that had my name on it and sat back down at a nearby table, scanning the hordes who came to the corner. The package I had was inexpertly wrapped and said TO LISA in an elementary school hand. There was a murmur and scraping of chairs and a lot of giggling as people tore wrappings off. I sat at the table, the present in front of me. Kevin, who had

Bonnie's present, paired with her. I was supposed to pair with whoever was left: a third grader named Mitchell, who was asking for me. Bonnie grabbed my arm and led me to him. He opened my present eagerly: a tin of brownies, cookies, and fudge, which seemed to suit him. I slowly opened his: a glass paperweight with the SAC logo on it and 'GO WOLVERINES!' atop. I let it fall to the concrete floor, where it shattered. Mitchell took his tin and ran to his parents.

"I need to get—a broom and dustpan," I sobbed in front of the suddenly quiet room, then ran into the Women's. Barb and Elizabeth came in a few moments later. Barb put her arms around me. I just cried.

I could hear Bonnie asking everyone to serve themselves at the potluck tables and heard the subsequent voices. A little girl came in and asked Elizabeth if she could use the bathroom. Elizabeth smiled and pointed to a stall.

"Do you want me to drive you home?" Elizabeth asked.

I did. "I'm sorry, Barb," I choked. "I can't face—Mitchell."

In spite of herself, Barb laughed. "Mitchell? He's probably forgotten about it!"

"That's good," Elizabeth said, her tone making Barb serious again. "We can leave through the back hall here. I'll get our coats and come back, Lisa. Barb, if you could keep track of my dish—" Elizabeth had made her enchilada casserole: one of my favorites.

Barb nodded, kept her arms around me, and let me cry. "Elizabeth told me that Dr. Brace gave an offer for the lawsuit against him—all our mortgages?"

I nodded.

"He wants to settle; do you understand, Lisa? We won't be losing the ranch!"

"In local news, Chuck Young, SAC quarterback, whose DVD, "Inspirations," has already earned a quarter of a million dollars, has been invited to the Cancer Survivor benefit in New Orleans on Christmas, where he will be keynote speaker..."

Mr. Sanders turned the television off. "They're making him untouchable," he remarked. "A celebrity is a lot harder to pin a charge on than a nobody."

...thus his father wept for him... (Genesis:37.35)

No one from the cast of Herpetology and You showed up for Christmas. An e-mail from Anh summed it up: "Snowed in in Idaho. What a crappy place!"

Candlelight Catering showed up an hour before they were to arrive, then seemed uncertain when Elizabeth told them that there was no one to serve: just Mr. Sanders, she, and I. "What the hell?" one of the caterers asked. "We're being paid; let's feed you!"

They took over the kitchen and an hour later we were all treated to fresh chicken cutlets, herbs, glazed carrots, green beans in a wine sauce: "the best we can cook," the caterer remarked. "Hope you like it."

"Will you leave the leftovers?" Elizabeth asked.

They wrapped and froze the leftovers and left. There was no reason for them to continue coming; they'd get their check anyway.

Although he seemed to enjoy the meal, Mr. Sanders was distant. "He got the word that he didn't have a case," Elizabeth told me. "The school can hire and fire for any reason at all."

The Letter to the Editor, signed by the students in Mr. Sanders' AP Literature Class, composed by Meg, was given a large headline in The Fondis Daily and The Divide-Review. We said we wanted him back. It was signed by everyone except Eddie Brace.

None of us wanted to attend first hour when we came back in January—well, maybe Eddie Brace did—but we went anyway; not just because we were good students, but because we wondered who'd replace Mr. Sanders.

"There's a chemistry between the teacher and students in an advanced class like this one," Mrs. Grimes began, "and I know Mr. Sanders was preferred."

"Not by all of us," Eddie said. "I couldn't stand him. He's trying to kill my—"

"Would you shutup?" Meg, normally quiet, turned on him.

"I know Mr. Sanders was preferred by most of you," she continued quietly, "and that was because he pushed you. He pushed you to learn to write; to read critically; to understand what a piece of literature might contain.

"I've been your counselor for all four years of high school. I know what you're capable of; I know about the scholarships some of you have conditionally attained; like the SAC scholarship you received, Kevin."

His ears turned red, which made me smile.

"I also know that a lot of scholarships aren't certain yet," she emphasized. The SAC scholarship is one of them; the Miscatonic scholarship is another." She shot a look at Meg. Those schools expect you to keep your grades up and to do well. If you don't, they'll be withdrawn.

"I'm going to be your English teacher this semester." She stated it flatly. "Because I know that most of you are interested in doing well, I'm expecting you will. I will be pushing you the same way Mr. Sanders did and I will expect the same level of work."

"So you'll be our teacher this semester?" Kevin asked. "Assigning what he would?"

"Yes; and with the same expectations." She paused. "Any questions?"

My teachers looked surprised when I showed up to classes the day after Winter Break. No: I was going to tough it out. Goddamn Coach Quintana. God bless Coach Quintana. She didn't look askance when I appeared: she put me to work pounding the mats on the floor for wrestling. "Girls: this is something that most of you will encounter only in this class: Women Wrestling. I include it because it's part of the larger culture and some people want to see women wrestling. They also want to see women on roller skates." I understood that. Chuck had asked one time that I wear a soccer jersey. Yeah, I understood that.

"So why don't we wrestle in a nightie?" I asked. "Give 'em what they want."

"Take five laps," Coach Quintana snapped, "then come see me. I'll let you shower later than the others. I want to talk to you."

I ran the five laps, angry; satisfied that I'd made her angry; and ready to give an explanation. After all, I was taking her class not because I had to; I wanted to be there.

Because she was preoccupied with helping the basketball team sort itself out, I went into the showers and took a long one: about fifteen minutes: just enjoying the heat and steam. When I got out, it was clear that I'd kept her waiting.

"I don't get you," she began. "You have the opportunity to graduate but you reject it; you can't stand my class, but you come back to finish it; your friend gets fired and why are you here?"

"Because I need to be here," I answered quietly.

"Something with your scholarship?" She looked kind of hopeful. It would have pigeonholed me for her. She would have understood that.

I shook my head. "I need to be here to finish what I started in August: no special favors; no offers to get ahead; nothing that sets me apart. I need to finish it."

"Why? You're not going to be a star athlete; I understand you're good in Chemistry and the other classes, but so what? You could be in college right now, taking courses toward a degree that would mean a job later. Why stay here, Lisa?"

I didn't quite understand it myself: a few sessions with Nancy made me realize I needed to be here because it was the scene of Chuck's triumphs and it should be the scene of my ending with Chuck. Everything seemed to exude the name and reputation of Chuck Young in Fondis High School: his jersey on the gym wall; the records he'd broken; the All State record: they were all there for anyone to read, just like the banners for state championship Rabbit Judging in the Ag. Building. I wanted to finish something that Chuck had dodged: I wanted to finish at Fondis High School without being given a special privilege: I wanted to finish the way most people should; not helped by my prowess on the field or my ability to charm.

"I know you helped Chuck with weight training," I answered, "and I know he missed his first hour to work down here a lot of times. Mrs. McGurky had to pass him because Dr. Hoeppner told her to because he was down here, working with you during first hour." I breathed hard. I'd never faced a teacher with these words before, but I thought of Mr. Sanders, who was probably waiting outside for me, and I got angry enough to say what I wanted. "I want to pass your class because I do what you ask, Coach; not because I'm a special athlete or a special kid. I want to be the one who finished because she could do it; not because she was special."

She shook her head in disbelief. "Did he really miss Biology to come work with me?"

I nodded.

"I didn't know," she said. She looked around. The Basketball Team was finished with layups. "I'll see you tomorrow, Lisa."

"I'm sorry I'm late," I told Mr. Sanders, who was waiting in his car outside the school.

"No problem;" he answered. "I've been catching up." He pointed to the copies of The Daily on the backseat. "Your mother has been sponsoring all kinds of luncheons in support of Chuck's DVD and his book: The Garden Club; the Debutante Society; the Art Exhibition Crowd: everybody except 4-H."

"She's good at that," I remarked, snapping my seatbelt. "She'll probably try Friends of the Hospital and the Art Museum next."

"Why do you think she's trying so hard?"

"Dunno. Maybe she's afraid he'll lose money."

"He has earned more money than I'll ever see in a lifetime," Mr. Sanders remarked. "Dozens of people have gone nuts over it: there's a table at Fuller's—" He shifted into second and turned on Main. "How was English class?"

"Oh—Mrs. Grimes had us tell her about a couple of poems," I answered. "They were both by John Donne and we had to draw what was going on."

"Hmm. Very good," he remarked. He'd been impressed with what I'd told him about her first day in our AP class: "So in a few words, she knocked the leadership out. It wasn't an accident that she'd single out Kevin and Meg. Once they were on her side, the rest would be easy."

He drove past the Sheriff's Office, where a sign pointed to ZEBULON COUNTY ANIMAL IMPOUNDMENT. "I'd had a call today from Charles Holmes," he remarked, "asking me if I would reconsider. I didn't."

I was reaching for the radio. I stopped. "So Eddie's dog is...?"

"Dead," he finished.

He stopped at the mailboxes and we both got out of the car. Elizabeth had a bunch of catalogues; Mr. Sanders had a credit card offer.

30

When the host goeth forth against thine enemies, then keep thee from
every wicked thing. (Deut: 23.9)

"I'd written your parents," Elizabeth said as she opened the letter, "asking if Arthur or I couldn't teach you to drive, and I also asked whether they'd fund your entry fees in the spring rabbit shows as well as the judging." She looked it over, shaking her head, then handed it to me. Yes: of course I could be taught to drive as long as she or Arthur had insurance; no, they wouldn't pay any of my fees because they were gratuitous. There was a sentence wondering why I needed to talk to a therapist as well.

"I got a call today," she said as she began looking in the freezer, "from Mr. Hazlitt at the DA's Office. He'd like to see us both tomorrow at ten."

That was during Chemistry class. "Anything important?"

"He told me that he had some information that might be of interest to you, especially."

"Anything else?"

"He didn't tell me." She pulled a bag of peas from the freezer and laid it on the counter. "Hey, isn't it Thursday? Why aren't you at Bonnie's?"

I shook my head. I'd told Bonnie I had too much homework, which was a lie, but truth was, I didn't want to watch Herpetology and You anymore; and not because of Iain. I was sick of remembering how Bonnie in her sweater had charmed them; how they'd all played along and just how temporary they were. I didn't want to watch "recent footage" in the snows of Yellowstone and Grand Teton National Parks knowing that I'd been hoping Iain felt something for me, while it was being filmed. "I just got tired of watching it," I said.

She pursed her lips. "Should we have chicken with the peas? We've got some mint. How about mushrooms, too?"

Eddie Brace put his book on his desk, then poked around inside his backpack, turning it sideways. Something shifted and a rush of pencils, a notebook, a photography magazine and a camera all fell out. "Shit," he announced, and began reaching for the stuff.

Kevin, who sat in the row next to him, jumped up and helped. Mrs. Grimes, who'd just come in, paused, her arms full of papers.

"Good to see you've got a pencil, Eddie," she said before going to her desk where she sorted out the assignments, her back to us. She put the page numbers on the board and turned around to see Eddie, his stuff picked up, looking into his backpack. "Missing something?" she asked, then pointed to the page on the board.

"Yeah; my camera," Eddie answered. "It cost a lot."

"Has anyone seen Eddie's camera?"

"Kevin—" Eddie looked up at him. "Do you have it?"

Kevin gave a "Search Me" gesture, then opened his book. Meg, who sat beside him, had her book open in one hand and toyed with the clasp on her purse with the other.

"Does someone have my camera?" Eddie demanded. "It's got a lot of stuff I don't want to lose on it."

"Your dog?" I couldn't help asking.

He nodded, looking at me, then "Fuck you, Lisa," he said as he left.

Mrs. Grimes closed her eyes then looked at me a moment. "In 'A Valediction Forbidding Mourning,' what paradox do we find?" she asked.

I thought about Kevin's strong arms and how he smelled like hay and cattle; not the smell of a feedlot, but the smell of dew on the grass; of sweet grains and clean dust in the afternoon sunlight. It kept me going as I stepped out the front door of Fondis High and into Elizabeth's van just outside after second hour. I thought of it when Mr. Hazlitt told us that an investigator had talked with all the girls Chuck had gone steady with during high school— "and only one— Charlene Hauptman—will actually say what he did. Most of them didn't say why. Do you know?"

"Lisa?" Elizabeth asked me.

"Do their parents have loans with the bank?" I asked simply.

He shook his head. "A lot of those loans were settled a long time ago," he answered. "We looked into the mortgages, too: fixed rates; no balloons; no unexpected surprises. Is there anything else you can think of?"

I could imagine what Chuck had made them do: all for love, he'd tell them. In my case, it was losing my virginity at twelve, and I thought of Bonnie and Elizabeth and cringed when I thought of them and their disappointment. I could think of a lot more humiliating things that would—

"You might ask them what Chuck asked them to do for love. It was always something embarrassing: something that a girl would cringe at inside. Chuck knew what it was. He always knew what it was."

"Like what?"

"If Desiree cut her hair for him," Elizabeth said, "it could show a mastery of her that she didn't even let her parents have. There are some things that really don't need to be sexual to humiliate a woman or a girl becoming a woman."

"So you don't know any specifics?"

"No, I don't," I answered.

He tapped his desk a couple of times, considering, then let loose a revelation: "There is a blog by a Barbie Vanest, student at SAC, who went out with Chuck Young, that describes all kinds of things—We're trying to get in touch with her. Do you know who she is?"

I vaguely remembered a bubbly girl named Barbie during Chuck's freshman year who leaned over the dinner table and giggled a lot at anything Chuck said. I shrugged. "She was one of many. There was a Janet; a Rachel; a Debbie. I don't remember who else."

"So I missed Chemistry class to see Mr. Hazlitt?" I asked as we climbed back in the van.

"The law takes a while to work," Elizabeth answered as she buckled her seatbelt.

TO: SHERIFF'S OFFICE, ZEBULON COUNTY
THE ATTACHED PHOTOS, FROM THE CAMERA OF EDWARD BRACE, JUNIOR, MAY BE USEFUL TO YOU IN THE CASE OF DESTRUCTION OF THE FELICIA DUNCAN MEMORIAL.

I'd been sent a copy. There were photos, dated, of the Memorial before its destruction, then after its destruction. There was a large black shape in one and a really distinctive-looking handle of a leash in the corner of another, where it had wrapped around a tree. How Kevin managed to send it anonymously, I couldn't figure. Kevin had caught Eddie Brace in the crosshairs and I smelled sweet hay.

I put on the curvy jeans that were sort of difficult to fit in; I put on the blouse with the touch of blue that looked good. I looked clean. I wanted to look good for Kevin.

"What's the occasion?" Mr. Sanders asked.

"I want to look good," I answered.

He put the car in gear. "The Sheriff's Office wrote me that they might have found a suspect who vandalized the memorial."

"I know," I answered.

"What do you know?" he asked. He'd become quiet; intense. I got a sense of the reporter who'd faced supporters for Sheriff Thompson threatening his house and livelihood.

"I know that the Sheriff got an e-mail with pictures on it," I said, "because it came from Eddie Brace's camera."

"How do you know that?"

"Because someone I know got hold of Eddie Brace's camera and found pictures on it."

"Did Eddie Brace know his pictures would be sent to the Sheriff's Office?"

"Probably not."

"Who stole his camera?"

I didn't reply.

"Eddie, were you missing this?" Meg held a small camera in her hand. "I found it in my bag yesterday, and I don't know how it got there—"

Eddie snatched it from her hand.

I noticed Kevin smile. He didn't even look at me. He looked at Meg instead.

"Why are you attacking your brother?" One of the tenth graders in Gym class came up to me, wondering. "He's such a star."

I smiled. That usually worked. With this one, it didn't.

"He's made Fondis such an athletic proving ground! I can get a scholarship in volleyball because of him!"

"Good," I said.

"So can Adriana," she said, pointing to someone else at her locker.

"Good," I said.

"And your attacking your brother is making our volleyball look worse!"

I found something in my locker to find. The piece of quartz Marla gave me felt warm in my pocket.

I had no answer. I never had an answer. She finally left as the bell rang.

"One of my classmates told me I was attacking Chuck," I began as I tossed my backpack into the back seat, "and making it harder for kids to get athletic scholarships."

"A lot of people are going to say a lot of things," Mr. Sanders replied. "Look at this."

The front page of The Fondis Daily bore the large headline:
CHUCK YOUNG: ABUSER?

The District Attorney's Office has confirmed that it's looking into allegations that SAC Football Star and former All-Around Fondis Athlete Chuck Young "has systematically and repeatedly abused every woman he's intimately known," according to

Ron Hazlitt, Assistant District Attorney, who gave a press conference in Fondis this morning.

Young, 20, couldn't be reached for comment at press time.

"Allegations have been made since Thanksgiving and an investigation has been ongoing into the charges," Hazlitt said, "and we feel there's a pattern here."

Two SAC coeds who dated Young have given sworn statements at the Ford County Sheriff's Department during the last two days, Hazlitt reported, and he feels certain that as the investigation goes deeper, more coeds from the Fondis area will step forward.

SAC is located in Ford County.

A spokesman for the SAC Athletic Department dismissed the investigation, telling reporters that athletic stars the caliber of Chuck Young are "always in the spotlight and sure to bear scrutiny"

"Look a little farther down," he suggested.

Above the reproduction of a photo I knew were the words: POSSIBLE VANDAL FOUND IN MEMORIAL DESTRUCTION.

"I need to stop by Whispering Pines with you today, Lisa," he said, parking at a meter along Elm. Dr. Philco says they're cleaning up the Memorial and Nirvana has been rehired to fix it. We're meeting to see what her new design looks like."

"Kind of a nice gift for the end of January," I answered.

He stopped the car and turned it off, looking at his watch as he did so. "You've still got some time. Why don't you come meet these important folks a moment?"

"I don't think—"

"C'mon!" He held my arm and steered me toward a door to the right of the Memorial. He opened it and followed me inside.

Along one wall was a shelf filled with books opposite a wall filled with paintings and photographs. There were chairs arranged for one-on-one discussions and end tables. At the end of the room, above a bar, was a cross-stitched sampler that announced the dates of birth and death of Felicia Duncan and the legend: "Furnished from her home in the hope that all may be comfortable who use this space."

A blonde professional-looking woman stepped inside accompanied by three others. "Arthur! So good to see you again!"

I put on my pleased to meet you look which I'd perfected during the Museum evenings and the Bank Christmas Parties and the hospital fundraisers, then noticed a quiet woman slip in behind them and take up a place in the corner. I shook hands, then went to her. "You're Nirvana," I said.

She nodded. "Lisa Young. Dannah told me she'd met you."

"I really like your sculpture. I used to sit there last fall."

"Yeah. I saw the Police Report," she said. "You said you liked to think and contemplate. Felicia would've liked that. She liked to contemplate."

"Did she do it here?"

"No; this building wasn't built. She contemplated on her back porch, she said, to the sound of windchimes."

"There's a sound that is so pure—" Felicia touched the large chime with her nail. *"Can you hear it?"* She tapped it again. *"We've got to get it."*

"You're a few minutes late, Lisa," Dannah said. "Go right in."

Nancy had asked me to bring my diary: "There's probably stuff in there you don't even know about, Lisa. I'd like you to look at it through your grown-up eyes."

At first, I hadn't wanted to. Who would? But then, as she led me through my first misunderstandings then my bits about school and rabbits and what was said by whom— "You used to spend two hours every day, writing?" Nancy asked with amazement. Yes: in the Rabbit House, mostly, where I kept the diaries among the 4-H stuff, where I knew no one would ever look: I even made a notebook look like a 4-H Rabbit manual, carefully gluing the 4-H four leaf clover on its binding then stenciling RABBITS AND THEIR CARE on it: writing, usually before dinner, my chair pulled up to the show table

333

and a folded up Divide-Review under the papers I was working on to give a stiffness against the pile of carpet.

I sometimes commented on what was in the paper as well: "Sheriff Thompson stole a lot of money from the government," one of my entries read. "A really funny article about a guy who took a kid's fire engine riding toy along CR 186 and got picked up by a deputy," another read. Nancy didn't mind my getting reacquainted with the memories: "But get acquainted with all of them," she advised. "From what I can see, you've known Arthur Sanders a long time; a long time before he was your English teacher."

Maybe, but I really didn't recall. "Um—maybe so," I admitted.

"And while you kept a portion of yourself tightly under lock and key, this volume and every other one showed the Lisa that engaged the rest of the world. It's a record of your personality—the personality that stayed in these volumes until Thanksgiving; or maybe before, when you met Iain.

"I'd like to keep this volume until next time, Lisa;" Nancy said. "I'd like you to look at it after not having it for a week and tell me what you've learned."

"Not have it?" I felt prickly inside. "What if you lose it?" I asked.

"What if I did?" she answered.

"My chickens," I said. "No: I want to keep it with me, please. Maybe next week." I took the diary and buried it in my backpack.

She nodded. "Re-read it with fresh eyes, Lisa. Bring it back next time. You'll be eighteen, then."

31 /

Then thou scarest me with dreams, and terrifies me through visions. (Job:7.14)

Mr. Sanders was waiting for me in the lobby next to a sketch of the Memorial. "This time, she's going to build a stone wall behind

334

it and the face is going to be longer," he said, "and the water's going to fall in such a way that it sounds like wind chimes."

"Very interesting," I answered.

"You know, I used to come here: for a whole year after it was put up, every day except weekends, taking care of some of the weeding, watching the plants grow; tending the roses. It was nice while I waited for Iain on Wednesdays."

"You came here every day after school?"

"Yeah. I had a lot of time," he concluded.

"Did Iain know you spent every afternoon here?"

"I don't think so," he answered. "He was so consumed by his mother's death that he couldn't do much besides concentrate on school. Then he and Charles Holmes' kid took a bunch of weekend trips, hauling around that little sailboat; and he and Jeff Prentice were doing something else during the week. It didn't seem like what I was doing was of much concern to him."

"But it was," I said, then wished I hadn't because I could see it hurt him.

"Yeah. I know, Lisa. I should have been a more interested father; or at least checked in on him more; but it wasn't an easy time for me, either. I worked to dull the pain. In some ways, I'm still working to dull the pain. Have you heard from him?"

"Not a thing."

"I haven't either. No e-mail; no call when I went to the hospital. He knows I've been fired because they get TV up there: Anh has this setup where he can beam into local channels, including Fondis."

"If I knew, I'd tell you," I said.

"I know you would." He turned into the driveway and we got out to open mailboxes. Elizabeth had a package from her grandchildren in Iowa; Mr. Sanders had a credit card offer.

"Eddie probably won't be coming in today," Bonnie met me in the hall before class. "He's being questioned in the Sheriff's Office, Vern just told me."

"About the pictures?"

She nodded. "Mr. Holmes is down there, too."

"Of course." I saw Kevin down the hall and asked, "Does he know?"

"Probably. He's probably pretty pleased about it. Eddie can be treated as an adult, now that he's eighteen."

"Treated as an adult?"

"Oh come on, Lisa—when you're eighteen, you can get your name in the paper if it's on a legal record! You knew that!"
Eddie turned eighteen January tenth, I remembered, from a birthday party I'd attended a long time ago.

February second. Groundhog Day. My eighteenth birthday. I took my seat, noticing that everyone else seemed preoccupied with whatever it was: Oh yeah: Examples of Moral Ambiguity in Dorian Gray. Due at hour's end.

I opened my notebook and the copy of The Picture of Dorian Gray, by Oscar Wilde, fully intending to write about it.

I found myself in front of the Rabbit Barn at the County Fairgrounds: all bare and locked up. I walked close to the wall, suddenly noticing the chilly wind that swept up into my coat that made me shiver. I looked through the wind. The corrals, the parking lots, the grandstands: all were empty and had a patina of snow and ice.

And I kicked the door of the Rabbit Barn. And it opened. Someone had not shut it properly last summer and it was waiting for me to come along seven months later. I went in, closing the door firmly behind me.

It was cold. I knew it would be. The rabbit cages were stacked along the far wall, away from the windows, which let in the white light of February and little else. Tables and chairs were stacked against the north wall and the banner: THE ZEBULON COUNTY RABBIT JUDGING TEAM IS SPONSORED BY THE FARMERS AND MECHANICS BANK OF FONDIS still hung from the ceiling, every now and then shivering when a draft from a broken window hit it just right. Some snow had gotten in through the broken window, but the rest of the barn was dry and a large table where Elizabeth Prentice sat and did registrations during the summers, stood in its patina of dust. I climbed on it, stretched, looking up at the dusty rafters above me, and fell asleep, listening to the wind whip around the Rabbit Barn.

"Chuck doesn't like lasagna, Lisa," my mother told me. "Too many layers. Besides, the recipe—" she looked at it distastefully "—calls for too much sauce. It's too pedestrian."

"But I wanted to cook for him tonight!" I said excitedly. "I'd promised him that I would."

She sighed and said no. She'd go ahead with her crepes, which were already laid out.

I was in tears. "I couldn't make the lasagna, Chuck, like I promised, "because—"

He hit me. It made me cry more. He held me. Then he made me feel guilty.

"Do you want to go shopping?" Felicia Duncan was self-possessed; determined; sympathetic. She wore glasses. "I've been working all week and I want to do something fun. Climb in, Lisa." She opened the back door of the car and I found myself seated next to a nine year old who told me her name was Janie. As the car started down the road toward Fondis, Janie told me she was on the Rabbit Judging Team and that she was trying "really hard to win blue ribbons and belt buckles." Janie was in third grade at Kutch Elementary and her father was a teacher in high school.

"Ya know," Felicia said as she started the car in the sunshine and the promise of a beautiful summer, "Lisa, you have the potential to really become something far beyond your brother or your parents if you decide to. You're still stuck in being Chuck Young's sister, which is an identity that a lot of people have. Like Anna Maria Mozart: World-class musician who did what her parents wanted her to do and was overshadowed by her younger brother. Do you really want to be known as Chuck Young's sister; especially now, since you've come so far?"

She turned to the back seat to look at me as a huge sand truck loomed in the front window of the car. I screamed and no words came out.

"Time's up," Mrs. Grimes said pleasantly. "Take your papers out of your notebooks and staple them if you need to."

I stared at what I'd written, turned to two blank pages, tore them out, went up and stapled them, then placed them in the folder.

"Blank?" Kevin asked.

"Blank," I answered.

Mr. Sanders was waiting for me at the entrance to Fondis High School. I wearily threw my backpack into the back seat.

"I was with Felicia and Janie, shopping," I told him. "We picked up a couple of candles, a heart shaped box, and some windchimes."

He stopped. "What are you saying?" he asked.

"I've got it right here," I answered, reaching in back and opening my backpack, pulling out the notebook. "Felicia told me about something I needed to do. Look; it's all here—" I opened my notebook.

He began reading.

Somebody honked behind us. "Damn," he said, putting his car in gear and pulling into the nearest parking place. He picked the notebook back up and continued reading.

I told him about how I was first riding in the car right after Eddie's dog had killed my rabbit; how I was in a trance at home the night of the Memorial vandalism; how I'd tried to tell Iain about it after Thanksgiving. "Can ghosts come back to tell you something?" I asked.

"Look what she said," he answered, tapping the notebook. "That I could be bigger than my brother and my parents—"

He gunned the car toward home; not even bothering to stop at the mailboxes. He opened his door and hurried me through it. "I've got some things to show you," opening the hall closet door close by. He pulled out a box, the only one inside, hesitated, then took it to the dining room table, where he opened it, revealing five bent windchimes: two flattened. He picked it up by the ring and flicked each with his thumbnail. Three rang. Two clonked.

"This was about all that was left," he said, "that wasn't completely crushed or covered with blood. The bag around it was a mess.

"Did you know that Felicia liked windchimes?" It was like he was speaking to someone else. "We used to have them all over the back porch. I took them down after she died. Just couldn't listen to them anymore." He tapped a flattened windchime. It clonked softly. "Just couldn't listen to them anymore," he repeated. "Now it sort of sounds like the water at the Memorial."

"You can be bigger—" I suddenly said.

"—Than your brother," he finished for me. "You know, Lisa," he said, a light in his eyes, "I don't think I ever told Iain that I had this." The chimes moved in a blast of cold air across the tabletop.

"The door's open."

"I could've sworn that it was closed," he murmured.

He placed the windchimes on the table as I let myself out the back door. I kept on hearing the words: "You can be bigger..."

...behold, it be true, and the thing certain, that such abomination is wrought... (Deuteronomy:17.4)

"Major breakthrough in the investigation of Chuck Young," the anchorwoman intoned. "Four more women have submitted sworn statements: two Fondis High School graduates; two current coeds at SAC. Zebulon County District Attorney Eric Saunders says they'll go ahead and press charges..."

Elizabeth turned the TV off, a small smile playing about her lips. "I don't think this is coincidence, Lisa. I think word got around that you'd left home and why—"

"How could it? Nobody's talking."

"Word gets around, even when it isn't supposed to." She picked up the grocery bag that proclaimed BIJOU GROCERY AT FULLER'S MERCANTILE REUSABLE BAG on its side and took it into the kitchen. "Everyone knows you moved out; why did you move out? It's a topic for endless speculation. Why is your brother suddenly the subject of news stories? Is there some connection?" She put the frozen peas and green beans in the freezer, smoothed the bag, and hung it on the peg by the back door.

"We've decided to keep the case open, Lisa," Mr. Hazlitt told me earlier that January, "because we're still convinced there's something here. In your diaries, you talk about everything except yourself. Why is that? You don't mention your feelings and there's very little poetry, except about birds and flowers. Most thirteen-fourteen year-old girls write about their feelings. You don't. We have no concrete evidence here—" he lifted a photocopy of my journal— "but still a suspicion that things weren't right. We're recommending that you remain with Elizabeth until you go to college in the fall."

I'd kept track of how often Chuck and my mother hugged or kissed each other. In that volume, 115 times. I'd kept track of how my life was like any books I was reading: zilch. I'd kept track of the times my father went out to "throw the ball around" with Chuck: almost as many times as my mother had kissed or hugged him. I'd kept track of how well my chickens were doing; I'd kept track of what Bonnie had told me about the boys she was seeing: some of them in high school, even then. "But what did you leave out, Lisa?"

"There's nothing about what Chuck did, and I know I started my diary when—a month after—"

Nancy nodded. "Did you look at all of your other diaries?"

"Yeah. I didn't mention Chuck doing anything to me until I was in high school."

"Fully a year after what, Lisa?"

"More like a year and a half after he gave me the locket and didn't bother me anymore. Then, I started writing about what he was doing with some of the girls—it was easy enough to listen with a car full of boys, who used to pick Chuck up every morning and he'd say stuff—"

"And you wrote about it."

"And I wrote about my mother's going to rehab once: I forgot about that; and how out of control she was, saying things about Chuck being her lover and how she was mad about him."

"Can you tell me why you keep referring to them not as 'mom and dad,' but as 'my mother and my father,' Lisa? You refer to your brother as 'Chuck,' too; not as 'my brother.' Why is that?"

33 /

For thou hast girded me with strength to battle; them that rose up against me hast thou subdued under me. (II Samuel:23.40)

"This is patently false and a pretense to either gain notoriety or money or both," SAC Athletic attorney Joe Norton was raging on the News the next night. "To take a fine, upstanding young man whose book has exemplified all the best the gridiron is capable of and smear him with these allegations is ludicrous!" He wore a lapel button that proclaimed in block letters: I SUPPORT CHUCK YOUNG, which glittered in the light at the cameras as he leaned forward to answer questions. "Of course, we don't know if these young women have come singly or conspired to bring Mr. Young down, but we do know that we'll fight these allegations with every truth we have. We consider these allegations baseless!

Elizabeth turned down the volume and went back to stirring the couscous and mushrooms on the stove. "Causing quite a sensation," she remarked. "It's on a number of the sports talk shows, too."

The wall telephone rang. I was told not to answer it; to let her do that. Since I'd turned eighteen, her voicemail and e-mail were full of requests to talk with me. The pushier reporters had just shouted their questions into the voicemail; the locals were polite and merely asked, if I had the time, could I call them?

"Don't talk to any of them," she said.

"It's Dorothea," she said as she picked up the receiver.

"Arthur's house in fifteen minutes." She replaced the receiver in its cradle. "Wonder what that's all about."

Dorothea stalked into the living room. " Liz, the reason I didn't want to go to your house was because I couldn't have a drink there. I can here." She produced a bottle of wine from a sack she carried and handed it to Mr. Sanders. "Open this and get the glasses while I take off my coat."

She shook off her coat and sat down on the couch, where Elizabeth and I joined her. Mr. Sanders, carrying three glasses and an open bottle of wine, began pouring for each of them and handed me a Coke.

"The reason I wanted to see you three," Dorothea began, "is because of this." She produced a button: I SUPPORT CHUCK YOUNG, that clattered on the coffee table. "That Norton guy, the SAC lawyer, had a bunch of these made and specially delivered to Fuller's, the liquor store, the feed store, and probably the school."

"And they'll be offered for free to anyone who wants to wear them," Mr. Sanders summed up. "Does the DA know about this?"

Dorothea shook her head. "I don't think so. I think it happened this afternoon."

Mr. Sanders took a drink and frowned, then went to the phone.

"I just called Sheriff Franklin," he rejoined us. "Someone should be by soon."

"Oh, shit," Dorothea said. "To find three old people drinking wine in the presence of a minor?" She drained her glass, then looked at the level of wine still in the bottle. "No use," she said. "Arthur, where'd you put the cork?"

The Sheriff himself arrived within a half hour, looked at the button, and asked, "You've heard of the First Amendment, Dorothea?"

"I can't think of anything to prohibit anyone from wearing one of these. If it was political, yes; but it's not incendiary; it doesn't have a pornographic image or suggestion; it doesn't suggest anything illegal."

"But how's it going to make people feel about Lisa when they put two and two together?" Elizabeth asked.

"Has anyone approached you or said anything?" Sheriff Franklin asked me.

"Just the phone," I said, "and Elizabeth answers that."

"Well, they have every right to try and talk to you if they can, Lisa. After all, many of them have already put two and two together, as you say, since Eddie Brace's dog attacked you. Even though none of the newscasters said anything, it was kind of obvious you were moving out and the next logical question is why."

He drained his glass. "Dorothea, you say that these are being delivered to Fuller's, the feed store, the liquor store,"

"—and probably to Coach Mecklinberg," she finished for him. "I only saw the delivery sheet a moment when I signed for them and didn't realize what it was until I opened the box. He came in at ten 'til six."

"Well. I'll inform the DA's office in the morning and tell the staff about the buttons. I can tell my staff not to wear them; and I can suggest to the Commissioners that the County staff can't wear 'em, either."

"Oh—it's okay, Mrs. Grimes," Eddie Brace said sweetly as he entered the class ten minutes late. "Coach Mecklinberg needed help from a lot of the football players to pass out these buttons. Can I pass 'em around?" He pulled one from his bag to show her.

"Give me the bag until the end of the hour, Eddie," Mrs. Grimes replied.

"Oh—if you don't want me to, I won't pass them around," he assured her. "I'll just keep it in my backpack."

"Hand me the bag," she said firmly. "You'll receive it by hour's end."

Kevin looked over at me and shook his head. Clearly, not all the football team had been recruited for this.

Mrs. Grimes quizzed us on the imagery in the Wallace Stevens poem and was just about to finish when "TEACHERS AND

STUDENTS, PLEASE PARDON THE INTERRUPTION. THIS IS DR. HOEPPNER. IF YOU HAVEN'T ALREADY GOTTEN ONE, THERE ARE SEVERAL BUTTONS IN SUPPORT OF CHUCK YOUNG, FONDIS GRADUATE AND AUTHOR OF THE HIT CD AND DVD MY INSPIRATION. AS FONDIS STUDENTS, YOU SHOULD ALL BE PROUD TO SUPPORT CHUCK IN BATTLING AGAINST EVERYTHING THAT'S BEING SAID AGAINST HIM IN THE PRESS AND ON TV. WE WILL HAVE AN ASSEMBLY HONORING CHUCK, WHO'S AGREED TO COME AND SPEAK TO US IN THE NEXT COUPLE OF DAYS, DEPENDING ON HIS SCHEDULE. LET'S SHOW OUR SUPPORT OF CHUCK YOUNG, LIONS!"

I saw a lot of buttons in second hour; by third hour, the room was a sea of I SUPPORTCHUCKYOUNG; by lunchtime, I couldn't find anyone who wasn't wearing one—except for Bonnie, who met me at the corner of the lunchroom. One of the freshman football players was handing the buttons out at the door: he was wearing two or three. With each one he handed out, I felt a penny dropping into the pit of my empty stomach.

"You hungry?" Bonnie asked, looking around.

"Not anymore."

"Then let's go."

We took off in her car to the Lassiters' ranch.

"He said what?" Barb asked in disbelief. "He should know better!"

In a second, she was on the phone, punching numbers furiously. "Superintendent Smedley," she asked sweetly, and was connected to his secretary, who evidently thought Barb was harmless, because she was put right through. "Just what do you mean by letting your principal stir up the students at Fondis High?" She demanded. "They're all being encouraged by Dr. Hoeppner to wear buttons in support of Chuck Young, and your principal has come over the intercom system to tell them that Chuck Young is worthy of all the support they can give! Do you know what you've unleashed by this? Any student not wearing a button is automatically singled out!"

Obviously, the Superintendent had no clue that this was happening in the high school.

"It started just this morning, when Coach Mecklinburg had the football team distribute the buttons. I understand they were made yesterday and sent by special delivery.

No; I not only want you to look into it; I want you to stop it. I'm going to call every board member after this and I'm also going to call the newspapers. Further, I'm keeping my daughter home until this is done and an apology made to those students who don't support Chuck Young!"

She was white-hot and had gone through four of the five members of the School Board when Bonnie's cell phone went off.

"Elizabeth," she announced. "Take it, Lisa."

I recounted everything that had happened that morning, then told her that Bonnie and I were at the Lassiters; "and Barb tells us to stay here because she doesn't want us to return to such a hateful environment."

"Hateful environment," Elizabeth repeated. She'd been taking notes all along. "I'll need these for Mr. Calkins," she explained. "Did anything happen to you?"

"No; nothing," I answered.

"Well! You're in good shape over there. Have you told Arthur where you are?"

"No; but I will."

"Good." She chuckled. "How's Barb?"

"Scary," I answered, watching Barb tell her fifth Board Member what was going on.

"Here's another number she might want to call," Elizabeth was flipping through her book. "Bill Hoefler, Fondis TV. Don't say where she got it, though."

She gave me the number and I passed it to Barb, who picked her phone back up and punched the number. "Mr. Hoefler? You don't know me. My name is Barb Lassiter and there's something going on today at Fondis High School that is seriously affecting the students. How'd I get this number?"

I frantically shook my head.

"Oh, a friend," she casually said. "What I wanted to tell you, though, is breaking news and involves pitting a group of students against a minority. You know those buttons that say 'I SUPPORTCHUCKYOUNG'? You do? Well, the Fondis High Principal, has encouraged every student to wear one and my daughter is a student who refuses. It's her right, of course. But in an atmosphere where the principal is telling the students to—"

She was interviewed that afternoon by Bill Hoefler and led the newscast that night; much more intense than the rather shocked and lost-looking Dr. Hoeppner, who ceded that he might have been a "bit overenthusiastic" and promised to address the student body the next morning about tolerance and had already withdrawn his agreement to feature Chuck Young at an assembly.

"Unless school authorities prohibit the wearing of the buttons," the Sheriff was quoted, "they can wear them as long as no safety issue is concerned."

"This on?" swept over the auditorium. "Guess it is," as several students clapped and cheered. A bunch were wearing buttons all over.

On center stage, in front of the assistant principals and the faculty who were all in chairs behind her, like the first day of school, a slight figure in a FONDIS ATHLETICS t-shirt and jeans stood. From where I sat, at the back of the auditorium, she looked like a guppy in a tank full of sharks.

She cleared her throat and held the microphone like a foreign object. "I'm Nicole Quintana," she began. "Coach Quintana, to most of you. I coach girls basketball, volleyball. I was asked to speak to you today because maybe you'll understand my story better through the lens of the last two days, when everyone has been wearing the I SUPPORT CHUCK YOUNG button to the exclusion of those who don't support him."

A couple of boos arose from the audience. Her intensity, however, made them fade. She had something important to say and we sensed it.

"I coached Chuck Young. I taught him weight training every first hour for two years and he was wonderful. He did rings around me and could bench-press three times his own weight. To those of you who don't know weight training, it's a skill developed over years, carefully, to develop just enough muscle to use, but not too much muscle so that it's extra flab. And Chuck Young was brilliant. He knew just how much to push himself; just how much to let go. It was sheer pleasure to work with him. If anyone could support Chuck Young in a heartbeat, I'm the one."

The audience clapped and cheered.

"Now that's great," she continued. "Every time he caught a pass for SAC or ran a line, I cheered. There was some part of me that had made that athlete. God! When he beat Idaho almost singlehandedly by a score of sixty to ten, I was in heaven!"

More cheers.

"But is that a reason to think he's perfect?" She waited for the audience to stop. "Is that a reason to believe that he can't do bad things?" Again, she waited for the audience to stop.

"Let's look at a Mexican girl, seven years old, whose parents enroll her in an almost all-white school. Her dad, who used to be a

345

lawyer, gets a job mopping floors and her mom, who was a teacher, gets a job at McDonald's. This little girl goes to the almost all-white school and is immediately placed in Special Ed because she doesn't understand the language. This little girl, even though she's bright and quick in her native Spanish, cannot communicate in English, and cannot convince her teachers to put her into classes that aren't Special Ed. It's because she's brown in an almost all-white school; not because she's knowledgeable and skilled and becomes better and better every year."

"It wasn't until seventh grade, when a teacher named Mrs. Fox, who didn't know her and refused to read her files, really looked at her, and realized that this girl was pretty bright and not a Special Ed student at all. Mrs. Fox gave her a bunch of tests, talked to her, and then got her into regular classes, where she excelled.

"You all know this story. It's called stereotyping. Anybody who's different is a weirdo. You can call them whatever you want to: I've heard them all: the worst I ever heard was "beaner," or "spic." Both those words show ignorance and hate.

"There was a boy who asked, sometime after she was in his English class, 'What's that Beaner doing here reading our books? Does she even understand them?' And she was hurt. She didn't show it. Every one of you has been hurt by a stupid word, right?"

There was a cheer and some imitation, which she stopped by looking directly at the audience.

"I was that girl who struggled in an almost all-white elementary school and who finally took her place in middle school." She paused, "and I want to ask you why the system was so against me as a brown Mexican girl, then, after you answer that, tell me why you, with all your advantages of tolerance, understanding, your knowledge, couldn't realize that some folks in this school won't wear that button? *¡VIVA LA DIFERENCIA!*" she shouted.

Students gave her a standing ovation.

Goddamn you, Coach Quintana; God bless you, Coach Quintana.

I worked out extra hard that eighth hour. If she noticed, she kept it to herself, outside of "Good job, Lisa: hope to see the same tomorrow!"

God bless you, Coach Quintana.

The buttons disappeared from most of the students after a while. A few were seen on backpacks, like Eddie Brace's, which had five of them. I saw a bunch on the wall underneath Chuck's photo at

Fuller's. Otherwise, they were retired to sock drawers and the trash pile.

ORGANIC FARM TURNS 110% PROFIT
By Arthur Sanders
March is not a time to be lazy on the Mellon Farm, according to Judy Mellon, who raises a breed of Navajo Sheep that is only found on the plateaus of New Mexico and the eastern plains of Colorado..."

Elizabeth folded the paper and put it on the table. "Probably a great article," she observed, "if you're into organic farming."
Mr. Sanders shrugged. He sipped his coffee. School was ready to begin in twenty minutes and he'd stopped by to drop off a copy of the April issue.

"Ready to try to get us there?" he asked me.

I nodded, grinning. I'd stopped grinding the transmission of his car after having spent afternoons going up and down the driveway, then up and down Road 17. He'd had me drive us in little traffic to the Fairgrounds on Sunday evening and then to the shopping mall west of Fondis. Today would be my inauguration in daytime traffic.

I got us to the front door of Fondis High and stalled. He waved me away as he resignedly took the driver's seat and coaxed the ignition. I was off to first hour that Monday, knowing that Chuck's first court appearance would be soon: "a couple of weeks," and I could say something.

For five months, I'd made sure I didn't say anything regarding Chuck. "First of all, he's your brother," Elizabeth had said, "and whatever you feel about him, you want what's fair." I agreed with her. I also agreed that I had a certain loyalty to myself. "What kind of a hash would the TV station or a magazine make out of what you put up with?"

I ignored the growing list of voicemails and e-mails that Elizabeth kept: "So far there are sixteen girls who have been willing to testify," one of them had pleaded. "Please call us!"

"Do you have any comments on Edward Brace, Jr.'s conviction for vandalism?"

"Is Iain Sanders involved at all?"

I'd been silent to all of them.

347

Mr. Sanders answered the phone once, and a reporter asked what his "secret" was for finding out information. "Trust," he answered, and hung up.

The public record that was released and reported in The Fondis Daily said Eddie Brace had to clip the grass and clear trash every day from the Duncan Memorial once it had been restored. He had to do this for a year. Did he have anything to say? No. He would be stuck in Fondis, according to his probation. Did he have anything to say? No.

"Been really busy," Iain e-mailed Elizabeth, "In Fairbanks, if you haven't been keeping track. Really cold up here. Followed news of Memorial but could get nothing about Lisa vs. her brother."

Elizabeth showed me the e-mail in disgust. "Arthur's been sending him stuff regularly and telling him what's been going on in e-mails. He wrote about his firing; his hearing; his latest stories: and this is the reply? You're well rid of him, Lisa."

Zebulon County always hosted the first Rabbit Judging Event of the year: the Eastern Slope Rabbit Judging Contest, where any of the counties that had 4-H Rabbit Judging Teams could participate. The awards were not as lavish; the belt buckle that had been awarded in past years was silver; this year, it was copper. The food at the concession stand was pricier and the donations from various merchants for the raffle were smaller. That was the effect that the Bank's pullout from sponsorship had. Elizabeth had asked the parents to donate money on a meet-by-meet basis to cover expenses and entry fees; most were willing, or worked in-kind by building cages or cooking for the concession stand. I worked by keeping records and organizing most of the event until it was time to compete. Then I pulled back my hair, checked to see if I had any smudges on my face, washed my hands, and put on my rabbit judging coat: a sort of medical coat that was white and ended at my knees. It had my name above the right breast pocket and patches and pins from my time in 4-H.

Another competitor came in to check herself in the mirror. "You're Lisa Young," she stated.

I nodded. I still wasn't happy about being recognized; much less in the bathroom. "Hi," I said.

"I just wanted to tell you that I think you've got a lot of courage," she said. "Good luck."

I smiled as I checked the folds of my coat. I was a rabbit judging professional. "Good luck to you, too."

"You'll find a lot of people coming up to you in the next few months," Nancy told me after I recounted the story. "Many of them will thank you. They all won't be worrying about athletic scholarships or whether or not you're smearing someone they think is a good guy. How you let it affect you is what's important."

We'd been going through my diaries, looking at me as a character rather than me. "Besides being self-absorbed, Lisa, have you seen some themes in your diaries?"

I was scared of everything; mainly incurring someone's displeasure. To avoid my father's displeasure, I did well on tests and got straight As; to avoid a teacher's displeasure—Mrs. Harris in seventh grade Home Economics—I became President of the Junior Chapter of Future Homemakers of America, which post I held all through Middle School. To avoid Barb's displeasure, I did the jobs no one else wanted to do for Whispering Pines 4-H; to avoid my mother's displeasure, I went to receptions and parties so she could lean on me.

"You've been a good girl," Nancy observed. "The only person you weren't afraid of was Elizabeth Prentice."

"And she's—and Bonnie and Barb—the only one who's stood by me."

"More than that; she's the only one you can still be yourself with. These books, up until about your fourteenth year, are full of your letting yourself in through Elizabeth's back door and helping her make cookies on Saturday afternoons; always enough for you and Bonnie; no one else. Elizabeth must have spent a fortune in ziplock bags during those years. Any other themes you found?"

"I kept counting all the times my mother and Chuck touched each other and all the times my father and he did something. I also kept track of his sports career. I went to a lot of games." They were a blur, probably because I was wondering who his current interest was every time, dreading that I'd be the new one.

"Exactly," Nancy said. "You describe every one of these girls all through high school. There's even one where you have her address and phone number. In some margins, you have a hope or two that 'THIS IS THE ONE!' You also write about the break ups Chuck has, giving every detail. Why, Lisa?"

"I was always the spectator; never in the play."

"So do you feel guilty anymore about getting a scholarship away from here?"

"I feel more guilty about the money Elizabeth's spending on me," I answered. "She even paid for my driver's license registration and she's paying extra on her insurance so I can use her van. And you know—even though I'm eighteen now, she and Mr. Sanders have still agreed not to live together until I'm gone in late summer: the contract they signed so I could live with Elizabeth." I paused. "I don't know how I'm going to repay her—or him, for that matter. He taught me to drive."

"Did you ever think that might be something they did themselves?"

"Why?"

"They did this all willingly, didn't they?" She paused. "People show their love for you in different ways. You'd told me Dorothea, that cashier, always looked out for a new article in the paper for you. Isn't that a form of love?"

"So do I need to see you anymore, Nancy?"

"Your choice, Lisa. If you feel you need a few more weeks with me, then let's go ahead, but if you feel pretty good about what we've done here—"

"It's not like I'm cured, is it?"

"No. It's more like having a base to build on and whatever you build is your responsibility."

TO: ARTHUR SANDERS, ELIZABETH PRENTICE, LISA YOUNG
FROM: IAIN SANDERS
@HERPETOLOGYANDYOU.COM

It's about time I told you all why I haven't contacted you since Thanksgiving; and you can be assured it's entirely selfish. I was offended by the fact that you two rallied around Lisa, like I didn't exist, and so I figured I wouldn't exist for a while, thinking that I'd show you; or something similar.

A couple months ago, when the contract came up for renewal, Charles, our director and producer, asked each of us if we really wanted to continue for another year, going round the globe, falling into rivers, swimming with sharks and so on—and except for me, they all wanted to go home. I was the only one still willing to charge along over rocks and trees and dangle out of a helicopter or ride a skidoo in Antarctica.

After talking for hours to Charles about what my own show would look like, we both agreed that I couldn't draw the audience that the four of us could and I wrote some of my former professors at Columbia. Dr. Rogers, who'd supervised my dissertation, told me that I needed to grow up. The reason I was globetrotting for five years, he said, was because I was running away from the truth. That hurt; but it really got me to thinking. Lisa, you were the first girlfriend I'd ever had. I don't know if you knew that. I was wrong not to understand that you got strength enough to really say what had happened to you at Thanksgiving dinner because of me. Does this make sense?

If you'll have me, I'd like to come home when filming's over. I can probably find a job at one of the universities; maybe even try teaching high school. I just don't know yet. I want some time to think."

"He thinks he gave me the juice to say what I said?" I asked Elizabeth. I was irritated at his arrogance.

"No, the waiter was pouring it," she answered, laughing.

34 /

I have heard of thee by the hearing of my ear: but now mine eye seeth thee. (Job:42.5)

"The cattle show's this weekend, isn't it?" I looked at the headline of the June Divide-Review, which was being read by Elizabeth at the breakfast table opposite me:

THE LONG REACH OF DOCTOR BRACE:

How A Single Urologist Controls A County
By Arthur Sanders

"Yes. Yes it is. Thinking of going?"

"I thought I'd like to go cheer Kevin on." I absently looked at the quartz crystal before replacing it in my pocket.

"I think he'd like that," Elizabeth said, taking a bite of her cereal and turning the page. Chuck was going to appear in court in a couple of weeks to face twenty one women; what I'd said and done, short of some "very interesting answers from your parents and teachers," Mr. Timmons had said, "really doesn't amount to much, Lisa; except that it opens the door to some recent complaints that we can address." Mr. Calkins had successfully concluded negotiations on behalf of the mortgage holders with the Farmers and Mechanics Bank. "Arthur's story's thorough, as usual," she said. "He contacted a bunch of former associates of Dr. Brace; Eddie's former teachers; everybody who's ever dealt with him." She continued reading.

"June first," I murmured. "Iain's s'posed to be here today."

"I'm having enough problems with the father; I don't want to deal with the son, too."

It was April when the contract was stopped. Iain had first stopped in Sacramento; then slowly made his way down the coast: San Francisco; San Diego; even Guymas, Mexico. He kept sending along photos of the places he stopped. His last one was from Shiprock, New Mexico, two days before.

"If we don't see him for a while, it'll be just as well," Elizabeth observed. "He and Arthur are regularly sending each other e-mails again and that seems sufficient." Meanwhile, various packages had been mailed to the Sanders home: some large, some small, from points all over the country, all addressed to Iain; most from the cable network. There were boxes from his show mates, too; probably all the stuff over the years that had gotten jumbled together as they travelled from one place to another. "I'll bet the only one who had all her stuff when the show ended was Marla," Mr. Sanders noted as he carried another box in, leaving it atop three already in the living room. "If this keeps up, I'll pile all the boxes in a pattern and make a maze."

When Elizabeth asked who I'd like to invite for my graduation party, I asked, quite sincerely, if she could afford it.

"Of course I can," she answered, surprised. "Why would you ask such a thing?"

"Because I'm costing you more money than my parents are sending you," I answered. "Even though they paid for my AP Calculus test, you paid for the calculator rental; they paid only half for the AP Literature test. You've paid all my entry fees at the Judging tournaments; you paid for my entry at the Greeley Rabbit Show two weekends ago: I don't want you spending money on me if you can't afford to."

"But I can afford to, Lisa," she answered.

"But money is an issue," I remonstrated. "Why else do you make and bake Christmas gifts for people; and why do you always look for the sale items when we go shopping at Fuller's?"

"Because I'm smart," she answered. "Sure, I know what it's like not to have money in the house; but we're far from that, Lisa."

I thought back on those Thursday dinners for my father and realized that I'd spent almost as much on one dinner as Elizabeth spent on a week's worth of food.

"But I want to celebrate your graduation," she continued. "It doesn't matter how much it costs. I thought you'd have a few friends over if you'd like and we'd barbecue some ribs and chicken. Nothing big, Lisa. Probably the Saturday or Sunday after the ceremony. What do you think?" She was really pretty excited about celebrating it, I thought, and she told me to stop feeling guilty "because I imagine you'll find a way to pay me back if you want to."

It was small, but there were still plenty of people and Elizabeth circulated among the old ladies of her circle; the clerks and paralegals she knew; the various people who made Fondis run. She'd included a bunch of people I'd not even thought about, like Dr. Rural, Mary and Caroline from the Library, Dorothea Harris, Mr. Calkins, and Nancy, my therapist, and Dannah Davidson. Of course, Kevin, Bonnie and all the Lassiters showed up; Meg, the Lood Twins, and Wendy Simpson came.

"I've never seen such a collection of rogues in one place outside of the paper I work for," Mr. Sanders joked as he turned the burgers on the grill.

On Monday the following week, the telephone rang, and it wasn't a reporter. "Go ahead, Lisa, pick it up," Elizabeth said. "It's for you. It's Dottie Hawkins."

Mrs. Hawkins had been looking for someone to walk her dachshund, Frankie, twice a week, and she understood I was responsible. "Would you accept twenty dollars to play a couple of hours with him in the park? Oh, every Tuesday and Thursday? That would be forty dollars."

And five more calls came in that day. Dannah Davidson needed someone to organize one of her two storage units because her house was too small for all those canvases. Could I do that on Wednesday? One hundred dollars too little? Could I take care of Caroline's house while she was on her two-week vacation? Yes: someone needed to stay there nights because of the possibility of burglars; to mow the lawn and pick up the papers and the mail. Was one hundred dollars a week too little? There'd be free food. I didn't smoke, did I? Oh: that was good. Could I do part time custodial duties in the Church of the Redeemer? Mainly bathrooms, unfortunately; but floors as well because old Rufus can't bend like he used to. Every Saturday afternoon, one to five. Usually, Rufus got a stipend of fifty bucks. Was that okay?

Elizabeth tossed me another pen when the one I was writing with failed. "You got enough jobs?" she asked as I replaced the receiver.

I looked over the three pages of notes I'd taken. "I've got every Saturday this summer taken care of; two weeks of evenings at Muriel Sibley's house—" I sat down as she laughed.

"Feel like you can pay me back yet?" she asked.

I nodded. "And keep some for myself," I replied.

"There are a lot of people who will hire a responsible eighteen year-old for all kinds of things, Lisa. Getting money doesn't mean you have to spend summers at a bank filling in, although I imagine you're going to be missed by Inez and Dennis and some of the others you used to cover for."

Mrs. Hawkins lived only a couple blocks from Schley Street and because our route wasn't predetermined, I often walked Frankie through my old neighborhood, staying away from the block my parents' house was on, but walking to the north of the block or the south of it, until one Thursday, when Frankie, who was usually pretty docile, found a squirrel to chase, jerking the leash from my hand. I chased him to a tree at the Harris' house, where he barked incessantly, standing on his hind legs.

The neighborhood looked the same. My parents' house stood in its quiet majesty, the porch bedecked with the imitation wicker chairs that no one ever sat on; the garage matching the paint of the house, and—I shaded my eyes. Something was missing.

There was no Rabbit House.

I pulled Frankie along behind me as I crossed the street to get a better view, then quickly walked opposite where the Rabbit House had been. There was no sign of it: just the outline of a rectangle made by the trees and roses surrounding a patch of freshly-laid grass, sunken in proportion to the rest of the yard by a few inches, I noted, but nothing marked its existence. Even the place where the door had been was barred by a new rosebush with a trellis behind it.

The back door slammed and Chuck appeared, basketball in hand. He went over to the driveway and shot some hoops, completely unaware I was watching him.

"C'mon, Frankie," I murmured, tugging at the leash.

Iain Sanders did return to live with his father, finally; although he didn't arrive until mid-June, a day before I was to testify for the District Attorney, so I didn't pay much attention at dinner with him, Elizabeth, and Mr. Sanders. Mr. Hazlitt had just told me to tell the truth and I'd gotten caught up in wondering what the truth was. Nancy had told me that although it was seen through imperfect eyes, it was probably truer than most adults saw. "Just tell the truth, Lisa."

"I'll probably stay for at least a week, Dad," Iain said through my thoughts.

"And clear out all the stuff in the living room?"

"Comes from not having a permanent address," Iain grinned. "When I wrote Hal's parents, they wrote back, 'O thank God, we can finally clean out our garage!'"

"You'll miss those guys, won't you?" Elizabeth asked.

"Not the production meetings or script editings," Iain answered; "but the nights we had to bed down in intense cold; the afternoons on a beach in Mozambique; the canoeing on the Yellowstone River: I'll miss that for sure."

"Why just a week, Iain?" Elizabeth continued asking. "You're home."

"Maybe more," he answered. "I don't know yet."

"Why don't you put your feet up, sort out your stuff, have a couple meals here, help out with the animals, and then decide?" Mr. Sanders asked.

Elizabeth stopped the van in the back Courthouse parking lot, away from the front door, "where we won't be mobbed," Mr. Sanders pointed out. "We can come and go as soon as Lisa's done."

We entered the warren of hallways and offices at the back door and reported to the Court Clerk's office, then were escorted to a room with a large table. Mr. Hazlitt appeared, looking a trifle flustered. "There have been some developments," he said as the door closed behind him, "and Lisa won't be needed after all."

Although I didn't want to say anything in Court, I'd prepared for it; I'd discussed it with Elizabeth, with Nancy; with Mr. Sanders: I was disappointed. "How come?" I asked quietly.

"It's not recent evidence," Mr. Hazlitt answered, "and it might be a distraction from our case."

"Just like that?"

He nodded. "Of course, you're welcome to sit—"

"Thank you," Elizabeth answered. "We'll see, Mr. Hazlitt."

"You want to watch?" Mr. Sanders asked as the door closed behind Mr. Hazlitt.

I wiped a tear from my eye. "Maybe for a while."

Chuck sat in his blue suit, looking gorgeous and muscular: the inspirational author of "My Inspiration," which newscasters were fond of saying had become a "million-selling bestseller" since the trial began. Right behind him were my parents: my father in a severe black suit; my mother in dark colors with a tasteful blouse, and Coach Mecklinburg with the head coach from SAC.

In the seats behind them were family and friends of the females from SAC, some of whom I recognized, like Barbie VanNest's father from her blog, all watching intently. Behind them were members of the public. The Press, represented by a camera crew, a sketch artist, and two print reporters, crowded behind the bailiff.

"Kinda' crowded in here," Mr. Sanders remarked as we squeezed in. "Maybe we'll get a better view on the television."
Elizabeth agreed. "Let's go, Lisa, okay?"

"Determining whether superstar college athlete Chuck Young abused coeds here in Fondis and at SAC during the last three years is going to take some time," the newscaster droned, "with Assistant District Attorney Ron Hazlitt leading the prosecution. Reports of the length of the trial vary with a month or a month and a half being the general speculation."

"We will fight for this young man's innocence," a feisty Mr. Norton was telling the camera, "No matter how long it takes."

"Reports that Chuck Young's sister, Lisa, was going to testify for background have not been confirmed, but she was briefly seen at the start of the proceedings..."

"Well!" Mr. Sanders flipped the television off. "It's probably going to be this way for a month at least: claim and counter-claim. Thank goodness that you don't have to be in the middle of it, Lisa."

"I started it." Shouldn't I be there?

"Understandable," Elizabeth answered. "What good would it do, though?"

Nancy asked the same question. "Sometimes, we have to step back and look at what's best," she said. "Like what happened between you and Iain. He wasn't ready for a relationship."

"Brooding," Elizabeth remarked. "Too preoccupied with himself. That's why I haven't really told him a lot about what Jim's doing in Australia, even though he'd like to renew Iain's friendship: it's just not the time. Selfish."

She turned to see him in the doorway. He'd probably heard her. If so, he gave no sign. "I was wondering where the windchimes were that used to be on our porch," he said, "until I remembered that my dad gave them away, but do you remember the birdfeeder my mother used to have on our porch?" he asked. "Do you know what happened to it?"

"It might be in the barn," she answered. "I think your father gave me a box right after your mother—probably in there: corner of the attic, you know? but check with your father before you hang it."

"Thanks," he answered. "I'll find it."

"I'll help you," I announced, following him.

"Am I really as heartless as all that?" he asked as we climbed the ladder and began searching among the boxes.

"You are," I answered. "Stuck in your own little world."

"Save it, Lisa," he said. "Aren't you, too?"

"Yeah," I answered reasonably, "but it hasn't stopped me from growing away from it."

"Found it," he said as he hefted a box labeled BIRD FEEDER.

...thou art abhorred of thy father: then shall the hands of all that are with thee be strong" (II Samuel:16.21)

I was walking Frankie along Schley Street a couple of blocks above my parents' house, next to the pocket park that graced that area when Elizabeth tore up and stopped the van with a squeal of brakes. "I just got the call at the office," she called, rolling down the window of the van, "the trial's ending abruptly and I figured you'd like to be there to hear the sentence."

"What about Frankie?" I asked.

"Bring him," she ordered.

The radio, tuned to FONDIS AM, announced that "people were arriving at the courthouse in light of the unexpected plea bargain worked out by Charles Norton, attorney for football superstar Chuck Young after Young's testimony did not hold in light of witness after witness..."

"Did you know this was going to happen?" I asked.

Elizabeth shook her head. She turned onto Main around the Courthouse Square.

What I'd begun in November was small potatoes to how it finished in late June: Chuck was going to take a "leave of absence" from SAC and football altogether for a year, turn any profits of his book and DVD and CD work to funding Fondis Women's Shelter, and do a year's worth of volunteer work, supervised by a probation officer. He was to take classes about how to treat women and anger management. It sounded like he couldn't do anything except go to those classes. Any other time he had was to be spent at home, where he was to spend time with his parents.

"You realize that any infraction of your sentence, Mr. Young, will result in immediate jail time?" the judge asked.

Chuck nodded. There was no Mr. Holmes to get him off; Mr. Norton looked defeated. My father looked older than I'd ever seen him; my mother looked drained. Maybe, somewhere, she'd finally realized that what I'd been trying to say all those years ago, was true.

"Objections to the sentencing of Chuck Young come from some of his victims," the newscaster announced, "who feel that his sentencing is much too light in the plea bargain."

"I've had my life wrecked," one woman announced, "How's a year off football going to help that?"

"How indeed?" the editorial that followed began. "It's our opinion that the judge acted well and with great deliberation in how he handled this plea bargain. Not only is Chuck Young serving time away from his most favorite activity; those of us who have been amazed by his ability on the gridiron will always remember the year he was away and why. So will any sports franchise that hires him. We already know he will have to take classes that will essentially change his behavior. If they make him less abusive, then Chuck Young will be a decent adult after his football career is over. If he doesn't wise up and become an adult because of this experience, then his football career will be over."

"There's some truth to that," Mr. Sanders remarked as the TV news moved to coverage of a cat up a tree.

"But what community service will he do?" Iain asked.

"That's to be determined, isn't it?" his father observed. "I'll bet it's going to strike some people as ironic, however."

"Lisa, did you make this potato salad?" Elizabeth asked. "Really quite good."

I shook my head.

"I did," Iain announced. "Mom always had potato salad around during the summer. I found the recipe in an old cookbook and figured I'd make some."

"Iain's become quite the homemaker this past week," Mr. Sanders observed. "He's unpacked his boxes, thrown away a lot of stuff I had lying around for him; given a lot of sports equipment to the thrift store—"

"—and won a bunch of rabbit judging ribbons," I said, looking in a box on the counter as I opened the refrigerator for some milk.

"Those were my sister's," Iain answered. "I wanted to hang 'em up in a cabinet or frame 'em."

"And maybe put it up where that painting by Felicia used to hang." Elizabeth pointed to a blank wall. "Or put it in the Whispering Pines Conference Room."

"No; I'd rather have those here," Mr. Sanders said. "I only have those and a few pictures of Janie. I'd like to keep them. Did you ever find her first ribbon, Iain; that fourth that she won?"

Iain shook his head, then cut himself a slice of ham. "There's a lot to do around here. Brush to cut back; rosebushes to trim. I'm going to turn that old hutch out back to firewood, if that's all right."

Mr. Sanders paused in chewing, then nodded. "Go ahead. I don't have any use for it."

It was two days later when I heard a yell and a tousled Iain Sanders appeared at the back door, holding a cobwebby box in his work gloves. "Lisa! Do you know what this is?" He hopped on one foot then the other in his excitement.

"Are you okay?"

"Do you know what this is?" He waved the box, then opened it, carefully pulling out a green ribbon. "Found it in the rabbit hutch, between the cages where it didn't fit right. This box has been there fifteen years!"

There was a folded note, which he opened: "First rabbit juging ribbon won by Janie Sanders, age eight at the Estern Slope Rabbit Juging Contets."

He pushed aside the Fondis Daily: "Chuck Young's Community Service? He Gets To Clean Up After Sports Events at Fondis Stadium!" and carefully laid out the note next to the ribbon on Elizabeth's kitchen table. "I never thought I'd see this, ever."

"Why didn't she keep it with her other ribbons?"

"Probably just forgot. She started really winning the next year and maybe it just wasn't as important."

"But it was to your dad."

He nodded.

...and the soul of the child came into him again, and he revived. (I Kings: 17,22)

"Fair's in a week," Elizabeth announced. "Do you know which rabbits you want to show?"

"Seven," I answered. "I can show seven at five dollars a rabbit; that's thirty five dollars, Elizabeth."

"You can show eight; or ten, if you'd like. I'll pay for it, Lisa."

"I want to pay for it."

She smiled. "Choose the ones you'll show, carefully," she suggested. "Oh—" the wind knocked some papers from the kitchen table onto the floor. "I wish it would stop!" she said. Then, "What's that sound?"

I heard wind chimes: ring, ring, ring, klunk. Ring, ring, ring, klunk. "Coming from Mr. Sanders', I think," I said.

"And Iain's," she said. "What is that?" as it clunked again.

"It's a twisted windchime pipe," I answered, listening for the clunk. "He finally put it up."

...when I begin, I will also make an end. (I Samuel:3.12)

Afterword

Tying Expressive Arts and Healthcare:

NEW DEPARTMENT AT FONDIS UNIVERSITY

By Arthur Sanders

If you ask 23 year-old Lisa Young what she's planning on doing, she would say: "Helping others help themselves," which is more or less the answer you'd receive from the other 49 graduate students gathered in the Main Hall at Fondis University's newest department: Integrated Studies of the Expressive Arts for Healthcare Professionals, located in the "Old Stone Monastery" building at the north end, the "woodsy part" of campus.

The Monastery, refurbished and remodeled, will retain its granite exterior, but within, it has been fitted with the latest technology, including satellite teleconferencing, and wireless internet capability. The building, which was built with room for a chapel, meeting room, granary, brewery, mill and storage area in addition to 50 monks' cells, now has a series of classrooms, lecture centers, and state-of-the-art spaces where art can happen right next door to modern diagnostic areas.

This configuration is not accidental. Gwyneth Walsh, PhD., program director and Department Chair, points out that "artists and healthcare professionals need to have space to collaborate and learn from each other in order to enhance the treatment experience for patients." That's why an artist is paired with a professor; not as a "buddy," or "teaching assistant," but as an equal colleague. Walsh adds: "And what better space than in a building devoted originally to prayer and meditation? The goal of our program is to integrate artistic creativity into the healthcare field so healthcare providers are more responsive to their patients' emotional and spiritual needs."

These artists, many of them locals, such as Dannah Davidson, Nirvana, Brendan O'Donnell, Roger Rural, Epona Maris, and Deirdre Moon, are joined by visiting performance artist Michael Berg and musical groups The Calfbranders and Bodies We've Buried, whose presence will round out the faculty. Collaborating with them will be professors from Fine Arts, Music, Psychology, Medicine, Biology and English as well as Fondis University Hospital Staff. A partial list includes Talia Master, M.D., Raul Rural, M.D., Mary Lucero, PhD. and Janice Redwood, PhD. from Whispering Pines Mental Health.

The idea of having Expressive Arts paired with Health is not new: it was embraced by Aristotle and Plato; but its implementation at Fondis University is unique and its scope is unique. Beginning with a paper jointly written by Dr. Walsh, Dannah Davidson and Dr. Rural, the idea of healthcare was discussed and studied toward a more holistic approach. The paper, which was initially presented at the Fondis Lyceum, was later that year presented at the National Behavioral Research Council Convention in Boston where its tenets were widely discussed and applauded. This brought donors and grantors: from a stipend by a local mental health center to a five year, $5 million grant from Abajo Healthcare.

"Keeping the Department in Fondis was also important," Walsh explains. "It began here; we decided to keep it here; but make sure we could gather students from all around the world who were interested, from all disciplines."

Lisa Young, who just graduated from Siwash with a Bachelor's Degree in Biology with a minor in English, is one of these. Like her peers, she began with an essay and two recommendations from professors. Then she and 200 others were given a series of tasks to perform, both alone and with others: all requiring some degree of logic and creativity. Tasks ranged from preparing a meal to carrying stones across a river without the aid of a bridge. The incentive, besides being part of a dynamic new program leading to more engaged and responsive healthcare providers, was a scholarship for the final 50 candidates: the best of the best.

"We have several majors you wouldn't directly associate with healthcare," Walsh explains, "such as engineering and graphic design; we've even got a Latin scholar among our students; but all of them had a passion to improve the delivery of healthcare, to bring more creativity, more humanity to the field. I am really excited to get started with them on this adventure."

The course, which culminates in a PhD, requires four years of study and classroom experience with laboratory work included, then a yearlong residency at Fondis University Hospital.

"By the close of the five years," Dr. Walsh says, "we'll have fifty dedicated and committed professionals ready to take on an ever changing world."

Acknowledgments

William C. Thomas

I am grateful to Joanne McLain for her perseverance, dedication, work, questioning and editing. I am grateful to Susan M. Fox for her suggestions regarding characters. I am grateful that a host of students showed me how brilliant and clear a high school senior's voice could be.

C.J. Prince

Thank you to the wild, wonder-filled, dedicated writers in the Womyn's Centre Writing Group: Laurie Marr Wasmund, Karen Steinberg, Victoria Motazedi, Jesse Kuiken, Barbara Miller and Mark Putch.

Thank you to WOW, Write On Women, who encourage and help me when the Muse is out to lunch: Sue Erickson, Rae Ellen Lee, Carol Austin and especially Nancy Canyon, who edited "Canvas Angels".

Thank you to the Muse-icians writing practice for keeping it real every week: Pam Weil, Ann Edmonds, Linda Hirsh and Barbara Gobus.

Thank you every day to Michael E. Berg who never questions my hours dancing with the keyboard and always supports my creativity.

Beyond words gratitude to Joanne McLain and William Corbin Thomas without whom this volume would have never seen the light of day: for endurance and patience, for creativity and vision and especially, Joanne, for her technical skills and encouraging emails when I was lost on a cul de sac in the forest.

Joanne McLain

Thank you to C.J. and Bill for sticking with this book through the years that it was just a project, until it was finally birthed to the world. Thank you to Jennifer Walker for her comments filled with the insight from her years of marvelous work at the Women's Crisis and Family Outreach Center. And thank you to all of the women (and men) who shared with me their pain, their grief and their burden of shame so we could work together to find the meaning in it all.

Made in the USA
Charleston, SC
20 September 2012